A GIFT UPON THE SHORE

M. K. Wren

Ballantine Books • New York

The excerpt from the letter of John Adams to John Taylor is taken from the Adams
Family Correspondence, Vol. I, edited by L. H. Butterfield, et al., published by the
Belknap Press of Harvard University Press, Cambridge, Mass.

Grateful acknowledgment is made to the following for permission to reprint previously
published material: Harvard University Press: Excerpt from poem #883 from *The Poems of
Emily Dickinson* edited by Thomas H. Johnson. Published by the Belknap Press of Harvard
University Press, Cambridge, Mass. Copyright 1951, © 1955, 1979, 1983 by the
President and Fellows of Harvard College. Reprinted by permission of the publishers and
the Trustees of Amherst College.

Macmillan Publishing Company: Excerpts from: "Watch the Uneasy Landlords" from *The
Innocent Assassins* by Loren Eiseley. Copyright © 1973 by Loren Eiseley. Reprinted by
permission of Charles Scribner's Sons, an imprint of Macmillan Publishing Company;
"The Second Coming" from *The Poems of W. B. Yeats: A New Edition* edited by Richard
J. Finneran. Copyright 1924 by Macmillan Publishing Company. Copyright renewed 1952
by Bertha Georgie Yeats. Reprinted by permission of Macmillan Publishing Company.

W. W. Norton & Company, Inc.: Excerpt from *The Future of an Illusion* by Sigmund
Freud, translated by James Strachey from the German. Copyright © 1961 by James
Strachey. Reprinted by permission.

Wren, M. K.
A gift upon the shore / M. K. Wren.—1st ed.
p.   cm.
ISBN: 0-345-36341-8
I. Title.
PS3573.R43G5   1990
813'.54—dc20   89-90890
CIP

Design by Holly Johnson

Manufactured in the United States of America

First Edition: March 1990
10 9 8 7 6 5 4 3 2 1

For Lyle Ardell Taylor—

Dreamer. Healer. Catalyst.
You loved not at all wisely.
A knight without armor—
Not even a scrap of steel
To shield your heart
Or hide the scars.
You left behind the enigma
Of your absence
And the sure knowledge
That I shall never meet your like.
If I could, for you,
I would believe
In heaven.

ACKNOWLEDGMENTS

A book is not the work of its author alone. I've had a great deal of help with this one, and everyone who so willingly offered their support and expertise deserves to be recognized if only with a few words.

For their expertise in a variety of fields, my thanks to Glen Mills of the Oregon Museum of Science and Industry; Bill Rogers of the Lincoln County Extension Service; pharmacist Carol Griggs; Morris Kauffman, of Kauffman Quarries, Inc; Lee Crawley Kirk, who provided information on livestock in general, Jane Thielsen on horses in particular, and all the Finks of the Fink Family Farm on goats in particular; and Meg Portwood, FNP, who not only provided medical expertise and textbooks, but patiently read parts of the manuscript.

My thanks also to Kaj Wyn and Don Berry, who listened and asked the key question.

And to Jean V. Naggar, the adroit matchmaker, who insisted on certain standards, and she was right—as she always is.

And above all, to Ruth Dennis Grover and Katharyn Miller Renfroe, who not only didn't laugh when I devoted more than three years of my life to this endeavor, but offered the tangible and emotional support I needed—sometimes desperately—to complete it.

—M. K. Wren

A GIFT
UPON THE
SHORE

Every good and excellent thing in the world stands moment by moment on the razor edge of danger and must be fought for.
—THORNTON WILDER, *THE SKIN OF OUR TEETH* (1942)

I want to know what it says. . . . The sea, Floy, what it is that it keeps on saying.
—CHARLES DICKENS, *DOMBEY AND SON* (1848)

I will call it the Chronicle of Rachel.

It will be written simply, simplistically, with the cadence of the King James Version. The story of Rachel Morrow as told by her acolyte and apostle Mary Hope.

I can hear Rachel laughing at that—a gentle, comprehending laugh with a hint of cynicism in it, but no bitterness.

I think of Rachel's laughter as I put my back to the sea, and with the cautious pace dictated by age and arthritis, I make my way east across the beach toward the bank. It's forty feet high here, with salal and clumps of mimulus clinging to its striated layers of earth and clay and the cobbled ledges of buried beaches. I'd never be able to climb that slope if it weren't for the path that winds up through the ravine cut by the Styx. Not the River Styx. The small, stubborn creek Styx.

I pause at the foot of the path, my cane and moccasin boots sinking into the snowy, dry sand where the tide hasn't reached since winter. The air is weighted with dew, and on this April day, the early-morning sun shines clear as white wine on the blue-green face of the Pacific, makes rainbows in the spindrift arching off the breakers, but it will be half a day before the sun reaches this spot. At my knee, Shadow stands panting from her sprints along the edges of the waves, black and white and russet fur sea-wet, long nose pointed into the wind. The family thinks I call her Shadow because she is so often beside me, but in fact I named her for her ancestor, the first Shadow, whose ancestors were bred to herd sheep in the Shetland Islands, a place so hopelessly far away now that I'll never know if anyone, anything, still lives there.

I draw my brown wool shawl closer as I set off up the path.

Yes, I will call it the Chronicle of Rachel, but it will of necessity be my story. I am the viewpoint character. And I can delay it no longer. Last night I read something in Miriam's eyes that served notice to me. I must do it for Rachel, for all her hopes.

And for Stephen, that he may be emancipated, and his children and his children's children. Generation unto generation.

When at length I reach the top of the path, I stop to catch my breath, then, with Shadow at my heels, I walk into the sun across the unmowed grass, passing the house on my left. No one is there now. A covered breezeway connects the east wall to the garage. Rather, the church. I can hear voices singing in three-part harmony: "Rock of Ages, cleft for me . . ."

I don't attend the family's religious services. Early on I attended a few of them and found them annoying on many counts, not the least of which is that they were boring, even the daily morning and evening services that usually last only an hour. And they all remind me too much of the Doctor's sermons and his morbid visions of hell.

Jeremiah's hellfire lacks conviction. Despite his youth, he tends to long-winded and edifying parables. Miriam is more a preacher in the evangelistic tradition. I attended, out of curiosity, the first service she conducted. That was five years ago when Jerry had pneumonia. In his absence, Miriam flowered proudly as our resident high priestess, like her namesake, the sister of Moses. When Jerry recovered from his illness, he decided that perhaps it *was* possible for a woman to serve as preacher. For morning services, at any rate.

He decided that? Let's say he *thought* it was his decision.

But I avoid the services, whoever is preaching, and on this spring morning I sympathize with the children, who have no choice but to be confined in the church. The family hasn't done much to improve the structure since it was a garage—and for a while a chicken house and rabbitry, then a storeroom—except to put in two windows, a crude altar, a pulpit, and three hard benches. They replaced the garage door with a standard door, and on the peak of the roof mounted a wooden cross.

I hum along with the hymn as I walk on toward the barn and the labyrinth of pens and sheds and rabbit hutches around it. Cassandra, the grande dame of our goat herd, is at the watering trough. Since Shadow is with me, I don't venture too close to Cassandra, although I'm worried about her. She's pregnant and near term. At the chicken coop, I try to count the chicks, a hopeless task; they move so constantly. There are at least thirty. The rabbits are proliferating handily: two of the does have litters of seven. In the pigpen, Diana happily nurses her squealing litter of ten.

I turn and walk back toward the house and church. I can hear no music now. Miriam is probably giving one of her lessons. She has, so I've been told, made the morning service a Bible school for the children. Not only are they confined to that bleak building on this splendid morning, but they must be catechized by Miriam. But it gives them practice in memorization.

And I'll have them for three hours later this morning.

Stickeen and Diamond have joined us. They're both Agate's heirs and have his wolfish look, and they're still puppyish enough to tempt Shadow into a romp. I stop to watch their game, but a few minutes later I'm distracted by the opening of the church door.

The service must be over. I watch, unnoticed in the shade of an alder copse perhaps thirty yards away, while the family files out of the church, Jerry leading the exodus. Jeremiah. I find it difficult to think of him as Jeremiah. I will always, I suppose, think of him as Luke's boy. He has the same narrow head, deep-set blue eyes, and long bones, although his hair and beard are a wan brown. Jerry is thirty-one years old and our Elder. Since he's the only adult male here, he holds that office by default, really. I never remind him of that.

Miriam follows him, her imperious posture making her seem nearly as tall as Jerry, and she has Luke's copper red hair. The sun fires it, a candescent cascade falling to her waist. All the other women cut their hair short for convenience—in that, they've taken my lead—but I can't blame Miriam for letting her hair grow long. It is her glory. She'd be beautiful without it, but with it she is ravishing. Yet this Ishtar, this Astarte, this veritable Venus—and the first time I saw her she was standing on the verge of the sea— considers vanity a sin.

She takes her place at Jerry's side a few feet from the door, and as if the contrast were purposely staged, the next to emerge are Enid, Bernadette, and Grace. The three crones, so I call them, well aware that I am the fourth crone. Enid is holding Deborah's hand, and Grace is carrying three-year-old Rachel, who is crying disconsolately. Jonathan, Jerry's eldest, comes out next, with his half-brother, Isaac, at his side and Little Mary behind him. Then Esther emerges, tall and lithe, her dark skin the color of a Benin bronze. I call her our earth mother, and she is in fact five months pregnant. I see in her face none of her usual calm, and her distress, obvious even from a distance, sounds in my mind the first faint alarm. She rests one hand on her son's shoulder.

Stephen. He surprises me sometimes because I look at him ex-pecting to see a boy and instead see a youth nearing manhood. He's thirteen now, nearly as tall as his mother, and he has her dark, curling hair, her obsidian black eyes, her supple grace. But now there is an odd rigidity in his stance.

None of the family makes a move to go to the house. They all remain near the church door, and my curiosity is piqued. Something has altered the routine.

I realize that something is not only unusual, but seriously wrong when I see Esther appealing to Jerry. I'm too far away to understand what she's saying except for her last words: "He didn't mean to. *Please*—he's only a child!"

Jerry shakes his head, and Esther slowly retreats from Stephen, who stands with his back to the closed door. When Miriam holds out her hand, Jerry—reluctantly, it seems—unbuckles his leather belt and gives it to her. She speaks to Stephen, and I watch, baffled, as he takes off his shirt, turns, reaches out to brace his palms against the door.

I don't believe what I'm seeing, and that doubt paralyzes me. Miriam folds her hands over the leather strap and bows her head. *Her* voice carries easily to me. I hear every word. "Heavenly Father, have mercy on this our brother, who has blasphemed in Your presence. . . ."

Blasphemed?

The word impels me forward, rage rising from some capped well deep within me where memories and hatred are stored. I throw my weight onto my cane at every step, but I can't run. Old woman, half-crippled old woman, hobbling along on aching limbs.

Miriam stands in an empty circle whose radius is the length of the belt, and now she draws back her hand, the belt snakes out with a vicious whisper, cracks against Stephen's naked back, leaves its livid track burned into his flesh.

And over his muffled cry I shout, *"Stop it!"*

My protest goes unheard, and again the belt slashes through the air, snaps across Stephen's back, forcing out another cry, leaving another dark welt. I stumble on, while Miriam draws the belt back again, but I'm only a few feet away now, and I reach out for the flailing leather.

It hits my hand with a burning shock as it wraps around my wrist and pulls me off balance. I fall, hard and clumsily, lie clutching green spring grass in my hands, while my heart pounds against the constriction in my chest that stops my breath. Beyond the ringing whine in my ears, I hear the dogs barking, little Rachel wailing, all the women talking at once, and finally Jerry bellowing, "Enough! That's enough, everybody!"

At length silence prevails, except for Shadow, who stands by me, growling at Miriam. And Miriam glares at me, her ivory skin spoiled with mottled red. I manage to get enough breath to quiet Shadow, then Jerry helps me to my feet. He offers me my cane, never once looking me in the eye. The belt is still wrapped around my wrist, and when I remove it, I make no effort to hide the red weals under it. I hand the belt to Jerry, and he takes it, frowning as if he's never seen it before.

I glance at Stephen. Esther is draping his shirt around his shoulders, but he seems unaware of her. He's staring at me.

And I demand, "What's going on here, Jeremiah?"

Miriam answers my question. Blue eyes glacier cold, she says, "This is a just punishment! Five lashes, that's all, and he'd be better for it. He'd be cleansed in the eyes of the Lord!"

Behind Miriam, Grace nods emphatically. Her white scarf rekindles some of my rage. Enid and Esther seem bewildered, while Bernadette watches with narrowed eyes, like a spectator at a play waiting for the next line. And Jerry—he stands with his wide shoulders slumped, and now he seems annoyed more than anything else. The children watch, silent and motionless. Why should they understand any of this? No child has ever been punished here by any means other than a hand to the posterior, and even that was unusual. This is absurd.

I turn on Miriam. "A *just* punishment?" The words are burdened with dark memories. "What did Stephen do to deserve this?"

"He blasphemed!"

I demand of Jerry, "What did Stephen *do?*"

Jerry's big hands curl into fists. "He . . . asked questions he shouldn't have."

"*What* questions?"

8

Jerry looks at Stephen. "You tell her."

Stephen swallows, but his voice is level, uninflected. "I asked why Jesus was called the son of David if Mary was a virgin. The *begats*—there's two of them in the gospels, one in the third chapter of Luke, the other in the first chapter of Matthew, and they both go from David to *Joseph*, not Mary. Besides, they don't match up, and I—"

"Be quiet!" Miriam shrills. "You'll not *repeat* your blasphemy!"

I feel the binding ache in my chest again. "Miriam, he only asked a question! Why didn't you answer it?"

"Because there are some questions a child shouldn't ask!"

"What questions should a child *not* be free to ask?"

"Mary, please . . ." Jerry's quiet voice reminds me that I've let mine get out of control. He looks around at the family. "This has gone too far," he pronounces solemnly. "I'm making an end to it, and I never want to hear any more about it. Is that understood?" He waits for the expected nods, then: "Miriam, it's time for breakfast."

She stares at him, seems on the verge of protesting that dismissal, but her eyes narrow, anger retreating into calculation. Jerry is Elder here, and she won't openly defy him. The patriarchal traditions of her childhood are too well ingrained in her. I doubt such defiance has occurred to her as a possibility. Not yet.

She says to me, "I'm sorry about your hand, Mary, but you got in my way."

Then she turns and strides past the breezeway gate toward the house, and one by one the other women and the children follow her. Bernadette takes Stephen's arm. "Come on, I'll fix an aloe poultice for your back. Mary? What about your hand?"

"Later, Bernadette. Thanks."

When Jerry and I are finally alone, I ask, "How did this happen?"

He grimaces, nervously adjusts the headband confining his long hair—a strip of cloth on which is embroidered, white on blue, DO UNTO OTHERS AS YOU WOULD HAVE THEM DO UNTO YOU. He says "I'm . . . not sure. I mean, it happened so fast, and—well, I told Miriam

9

she could run the morning services. It means a lot to her, and I didn't want . . ."

"You didn't want to argue with her?"

"Mary, it's important to keep peace in the family. You know that."

"Yes, I know." I know that we're a fragile, profoundly isolated community, and that dissension could destroy us. But what does he consider a reasonable price for peace?

He seems encouraged by my apparent agreement. "And Stephen *did* blaspheme."

"Jerry, don't be silly. He only asked a question. Do you really think Stephen is capable of blasphemy?"

Jerry stuffs his hands in his pockets, frowns over that for a moment, then shakes his head. "Not on purpose, anyway."

"When you were his age, didn't you ever ask that sort of question?"

"Not in *church*."

"But didn't you wonder about some of the inconsistencies in the Bible?"

Finally, he meets my eye and nearly smiles. "Yes, I wondered, and I sometimes asked my father questions like that."

"How did he answer them?"

"He told me the Bible is full of puzzles, and he didn't know what some of them meant." Jerry shakes his head, almost angrily. "I *still* don't know. I've prayed for guidance, but I still don't *know*."

He isn't satisfied with his ignorance, but I am. That vacuum might be filled with something other than dogma. And it means he hasn't entirely embraced Miriam's dogmatism.

The danger is that he's blind to it.

Through breakfast, through the morning's activities and school, through the midday meal, the atmosphere is strained, and Stephen is subdued, but nothing is said about his so-called blasphemy. Nothing *will* be said about it, not in Jerry's or Miriam's presence.

I take a deep breath of sun-warm air, turn my face up to the sky.

I'm standing at the top of the Knob, the wind tugging at my berry-dyed wool skirt, while Shadow lies in the grass at my feet. I look out at scudding cumulus clouds that cast lavender shadows on the turquoise sea, and the blue of the sky is nearly the deep, transparent hue I remember from Before. The sun eases the pain out of my arthritic joints, and I bask in it like an old, gray tabby. In my youth I never cared whether the sun shone or not and even relished the recurrent rains of western Oregon, but now I dread the rain and cherish the sun.

I stand on this dome of solid basalt veneered in earth and grass, but only a step away is a sheer drop of three hundred feet. I lean on my cane and look down at the ocean smashing at the rocks, while they dissolve each attacking surge into swirls of foam. The flowing locks of bull kelp sway back and forth with the progress of the battle, and the surf murmurs: *I am here . . . I am always here. . . .* That was the song the sea sang to me in my childhood, sings still, and the colors and patterns I see call to mind a painting that hangs in my room, one of Rachel's encaustics. Yet I know the point of departure for that painting was a piece of jasper she found on the beach.

And I think about the Chronicle, Rachel's story.

It must be written. And Stephen must take part in that. He must understand.

I gaze down into the caldron of battle between sea and land, and I know my battles aren't over—as I had once believed and hoped. Miriam made that acidly clear this morning. I must relive the old battles and gird my loins for a new one. My last, probably.

I turn and face south where the beach stretches, smooth as suede, a mile and more past the vine-shrouded ruins of Shiloh Beach and on into blued distance. But my old eyes seek nearer distances. There, perhaps two thousand feet down the beach, my gaze moves landward, past the eroded slope of the bank, the dark glades of spruce above it, and I survey the domain that was so long mine alone and was always Rachel's. Amarna, she called her fifteen-acre subsistence farm, and she named the two creeks bordering it Styx and Lethe.

Rachel enjoyed her little ironies.

The house is only twenty feet back from the bank. To the northeast, on the Styx, is the round, slab-sided water reservoir. East of the reservoir, the garden, with its high, sturdy deer fence, and farther east, the orchard. South of the orchard, the barn. The house is gray with weathered cedar shingles, and from this distance, the geometry of its hipped roofs is cleanly evident. It was built in a symmetrical U, the open side facing the sea. There was once a patio within the U, but Rachel had it roofed with angled glass panels and the open west end closed in with more glass to make a solar greenhouse.

From this vantage point Amarna looks much as it did when I first saw it forty years ago. The most profound change, the conversion of the garage into a church, isn't obvious from here. The only obvious change is the one that disrupted the geometric symmetry of the house: the addition that doubled the width of the north wing. Most of the new section is a storeroom, the remainder a room that Enid, Bernadette, and Grace share. That's the wing Jerry plans to enlarge this summer. Miriam and Esther are complaining that the basement—the half of it they've converted into an apartment—is too crowded with the six children, which will be seven when Esther's baby is born this summer. I've heard Miriam's complaints, seen her cold looks at me. I occupy the larger of the two bedrooms in the south wing. Alone. Yet I'm not inclined to give it up. They'll have it in due time.

The orchard is in flamboyant bloom, but I can only see patches of pink and white through the jack pines that provide a windbreak at the old fence line. That fence once marked the north boundary of Rachel's property, but after the End we appropriated the adjoining meadow where sheep, goats, cows, and horses graze now. There are six new lambs, and I smile as I watch them trying their spring-coiled legs. Only one calf this spring. The goats have done better: there are three kids. No colts yet, but Scheherazade is pregnant.

Thirty feet below me on the steep slope of the Knob is a stone-walled structure ten feet wide and twelve feet long. The vault. The vault, the crypt—treasure or tomb. It is set back into the slope, the front wall facing southeast, and from this point I look down on the peaked roof and upper part of the back wall. The rest of the wall is buried in the hillside. I start down the slope, bracing myself with my cane at every step, while Shadow runs headlong through the grass. She pauses at the vault, as she knows I will. I make my way to the thick, cedar door, touch the brass hasp and stainless steel padlock. Both metals have suffered with the years. And I wonder if these stone walls, this hasp and lock, will be enough to safeguard—

But such speculation is futile. The Chronicle and Stephen. I must focus my energies there. Is he old enough to understand? Perhaps I'm asking too much of a child.

But he's not a child. Again, I remind myself of that. He's thirteen, and the exigencies of life in this new Stone Age preclude a protracted childhood. And he'll understand. There are qualities in him that are in this place and time unique. I have no choice but to make Stephen heir to this legacy.

As my apprentice.

Yesterday was the sabbath, and we ended the day, as we do every sabbath, with the family meeting, the seven adults gathered around the long table in the dining room. Last night we discussed expanding the north pasture, adding a room to the new wing, whether the old buck goat should be slaughtered so that one of the younger bucks can take his place, and the advisability of planting corn in the old quarry this year. Then I broached the subject of taking Stephen on as my apprentice. Jerry thought it odd, the idea of an apprentice at teaching. I pointed out that Enid has Little Mary as her apprentice at weaving, that Bernadette has Deborah as her apprentice at herbal medicine, that Jonathan is in fact Jerry's apprentice. Jonathan is Jerry's oldest son and will inevitably be his successor as Elder.

It was a question of time, really. I asked for two hours every afternoon to spend with Stephen in private tutoring. That would be time taken away from his assigned tasks, and he needed the blessing of the family for that. At least Jerry's blessing; this is not a democracy. He finally agreed that Stephen and I could have the time between the midday meal and the afternoon break every day—other than the sabbath, of course—and no one raised any objections. Except Miriam.

Miriam in candlelight, golden light lambent in her hair, and I thought then that her color and the chiaroscuro light might inspire a Rembrandt, someone who would understand the shadows in her incandescence.

She recognized in my modest request a larger plan, and what I read in her eyes was elemental and frightening: a righteous rage.

Miriam, did you think it would be over when the old woman died?

No doubt she hoped so.

And so this morning she tried to put the fear of god into Stephen, to bring him—and perhaps the rest of the family—to heel.

I continue down the slope, grateful when it gentles into the pasture, giving me nearly level ground to walk on. I pass the pond near the fence and remember its genesis. There was always a seeping spring here, a slough of dampness where skunk cabbage flourished. Jerry made a pond of it to provide water for the livestock by blasting out the earth. With dynamite. He brought it with him from the Ark, and I remember clearly that crashing fountain of dirt and sod. Jerry was inordinately proud of it. But the dynamite—and there are still fifteen sticks of it in the storeroom—made *me* uneasy. I knew all too well how such plowshares were beaten into swords.

I turn my back on the pond, walk through the tangy new grass to the gate, remembering how little Jerry knows of swords.

When I reach the house, I find Enid and Grace sitting on the deck off the living room in the north wing. Grace rises when I approach. "Sit down, Grace," I tell her. "You needn't leave just because I've arrived."

Grace is ten years younger than I, yet to me she seems older. Of course, we all seem older. I'm older than my grandmother was at sixty-five; the medical and cosmetic miracles she took for granted died with the golden age. Grace hides her thin, gray hair under a white scarf tied at the back of her neck. There was a time when that scarf aligned her with community tradition. Now I suspect there's a sad vanity in it. I once heard her say that in her youth her hair was like spun gold. But the gold is gone, and Grace is a lost soul who can never find her way home again because her true home is gone.

And in her heart, I know, she blames me for that.

Grace stays, although she remains standing, and we three old women chat about the weather and other safe subjects, then she says she must go help in the garden. The weeds are growing like— well, like weeds, and she laughs unconvincingly as she makes her retreat.

I sit down in the cedar-slat chair next to Enid's, and after a long silence she looses one of her expressive sighs. "I suppose Jeremiah's right," she says. "We should all just forget about it."

Enid tends to misplace antecedents, but I know exactly what she's talking about. Enid is tall and ungainly, her brown hair shot with gray, her face too angular to be called anything but plain, yet her smile is magnificent, a revelation of gentle solicitude. But she's not smiling today. The lines around her eyes and mouth seem deeper.

"Enid, we can't just forget about a boy being whipped."

She shakes her head, callused hands rubbing against each other dryly. "No, and I never wanted to see Stephen hurt, and yet . . ."

"And yet you think he deserved it?"

"Well, he *did* blaspheme. I guess he did. But it seems to me the Lord would forgive a boy. I mean, I'm sure he didn't really know . . ."

She can't seem to bring that thought to a conclusion. I don't pursue it. "By the way, where *is* Stephen?"

"Well, I suppose he's out in the garden. Such a lovely day, and high time we got the ground ready for the seedlings." She rises, as if goaded by that reminder of her own duties.

"And high time Stephen was here." I try to keep the annoyance out of my voice, but her look of dismay tells me I've failed.

"Oh, I'd forgotten. Stephen begins his special lessons today. I

15

guess Miriam just . . ." Enid hesitates, then hurries toward the steps at the south end of the deck. "I'll go find him and tell him you're waiting."

"Thanks, Enid." I push myself to my feet. "I have to get something from my room. Tell him I'll meet him here."

When I return to the deck, Stephen still hasn't appeared. I sit in one of the chairs while Shadow circles and settles at my feet. Two of the cats, Juliet and Emily, are sunning themselves on the deck railing. In the pocket of my skirt is a small magnifying glass, and I hold in my lap a black-bound, five-by-seven-inch sketchbook. It's only one of eight that have been hidden for many years in the bottom drawer of the chest in my room. My souvenir drawer, I call it, where I've consigned memories I no longer wish to be reminded of.

Rachel gave me the sketchbooks, and I filled them not with drawings, as she would have, but with words, with a sporadic, disorganized, occasionally agonized history of the last forty years of my life. They might as well have been written in blood.

I'm not looking forward to unleashing the memories locked within these diaries, yet I need now to make sense of them, to find the meaning, the legacy in them. To *write* them. I was a writer Before. I just saw the proof of that in my souvenir drawer, a paperback novel titled *October Flowers*. A trivial thing, so it seems now, about fathers and daughters and the men daughters love. It was dedicated to *my* father. Posthumously. He died when I was eleven, only three months after he and Mother and I came to Shiloh Beach for that long summer week at Aunt Jan's house, the house by the sea that was her legacy to me when she died thirteen years later in a nursing home in Portland.

I open the diary, reach automatically for the magnifying glass, but I don't need it. The writing is large and legible. Still, I don't at first recognize it. Yes, it's my handwriting, but the years have separated me from these loops and lines. The Mary Hope, twenty-four years old, who wrote these words was not the same Mary Hope who reads them now.

The squeak of the sliding glass door that opens into the living room rouses me. I look around and see Stephen. He wears a shirt of fine, pale wool, pants of dark leather thrust under the tops of laced moccasin boots, and a headband of goldenrod yellow. His Christian mantra, embroidered on the headband in brown thread, is ENTER YE IN AT THE STRAIT GATE. It's all standard attire for the male members of the family, but the earthy colors suit him well. No, he's not a child, and it seems to have happened suddenly, his growing up. And like his mother, he has a face that seems as if it has been cast in burnished bronze. But in his eyes—large, slanted into heavy lids, black and deep as night—is life and intelligence and curiosity. He reminds me at this moment of a young man I once loved when I lived in Portland, a man named Dean, who called me Green Eyes and sent me oblique smiles—leopard grins, I called them—full of wry laughter and knowing sadness.

But now Stephen's hooded eyes are reflective, revealing nothing. I motion him to the chair beside me. He sits down, but doesn't lean back. I wait out his reticence, and finally he asks, "Did I do wrong, Mary?"

"What? You mean in questioning the lineage of Jesus? Well, did you intend to hurt anyone when you asked your questions?"

He frowns at that. "No, of course not."

"Then I can't see that you did wrong."

He shifts his shoulders slightly, grimacing. "You always said we should ask questions."

"And I still say it."

"But Miriam said it was wrong. And Jeremiah agreed with her."

"And I say it was *not* wrong," I answer bluntly. "Stephen, things aren't as simple as you were led to believe when you were a child. You're on the edge of adulthood now, and there are some hard truths you'll have to recognize. One is that good and bad are not absolutes. They're entirely subjective. They're judgments. Opinions."

He shakes his head and for a moment seems on the verge of tears. But he won't cry; he won't let himself cry.

"Then how am I to know what's good or bad?"

"You'll have to decide that for yourself, and it will never be easy. Never, as long as you live."

He sighs, but there is no resolution in his features. He remains silent for a while, staring out at the sea, then he turns. "I'm sorry you got hurt. For me."

I look down at my hand, at the diagonals of burning red. "Well, you'd do the same for me, wouldn't you?"

He smiles, no doubt finding it incongruous that I might be in the same situation he was. "Yes, I'd do it for you, Mary."

"Anyway, we've both learned something from all this. I said you should always ask questions, but I should've qualified it. There are some questions you don't ask in church." Then I add with a crooked smile: "At least . . . not out loud."

"But I can still ask questions to myself?"

"I doubt you'll be able to stop yourself. I hope not." I pause a moment, then: "Do you know why you're here now?"

"Enid just said you wanted to talk to me."

"Did she tell you I've chosen you to be my apprentice?"

Stephen stares at me. "No."

"My apprentice and someday my successor as teacher."

He seems stunned, and at first I don't realize why, until he turns away and asks, "Why should you need anyone to be your successor?"

And now I am surprised. "Do you think I'm immortal, Stephen?"

He doesn't look at me, nor even move. "It's just . . . well, it'll be a long time before you have to worry about anyone being your successor."

"Let's hope so, but it takes a long time to learn what you must to be a teacher. That's why I'm starting with you now. We'll have two hours every afternoon. Except the sabbath."

"But I'll never be able to learn enough to be a teacher, to . . . take your place."

"Yes, you will, because you'll never *stop* learning. You have it in you, Stephen, or I wouldn't have chosen you."

He faces me, his dark eyes reflecting the sun on the sea. Finally he nods. "Where do I begin?"

"You've already begun. You began when you read your first word.

18

In the future you and I will cover a lot of subjects I haven't touched on in school, but first . . ." I look down at the diary. "There's something I have to do, Stephen. I'm going to write Rachel's story. The Chronicle of Rachel. But it's my story, too, and I want you to help me, to experience it with me so you'll understand . . ." What? I don't know how to explain what I want and hope of him. " 'To see a world in a grain of sand . . .' Remember that?"

He nods, smiling. "William Blake."

"Yes. Well, maybe Rachel and I are like a grain of sand, and maybe you can find the world of . . . of humanity in our story."

"That book—is that your story?"

"Only fragments of it, and there are more of these books. But I never kept a proper diary. I only wrote about things that were especially important to me. The story is mostly in my head, Stephen. I have to search out the memories, then I can write the story."

"But how can I help you?"

"By listening, by making my memories part of your memories."

He doesn't yet understand what I expect of him, but he's curious. He wants to hear the story. I can ask no more now.

He pulls one knee up, wraps his arms around it. "When does the story begin?"

I have to think about that, and I realize that nothing in my life or Rachel's is important to this Chronicle before I came to Amarna. I've tried to tell the children what life was like in the time before the End, to give them a taste of that infinitely complex, glittering, and terrifying civilization. I lived in a dying golden age, a time of miracles and mania. Rachel said that one of the most profound tragedies of human existence is to live at the end of a golden age—and know it.

She recognized both the miracles and the mania. Enid, Grace, and Bernadette lived in that golden age, too, but only on the edges of it; the edges of mania. They remember almost nothing of it.

I remember.

"The story begins, Stephen, when I left Portland."

He nods. "Why did you leave the city?"

"Because I wanted to write. Not just bureaucratic semitruths and useless bulletins." I smile at his look of confusion. "I worked for the government, Stephen, for IDA: the Information Dissemination Agency. And I left the city because it had become a place where you couldn't breathe for the smog, you couldn't move for the people, the homeless, the unemployed, the huddled masses longing to be fed. This country—the world, in fact—was in an economic depression. The sheer numbers were finally catching up with the resources, and what resources were left were squandered in wars. If only we could've . . ."

He's still looking at me in confusion, and I stop to remind myself: simple, Mary, keep it simple.

"I left Portland because I had a dream of living and writing in a house by the sea. I thought if I couldn't make a living at writing, I could get a job cleaning motel rooms, if nothing else. Shiloh Beach was a resort town, a place people came to stay for a while to enjoy the sea and the beach."

"Didn't you come to live with Rachel?"

"I didn't know Rachel then. I didn't know anyone in Shiloh. I hadn't been there for thirteen years, since I was eleven. The house by the sea was my aunt's; she willed it to me when she died. It was so naive, that dream. There was so much I didn't know. I didn't know how hard the depression had hit the coast, I didn't know about the road gangs—Rovers, Gypsies, Goolies, they had various names for themselves—I didn't know about the squatters and migrants. Well, I knew of their existence from television and newspapers. But I didn't understand. . . ."

So much I didn't understand then, still don't. I left the city in search of a place to write because it was the one thing I did well, the one thing that seemed to justify my existence. In search of the sea that I loved with the passion of childhood. In search of a dream.

Before the beginning of years
  There came to the making of man
Time, with a gift of tears;
  Grief, with a glass that ran;
Pleasure, with pain for leaven;
  Summer, with flowers that fell;
Remembrance, fallen from heaven,
  And madness risen from hell. . . .
        —ALGERNON CHARLES SWINBURNE,
          "ATALANTA IN CALYDON" (1865)

Mary Hope stared through the glass only inches from her right shoulder. Beyond the window—fogged with the heat of the bus, smeared with fingerprints, streaked with yellow spears of reflected light—was another world, and it sustained her. Phosphorescent silver shapes whisked, fragmented, past the black span of glass, but she knew them and in imagination made them whole: meadows of velvet grass; groves of alder, pale limbs winter bare; fir and hemlock catching stars in their crowns, their trunks black columns for temples consecrated to their own existence. Sometimes, when the winding of the road turned the bus southward, she could

21

see the moon, a perfect disk of ultimate white, flickering through the black smoke of trees.

Mary sat squeezed into a seat once meant for two, now, with the center armrest removed, occupied by three adults and a baby. She hugged her duffel bag to her chest. The strap angled around her body, the buckle digging into her backbone. All her worldly possessions—all that she hadn't sold or given away—were in this canvas bag. Clothes and cosmetics, three books, and the few thousand dollars that were her grubstake for a new life. She felt her shallow breaths on chapped lips, wondered if she could ever get used to the sour-sweet smell of tobacco and emjay smoke and liquor—all illegal here, all tolerated indifferently. Tolerated like the fetid air and the odors of overheated bodies, of mold and urine that clung to the upholstery.

Mary Hope considered the relativity of time.

Rather, the subjectivity of it. Her watch informed her that five hours and forty-four minutes had passed since the beginning of the twentieth day of February, that twelve hours and twenty-one minutes had passed since she left her apartment to wait in the hellish limbo of the terminal for a coast bus, that two hours and thirty-six minutes had passed since the bus left Portland. And every one of those hours and minutes, every second of them, she had experienced separately and distinctly. She had learned that boredom and fear can coexist and that they make a mind-racking alchemy.

The fear was the ancient fear of strangers. Too many strangers, any one of whom could be mad. There was no way to know which among the pressing thousands might be over the edge past sanity.

But that was one of the things she was leaving behind.

Her left arm from the elbow up was numb. Laura's *right* arm was undoubtedly equally numb where it pressed against Mary's.

Laura. Mary didn't know her last name, but Laura wasn't one of the strangers to be feared. To be pitied, perhaps. Laura, alone and lonely, sixteen years old, her baby only three weeks old, trying to return to her family in Coos Bay. The baby began crying, a fretful wail against the rumble of the bus's motor. Laura sang, "Hush you by . . . don't you cry. . . ."

Mary closed her eyes, listening to that frail lullaby. The baby was sick. Probably one of the viral mutations that seemed to appear magically every winter. This year's model was called L-flu. Someone would come up with a vaccine, and she'd have to get a shot. There must be a USMA hospital in Shiloh Beach.

The bus slowed for a wide turn to the south, and Mary, suddenly alert, stared out the window. A plain of silver grass . . . there, the moon glinted on water. It must be—could be—the Coho River estuary.

Reflected moonlets raced over the water at the speed of the bus, and Mary held her breath to avoid fogging the glass. She couldn't doubt it now. The Coho River estuary. That was only—how far? No more than three miles from Shiloh Beach. Her breath came out in a sigh that caught in muscular tremors. *Aunt Jan—oh, finally, I'm almost home.*

The beach house—that was all Mary could see now. She could even smell the misted scent of sea winds. It was gray, the house, shingled in weathered cedar. There was one bedroom; a kitchen with minimal, almost antique appliances; a living room with a fireplace and big windows looking out on the sea. The furniture was made of wood, real wood in unique varieties, like the cherry dining table, the rosewood rocker, the nested teak tables. And the clock on the mantel, the old Seth Thomas that clanged the hours so steadfastly—

"Mary? Are you okay?" Laura was nearly shouting over the spitting of the motor and the baby's crying.

Mary tried to control her trembling, tried not to laugh aloud, but she didn't have time to answer Laura's query. The ampsystem blurted the bus driver's announcement: "Passengers for Shiloh Beach, we will arrive in approximately five minutes. For continuing passengers, there will be a twenty-minute stopover. Rest rooms and vendor refreshments will be available. There is also a Federal Transit Administration infocomp at the terminal. Shiloh Beach, five minutes."

Along the aisle, people began shifting, pulling themselves out of cramped squats. Laura said plaintively, "I wish it was Coos Bay."

"It's only a few more hours, Laura. You'll be all right."

"I wish you were—oh, Jamie, *please* shut up."

The baby wailed louder, and Mary turned to look out the window. Black smoke of trees rushing past; ahead, another open area. That would be the golf course—

The ampsystem came on again at the same moment the driver hit the brakes, hard. *"People, we got trouble!"*

Mary threw her arms out to brace herself against the seat in front of her, caught a split second's glimpse of the highway ahead, of two cars barricading the road, glittering in the bus's headlights.

"Hang on!" the driver's amplified voice shrilled. *"Rovers!"*

The terror in that word shivered through her. The bus lurched to the right, tires screaming. Its murky interior erupted with cries of alarm, while Mary pounded desperately on the window. It was a breakout window. All bus windows were breakouts. It *had* to be—

The bus careened left, then right again, and Mary was crushed against the window under the pressure of flailing bodies. The baby shrieked, and the hammering, grinding crash seemed endless. The window gave way as the bus thudded to a halt, listing to the right, and she tumbled out, breath choked off at the impact when she hit the ground. She rolled in a tangle of bodies to the bottom of the ditch, staggered to her feet, and there stood rigid.

From behind the barricade of smashed cars at the front of the bus surged a troop of human figures as irrational as monsters born of a medieval imagination. Howling insensately, faces limned in fluorescent colors in the shapes of skulls, they brandished guns, axes, machetes, all strobe-lighted in the glare of hand spots dancing jerkily toward her.

Mary shouted, "Laura!" But she couldn't even hear her own voice in the din of cries and screams, couldn't see faces in the darkness where more passengers spilled out of the bus's windows in heaving avalanches. The Rovers plunged into the crowd as she scrambled out of the ditch, and she heard the spit of automatics, heard bullets pound into flesh. A man toppled against her in a rain of blood, and she broke away, struck out at an adreneline-charged run into an open field toward the haven of the trees beyond. How far? She couldn't guess. She could only run. The guns stuttered amid cries of agony, banshee paeans. Stumbling, blinded by the searing afterimages of the lights, she ran toward the pallid fringe of alders.

A sobbing yelp of pain, and something knocked her right leg out from under her. Drowning in dead grass, hands clutching a barbed vine, she lurched to her feet and ran.

Alder ghosts ahead of her and finally around her. Silver branches in silver light, darkness pooled around them. Hands stretched out before her, she caromed from one dappled trunk to the next, the dense underbrush a riptide miring her legs. She swam into the shadows of the conifer forest beyond, where moonlight filtered icily into the depths. Branches raked her face, battered her body, roots caught her feet and threw her down again and again, and she pulled herself up again and again and thrashed on through the tangled darkness. She couldn't hear beyond her own crashing progress, beyond the reverberations of her pulse and the hoarse rale of her panting. She plunged into a lightless ravine, terror intensified by the absolute blackness until she swarmed up the far slope, clawing at roots, toward the glimmer of moonlight.

The light drew her on finally into a treeless aisle, and she followed the light as a flower follows the sun, followed it until she could no longer run, until she could no longer walk, until at length her legs gave way, and she lay with her cheek pressed into bladed gravel.

She still didn't hear the silence. That came only when her panting slowed and her pulse ceased pounding in her ears. With her awareness of silence—of safety—she awakened to pain. Her throat and lungs burned, her muscles quivered, her body ached with countless bruises and abrasions.

But her right leg—that was more than strained muscles and battered flesh. The pain was so intense it kindled a new kind of fear.

She tried to sit up and realized that the constriction around her chest was the shoulder strap of her duffel bag. All her worldly goods. She had somehow held on to that. No, not held on. It would have been difficult to rid herself of it; she had only managed to push the bag around to her back. She maneuvered into a sitting position, grunting with the effort. Below her right knee, the pant leg was wet. Her palm came away dark and glistening in the pallid light.

Wind moved the black plumes of branches above her. She shivered, dizzied by their stately bowing and rising. The sky was perceptibly lighter than the trees, and the moon was sinking behind them. She could see, dimly, the ephemeral clouds of her breath. Dawn. The dawn's early light, pearly light, first light I see—

Damn, she was getting hysterical. No, that was over now. But the shivering wouldn't stop. Laura. Poor Laura. And Jamie, only three weeks old. They couldn't have survived.

Those bastards! Those inhuman, insane—

She couldn't find words adequate for her rage. Perhaps the words to encompass it had never been invented, not in all the centuries that humankind had suffered at its own hands.

She looked around in the ashen light that bordered on darkness. A road. She was on a road. Winter-dead weeds at the sides and in a fringe down the center, but it was a road, and it must lead somewhere.

All she had to do was walk down the road until she came to a house, ask the residents to call the local or Auxiliary Police. Must be an Apie station in Shiloh Beach.

All she had to do was walk. . . .

Her teeth chattered uncontrollably, and it seemed that ice crystals were forming under her skin, exquisite fronded patterns slowly coalescing. She struggled to her feet, the effort wrenching out cries of pain, took two steps, and fell to the ground. She didn't try again. The neural links between her muscles and brain were frozen.

She looked up at the bowing plumes. *I'm going to die here.* Some bleak, unfathomable irony lay in that.

In the distance a sound. She wasn't sure whether she heard it or imagined or remembered it.

The murmur of the sea.

I am here . . . I am always here. . . .

Under a white sky in a white, frozen ocean, she lay on a white ice floe waiting for it to melt out from under her. It seemed fitting.

26

Broken and useless things must be discarded for the good of the tribe.

But the sound was puzzling. Sniffing. A soft whine. Something touched her cheek. She opened her eyes, and the creature drew back, watching her with amber brown eyes, cabochon gems trapping golden light. How did a fox get on her ice floe? Fur of russet blending into brown; under the chin, a ruff of white. Ice white . . .

She realized then as her mind and eyes came into focus that her ice floe had vanished, that she lay in a place full of color: sky blue, looming conifers deep ever green, grasses winter rose and gold.

With a cry, she jerked away from the animal, and it jumped back, teeth bared. She tried to get to her feet, but she was too weak, and the pain hit too hard. She only managed to prop herself on her left elbow, right arm raised to fend off the dog. And now there were two of them, the second smaller, blacker. They danced and whirled and barked, the sounds like bludgeons. The piercing whistle cut into her skull.

"Topaz! Shadow! Here—come *here!*"

Mary numbly watched the dogs retreat to flank the figure moving toward her.

A woman. Age indeterminate, but past forty certainly. Small, compact body clad in jeans and a red jacket, both faded with wear. Below her knit cap, fine hair the color of sand lay on a high forehead; her face was all one color with her sandy brows, the weathered skin lined as if she turned her deep brown eyes often to distant vistas.

Mary's fear dissolved as it would if she'd met a friend of many years on this remote, forest-girded road. She didn't understand that, but neither did she question it.

The woman knelt beside her, regarding her with concern but no surprise. She asked, "What happened to you?"

Mary didn't try to answer that. She wanted to say, *I know you.* Instead, she asked, "Who are you?"

The woman answered, "I'm Rachel Morrow."

27

Therefore to this dog will I,
Tenderly not scornfully,
  Render praise and favor:
With my hand upon his head,
Is my benediction said
  Therefore and for ever.
                    —ELIZABETH BARRETT BROWNING,
                        TO FLUSH, MY DOG (1844)

S hadow stretches every fiber for her tumultuous runs after gulls, unaware, apparently, of the insurmountable advantage wings give them. At the end of each chase she returns to me, pattering along on the delicate feet of her mirror image in the sea-wet sand, and I remember the first Shadow. Rachel's Shadow. Like her name-sake, this Shadow is mostly black, a silky black like the waters of the night, with white stockings, belly, and ruff, white at the tip of her plume of a tail. Russet marks the divisions of black and white, forms expressive commas above her eyes. She is a replicate of the first Shadow, and from the moment I saw her as a blind, wavering

28

pup, I claimed her as my own and named her for her ancestor, the good mother of our canine tribe.

Topaz would have been a good mother, too, but there are no throwbacks to remind me of her.

How many generations did the first Shadow and Sparky beget? I can't remember, and the bloodlines were muddied—or invigorated—by feral dogs and by Agate, whom Rachel and I stole as a pup from a feral bitch. The dogs at Amarna now—there are only six since Desdemona died this winter—tend to pointed noses, long hair, upright ears, with black the predominant color, although Agate's genes manifest themselves occasionally, as they have in Stickeen and Diamond, in a leggy sturdiness and tawny coat. Sparky was a mongrel, part spaniel, part terrier, black except for the white locket on his chest; he had the tenacity typical of terriers. I see his personality in his descendants more than his physical attributes.

Is that anthropomorphism, to think of personality in animals?

Perhaps. But I've lived too intimately with animals not to recognize in them the existence of unique characteristics of mind.

I look down at the sand, at my tracks: drag lines between each print, the holes made by my cane like periods punctuating terse sentences. Then I look ahead and choose a log as a convenient resting place. I make my way up the slope of the beach and ease down on the weather-polished back of the log. To the north looms the dark, basalt wall of the Knob, at its base a tumble of rocks terraced by the sea that even on this calm day strikes with white detonations and rains spray into the tide pools.

Shadow is sniffing about in the rocks, and I reach for the silent whistle on its chain around my neck. What she might find to eat on the beach can harbor salmonella and prove a deadly repast. I blow at the whistle, hearing only a faint wheeze, but Shadow looks up and lopes toward me. The whistle was Rachel's, and it has served well through all the generations the first Shadow and Sparky begat.

When she reaches me, fur beaded with water and sand from her futile pursuits of gulls, she lies down at my feet and smiles at me.

Anthropomorphism again?

I am the alpha in Shadow's mixed species pack. She trusts me and lets me dominate her and seems to enjoy physical contact with me. She moves closer, presses her forehead against my leg, and she knows I'll stroke her head, scratch her back. It's bonding behavior, I suppose, and it works. I'm bonded to her as I seldom was to humans.

But she stiffens now, looks intently to the south, gives a sharp bark, then catapults into a run toward the figure walking up the beach.

Stephen. I told him to meet me here this afternoon. I watch, laughing, but a little envious, as he runs exuberantly, with the unaware grace of youth, to greet Shadow, then runs with her until they reach me, waiting inert and weary on the log. He isn't even panting.

"Good day, Mary."

"Good day to you, Stephen. You and Jeremiah and Jonathan certainly did yourselves proud on your fishing expedition."

He nods, grinning proudly. "The salmon run's the best I've ever seen. We could've brought back more than the one wagonload, if we had a way to take care of them. Jeremiah says we should build a bigger smokehouse."

Jerry and the boys were gone for two days collecting their bounty. They returned with it yesterday evening, and this morning the women and girls were busy cleaning the fish and hanging them in the smokehouse.

I remember a time when Rachel and I wondered if we'd ever see another salmon running the Coho River.

Stephen sits beside me, legs stretched out, heels digging into the sand. "Are you going to tell me more about your story, your . . . Chronicle?"

His interest pleases me, even if it's still only curiosity. "Yes, of course. But most of this part still has to come out of my memory. I hadn't begun my occasional diary yet."

"How can you remember things that happened so long ago?"

"Sometimes—at least, at my age—things that happened long ago are more vivid than things that happened just yesterday."

He seems to consider that, then: "What happened after Rachel found you?"

I look out at the tumbling breakers and back into memory. "Well, she went to get Jim and Connie Acres. They were her nearest neighbors. Jim brought his old brown Dodge van. He was a big man, hair like those clouds, white on top, gray on the edges. I remember when he carried me to the van, I held on to him like a frightened child, and he smelled of soap and . . . it seemed like sage. He reminded me of my father, and that made me cry." Now I can smile at that memory, at Jim assuring me I was safe. He didn't understand why I was crying, and I was too weak to explain.

Stephen prompts me. "Did you come to Amarna then?"

"Yes. When we reached the house, Jim carried me inside and put me in the bed in the spare room. Well, it's Jeremiah's room now, and it was mine until after Rachel died. Anyway, once I was in bed, Connie took over. She was a paramedic. A doctor of sorts."

"What did she look like?"

The memory is poignantly clear. Constanza Jensen Acres, of mixed ancestry that combined so beautifully. "Well, she was tall and thin, Stephen, and her hair was salt-and-pepper gray. She moved like a dancer. An amazing woman. And within an hour she had me numbed with a local anesthetic and the wound cleaned, sutured, and bandaged. She plied me with antibiotics and gave me a tetanus shot. The wound wasn't serious, but I'd lost a lot of blood. Anyway, I went to sleep, and it was a long time before I woke up enough even to know where I was. I remember lying on that narrow bed wondering what kind of hospital they had in Shiloh where the walls were wood-paneled and lined with bookshelves. Then it began to dawn on me that I wasn't in a hospital at all when I saw the paintings on the wall across from me. They were all abstracts: amorphous forms and colors that seemed to glow. I thought I saw images in them I recognized, yet when I tried to name them, they vanished."

Then I look down at Shadow. "I was *sure* I wasn't in a hospital when I saw Shadow asleep at the foot of the bed. The first Shadow, I mean. As soon as I moved, she jumped off the bed and started barking, then Topaz appeared in the doorway, barking too. Finally, Rachel came to quiet them. She sat in a chair by the bed and answered questions for me. You know, where am I, what happened, that sort of thing."

Stephen leans down to stroke Shadow's head. "You knew then you'd come home, didn't you?"

I consider his question, knowing that to him it is rhetorical. He doesn't understand that I lived in a world of myriad alternatives, that I had another vision of *home*.

"No, Stephen, I only knew then that I'd found a friend. That was miracle enough."

Nor does he understand how rare it was then, finding a friend. I wonder if he really knows what the word means. There are so few people in his world, and they're all family, all part of his tribe.

He turns, studying me intently. "Mary, what was Rachel like? I mean, you talk about her all the time, and you showed us the pictures of her, but I don't really know what she was like."

I nod, pausing before I answer. "Well, the first thing you should understand about Rachel is that she was an artist. Her life centered on art. Sometimes people bought her paintings. Not many by the time I met her. Most people didn't have the money to spare for what was considered a luxury. Yet art was one of the first expressions of our humanity, Stephen. Cro-Magnon didn't consider it a luxury. Anyway, Rachel was fifty years old when I came to Amarna. She'd lived alone here for twenty years and never married or had children."

"Why didn't she have children? Was she a Barren?" Stephen doesn't ask why she didn't marry. That institution means little to him.

"No, she wasn't a Barren. She chose to remain childless because at that point in our history, she considered bringing more children into the world a crime against humanity."

His dark eyes widen. "A *crime*?"

"Yes. I've told you about the billions of people burdening this small planet, but I know it's impossible for you to imagine them. Rachel said that nature wouldn't tolerate too many of anything, wouldn't tolerate imbalance. The scales were shifting even then. She didn't have children because she was too capable of loving them, and she'd seen the writing on the wall."

"Like Daniel. *Mene, mene, tekel, upharsin.*" Then with a perplexed frown: "But what writing did Rachel see?"

"A balance *will* be struck. That's what she saw."

The breakers turn slowly like liquid green glass, crash into white froth, and I remember the seas of years past, remember watching them with Rachel. The balance was indeed struck. But waves have broken on this shore for millennia and will continue to do so for millennia to come, whatever humankind's fate. Rachel understood that splendid indifference, and she wasn't afraid of it.

"And yet . . . she hoped, Stephen. She always hoped that humankind would learn tolerance and kindness and restraint, that we wouldn't throw away everything we'd learned and built. I think painting was her way of expressing her hope and her amazement at the world. And painting gave her sharp eyes." Stephen smiles tentatively at that, and I add, "It trained her to see things most people missed and in ways most people wouldn't think of. Yet she also approached the world as a scientist would, and she never considered that a paradox."

"What do you mean, as a scientist would?"

Do I detect an edge of suspicion in spite of all my teaching? Perhaps. I'm not his only teacher.

"I mean Rachel wanted to understand the world around her as it really is. She thought it was magnificent and wanted to know about it. Of course, no one can understand everything there is to know about the world, even if everything were known. She said reality is always in the process of being defined. But she learned everything she could."

Stephen picks up a strand of sea grass weathered to translucent fibers and absently wraps the pale ribbon around one finger, while I wait for the question he hasn't yet decided to ask.

In time, he puts it into words. "Miriam says there are some things people can't know. *Shouldn't* know."

No doubt she would add, some things people must take on faith.

I ask, "Do *you* believe there are things people shouldn't know?"

He unfurls the ribbon of grass. "Miriam says it's written in the Bible."

"Maybe it is. That doesn't answer my question."

He looks at me, and the grass slips from his hands, snakes along the sand with the wind behind it. Perhaps it's because we're alone and away from Amarna—away from Miriam—that he considers the question carefully and at length answers, "I don't see why it should be wrong for me to know *anything.*"

And I close my eyes, let my breath out in a long sigh.

"It isn't wrong, Stephen. Don't ever let anyone make you think it is. Anyway, I was telling you about Rachel. She wasn't doing much painting when I came to Amarna, but the house was still more a studio than a home. The big workroom in the center—that was a living room before she bought the house, but she made it into a studio for encaustic painting. Those are the ones done with wax and heat. And she made the dining room into a watercolor studio. Sometimes I still call it the north studio."

Stephen is intrigued. Perhaps it hasn't occurred to him that the house wasn't always exactly as it is now and has been all his life. "What else was different?" he asks.

"Well, nothing, really. Before she bought the house, the living room was a sort of sun porch, I think, but when I came it was much the same as it is now, except we replaced some of the furniture."

"Was the fireplace still there?"

"Oh, yes. Rachel heated the house entirely with wood. That was the cheapest source of heat for her since she had plenty of trees on her property. In fact, the old wood cookstove in the kitchen—well, it was an antique then, but she used it. I remember how amazed I was at that stove when I took my first look around the house. But the thing that amazed me most was the books. Nearly every wall had bookshelves, and more books were stacked on every table and even on the floor. I knew then I'd found a kindred soul."

"How many books did she have?"

"I don't know exactly. Thousands. What we have in the house now is only a few hundred. The duplicates."

He looks up toward the Knob as if he could see the vault, but doesn't seem to find it necessary to say anything about it. "Her neighbors—Jim and Connie—where did they live?"

"About half a mile south toward Shiloh. The ruins of the house are still there. They helped with Rachel's garden and livestock and shared the harvest. Jim was a retired engineer, and his pension couldn't even keep them in food. Rachel had a small income she'd inherited from her parents, but it was a pittance with the inflation that hit in the years before the End." But I see that I'm not making sense to him. He doesn't fully understand the concept of money. How could he understand inflation and a world economy skewed by a glut of population and by small, vicious wars that destroyed industries, cut off most of the world's oil supplies, and disrupted trade networks?

"Did Rachel have a lot of livestock?" he asks.

That's the economy Stephen understands, the elementary economy of food production. "Not as much as we have. Let's see, she had chickens, rabbits, bees, goats, and one horse, a bay mare she called Silver. The mare was about as far as you could get from the original Silver." His puzzled look tells me I must explain the Lone Ranger, and before I've finished that, Rachel's choice of a name for the horse loses its humor. Finally, I add, "She also had the two shelties, Shadow and Topaz."

"Didn't you tell us one of her dogs was named Sparky?"

"Well, Sparky was Jim and Connie's dog to begin with. The shelties—Jim told me they came from a kennel in Oldport that got burned out by a road gang. The two pups were the only survivors, and Rachel adopted them. Same story with Silver. She came from a stable in Shiloh. The owner rented horses to tourists, but he went broke and sold off the horses. For dog food, probably. By the time Rachel heard about it, Silver was the only one left. Rachel didn't need a horse—couldn't afford to keep it in hay—but she took Silver in. Just like she took me in."

Stephen smiles gently at that, but his smile fades as he says, "You still grieve for her, don't you?"

"Yes, I guess I do."

35

He nods. "I still want to cry sometimes for Rebecca."

We're both silent for a while, sharing the pain dulled by three years, but still persistent. I loved Rebecca like the daughter I never had. So frail and fey, she argued nothing, accepted everything. Even death when it came in the trappings of agony. She left us little Rachel and the memory of music, of the clear honey of her singing.

Stephen's hands close into fists. "I don't understand why Rebecca had to die."

Miriam called it the will of god.

"I don't understand it, either, Stephen."

"Maybe that's something we're not supposed to know."

I hesitate, wait until he looks around at me. "Stephen, reasons are human inventions. I mean, reasons as opposed to explanations. You can invent a reason that will satisfy you, but you should be aware that it's an invention."

I let him think about that a moment, then I look out at the surf. "I've lost track of my story. Where was I? Somewhere in the middle of my recovery, I guess. I was bed-bound most of the time for about a week, and Rachel and Connie and Jim took care of me like I was a long-lost relative. I told them about the house Aunt Jan had willed to me, about my plans to live there and write. And they tried to warn me. Shiloh was a shadow of what it had been when I was there as a child. That's why Connie took care of me at Rachel's house instead of sending me to a hospital. There *wasn't* a hospital closer than Portland. The USMA hospital in Shiloh had closed six years before. Connie ran a small clinic, and that was the only medical facility in the area. The town of Shiloh wasn't even incorporated by then. Jim was the last mayor, by the way. He was also chief of the local Veepies."

"What does that mean—Veepies?"

"Well, it was from the initials VP, for Voluntary Police. They were townspeople who helped the Federal Auxiliary Police, the Apies. Anyway, all Jim ever got out of ten years as chief of the Shiloh Veepies was a set of engraved handcuffs." I have the handcuffs now; they're among the memorabilia in my souvenir drawer.

Stephen watches me, but remains silent, and at length I continue: "They tried to prepare me for what I'd find at my aunt's house, but I didn't listen. I didn't *want* to listen. I'd quit my job in Portland, left the few friends I had there, left a man I loved, left my mother. Poor woman, she never got over Dad's death, and then I left her. I asked her to come with me, but she wouldn't. She was afraid. She didn't know why, and that was the saddest part. But *I* couldn't stay in the city. I had my dream—my dream of living by the sea and writing. And I had a house. All mine, free and clear. My house by the sea . . ."

Ah well,
this is the blind world swerving to its end, all balance gone,
deer starving in the trees, cougars in distant hills,
small puppies, bought for boys' vacations, left
by loving parents on New England's shores
at summer's end to starve or grow up wild.
I hope they live to stalk us once again.
—LOREN EISELEY, *"WATCH THE UNEASY*
LANDLORDS" (1973)

A gray day, the clouds like fog waiting to settle on the land. It was the first time Mary Hope had been outside the house, except for occasional forays onto the deck. Yet she felt strong today, ready to get on with her new life. She knew she could deal with anything now. She had survived her trial by fire—with a little help from her friends.

Mary accepted the cane Rachel offered, declining the crutches Connie had provided. She didn't need them now. Nor did she need any medication stronger than aspirin. On this day of all days, she didn't want her head muddled. Rachel was quiet, almost taciturn.

She didn't argue with Mary about forgoing the crutches, nor comment when she had to help her into the old, red VW van.

Rachel backed the van out of the garage down a long driveway to a turnaround, then headed east, and Mary saw Amarna for the first time, saw the whole of it: the house weathered into its setting, the spruce trees on the bank ragged silhouettes, the bamboo south of the house lushly exotic. In her mind, bamboo was a tropical plant, but that giant grass flourished in this wet, temperate climate. She saw the high deer fence surrounding the garden; the orchard, veiled in the pink of furled buds; the barn, built by a carpenter, simple and functional, and like the house, covered with gray cedar shingles tinted green with microscopic moss. Silver was at the watering trough by the barn, flanked by three brown, lop-eared Nubian goats.

Rachel's domain was fenced with barbless wire. When she reached the gate in the southeast corner, she had to stop and get out to unlock and open the gate, drive through, and get out again to close it. Then she drove along a gravel road that curved to the south. At one point she gestured toward the side of the road. "That's where I found you."

Mary didn't remember the place, only what brought her to it, and she shivered. "You're a true good Samaritan, Rachel."

Rachel laughed. "I doubt that."

"I mean it. I'd have died if you hadn't found me."

Rachel glanced at her, but made no comment, concentrating on shifting gears where the gravel road met a paved loop. Mary leaned forward, hands braced on the dashboard, her pulse quickening. She remembered now. This loop marked the end of North Front Road, which ran parallel to the beach for a mile before angling inland to make a Y with Highway 101. Aunt Jan's house was at the south end of town, but in that childhood summer she and her parents had explored all of Shiloh by bicycle or on foot. Rachel pointed out the Acres house northwest of the loop, but Mary was too distracted by memories and anticipation to garner more than an impression of ochre-stained wood and great spans of glass. Nor was she interested in the other houses as they drove along North Front

Road. Maybe there were a lot of FOR SALE signs, but she ignored them.

The shopping mall at the junction of North Front and the high-way surprised her. It had been built since she was last in Shiloh. Rachel said, "This is really Shiloh's downtown these days." Yet half the mall's shops were vacant. Mary ignored that, too.

And on the highway, which served as Shiloh's main street, she ignored the empty buildings and boarded-up windows. There were still shops open for business here. The bakery—yes, she remem-bered that and its rich crumpet bread—a barber shop, a laundromat.

After three blocks, Rachel turned left into a parking lot. On the south was an aged building with scarred, brick walls. That, Rachel informed her, was Connie Acres's clinic. Mary only glanced at it. North of the parking lot stood a new building, flat-roofed, olive drab cement block, metal letters above the entry: U.S. AUXILIARY POLICE STATION, CENTRAL OREGON COAST DIVISION. A communication tower loomed over the building, its dish antennas bizarre blossoms on the latticed steel stem. Six black Apie patrol cars were lined up in front of the station.

Mary still didn't understand why Jim Acres insisted on going with them to her aunt's house, why he further insisted that they meet him here. And when he came out of the station, it was in the company of an Apie captain who looked like a model for a recruiting poster.

When Rachel and Mary got out of the van, Jim made the in-troductions. Captain Harry Berden, tall and hard and handsome. He spoke with a Western drawl and hailed from Boise, Idaho. Mary found herself pleased with his assessing gaze as he courteously ex-pressed regret that she'd been caught in the Rover ambush.

But she was less than pleased when Jim put in casually, "Harry's going to drive us down to your aunt's house in his patrol."

Mary looked at Jim sharply, but he seemed incapable of meeting her eye. She smiled at Harry Berden and said, "Well, we'd enjoy your company, Captain, but I don't really think we need a police escort."

"You do, ma'am," he answered soberly. "Take my word for it."

Then he explained in his easy drawl that after the oil crunch hit Shiloh so hard, the few people who stayed—no more than five hundred, he estimated—had moved into the north end of town. There was safety in banding together. The south end, well, it had been left to the squatters. And he explained that 101 was a hobo's highway, a migration route for the homeless and hopeless. And he explained that the Apie garrison here was understaffed, under-equipped, and they had more pressing problems than what he called the wild geese. The highway was turf to road gangs; the Rovers that attacked her bus were still holed up somewhere around Shiloh. And he explained that he knew from the address that her aunt's house was within the area occupied by the nomads. Forfeited to them.

Squatters' land, he called it.

Mary listened, feeling unexpectedly dizzy, and she wanted to deny it all with a laugh, but she read something in Captain Berden's eyes that made any denial a delusion. Those young eyes—he was no more than thirty—were suddenly old. There was no despair in them; only a bleak acceptance that was as much a witness to old wounds as a scar.

Yet she couldn't surrender her dream. She had nothing else to hold on to. She had to see the house for herself.

And she did.

Squatters' land. It had been a pleasant neighborhood, most of the houses weekenders, but well kept. Now it was as desolate as a war zone, half the dwellings burned ruins engulfed in blackberry vines. Mary sat in the backseat of the black car and stared out through bullet-proof glass, her mind denying the reality her eyes presented her. She caught glimpses of the squatters, ragged wraiths peering through broken windows, running across yards inundated by brittle, gray weeds. One of them—an old man with a prophet's beard—paused to give the police car a defiant finger before he disappeared behind a burned cottage.

She wondered numbly why the captain finally stopped the car. She didn't recognize the house. This was only a shack giving way to weather and weeds, shingles blown off the roof, a climbing rose gone wild festooning the porch, growing through the broken windows.

It was Aunt Jan's prized climbing Peace rose. This was Aunt Jan's house. Mary felt that realization reverberating within her at the same moment she saw three shadowy figures burst out of the front door and vanish within seconds.

She knew she should surrender then. But she couldn't. Not yet.

At the captain's suggestion, Jim stayed in the car. He knew how to use the radio. Berden and Rachel went into the house with Mary.

The musty emptiness, the sour smell of filth and mildew, made her skin crawl. All the furniture was gone—except for the charred fragments of carved table legs and chair backs in the fireplace. The sound of the surf echoed hollowly against the smoke-grimed walls; the west windows were empty rectangles. She made her way to the kitchen in the northeast corner. No stove or refrigerator, no cabinets, not even a sink. Pipes thrust out of scarred walls, and in one corner three rats foraged on a mound of garbage. Mary stumbled back, caught her foot on a loose floorboard, and gasped with a spasm of pain.

The bathroom door was missing and so were the fixtures, except for the toilet that overflowed with foul, brown liquid. She went to the bedroom door. Where the door had been. A mattress, strewn with tangles of dirty blankets, lay on the floor. Torn organdy curtains writhed in the wind that blew cold through the empty window frames.

A shadow of movement drew her to the north window. Behind the house next door, three people were standing, waiting. Two bearded men. A woman. No, a girl. Maybe seventeen. She stared at Mary with dark, unblinking eyes, and Mary read there fear, anger, resentment, and a hunger that transcended the simple need for food, a hunger Mary knew to be beyond appeasement, and perhaps the girl knew it, too.

They stared at each other through the empty window, each looking into another plane of existence, and all that stood between Mary and that hungry-eyed, feral creature was a distance of a few yards.

Then abruptly the squatters turned, ragged clothes flapping, and they disappeared.

And at that moment the dream died beyond hope of resurrection.

The wreck of the house might be repaired—if she had the tens of thousands of dollars to spend on it—but the squatters, the wild geese, would still be here, waiting. The deed that had been the lucent focus of all her hope was only a scrap of paper. This house was theirs now.

Rachel and Captain Berden were waiting for her when she returned to the living room. They didn't speak, nor did she. She was looking for something, although she didn't understand what, not until she found it. A memento of the dream.

It was on the mantel. She wondered how she'd missed it before, how—and why—it had survived.

The old Seth Thomas clock.

It was made of quarter-sawed oak, its design stringently simple, the face set in an arch from which the sides fell straight to a curved base. The wood and glass were coated with grime. Mary opened the small door on the front panel. The hinges were stiff, but nothing inside seemed to be broken. She pushed the pendulum. It swung, ticking at a stately pace.

Aunt Jan's great-grandmother brought this clock with her when she came west as a bride, from Portland, Maine, to Portland, Oregon, by ship around the Horn. Aunt Jan had told Mary that long ago in the summer of her childhood, when she let Mary wind the clock.

Now Mary picked it up, held it against her body, saw her tears fall onto the begrimed wood, and she knew it would have been simpler if the Rovers had killed her, too. Like Laura and her baby. That had seemed so cruelly meaningless, but death has no meaning if life is meaningless. And her tears were equally meaningless, but she couldn't stop them. She knew the feel of these tears. Grief. She grieved again for her father, even for her mother. Grieved for Aunt Jan. Grieved for that feral-eyed girl.

Grieved for a dream.

She felt Rachel's hand on her shoulder. "Mary, let's go home."

Earth knows no desolation.
She smells regeneration
In the moist breath of decay.
                    —GEORGE MEREDITH, *THE SPIRIT OF*
                              EARTH IN AUTUMN (1862)

S tephen latches the east gate, then, with Shadow sniffing out the way, he walks ahead of me north up the alder-shaded quarry road. It's little more than a footpath now and wouldn't exist at all except for our continued use of it. In dry summers we grow corn in the shielded bowl that was once a gravel quarry. Stephen stops about a hundred feet up the road, then turns east through a break in the foliage. He looks back, patiently waiting for me to catch up. Then again he leads the way, following a trail I first walked with Rachel forty years ago.

The trail winds up the valley of the Styx. The sound of water rushing over its stony, brown bed is constantly at my left, yet I seldom see the creek; it's too densely curtained with foliage. We've entered a world that seems far removed—although it's only half a mile away—from the world of the sea and the littoral. This is the forest primeval. The rain forest.

This is, Rachel told me, climax forest, the kind of forest common in the Coast Range before European immigrants razed them for houses and toilet paper. Sitka spruce and hemlock dominate here, thrusting thick boles over a hundred feet skyward. I can't see the top of them, only the fretted pattern of twigs and needles that makes up the canopy, a pattern of exquisite complexity that's only a blur in my old eyes.

At the feet of the giants grow thickets of thimbleberry, salmonberry, elderberry, and salal, all leggy and sparse here, not the dense growth typical of the same plants in sunnier sites. And red huckleberry. It seems to be a native son of the rain forest. Its slender trunks are brown and smooth, its branches warm green, bearing myriads of tiny, oval leaves that arrange themselves in artful clusters. I know the only art in those compositions of leaf and limb is a strategy to catch the sunlight so precious here, yet I always see a self-conscious aesthetic in red huckleberry.

At the feet of the shrubs, ferns grow extravagantly, and in miniature marshes by the creek, the gigantic, ovate leaves of skunk cabbage spring incredibly out of the mud. The ground everywhere is blazoned with the torn umbrellas of coltsfoot, miner's lettuce starred with blossoms, oxalis like fields of shamrocks, and sweet-scented wild lily of the valley. And at every level is the moss. It furs the trunks of the trees, sleeves their branches in velvet, hangs in gossamer festoons.

The earth is rusty brown—burnt sienna, Rachel called it, verging into umber. Duff is its proper name, and if I step off the path, my feet sink into its spongy substance, and I wonder, as I always do: how many centuries of fallen needles, leaves, bark, and rotting wood, how many layers of moss, fungi, and lichen, has it taken to make the resilient texture of this ground? How many moles, worms, ants, and termites? How many billion generations of bacteria.

That's the ultimate layer of life here. I can't see it, but I smell it in the moist, fecund air. In this context there is nothing horrific about decay. It's the source of the richness of life here. Nurse logs. They are peculiar to the rain forest: fallen trees dissolving slowly into green mounds, supporting colonnades of young trees. Nurse logs represent an essential of life: nothing wasted, nothing lost, however profligate death might seem.

Stephen is still ahead of me, expertly wielding a machete. He wears only short, buckskin breeches on this warm day, and as he strides down the trail, slashing at encroaching salal and fern, he is as graceful and beautiful as any young creature in its true habitat.

And I, neither graceful nor young, carry no tool to keep this trail clear, but I've put in my share of hours tending it; Rachel and I always kept it passable. Before the End this area was part of a national forest, and the trail was built by the Job Corps. There, around the next curve, is a cement slab inscribed with the names of the six youths who were plucked from the ghettos of Brooklyn or Chicago or Los Angeles to hack a path through this temperate jungle. I wonder if any of them survived, if any lived to teach their children what they learned here.

Stephen's machete whistles and chunks in the rich silence, while Shadow rustles through ferns, following her nose. The path angles up to its highest point, and my pace slows, my cane digs deep with every step. The light, tinted green in its passage through hemlock lace and garlands of spruce, through huckleberry spangles and veils of moss, all moving in the gentle breeze, shimmers, and it's much like being underwater. I seem to feel the drag of it. At last, the trail slopes downward, then, finally, rounds a curve, and suddenly we are there.

It always seems sudden, the arrival here at the end and destination of the trail. Even Stephen, who has been here many times, has stopped still, staring upward.

This forest is full of giants, yet this magnificent Sitka dwarfs them all. It is two hundred feet tall, ten feet in diameter at the bole, and over five centuries old. The Forest Service provided those statistics.

But statistics don't convey the majesty of this towering column of living wood, thick sheathed in bark as impervious as weathered granite. Its roots flare from the bole, buttressing the massive trunk, then sink into the ground in brown hills and valleys. I must tilt my head far back to see the first branches a hundred feet above me. Beyond is the crown, its immense, mossy limbs spreading masses of needles to the sun. The light is trapped there, and little escapes to warm the foothills of the roots where Stephen and I stand in silence and constant shadow.

Running entirely through the base of the tree is a tunnel at most a yard high. When I was young, I crawled through that space. The earth within was lifeless and fine as powder. I lay surrounded by stony bark, and I felt an inexplicable uneasiness, not because of the impending tons of wood above me—the collapse of that tunnel didn't occur to me as a physical possibility—but because I sensed that I was in a place I shouldn't be: a womb to which I shouldn't be allowed to return.

That tunnel speaks of the beginnings of this giant among giants that seems immutable, something that has no end and no beginning.

It had a beginning. It was born on the mossy corpse of a nurse log. Its roots year by year grew down and around its source of sustenance until they sank into the earth. And in time the nurse log rotted away, leaving this tunnel, a negative space to witness its existence.

And this tree will have an end. It will fall, and what a sundering of sky and earth that will be, and it will in turn become a nurse log to nurture other giants.

Jerry has made a simple slab bench and placed it a few yards from the base of the tree. It replaced the one the Forest Service installed here, which has long ago rotted into duff. I ease down on the bench, smiling at Stephen, who sits down beside me, but doesn't speak, waiting for me to break the silence.

And finally, I do. "Rachel first brought me here the morning after I saw my aunt's house."

He nods. "It's a place of healing, I think. Bernadette says some places are like that. They heal the mind, so it can heal the body."

I'm surprised at that. Bernadette, our herbalist, healer, and nurse, seldom reveals her capacity for profound understanding.

"Yes, Stephen, it's a place of healing, but for me, Rachel was the healer." I pause, considering what to tell him. There is so much he must understand about Rachel, yet there is one aspect of her I know he isn't capable of understanding. I doubt he can imagine a philosophy so inimical to the religious traditions he grew up with. The day will come when he must come to terms with that, but he's not ready now.

For now, I'll tell him only what he must know.

I look up into the sun-gloried crown of the tree, then down through all its green stories, down the stone gray trunk to the heart of emptiness at its base, and I remember; the images are haloed with my tears.

If this tree were capable of sound, it would resonate in harmonies of a minor key in the deep ranges beyond the edges of my perception.

Perhaps it does sing: centuries-slow songs that I will never hear.

*Not one man in a thousand has the strength of mind or the goodness
of heart to be an atheist.*
—SAMUEL TAYLOR COLERIDGE, *LETTER TO THOMAS ALLSOP*
(ca. 1820)

*The most beautiful thing we can experience is the mysterious. It is the
source of all art and science.*
—ALBERT EINSTEIN, CONTRIBUTION, *LIVING PHILOSOPHIES* (1949)

S he could taste the green air. Mary Hope stared up at the tree,
her mind stretching to encompass its dimensions, its stunning
presence. She turned finally, found Rachel sitting on the bench,
watching her with a shadow smile that manifested itself primarily
in her dark eyes. She had been waiting, Mary realized. Waiting for
her reaction. She seemed satisfied.

Mary walked to the bench, leaning into the cane to keep her
balance among the sinews of roots, and sat down next to Rachel.
Neither of them spoke. Mary could find no words to express what
she felt, and Rachel didn't seem to need or expect any.

This was the second gift Rachel had offered her today.

Mary had wakened this morning to be ambushed by memories of the ruins of Aunt Jan's house, the ruins of her dream. But no new tears came with the memories. It was as if the night and sleep had dropped the curtain on that act of her life. She wasn't yet capable of raising the curtain on the next act, or even imagining it. She lay in the narrow bed listening to the murmur of the sea. *I am here . . . I am always here. . . .* She thought about dreams. Dreams were hope specified. Fragile fallacies.

But at length she left the bed, dressed herself, took up the cane, and opened the door to music. The third movement of Beethoven's ninth. The Adagio. Shadow came trotting out of the south studio to greet her, and that made her smile. Sweet Shadow, so loving and fey. *Highstrung* was the old-fashioned word Rachel used to describe her. Topaz was the steady one, reserved and dependable.

Mary found Rachel in the kitchen stoking the fire in the old, iron cookstove. She shut the firebox door and looked around at Mary. "How are you?"

"I'm all right."

Rachel studied her a moment. "Would you like some coffee?" Then at Mary's nod: "I'll bring it into the living room."

Mary went into the living room, with its fireplace built of beach cobbles backed to the kitchen wall, a bamboo-framed couch facing the hearth. Two armchairs, their ochre upholstery frayed at the seams, flanked the couch. On the south wall a door opened into the greenhouse. The west wall was almost entirely glass, with a sliding door opening onto the deck. Bookshelves took up every remaining space on the walls except for a small section on the north wall left for paintings. On the small table in the northwest corner, two places were set for breakfast. Topaz lay on the Persian rug; she rose and came to Mary, waited for her to lean down and pet her. Then Mary walked to the glass doors and looked out at slow, white breakers under a clear sky. At length she turned. That's when she saw it centered on the mantel: Aunt Jan's Seth Thomas.

Her breath caught, and she made her way to the mantel, mouth open in silent amazement. This couldn't be the grime-rimed clock she'd found in that ruined house. The wood gleamed like satin, the glass over its face was shining. And it was ticking steadfastly, the scrolled hands pointing the time as it was now, not a leftover hour marking the last pulse of its spent mainspring long ago. She touched the glowing wood, then looked at Rachel. She was standing by the fireplace, a mug of coffee in each hand.

"Oh, Rachel, how did you do it? How did you bring it back to life?"

"Well, it wasn't dead, Mary." She handed her one of the mugs. "I just gave it a little wax and oil. It's a beautiful thing, and like they say, 'hell for stout.'"

Laughing because she was so close to crying, Mary embraced her. "Thank you, Rachel. *Thank you.*"

Rachel returned her embrace, but with a certain awkwardness, as if she weren't used to such physical displays. She cleared her throat and said, "Let's have breakfast, and after that I'd like to take you for a walk."

And now Mary watched Topaz and Shadow sniffing out pathways of scent through the tunnel at the base of the tree, and her gaze moved up the scaly, granitic bole. She heard the impatient chirking of squirrels as she stared into the rose-window pattern of green and sky blue in the black fretwork of branches. "It's like a cathedral here."

Rachel was looking up into the crown, too, and she seemed to find there both wonder and comfort. "Maybe cathedrals are like *here,*" she said. Then she turned to Mary. "This is a very special place to me."

Mary nodded. "I'm grateful that you'd share it with me."

"It's my pleasure. I don't have many friends—none left in Shiloh except Jim and Connie—so I enjoy having someone to share this with. Strangely enough, it's Jim who loves this tree almost as much as I do."

"Why strangely?"

"Oh . . . because he's so thoroughly pragmatic. He's our resident survivalist, you know."

"Survivalist? Jim?"

"Yes. He's a paradox, really. A *liberal* survivalist. He has a radiation shelter behind his house fully stocked for the end of the world."

Mary felt a chill in the shadowed air. "I don't think that's something you can stock up for."

"Maybe not." For a while Rachel was silent. She seemed to be mulling over something, and Mary waited patiently.

Finally Rachel said, "There's something I want you to understand."

That had a nearly ominous cast to it. "What, Rachel?"

"Well, just that you have a home at Amarna for as long as you need or want it. What I want you to understand is that you shouldn't feel any obligation to me. That's probably impossible, I know. I'm just saying that if you want to stay here, you can. At least, it's an option."

Mary couldn't think of an adequate response. Rachel seemed oddly embarrassed, as if she were *asking* for something, not offering a gift—yet another gift—of great magnanimity. Her home wasn't just a place where she ate and slept; it was the context of her life.

Mary said huskily, "Rachel, I can't impose on you. . . ."

But Rachel only laughed. "It's not a question of imposition. If it is, then it won't work."

Mary listened to the wind sighing in the harps of needles and remembered Rachel's words to her just before they retreated from Aunt Jan's house: "Mary, let's go home."

Home.

It was a word to make her weep. Yet she had lived too long in the city, too long among strangers who had never, with few exceptions, become friends; people whose minds she couldn't touch and whose motives she could neither fathom nor trust.

Why? Why was Rachel offering a share in her home, in her life?

Rachel leaned forward, resting her elbows on her knees. "I'm twice your age, Mary, and one thing I've learned over the years is that loneliness can be—sometimes literally—deadly. But on the other hand, I've learned that just having someone else around isn't the solution, not if you don't have some affinity for that person.

I've learned to live alone. It's the price I've paid for certain things I value."

Mary considered that. "What are you saying? That you don't need me? That you're not asking anything of me?"

"I suppose I am. And *you* don't need *me*. Well, at the moment you need a place to stay until you're fully recovered, but after that, you could go back to Portland, couldn't you? Back to IDA? The government has a hard time these days finding people who can read, much less write, and with its penchant for verbosity, it'll always need writers."

Mary hadn't thought about going back to Portland or IDA. That was part of the next act, the one on which she hadn't raised the curtain. Yes, it was possible. And maybe that's what she should do. No more dreams.

Yet Rachel was offering another dream. Rather, the old dream in another setting: a house by the sea where she could write. And a home to share with a friend. A *friend*.

Rachel straightened and turned to face her. "This isn't the time for you to make any major decisions. I just wanted you to know there's an option here. That's all."

Mary felt the stifling approach of tears, but she kept them in check. "Thanks, Rachel. From the bottom of my heart . . . thanks."

Rachel smiled at her, then leaned back and contemplated her surroundings, totally absorbed, and Mary knew she would speak no more of her offer. Jim Acres called her "damned independent." But there was more to it. Maybe it was simply courage.

"Rachel, have you always lived alone at Amarna?"

"Well, I've always been the only *human* occupant, except when . . ." She paused, as if she weren't sure she wanted to go on. But she did. "About twenty years ago, not long after I moved to Amarna, I shared it with a young man. A lawyer." She laughed as she added, "If you're going to have a live-in, pick a lawyer, a doctor, or a plumber. They're handy to have around. Anyway, that lasted two years, then Ben had a chance to join a law firm in Portland. Very prestigious and all that. So, that was the end of it."

"He wasn't willing to join his prestigious law firm with a live-in?"

Rachel shook her head. "That wasn't the problem. Ben was willing to flout the stodgy mores of the firm. Or he was willing to marry me, if that's what I wanted. The trouble was, I wasn't willing to give up Amarna, to give up the sea, to give up my painting. It would've been a disaster, really, and I guess we both knew it."

Mary was silent, watching Rachel. The years seemed to have smoothed out the regret, leaving only a patina of melancholy. "Haven't there been other . . . Bens in your life?"

Rachel sent her a bemused smile. "No. I guess I expected too much—or needed too little—of men. Anyway, Shiloh was always a small town, and now it's even smaller, so my choices have been limited. Actually, Shiloh attracted some very interesting people. You get odd demographics in a coast town. But I never met that interesting man who was also interested in me. That's one of the disadvantages of living here, and it's something you'll have to consider."

Mary tried to consider it. But what had her choices been in Portland? Brief meetings and partings, firefly encounters that left her unchanged. Except for Evan. That was in her college days. Everything seemed to mean more then. And Dean. Yes, but that relationship always had its portents of disaster, however sweet it was to be so intensely in love. "It will not last the night. . . ." Dean made that his watchword. Yet it had, for them, lasted a year. Off and on.

She let her breath out in a long sigh. She would miss Dean, miss the constant shots of emotional adrenaline, the physical high he brought to love and making love.

Rachel said, "You're thinking of someone you left behind."

"Yes. Someone who preferred it that way, I think. Rachel, don't you miss having a family, children . . . that sort of thing?"

"No," she replied emphatically, "not children. I'd have been a lousy mother."

"I don't believe that. The way you treat Shadow and Topaz—not many children get half that much love and care."

"That may be true. Unfortunately, it probably is. But there are already too many children in this world. As for family—yes, I miss that. My parents are both dead and have been for over twenty years. Plane crash. They went down together. I was an only child, so I don't suppose I'll ever really understand—or miss—sibling relationships, and I have no other relations this side of the Mississippi. As for sex . . ." She glanced obliquely at Mary, a hint of irony in her eyes. "That's what you meant by 'that sort of thing,' isn't it?"

Mary had to laugh. "Yes, I guess so."

"Well, I don't miss that as much as you might think. It's one part of living, but I don't believe you *can* have it all. You have to consider the cost of things. I am a serious painter. Since I was a child, that's all I ever wanted to be, and that takes more than brushes and paint."

Mary nodded, thinking of *October Flowers*, of the disks of short stories and essays she'd left for safekeeping with her mother. "I understand that."

"Yes, I know you do." Then she turned her absorbed gaze on the tree, letting the silence move in, and Mary accepted it, savored this silence that asked nothing of her, that sustained and healed her.

A rustling in the green starbursts of sword fern. But it was only the dogs still exploring. Mary pulled in a deep breath of earth-scented air and asked, "Wasn't it the Druids who worshiped trees?"

Rachel nodded. "I guess they thought some trees had godlike attributes or were the sites of gods. If you're going in for divinity, it seems like a good idea, spreading it around that way. I mean, investing plants and animals and natural phenomena with godhood. I think the people who put all their divine eggs in one basket lost something."

Mary asked dryly, "What? Other than whole pantheons to keep track of."

"Yes, well, monotheism *does* simplify things. But when people conglomerated their gods into one grand old man in the sky, they lost all respect for natural processes. It's a very dangerous philosophy, because we are *not* a special creation. We're products of the natural world, and if we're going to survive, we have to live by its rules." She paused, looked levelly at Mary. "If you're a good literalist Christian, don't bother trying your evangelistic wings on me."

The dogs had concluded their explorations. Topaz lay down at Rachel's feet to wait with steadfast patience, while Shadow leapt up on the bench beside Mary and nudged her elbow for attention. Mary met the demand with gentle scratching behind Shadow's ears.

"Rachel, I don't have any evangelizing urges, and I don't really qualify as a Christian—literalist or otherwise."

"How *do* you qualify yourself?"

"Oh, I suppose as an agnostic. That's my father's influence."

"And your mother's influence?"

Mary winced, remembering her last long, futile phone call to her mother. She had been so painfully anxious, but for all the wrong reasons. "Mother was always a professed Christian, but she wasn't really serious about it, not until Dad died. That changed her. I think she got deeper into religion after that because . . . well, she *has* to believe that someday she'll be reunited with Dad. She has to believe he still exists somehow."

"Yes," Rachel said, the word a sigh. "That's the real source of religions. Grief. And fear of death. Most people find their mortality so terrifying, the only way they can deal with it is to deny it."

Mary asked quietly, "But you've accepted your mortality?"

"Well, I can't see any rational alternative to acceptance."

"No immortal soul?"

"No. Nor heaven or hell or the bureaucratic convolutions of purgatory or nirvana or whatever. They're all human inventions designed to avoid facing reality. I will not voluntarily blind myself."

Mary stared into the tunnel of shadow at the base of the tree and felt a lump of dull pain in her leg. "But reality is hard to look at sometimes."

"Yes. At least, the reality humankind has created for itself. It's hard to look at and hard to survive. But no living organism is guaranteed an easy life. Or death. And there's a reality beyond what we've created." She paused, studied Mary for what seemed a long time. "I'm not talking about any version of a god. The idea of a god doesn't answer any questions for me. I'm talking about what I call the real world. We're a very small part of it, but we're capable of comprehending it at least enough to know that it's magnificent. What else can a human being ask? And yes, you can assume from all this that I'm an atheist."

Rachel didn't seem to expect Mary to be shocked at that revelation, and if she was surprised, it was simply because she realized she'd have been more surprised to find Rachel professing any religion.

Nor did Rachel seem to expect a response. She leaned down to stroke Topaz's head. "I never talk about religion—or my lack of it. But I think you should know where I stand." She smiled wryly. "What you believe is your business, and I may not like what you say, but I'll defend to the death my right to disagree with you."

Mary laughed. "I don't think we'll find much to disagree about." A bird, invisible in the patterned ranks of foliage, piped a song that ended with a plaintive trill. Mary looked up, seeking the singer. "You know, there's a paradox about you I don't understand, Rachel."

"Oh? What is it?"

"You said human beings are such a small part of the real world, yet you've devoted yourself to a particularly human endeavor."

"I am what I am," Rachel replied with a shrug. "I'm a human being, and I paint because that's an expression of my humanity. I build each painting to last for centuries. And yet . . . well, sometimes I wonder if there'll be anyone around to enjoy those paintings in the future. But I have to hope, Mary. I have to hope people won't be ignorant and arrogant enough to throw away thousands of years' worth of civilization."

The bird piped its plaintive song again, and Mary thought of the city she'd left, of the foul air where that bird would soon die, where too much had already been thrown away.

Then Rachel stretched and came to her feet. "We'd better start home. Connie told me not to let you get too tired, and her word is law around here. By the way, she and Jim are coming for dinner, and she's bringing her guitar. She says she's sure you're a passable soprano. Topaz, Shadow, come on." Topaz stood up and shook herself, scattering spruce needles. Shadow was already off the bench, circling in anticipation.

Mary rose stiffly, leaning on her cane, and looked up into the green reaches of the tree's crown. "I hate to leave it."

Rachel nodded, her gaze sweeping up the massive trunk. "It's a microcosm, really. An archetype. To know everything there is to know about this tree, you'd have to know everything there is to know about the universe." Then she shrugged self-consciously. "Well, you can always come back. You know the way now."

Mary held those words in her mind as she would a hummingbird in her hand: gently, because it was fragile. And uncommonly beautiful.

Yes, she thought, I know the way.

Famine seems to be the last, the most dreadful resource of nature.
The power of population is so superior to the power of the earth to
provide subsistence . . . that premature death must in some shape or
other visit the human race.
　　　—THOMAS ROBERT MALTHUS, *ESSAY ON THE PRINCIPLE OF*
POPULATION (1798)

T he tide is low. From the deck, I look down through the V of
the ravine and the tall spars of spruce trees to the beach, note
the color of the sand, and know that if I were walking there, I'd
see the herringbone patterns of deep green and purple black on tan
made by the waves as their ebb and flow sorts the heavier, dark
sands, laden with microscopic crystals of magnetite and olivine,
from the lighter, paler silica sands.

Shadow and I will walk those sands later this afternoon, but now
I'm waiting for Stephen, and Shadow is sunning herself beside me
on the deck. And while I wait, I sit with a wooden crate upended

in front of me to serve as a chopping block. The cedar-root basket next to the box is nearly full of sliced bull kelp, and coiled in the grass below the deck with their bulbous heads hung over the railing, letting down their hair of shining ribbon leaves, are snakes of kelp ready for my knife. The high tide deposited them on the beach this morning, largess from the sea. Kelp makes good fertilizer and provides vital nutrients for the goats and pigs.

I see a movement on the beach and pause, knife poised for the next cut. Despite my failing eyes, I can identify the two people. I recognize Miriam's long, bright hair, and the bearded man can only be Jerry. They both have buckets, heavy, from the way they carry them. They've been to the tide pools at the foot of the Knob to gather mussels. I watch them, remembering a day of my youth, and it seems in keeping with my thoughts when they stop to talk, free hands clasped, when Miriam stands on tiptoe to kiss Jerry.

A chaste kiss, no doubt. At least, Jerry will think it that.

They are half-siblings. Luke was their father, but they had different mothers. I wonder what Miriam would've been like if they'd had the same mother, if they'd both grown up in Luke's household.

I watch them walking toward the bank until I can no longer see them. The house is set too far back from the ravine for me to see the foot of the path. I return to my chopping.

Jerry is, in a sense, Miriam's lover. But then he's also Esther's lover, as he was Rebecca's before she died. I don't suppose I'll ever forgive him for his part in her death. I know she wanted to try again to have a baby, but she'd had two miscarriages already.

But Jerry still has his two lovers. That is, he has sexual intercourse with Miriam and Esther at intervals determined by their menstrual calendars and the days they are most likely to conceive. That calculated approach to coitus is unavoidable. Jerry is the only adult male here, Miriam and Esther the only fertile adult females. Even the risks inherent in inbreeding between half-siblings must be accepted if new generations are to survive. There are six children now, but that's not enough, especially since Isaac may not live to produce any offspring.

My knife slips, missing my finger only by good luck.

Yes, it all sounds so calculating, like breeding livestock, but these people grew up with that kind of calculation. And in fact, Jerry does love both Miriam and Esther, but in the same sense that he loves the children, he loves the crones, he loves me. He doesn't know what it means to be *in* love, but he loves, deeply and steadfastly.

And Miriam? If what she feels for Jerry can be termed love, it is a jealous love, as her god is a jealous god. No doubt she feels maternal love for her children. Or is that possessiveness? Or am I coloring her with my fear? All I know is that she seldom laughs, and I've never seen her weep.

I fear that absence of laughter and tears. It doesn't indicate a lack of passion, but rather the opposite: a passion that is too volatile for its vessel.

By the time Miriam and Jerry reach the top of the beach path, I've filled the basket. I rise, grunting at the aching stiffness that occupied my knees while I sat. Jerry waves at me, strides across the grass, while Miriam approaches more slowly, watching Jerry, watching me.

I see Luke in Jerry always. He's tall and thin like his father, but that thinness is deceptive. He is all muscle, flat and hard, his hands strong and armored with calluses. Shadow runs to him, and Jerry feints playfully with her until he has her galloping in wild circles, then he calms her with a few words. When he reaches the deck, he offers me an ebullient, "Good day, Mary!"

"Good day to you, Jeremiah. It looks like you and Miriam had good luck in the tide pools. Good day, Miriam."

She smiles, although it doesn't reach her eyes, but before she can speak, Jerry says, "Miriam, you'd better go take care of the mussels."

That rudeness is typical and particularly annoying because he is always blithely unaware of it. I see resentment congeal in Miriam's eyes, but it isn't directed at Jerry. *I* get the brunt of it, deep and laced with jealousy. She picks up his bucket and hers, mounts the deck steps, but at the door pauses to say, "Jeremiah, we need some wood split for the stove."

I restrain a smile. She's restoring the real chain of command as it pertains to household tasks. Such things are her domain.

But Jerry only nods. He doesn't recognize the subtle reprimand in that reminder. When the door closes behind Miriam, he says, "Mary, we saw some whale spouts today."

That's something else I've lost with my failing sight: the brief puffs of mist that mark the passage of the gray whales on their migrations from Alaska to Baja in the spring and back again in the fall.

"Did you? Well, that's always reassuring."

"Yes, I guess it is, but I keep hoping one of them will get beached close by where we can get at it. I know how much you love them, but we could use the oil."

I laugh at that, then lean down to pick up the basket of kelp. "I'd better get this to the compost."

"No, Mary, *I'll* take it," he insists, reaching for the basket.

But I refuse to relinquish it. "Jerry, I'm quite capable of carrying it. I may be slow, but—"

"You can't carry it with your cane."

"I *can* walk without my cane if I'm careful."

He smiles, placating now. "I know, but I'm going out to the garden anyway."

With a sigh I surrender to his kindness. Besides, Stephen is coming around the corner of the house with Isaac tagging along behind him. "All right, Jerry. Thanks."

He departs, pausing on his way to talk to the boys, and I go into the house to wash the kelp slick off my hands. When I return, I find Stephen occupying one of the chairs, while Isaac sits cross-legged on the deck beside Shadow, and she patiently tolerates his unintentionally rough petting. Stephen watches him with the protective eye of an older brother, although Isaac is not his brother. Not genetically.

Stephen looks up at me. "Isaac isn't feeling good today. Bernadette said he shouldn't work in the garden. Is it all right if he stays with us?"

Isaac grins at me, blue eyes clear as the sky, his copper red hair shining in the sunlight. Freckles are powdered dark against his pale skin, and he is too thin, too small for his ten years. He constantly coughs and wheezes and doesn't seem to notice it, nor does he seem to notice the malformed foot that makes him limp when he walks, stumble when he runs. He is Miriam's child by an Arkite, and she's the only one here who doesn't dote on him.

Miriam mistrusts imperfection. Perhaps she fears it. But she probably won't have to deal with it much longer in the form of her asthmatic, crippled son. He won't survive another winter if it brings another onslaught of pneumonia.

She calls him god-marked.

I lean down and press my hand to Isaac's forehead. It seems cool, rather than hot with fever. He says, "I'm all right now, Mary. Bernadette gave me some tea."

"Well, if she says you're not to work, you won't. Not today." I go to the chair next to Stephen's, reach for the diary in my pocket. "Isaac, did Stephen tell you what we've been doing?"

He shakes his head, and Stephen answers, "No, I didn't tell him. I haven't told anybody."

I'm a little surprised at that. And a little relieved.

I nod without comment. "Stephen and I have been studying some history, Isaac. Mine and Rachel's."

"Is that history?"

"On a smaller scale, it's as much history as the fall of the Roman Empire."

"But that was a *long* time ago."

Stephen puts in quietly, "Just listen, Isaac. Don't argue with Mary."

Isaac draws his knees up, wraps his arms around them, and looks up at me expectantly. I open the diary. It's more a prop for me than a necessity. I read it last night, polished each shard of memory. "All right, Stephen, where were we?"

"When Rachel asked you to stay at Amarna. But you didn't give her an answer then."

"No. I couldn't. I think I knew my answer, but I had to wait until I felt stronger physically and emotionally. A week later I wrote to my boss at IDA. She telephoned me within a few days and offered me a promotion if I'd come back to Portland." I laugh, remembering that small, but vital triumph. "That's when I told Rachel I'd like to stay, to make Amarna my home. And then . . ." I turn a page. "Then spring came to Amarna."

Isaac objects, "Spring *always* comes to Amarna."

"I remember a winter when we weren't sure of that. But my first spring at Amarna was a revelation. I discovered what seasons meant. You two don't know what it's like to live in a city where changing seasons really don't mean anything. Here I watched trees flower and leaf, daffodils bloom, and cow parsnips unfold those huge, soft leaves, their stalks reaching up—well, they were higher than my head by summer. And horsetails. You know them, Isaac. They look like green bottle brushes."

Stephen nods and says, *"Equisetum."*

Isaac wrinkles his nose. "What does that mean?"

"That's their proper name," Stephen explains.

And I add—ever the teacher; I can't seem to help myself: "They're descendants of a plant called *calamites* that lived about three hundred million years ago and grew to be thirty feet high."

Isaac's eyes widen. "Was there dinosaurs then?" But as soon as the question is out, he looks apprehensively toward the house as if he's afraid someone might hear him. His mother, no doubt.

"No, Isaac, there were no dinosaurs yet. Anyway, in that first spring I learned about farming—preparing the soil, planting the seeds, watching them grow, and all the while battling weeds and moles and bugs and slugs. I saw a litter of rabbits and a kid born. I saw chicks hatch. That was a new project of Rachel's that year, raising chickens from scratch, so to speak. I learned to extract honey from the combs—no, that was later, in the summer. I learned about fishing and mussel collecting and clam digging from Jim Acres. I learned folk songs from Connie. She'd play her guitar and sing harmony to my lead. From Rachel I learned about the sea. She showed me the way wind and current and tide work together, the patterns of the sand, the creatures that leave their tracks on it. She called it calligraphy, and every animal has its own signature. She showed me the birds that call the sea home, the plants and animals that live in the tide pools. I even did some writing—Jim loaned me his old word processor—and I sold a few articles. And I saw quite a lot of Captain Harry Berden. Yes, that was the most beautiful spring of my life. But old people always say that about the springtimes of their youth, don't they, Isaac?"

He laughs uncertainly. "I don't know." Stephen only smiles and waits for me to go on.

"I lived in a microcosm, a lovely little island. Beyond Amarna the world was falling apart. Almost literally, when you think about the California quake. Rachel said the planet was simply adjusting its skin a bit, but what a price the insignificant creatures living on the Earth's skin paid."

Stephen frowns thoughtfully. "Miriam talked about that earthquake in one of her morning sermons. She said it was a prophecy of Armageddon."

"It wasn't a prophecy of anything," I reply irritably. "The San Andreas fault finally gave way. The epicenter was south of San Francisco. I remember seeing skyscrapers swaying like grass in a wind, and the dust rising where buildings collapsed, and the Bay patterned with intersecting waves like a huge moiré pattern."

Isaac's mouth sags open. "Were you *there*, Mary?"

I laugh at that. "No, I wasn't there, or I probably wouldn't be here. I saw all that on television." That garners only a blank look from him. I've explained television to the children—even shown them our old set—but they can't really understand it. Or believe it.

I go on. "Two million people died in that quake and the tsunamis that hit the coast towns and the orgies of looting that followed. The government sent in an army of Apies and National Guard troops. Food and clothing and medicine flooded in from all over the world, and refugees flooded out. And in the midst of that appalling wreckage, Lassa fever turned epidemic."

"What's Lassa fever?" Isaac asks.

Stephen is quick with a reply. "I think that's what Jeremiah called the great plague."

No doubt that came from one of Jerry's sermons, secondhand from sermons he heard as a child. He has no more comprehension of Lassa than Miriam does of the California earthquake. Those events are part of our mythos now.

"Yes, Lassa was a plague of sorts, Isaac. It was a contagious, viral disease. At first, people called it L-flu. But it wasn't flu. Connie Acres showed us a bulletin from the Center for Disease Control. It wasn't even the original Lassa fever. That was first identified years before in Africa, and it was spread by infected rats. The mutant originated in Africa, too, and by the time I read the CDC bulletin, millions of people had already died of Lassa there. In this country— we were so smug. There'd been around ten thousand deaths here from Lassa, but we thought we had the best medical system in the world. Hadn't we finally developed a vaccine for AIDS? But this new Lassa fever wasn't only transmitted by rats. Once it infected a human being, it could be transmitted just by personal contact, and it was almost always fatal."

Stephen leans forward. "But Bernadette said she had the great— Lassa fever, I mean, and she lived through it."

"Yes, some of the people who contracted it lived, *if* they got good care. But without hospitalization, the symptoms were lethal. Hemorrhaging, for instance. Bleeding that can't be stopped, Isaac. Anyway, Lassa seemed to explode after the California quake. In the epidemic areas, it disrupted everything. In some of the cities, it was like a return to the dark ages. By late summer it was totally out of control. I made a note in my diary. . . ." I pause to flip through the pages. "Here—on September first. Twenty million people had died of Lassa in the United States." Stephen and Isaac gaze at me in awe, yet they can grasp only a minute fraction of the hopeless terror underlying that figure.

Not that I could grasp it any better at the time. I take a deep breath. "Lassa wasn't the only apocalyptic plague humankind was suffering. There were the constant small wars, of course, but the other plague—and it was more deadly than Lassa, really—was starvation. I remember seeing a television news feature that showed a food drop at a camp near Mexico City. Big helicopters with bales of food spilling out into a whirlwind of dust. And the people—they looked like dry sticks hung with rags, and it seemed impossible that they could even walk. Yet they all got up and began running toward the whirlwind, toward the food. There were so many of them, they were like a dark tide. I remember Rachel said, '*There is the future.*' And she was crying." I clear my throat of the huskiness in my voice. "We stopped watching the television for a while after that. We closed our window to the world. But eventually we opened it again. In June the president was killed. Someone bombed the White House."

"What white house?" Isaac asks.

"That was what they called the big house where the president of the United States lived. There's a picture of it in the encyclopedia. Anyway, they never found out who did it, but the Bill of Rights was suspended, and the Apies rounded up tens of thousands of 'suspected terrorists'—most of them guilty of nothing more than having no home or job—and threw them in detention camps, which were perfect breeding grounds for Lassa. The rampant stupidity! That was the real epidemic. *Pandemic.* What was happening in this country was happening all over the world." I close my eyes, wondering how the frustration can still sting me like a thicket of thorns even after all these years. I call up a smile for Isaac and Stephen, to whom so much of this is meaningless. Yet they must understand what they can. At least, Stephen must.

I go on, "But here at Amarna the weather was ideal, the garden flourished, and I'd become very fond of goat's milk and learned to look a rabbit in the eye and slit its throat—*and* gut, skin, and dismember it. Isaac, don't laugh. That was a real accomplishment for a city girl."

Of course, he does laugh, then he asks, "Who was a city girl? What does that mean?"

"I was a city girl. I came from a city, and I was—loosely speaking—a girl." His smile is edged with uncertainty at that. No doubt he can't imagine me as a girl. "Yes, I was young then, but the world was still falling apart. We could close our window to it, but one day it came crashing through our front door. Not literally, Isaac. That's just a way of saying something . . . terrible happened."

Stephen's breath catches, and Isaac looks up at him, blue eyes wide. Stephen asks, "Was it Armageddon?"

He persists in calling it that because he hears the adults use that term. Yet our Elder, the arbiter of all things religious and moral here, declares that the true Armageddon, the one prophesied in such lurid detail by Saint John, is yet to come. Jerry denies the End as Armageddon because his father denied it. Finally.

"No, Stephen, not Armageddon. Rovers."

"What's a Rover?" Isaac asks.

"They were road gangs, Isaac. Groups of people—most of them young and into heavy drugs—who lived along the highways and attacked cars, trucks, or buses. They usually killed the people in them."

Isaac stares at me, aghast. "Why did they do that?"

"I don't know. Maybe because they were insane. Insanity is one of the symptoms of too many. Anyway, the gang that attacked my bus stayed in the area all spring. The Apies sent reinforcements, and that kept them under control, but by late June the extra Apies were needed elsewhere, and the Rovers came out of hiding." I look down at the diary, turn the pages back to June, but I'm not really seeing the writing that on these pages has become so cramped, nearly illegible.

"It was the day before the summer solstice. A grocery day. Food deliveries had been erratic for months, but usually a Safeway convoy came in Thursday night, and everyone in Shiloh did their shopping on Friday. Rachel and I always drove down to the mall with Connie and Jim, but that Friday morning Jim phoned and said there'd be no grocery run. The night before, the Rovers hit the supermarket just as the convoy arrived. There was a small, bloody battle—Jim rather bitterly called it the battle of the mall—and a lot of people were killed or hurt, including four of Captain Berden's officers. The Rovers blew up all three trucks. That was typical of them with cars or trucks. They just kept shooting until the gas tanks exploded. We didn't see Jim and Connie that day. They were both busy at the clinic with the casualties. Rachel and I worked in the garden and walked on the beach, just like any other day. That night Jim called and said everything was under control in Shiloh, and another Safeway convoy would arrive Monday. So we went to bed."

And slept the peaceful sleep of the muscle-weary, slept in the bliss of ignorance.

Things fall apart; the centre cannot hold;
Mere anarchy is loosed upon the world,
The blood-dimmed tide is loosed, and everywhere
The ceremony of innocence is drowned. . . .

—WILLIAM BUTLER YEATS,
"*THE SECOND COMING*" (1921)

As befitted the first day of summer, the sky was clear, the sun hot, and it was on this day that Josie Pearl, the white-and-tan Nubian doe, chose to go into labor. But Rachel didn't discover that fact until noon.

Mary had called Connie and Jim after breakfast and gotten a busy signal. There was an implied assurance in that, and she and Rachel went about the morning's work, feeding and watering the animals, weeding the garden, cleaning the chicken house, and collecting eggs. The hens were producing extravagantly with the long summer days. It was when Rachel went to the barn to get fresh straw for the nests that she discovered Josie Pearl's plight.

And again Mary found herself an assistant midwife.

The impending nativity attracted an audience. Rachel always left the barn door open during the day so the goats could come into its shade. Now they all gathered, drawn by the insatiable curiosity of their kind. Pan—black as night, silky beard bearing stars of dandelion seeds, the noble, fecund lord of this small harem—loudly demanded a rail position, but Rachel asked Mary to take him to his shed north of the barn. When she returned, Rachel had Josie inside the stall in the corner of the barn, while Persephone, her kid, and the three remaining does peered through the slats.

Persephone's delivery had been so easy, but Josie was having a hard time of it, since she had, with typical perversity, initiated herself into motherhood with twins. Once the necessary preparations were made, Rachel and Mary settled into the stall, Rachel constantly talking to Josie, stroking her head, giving her something to brace against when the contractions came. Josie, between contractions, crooned softly, talking to her kids.

The alternating contractions and crooning continued for over an hour before the front hooves of one of the kids appeared in the vulva, then retreated, while Josie stood panting, gray tongue hanging. As the afternoon stretched on, the kid made its teasing appearance, only to retreat, again and again, and as inexperienced as Mary was as a midwife, she knew Josie was weakening, her kids' chance at life dwindling. At length Rachel had to offer more than reassurance.

"Mary, hold her head for me. Just keep talking to her."

Mary knelt in front of Josie, stroking her rough coat, trying to keep the anxiety out of her voice as she murmured reassurances. Rachel moved around to the doe's hindquarters, and when Josie began straining with another contraction, Rachel said, "I can see the head!" She grasped the protruding legs with one hand, worked the other slowly, gently into the birth canal, while Josie panted and heaved, and finally on the surge of a last contraction, Rachel pulled the kid out.

A double handful of wet hair slicked in the remains of its embryonic sac, and Mary's pent breath came out in a sigh of relief.

Rachel shouted, "Give me a towel, Mary—hurry!" And when Mary brought a terrycloth towel from the shelf on the wall, Rachel cleared the kid's throat and nose with her finger and toweled it vigorously, smiling at its outraged bleating. Then she laid the kid under Josie's nose, and the doe began licking it. It was a black buck, so small and shaky Mary couldn't believe it might survive. Yet second by second it drew strength from its mother's tongue, and soon it was staggering to its feet. Rachel cleared Josie's teat with a few pulls, then squeezed the first drops of thick colostrum into the kid's mouth.

The second kid, a doe, came with relative ease, and Mary was ready with a clean towel. Rachel surrendered the kid to her, and Mary rubbed it, laughing at the novel sensation of this new life warm and vital in her hands. It was entirely perfect, black like its sibling, its exotic, horizontal-pupiled eyes bright and strangely knowing. Almost reluctantly, Mary offered the kid to its mother.

A few minutes later Josie rid herself of the placentas, and Rachel wrapped the pink-gray masses in newspaper and took them outside to bury them. Mary stayed in the stall, watched Josie licking, nudging, crooning to her newborn, while they wobbled about on fragile legs. So natural and inevitable, this age-old cycle of birth, and Mary knew she must one day take part in it. These infant animals were exquisitely beautiful in some sense that transcended aesthetics, and her yearning for that beauty was at this moment intense and undeniable.

She looked up, distracted by a rustling in the straw on the earth floor of the barn. Rachel had returned and stood leaning on the stall's gate. She said, "Josie, you did yourself proud." The doe was too occupied with her offspring even to look up. Rachel took her watch out of her jeans pocket where she had put it for safekeeping during the birthing. It was a mechanical watch with a dial on which the date was revealed in a tiny window. She insisted she liked to see time in a circle; it reflected the realities of existence on a spherical, rotating world. Now, as she buckled the strap to her wrist, she frowned. "Damn, it's nearly three. We'd better try Connie and Jim again."

On their way to the house, they were joined by Topaz and Shadow, who had kept their distance from the barn for the last few hours. Goats had no tolerance for dogs, nor any compunction about butting or trampling them. Once inside the house, Rachel washed her hands and put fresh water down for the dogs, then went to the telephone in the north studio. Within a minute, she returned to the kitchen, where Mary was at the sink downing a glass of water.

"Still busy. Damn phones are probably out of order again." She took the glass Mary offered and drank half of it, then went back to the telephone.

Mary felt her mood of quiet elation undermined by a whisper of apprehension as she followed Rachel into the studio. She listened to Rachel's end of the conversation, heard the name Joanie. One of the nurses at the clinic. When Rachel hung up, her eyes were narrowed, focused inward. "Joanie hasn't heard from Connie today, but she didn't expect to. It's Connie's day off. I think . . . maybe we'd better walk down to their house."

"But if you got a busy signal . . ." Yet Mary could find no assurance in that to dispel the fear taking root in her mind.

"It probably means Connie or Jim were on the phone when we called." She mustered a smile as she added: "We'll just go check on them, and if everything's okay, they can give us a cup of coffee."

Mary heard the dry, gravel crunch of their footfalls as she looked south at the distant, silent blocks of houses. They might all have been empty for any sign of life in them. She turned, stared up at the Acres house, and stopped, realizing she was holding her breath at the same moment she realized what sound she was listening for and not hearing: Sparky's bark. They were close enough to the house for Sparky to be aware of them and raise his usual strident alarm. She glanced at Rachel, who had stopped with her. She seemed to be listening, too. Then, as if Mary had asked a question, she nodded and continued toward the house.

Jim's brown van was gone. There was no garage, so if the van wasn't in the driveway, it wasn't here. The dogs paused a few yards ahead in the driveway, sniffing the wind. Then Topaz curled her lips to show her teeth, Shadow retreated toward Rachel with an uncertain whine. And Mary felt her skin crawl with dread. She shivered as she walked with Rachel along the tree-shadowed path to the south side of the house. The front door was open a few inches. She thought, *I don't want to go in there.*

Rachel ordered the dogs to stay, then: "Mary, wait here. I'll go in."

Mary shook her head. "No. We'll go in together."

Inside the door was a small foyer. On the wall opposite the door, Connie had proudly hung a painting, one of Rachel's encaustics. Now it lay on the floor, its frame splintered, bone white gesso ground exposed in a hectic pattern of crisscross streaks.

On the wall where the painting had hung was a huge hieroglyphic of a skull executed in spray paint in black and blood red.

Mary pressed a hand to her mouth, gasping for breath, eyes closed to shut out that monstrous image, but the skull icon was limned in memory with a night of terrified flight.

Rachel turned away, crossed to the double doors on the left that opened into the living room, and Mary swallowed at the constriction in her throat, fighting the resistance of her muscles. But again, she followed Rachel.

Some maniacal beast had been unleashed in this room: furniture was overturned, smashed, slashed; bookshelves toppled; the white walls hideously muraled with obscene, spray-painted graffiti and stitchings of bullet holes; the cabinets where Connie kept her china and crystal empty, doors ripped off; the floor graveled with shattered glass and porcelain.

Rachel's whispered *"No . . ."* echoed in the silence, and the sheer agony in her eyes made Mary want to cry out. Then it was gone, and nothing took its place. Nothing.

And where was Connie? Where was Jim?

There on the far wall—that wasn't just more demented graffiti. Spattered red brown and a curving, downward smear. Mary couldn't see the bottom of the smear; the overturned couch blocked her view. She made her way toward the wall, glass grinding under her soles.

Jim lay with his back against the wall, and he looked like something old and tattered that had been tossed away, his clothing and flesh riddled with bullet holes, caked with dried blood. Even his face had been smashed by craters of bullets.

For a long time Rachel stood motionless, staring at Jim's body, then without a word, she turned away, walked slowly toward the kitchen.

Rachel, don't go in there. Don't go . . .

Mary followed her. And they found Connie.

On her back on the floor, naked from the waist down, legs splayed, cold, dusky skin smeared with blood. Around her neck, the telephone cord cut deep into swollen flesh. Her face was bloated and purpled, tongue protruding, open eyes filmed like acid-dipped glass.

Mary felt darkness suffocating her, and perhaps she screamed, but she didn't hear it; she didn't hear or see anything until finally she recognized Rachel's face only inches away, felt the hard grip of her hands on her arms. But Rachel's eyes were as devoid of life as Connie's.

She said, "Mary, we have to go back to Amarna to get the van."

And Mary accepted that not because she understood it—she understood nothing at this moment—but because it imposed some semblance of structure on the chaos in her mind.

She didn't remember the walk to Amarna. She was only vaguely aware that Rachel left the dogs there, vaguely aware after a passage of ambiguous time of Rachel backing the VW into the driveway at the Acres house.

Rachel took the machete from the van, and Mary followed her to the back of the house and watched with neither comprehension nor curiosity while she hacked at the blackberry vines shrouding a mound of earth. Beneath the camouflage of vines, a metal door lay at an angle in the earth, brown paint rotten with rust. Rachel had a key for the lock. Together they pulled the heavy door back, hinges wailing. Under it, nine cement steps, another door. Rachel found the kerosene lamp and matches in the niche at the foot of the stairs. The yellow light went before them into a cell of a room. Jim's radiation shelter. Shelves filled with boxes, jars, canisters lined the walls. The air was chill and sterile.

Rachel went directly to a cabinet by the door, and it was then that Mary realized that all this had been rehearsed in a sense. Rachel had been *told* what she must do in case . . .

Mary couldn't hold on to that train of thought. Rachel opened the cabinet. A gun rack. Two rifles, a shotgun, three handguns. Two slots were empty. She thrust a rifle into Mary's hands. It was heavier than she expected, black metal, polished wood, the lens of the telescopic sight all gleaming with exquisite menace. In front of the trigger guard was mounted a flat, curved magazine, its steel dull and gray.

Rachel's voice was as dull and gray as the steel. "It's semiautomatic. That's the safety there. You have thirty cartridges in the clip."

Mary nodded, accepting those terse instructions as if this weren't the first time she'd handled such a weapon. Yet its lethal potential didn't take shape in her mind. She saw Rachel pull another rifle out of the cabinet, put the sling over her head, and shift the gun so that it angled across her back. Mary followed her example.

Then together they set to work.

Rachel and Mary became looters—purposeful, conscienceless, and guiltless—programmed by imperatives Mary still didn't understand.

We'll need these things.

Perhaps Rachel actually put it into words. Mary was sure she didn't add: *to survive.*

Through the summer afternoon under a blue sky dappled with opaline mackerel clouds, they looted the shelter and house, loaded the van time and again, drove to Amarna, emptied their plunder into the garage, then returned for more. They didn't touch the bodies except to cover them with sheets. And Rachel didn't shed a tear, didn't speak an unnecessary word. She moved, as she always did, at a deliberate pace, but she didn't once stop moving. Her eyes remained lifeless, and sometimes Mary was convinced she'd been struck blind by shock. Yet it was obvious that her eyes did at least register the images necessary to her. Her whole body seemed to function on that basic level. No doubt her heart still beat. She still breathed. Mary could see that: shallow breaths through parted lips.

Food, clothing, linens, tools, paper, books—all the books—anything the Rovers hadn't destroyed went into the van, then into the garage at Amarna. Mary didn't look at any of it, refused to recognize it as touching the lives of two people she had called friends. Only one thing briefly commanded her attention: the engraved handcuffs Jim was awarded when he retired as chief of the Shiloh Veepies.

And finally, when the last load had been piled into the van, Rachel climbed into the driver's seat and asked, "What happened to Sparky?" But she didn't seem to expect or want an answer to that question. Eyes fixed ahead, she drove away from the Acres house for the last time.

When they reached the gate at Amarna, Mary got out to open it, then after Rachel drove through, she pushed it shut. Her hands shook as she fumbled with the chain and lock. Pulling up the drawbridge, letting down the portcullis. She should call Harry Berden. Not that Harry could do anything. The cavalry was under siege, too, and the captain had lost a third of his troops two nights ago in the battle of the mall. But he could send someone to decently dispose of the bodies.

She turned away from the gate, looked up, seeking the sun, then looked down to the glow behind the wall of clouds in the west. Her watch blinked the time: 8:14. She got into the van, tried—and failed—to think of something to say to break Rachel's terrible silence.

Rachel stopped the van in front of the garage, but all she said was, "We'd better move some of the stuff so we can get the van inside."

Shadow and Topaz came to greet them, but they were subdued, panting despite the evening chill. Rachel and Mary worked in the waning light, shifting cartons and sacks into the north studio or the basement, until finally there was enough room in the garage for the van. The van was still full, but they didn't try to unload it. All they took with them when they left the garage was their rifles. The door rumbled shut, and Mary leaned against it, her knees on the verge of giving way.

"Where are the dogs?" Rachel asked.

Mary found it an effort to speak. "Shadow's in the house. I saw her when I took the last load to the basement."

Rachel nodded, called Topaz. She seemed to materialize out of the fading light from near the breezeway gate, and Rachel knelt to stroke her head. "Sweet lady, you don't know what the hell's going on. Neither do I, love, neither do—" Her voice caught, and Mary expected the break in her underlying silence, the iron silence that bound her grief.

But it didn't come.

Rachel rose and went to the gate. Mary followed her into the breezeway. The astringent smell of the firewood stacked against the house was oddly reassuring; she could hear a soft chirking from the chicken coop behind the garage.

And a throaty, distant rumble.

She thought herself inured to terror now. But she had only become inured to horror. *This* was terror, striking hard at the solar plexus.

What she heard was the sound of a motor. A car.

"Rachel?"

She had heard it, too. She turned and went back to the gate. Mary stood beside her, breath caught, listening.

Rachel whispered, "It's coming up our road."

Mary nodded. It could, of course, be quite innocent. A lost tourist, perhaps. It might even be an Apie patrol.

There. Lights glimmering through the trees.

Topaz whined impatiently, but she didn't bark. Maybe the car was familiar to her. Now the lights flashed around the curve; the pitch of the motor changed as the car slowed. The gate. Whoever was driving had seen the gate.

Mary stared at the twin points of light. It occurred to her that she should go call the Apies, but at that moment the motor roared and the car hit the gate with a clanging crash, plunged through, one-eyed now, careened down the road toward the house. Topaz began barking, and Rachel shouted, "Mary, are there any lights on in the house?"

"No, I didn't turn any on except in the basement, and I know I turned that one off."

"Maybe they'll think the house is empty. That gives us the advantage of surprise." And she brought her rifle up into firing position, resting the barrel on the top of the gate.

Mary stared at Rachel, suddenly transformed into a steady-handed guerrilla soldier, ready to kill. The rumble of the motor reverberated in a numbing crescendo, and Mary was struck with a new kind of fear. *I can't kill anyone.*

It was then that she recognized the vehicle roaring toward them; there was just enough light left.

Jim Acres's old brown Dodge van.

And within her, after this day of hideous revelations, terror found a channel into rage.

Topaz barked manically, and the van lurched across the lawn, a hubcap spinning off, flashing away in the skewed light of the remaining headlight. Mary snapped off the rifle's safety, felt the polished wood against her cheek, relished the potent weight of the weapon as she watched the last seconds of the van's approach through the scope, cross hairs centered on the windshield, on the glowing skull mask behind it.

The van slewed to a stop, both front doors swung open, the side door slammed back, and Rovers spilled out. Six—no, seven, eight raffish scarecrows in fluorescent paint, all laughing and shouting in demented camaraderie, staggering stoned. *"Tice diggin for the take!"* Had they said the same thing last night at the Acres house?

Mary fixed one in the cross hairs, squeezed off a shot. The recoil pounded her shoulder, the muzzle flash startled her, and her ears were numbed by the report, yet she heard a yelp as the Rover jerked back, fell writhing. Rachel's gun cracked while Mary lined her sights on another skull-faced figure, this one with an automatic snugged in his hands. She fired, and a spray of bullets smashed into the walls of the house, but they were high, and the gun tumbled to the ground as he fell.

Another fluorescent apparition dived for it. Rachel's shot dropped him. Shouted obscenities and Topaz's barking filled a millisecond before Mary and Rachel pulled off shots almost in unison, before Mary saw another Rover move out from behind the van with another automatic. She fired, shouting, "Get down!" and crouched behind the gate as the top of it vanished in a shower of splinters. But the Rover was wounded, and Rachel sprang up to fire again as soon as the burst ended. Mary saw the remaining Rovers running for the van, fired five more rounds, and Rachel yelled, "Mary, let them go!"

Mary hadn't assimilated that command when something hit her shoulder. A piece of wood. Topaz had climbed to the top of the stacked wood, dislodging wedges of fir. Mary grabbed for her, caught only more falling wood, and Topaz leapt over the gate, landed running, charging the last Rover while he scrambled for the van. Rachel cried, *"Topaz!"* and fumbled at the latch. Mary tried to get a shot at the Rover as Topaz closed in on him. His steel-toed boot lashed out, and Topaz howled, hurtled backward. Rachel threw the gate open and ran for Topaz, but not before the Rover took a long step, and with vicious deliberation, kicked the dog again.

Mary fired without aiming, staying a few paces behind Rachel, and the Rover made a dash for the van, jerked crazily at the impact of one of Mary's bullets as his mates pulled him in the side door. The van wobbled into reverse, and Rachel fired shot after shot at it. Flashes of light in the open side window—another automatic— but Rachel stood firm, oblivious. Mary dropped to the ground to join Rachel's desperate fusillade, while the van lurched toward the gate.

And it vanished in a ball of blinding light. The concussion hit like a hard slap against Mary's ears.

Dazed, she stared at the incandescent ball, watched it expand, then shrink until the shape of the van emerged, black against yellow flames.

And she began to laugh. *Taste of your own medicine, you bastards!* She felt no remorse nor even pity for the people burned to death in that van. She lay in the clover-scented grass and laughed. Until she saw a face in the grass not a yard away, the fluorescent skull smeared, glowing in the light of the fire.

One of the Rovers. Dead. A woman. Strange, she hadn't really thought of the Rovers as being male or female any more than she'd thought of them as being human.

This face was human beneath the painted mask. Now it was human, now that it was dead.

Mary heard a sobbing cry, and it wasn't her own.

In the flickering glare of firelight, she saw Rachel huddled over Topaz. Mary stumbled to her, sank to her knees beside her.

Rachel's silence had been broken. She wept now, sobs that racked her body, made her seem frail and small. Topaz lay on her side, every breath a whimper of pain, her eyes edged with crescents of white. Mary touched her flank, felt the crushed ribs soft under her palm, and her hand came away wet with blood. Her eyes burned, but she wouldn't give in to tears now. Throughout this terrifying day, Rachel had held back her tears. Now, Mary knew, it was her turn.

Rachel said, "Damn it, there's no vet within a hundred miles. Connie—she could've helped . . . oh, Connie . . ." The name ended in a keening cry.

Topaz coughed and whined, blood spattering out of her mouth. Mary said huskily, "Rachel, she can't survive this."

"I know." Those two words seemed a tangible weight, and the speaking of them bowed her down into a crouch. She stroked Topaz's head, whispered, "But I can't . . . kill her. Oh, my sweet Topaz, I haven't the courage. . . ."

"I'll take care of it." And even as she spoke, Mary wondered if she *could* do what she must to put Topaz out of her misery. Kill her. Rachel at least didn't sink to the euphemism. Mary looked down at her own bloody hand. She had, with no remorse, taken part in killing eight people tonight. Yet she shrank at killing this agony-stricken animal out of kindness.

81

But Topaz's final act was, however unintentionally, an act of mercy. She didn't force Mary to kill her. A retching cough, then she shuddered and closed her jewel eyes for the last time.

Mary didn't try to stop Rachel's weeping. She waited, dry-eyed, and the only other sounds were the crackle of the burning van and the omnipresent murmur of the sea. *I am here. . . .* There was still a glow of red at the horizon and a bright star above the clouds. Venus, probably. Lucifer. The wind blew chill out of the west.

She sat cross-legged in the grass on this erstwhile battlefield, smelled the bitter smoke, the gunpowder and blood on her hands, and tried to recapture that sense of triumph she felt when she became a killer. Self-defense? Of course. And more: revenge. But where was the satisfaction that was supposed to accompany revenge, that glorious, righteous satisfaction that was stuff of epics and history?

She felt none of that now. She felt no guilt, but neither did she feel anything she could equate with satisfaction.

She remembered the birth of Josie's kids—was it only hours ago?—and tried to recapture her desire to take part in the mystical cycle of motherhood. But that was gone, too. She would bring no children into *this* world. Rachel was right. There were already too many children. And too many of them grew up only to starve or go insane.

Finally she rose, helped Rachel to her feet, and saw the dark patch on her jacket just below her right shoulder.

"Rachel, you're hurt!" And it occurred to her then what a miracle it was that either of them was still alive.

Rachel stared down at Topaz. "I have to bury her."

"I'll do that. Let me look at your arm first." But Rachel didn't seem to hear her, and Mary added, "Shadow's still in the house. She'll be terrified."

Rachel stiffened and abruptly set off for the house. "Oh, damn, she'll be over the edge."

And Rachel was nearly over the edge of endurance. She almost fell when they reached the backdoor. Mary got her inside and felt for the light switch, and Rachel began calling Shadow. They found her in the kitchen, huddled trembling in one corner. Rachel knelt by her, nearly fell again. Mary steadied her. "Rachel, your arm—"

"It's not serious, Mary. If I could just . . . sit down."

Mary helped her to the couch in the living room, then had to carry Shadow to her; she wouldn't leave her corner. Rachel took her in her lap and whispered reassurances, and Mary thought, it's not fair that Shadow should suffer this terror and that Topaz should die simply because the humans they live with were victims of the insanity of other humans. It's not fair that Jim and Connie, who were kind and loving, should be so cruelly murdered because of that insanity.

But if she had ever doubted it, it was a conviction now. *Fairness is the exception to the rule in life.*

Rachel looked up at her, studying her face as if she hadn't seen her for a span of years. "I'm grateful, Mary. For you."

Mary could only nod. Then she went to the kitchen and a few minutes later returned with two glasses and a fifth of Jack Daniel's. She put them on the side table, poured whiskey into the glasses. "Water?"

"No." Rachel took the glass Mary offered, closed her eyes as she sipped the whiskey. "I suppose we should call Captain Berden."

Mary wanted to laugh, but knew better than to allow herself that. She tipped up her glass, held the whiskey hot in her mouth. A poor remedy, she thought, wondering if there *were* any real remedies.

Clad in rumpled pajamas and robe, a rifle in her hands, Mary looked out over the broken top of the breezeway gate into the glare of the early-morning sun. Her head ached unmercifully. Only a few hours ago she had seen the light of dawn in the windows before she achieved the oblivion of sleep.

And a few minutes ago she had been wakened by the sounds of Shadow's hysterical barking and a car horn. Now she stood trembling, trying to put her thoughts and memories in order. An Apie patrol was parked in the driveway, and she recognized the officer approaching her. Harry Berden. She opened the gate and went out to meet him, but stopped a few feet away. If she let him take her in his arms, she knew she'd start crying, and she wasn't sure she could stop. For a moment he stared at her, then glanced at the rifle, and finally nodded.

She said, "Harry, you look terrible. When did you last sleep?" And he did look like a specter, pale and hollow-eyed.

But he called up a smile. "You don't look so good yourself, Mary."

She laughed, brushed at her hair with her fingers. "No, I don't suppose I do. It's been a long night."

"Yeah. Damn long. The Rovers split up last night. Hit ten different places." He looked around at the bullet holes in the walls, the bodies on the grass, the black shell of Jim's van. "Is Rachel okay?"

"She has a very sore arm. Got grazed by a bullet, but I patched it up. And she lost three of her dearest friends. Did you get my message about Jim and Connie?"

A flicker of pain accompanied his nod. "We went to their house a couple of hours ago. Hell, I never thought . . ." He didn't try to finish that. "Do you know about any next of kin for us to notify?"

"No. I think they had some distant relatives in California. They didn't have any children."

He stared at the van, then frowned. "You said Rachel lost *three* friends?"

"Topaz." Mary looked toward the mound of earth near the beach path. "One of the bastards kicked her to death."

"Oh, damn. I know how she feels about her dogs. But maybe I have—" He stopped, distracted. Rachel was coming out the back door.

Mary studied her as she approached, wondering what lay behind her encompassing calm. When she reached them, she had a smile for Harry. "Good morning, Captain."

"Morning, Ms. Morrow. I'm sorry for what you've been through here. If it's any comfort, I think we took care of most of the gang that was hanging out around Shiloh."

She nodded. "I hope you didn't lose any of your officers."

The muscles of his jaw tensed. "Two. Five hurt. Anyway, I radioed for a tow truck and a wagon to clear out this mess here. It'll take a while, but they'll be around."

"Connie and Jim? Did you—"

"Yes, we took care of that. Mary told me about your dog, and I've got something in the patrol—just a minute." And he set off for his car, with Rachel and Mary, nonplussed, in his wake. He opened a back door, leaned inside, and emerged with Sparky in his arms. The dog was dull-eyed, atypically quiet, his right front leg bandaged.

Rachel's breath caught, she reached out with a shaking hand to touch Sparky's head as Harry explained, "Some folks down on North Front found him this morning and took him to the clinic. Had a bullet in his leg, but Joanie says he'll be fine. Little doped up now. Anyway, I figured I'd better find a good home for him."

"You've found it, you know that," Rachel said huskily. "Come on, Sparky. . . ." And Harry gently transferred the dog into her arms, while Sparky whined and tried to lick her face.

"Well, I'd better get going." Harry looked around again at the evidence of carnage and shook his head. "My hitch is up in September, and I don't think I'll sign up again. Home is beginning to sound good." He looked at Mary, a direct, questioning gaze. "Boise's still a nice place to raise a family."

She could think of nothing to say. Harry Berden was the kindest, most honest man she'd ever known, and yesterday—the day before yesterday—that oblique query would have at least given her something to ponder. Now it fell like a pebble in a frozen pond, creating no ripples.

After a moment he opened the front door of the car, then paused, frowning. "Ms. Morrow, I figure you'd like to know. We got a report yesterday that there's been two cases of Lassa in Oldport."

Mary felt a chill at the back of her neck, and Rachel went pale. "That's only thirty miles away," she whispered.

He nodded grimly. "Right."

Neither Rachel nor Mary spoke as he got into his car and backed down the drive, not until Rachel said, "Mary, I think we'd better start making some plans."

O cease! must hate and death return?
  Cease! must men kill and die?
Cease! drain not to its dregs the urn
  Of bitter prophecy.

—PERCY BYSSHE SHELLEY,
HELLAS (1821)

Rachel said once—stated categorically—that it is impossible for a wave to make a shape that is not perfectly graceful. Now at evening I look down at the beach and consider her dictum. In forty years I haven't forgotten it; the sea reminds me of it each day.

On this clear spring evening, the tide has gone out with the day, the sun has just set, its final moments marked with a pinpoint burst of incandescent green. The sky above the horizon is rose orange shading into pale yellow made green by its context, shading into warm blue and ultimately into ultramarine. There is little light left for the sea; it is pewter gray. The beach is umber verging on black, a somber expanse deserted by the tide. At the sea edge of this newly revealed strand, the waves have scoured out a topography of miniature hills and valleys, every valley a pool of captured seawater, every pool a mirror set in velvet umber, reflecting in reverse order the ultramarine, warm blue, green-hinting yellow, and rose orange. The shapes of these sky mirrors are all unique, the relationships of concave, convex curves complex and elegant. They are perfectly graceful.

I sit at the end of the table in the living room, my chair turned so I can look out the window at the beach and watch the children playing tag on the grass beyond the deck. Jonathan, the oldest, is also tallest, and he runs like a deer. Yet he lets Isaac catch him sometimes, and they fall laughing into the grass. Jonathan even lets eight-year-old Mary catch him, although she's so quick and lissome I wonder if he isn't fairly caught.

The youngest children, Deborah and Rachel, are downstairs being put to bed. Jerry is helping Miriam with that task, while Esther, Enid, and Grace are in the kitchen cleaning up after the evening meal. I can hear their voices, the clatter of silverware and pots. Bernadette is in the workroom grinding herbs for her medicines. Behind me, the fire crackles in the fireplace, beside me Stephen sits with his chin propped in his hand, and I remember my years of solitude here and know I'm fortunate to have such warm and peaceful evenings in my old age.

On the table is a stack of Rachel's watercolor paper cut into small rectangles. My hand still aches from wielding the old, dull scissors. I haven't yet begun writing the Chronicle, only preparing the paper. Fine rag watercolor paper: D'Arches rough, Whatman's hot press, Utrecht cold press. I've saved this paper all these years. Now I know why.

Stephen picks up a piece, runs his thumb over the rough surface. "Did you say this paper is handmade, Mary?"

"Yes, some of it."

"Could we make paper here?"

How many times have I asked myself that question? "I think so, Stephen. I have a book on papermaking. Maybe you'd like to read it."

"Yes, I would. Someday we'll have to make our own paper."

I smile at that. The words right out of my mouth. "I'll find the book for you tomorrow."

Not tonight. This is the sabbath. And this isn't one of my sanctioned lessons with Stephen. Sunday is supposedly a day of rest. It's also the day of the sabbath service: at least four hours of sermonizing and hymn singing. The children have no choice but to endure it, and I always feel sorry for them. Perhaps Jerry does, too. He usually plans something special for Sunday afternoon, and today it was a picnic on the Coho River. I didn't go along, but I'm proud of Jerry for making Sunday afternoons pleasurable for the children. When he was a child, his Sundays offered him no pleasure.

"Mary, what did you and Rachel do after . . . after your friends were killed?"

This may not be a sanctioned lesson, but Stephen is still curious, and I've never limited my teaching to the hours designated for school.

"Well, we barricaded ourselves from the outside world, Stephen."

"Because of the Rovers?"

"Partly, although the local Rover population had been drastically reduced. No, what really drove us into isolation was Lassa fever."

"Isolation? What do you mean?"

"Just that we made ourselves entirely self-sufficient so we wouldn't have to go out among other people for any reason. We were already *nearly* self-sufficient. We had land and water and livestock. We pooled our money to buy everything we'd need to keep going for—I don't know. A year or so. We never committed ourselves on the length of our retreat." And never imagined it would, in a sense, be permanent.

"What kind of things did you buy?"

"Well, nonmotorized farm implements, for one thing, like the plow we still use. Of course, training Silver to pull it wasn't so easy. We bought seed, everything from clover to squash, canned goods by the case, flour, rice, and beans by the sack. Canning jars, kerosene, gasoline—for the chain saw, not the van. Medicines, veterinary supplies, clothing, and many more things I can't remember now. In a way, the preparation for our siege was good for us. It gave us something to take our minds off the grief, and we needed that, especially Rachel."

Stephen's dark eyes are clouded. He nods and pulls in a deep breath. "How long did it take you to make all your preparations?"

"About a month and a half. By then the edge was off our grief, and even in our isolation, life returned to a kind of norm. There was more work without Connie and Jim to help, but I still did some writing, and Rachel did some painting. It was an oddly peaceful hiatus, yet we were never free of fear. We were living through the death throes of a golden age." I look down at the blank sheets of fine rag watercolor paper, and Stephen waits patiently.

"It was reaching critical mass, Stephen, all the deadly factors coming together. We still had our window on the world. The television. We knew about the riots and revolutions and the cities surrendered to anarchy. We knew about the failure of the monsoon in India for the third year in a row, the locusts in the Mediterranean and Africa, the killer smogs in Europe and on the East Coast of this country, about the Sino-Russian War, the nuking of Jerusalem, the droughts all over the world. And, of course, there were always stories about the Lassa epidemic and starvation. It was falling apart out there, and yet Rachel and I kept hoping. Now I can't imagine why. It was too late for hope."

Stephen seems to be watching the children, but his frown tells me his thoughts are elsewhere. "Miriam says it was prophesied, all the . . . falling apart."

I make no comment on prophesies. "We were also aware, through our window, of the crisis over that Russian fishing fleet. Some American admiral decided they were too close to our coast and sank all twenty ships. There was a furor in the circles of power, and all the charges and countercharges had nothing to do with the fishing fleet. In fact, we'd been on fairly good terms with the Russians for a long time. But most wars began with a triviality. What was really happening was a kind of mass madness—the same kind of madness that developed in animal studies when a confined population increased past a crucial point. But we were supposed to be smarter than white rats. And yet . . . it finally happened." I feel my eyes ache with tears even after all these years. That grief can't be salved by time, not for those of us who lived through that ultimate human catastrophe.

I wonder how many of us are left in the world now.

Stephen asks, "What was Armageddon like here at Amarna?"

I look out at the clear, brilliant sky. "September fifteenth. Indian summer. That evening, Rachel and I watched the six o'clock news-cast—the one that came to us via the new Federal Information Broadcasting System. I always wondered what bureaucrat came up with that title, if there was one among them who had a sense of humor. I mean, I can't believe no one realized it would inevitably be abbreviated FIBS."

Stephen smiles, but uneasily. "What did the newscast say?"

"Well, FIBS lived up to its acronym. Two days before, it had reported that cities were being evacuated in Russia, but on September fifteenth, Rachel and I—and the rest of the nation—were assured that negotiations were under way with the Russians, that the crisis was in fact over. So, we went out to the garden to pick zucchini and butternut squash. I remember a storm was coming in over the ocean from the southwest, but the sky was still clear in the east."

"What did you see? How did you know what had happened?"

"We didn't know. We only assumed. First we heard the FEMA warning siren from Shiloh Beach. It was so far away, we could barely hear it. Then suddenly it stopped. That's when I looked at my watch. My digital watch. It had stopped, too. The numbers vanished. And in the eastern sky we saw the strange colors."

"What . . . what were they like?"

I hesitate, trying to call up the words for those evanescent colors. They were no more amazing than what I see now in this sunset sky and in the mirrors in the sand. But before I can speak, I hear hurried footsteps behind me. Stephen turns, and I watch wariness take shape in his face.

"Stephen, what are you doing here?"

I look up at Miriam, and she looks down at me. She seems to expect me to answer the question. I remain silent, and Stephen rises.

"I'm just talking to Mary."

"I can see that. You don't have a lesson today. It's the sabbath. Anyway, it's time for bed. Go out and tell the other children."

He nods, glances uncertainly at me as he goes to the door. When it closes behind him, Miriam asks, "What were you talking to him about?"

"About the End," I answer flatly. "About Armageddon."

"What do *you* know about Armageddon?"

She's thinking of Saint John, of course. "Miriam, I know a great deal about it. I lived through it." And she was born of the next generation. What I lived through is to her as much a legend, a mythic event, as Saint John's revelation. To her it *is* Saint John's revelation, whatever our Elder says, and however difficult it might be to explain the obvious discrepancies between revelation and reality. I wonder how she explains the fact that *I* survived. Only the blessed were supposed to survive her Armageddon.

Miriam's lips part to speak, and I read in her eyes a rankling rage unmasked. I don't know what I expect her to say, but I am for a moment afraid.

But it is never said. The rage is hidden behind cool indifference.

The children are coming in, faces flushed from their games. They each pause to wish me good night and kiss my cheek, then hurry past the kitchen and through the dining room to the basement door. Miriam turns and follows the children. I watch her until she disappears beyond the door, then I close my eyes to listen to the sounds of voices from the kitchen, the grinding of Bernadette's pestle, the crackling of the fire, but there's no warmth or peace here now.

At length, I look out at the beach. The color is almost gone. And I think about Stephen's question: what was Armageddon like?

I don't know what it was like anywhere else. I can guess, but I don't know. Here, it was a day much like this one, except at the other end of the year.

And it was a day of terror beyond comprehension. After all these years, I still grieve for it.

But I don't understand it. I will never understand it.

Every one of these hundreds of millions of human beings is in some form seeking happiness. . . . Not one is altogether noble nor altogether trustworthy nor altogether consistent; and not one is altogether vile. Not a single one but has at some time wept.
      —HERBERT GEORGE WELLS, *THE OUTLINE OF HISTORY* (1920)

W hen had night come?
Mary Hope tried to remember. Minutes ago? Hours? How much time had passed, and what time was it now?

Mary's hand stirred abortively under the comforter. She didn't make the error—again—of looking at her watch. It had stopped, its minuscule circuits burned out in one silent millisecond. In that same millisecond it seemed the circuits of her mind had been destroyed, grids of perception and comprehension charred to inert threads of ash.

Rachel's old mechanical watch would still be working. They could be grateful for that.

Why?

What difference did it make what time it was now?

This was the end. Time didn't matter. Or perhaps it was only the beginning.

What is it when there is no time?

No, that was ridiculous, to say something didn't exist because the means to measure it had ceased to exist. . . .

For all the time Mary couldn't now measure—a few hours; it couldn't be more—her mind had functioned erratically on two levels she couldn't integrate. Neither the events of the last hours nor her thought sequences had imprinted themselves coherently in memory.

What am I doing here?

Did she ask that aloud? No. It only seemed like a question that should be asked aloud.

She knew the answer. One part of her mind knew it. The other part couldn't make sense of it.

The lithium-cell emergency light glowed atop a stack of cartons. Foolish to leave it on. They should save the batteries. At the foot of the basement stairs, like the debris of an avalanche, bedding, clothing, food, tools lay in shadowed mounds. Something pathetic about the light falling on a ceiling of cobwebbed floor joists; on pocked, concrete walls where the peeling whitewash made blighted patterns; on the yellow, sawed ends of stacked firewood; on the cast-iron Franklin stove; on shelves jumbled with dusty tools and scraps of lumber and pipes and loops of electrical wire and rusted paint cans wearing their colors in serrated collars of old drips—the detritus that basements collect over the years, the kinds of odds and ends that Rachel never threw away.

What were you keeping it for, Rachel?

At least the old mattress and springs had proved useful. Mary made herself aware of herself, of exactly where she was, and knew that was what she'd been avoiding all these hours, wherever she was and whatever she was doing. She listened for her own heartbeat, for the sound of her own breath, and she thought, *I am alive, I am here, this is now, and it is real.*

Images flickered in the nether reaches of her mind: fire and blinding white caldrons of light, black bones of girders, towering monoliths warping, splintering, disintegrating.

She was alive, but her mother was dead. Everyone she had known in Portland was dead. The city was dead, and how many cities with it?

But she was alive.

At this moment, in this place, she was huddled with Rachel on the old mattress, buried under a down comforter, propped with pillows between them and the concrete wall. Rachel's right arm was free of the comforter so she could stroke Shadow's head, while Shadow panted her fear, ears back. Sparky lay at the foot of the bed, outwardly calmer, yet his eyes shifted constantly from Mary to Rachel. Beneath one of the small, high windows, sealed with boards except for the taped hole for the intake hose, Jim Acres's filter pump thrummed like an insensate pulse. The air seemed heavy, turgid with the smell of dust and mold.

And beyond the window, the night raged. It had its own pulse.

Mary had to think about that sound, and she found it acidly ironic that it was only the howling, lashing roar of the storm that had swept in from the horizon where it lurked this afternoon.

It was only the storm.

At this moment she had no proof that anything worse than a sou'wester had occurred beyond the sealed windows.

No proof except a watch that had stopped—along with every electrical appliance in the house—and the fact that Jim's radio, the one that had been stored in the basement in its lead-sheathed box, had offered nothing but stuttering hisses of static.

And the fear and despair that finally came into focus in her mind shook her body, choked off her breath while she strained to stop a cry.

Why?

That was the word she wanted to shriek against the hammering

of the storm. But she held it back, because she felt Rachel trembling, too. They clung to each other as if each were paradoxically
both the drowning victim and the rescuer. And Rachel said in a
sibilant whisper, "Those ignorant, arrogant *bastards!*"

Mary didn't attempt a response to that. She knew that anything
she tried to say would come out in a scream of rage and chagrin.

It would be a long night, and she wondered how they would
know when it was over.

And yet, hope pursues me; encircles me, bites me; like a dying wolf tightening his grip for the last time.

—FEDERICO GARCIA LORCA, *DOÑA ROSITA* (1935)

L ike all our meals, breakfast is served at the long cedar table in the dining room. There are thirteen of us at the table; enough for a coven. Today we are treated to eggs scrambled with goat cheese, and I am treated to a duet by Little Mary and Deborah, since I missed their debut as a vocal duo at morning service. They sing "Jesus Wants Me for a Sunbeam" with enthusiasm and an attempt at harmony on Mary's part. I respond with applause and words of praise. I'm always glad to hear the children make music, whatever the message in the lyrics. And I like to believe they respond to the music more than the message.

Miriam, of course, values the message above the music, and while the girls sing, she watches me as if to be sure I get that point. I smile and after the duet tell her how sweetly the girls' voices blend.

An hour later the same table serves for another activity: school. Six days a week, three hours a day, the time determined by the Seth Thomas, the only timepiece that still works. I'm not sure how accurate it is by now.

I have the children for these three hours because I once made a bargain with Jerry.

So, again I sit at the table with my children waiting. My children. At least, when it comes to their education, their humanization, they're mine. I look at them and think how beautiful they are, as simple and as accessible as the iridescent skin of a soap bubble, and as fragile.

I sit at the west end of the table with the blackboard on one of Rachel's easels behind me, and in my hand is a precious stump of chalk. There's one box of pastels left, but I'm always trying pieces of soft stone as a substitute. None I've found so far have worked. Nor have I found substitutes for paper and pencils for the children's use. What little paper is left I hoard like a Scrooge. Enid and Bernadette are allotted a share of the precious sheets, but only the machine-made notebook or typing paper. Still, that suffices for Enid's garden and livestock breeding records, and for Bernadette's formulas for her herbal medicines. The pencils are long gone, but there's still some of Rachel's India ink, and we make a passable ink from twinberries.

Instead of paper, the children use slates of sorts—small rectangles of untempered Masonite that Rachel had prepared for encaustics. The smooth, white gesso ground takes well the marks of the vine maple charcoal sticks I make, for which Enid knits minuscule sleeves to keep the children's fingers clean. Enid considers cleanliness next to godliness, but the children blithely smear their hands and even their faces with charcoal every day. But it's easily removed, godly cleanliness restored.

Jonathan sits on my right today. He's fourteen, Jerry and Miriam's first child, and inbreeding has shown no deleterious effects in him.

He is in every way his father's son, even to Jerry's tendency to naiveté and his intrinsic dependability. And like Jerry, Jonathan isn't particularly good at reading and verbalization; his forte is mathematics, and in that he'll soon surpass me.

Isaac sits next to Jonathan, his half-brother. My sweet Isaac with his asthma and club foot. He's a little slow mentally, and I don't expect much of him in school. I'm just glad to have him here, this loving, fey child. He teaches me, I think, more than I can teach him.

On my left, Stephen occupies his usual seat. My scholar, my hope for the future of humankind—or this small colony of humankind. He is also the family's hope genetically. His father was an Arkite, so he carries neither Miriam's nor Jerry's genes. All the other children do, and sooner or later, that will cause problems.

But sooner or later, this colony will find other survivors or be found by them. That's inevitable. And necessary, although I wonder if the family will survive discovery intact. Yet change is also inevitable.

Next to Stephen on my left is Little Mary, Stephen's half-sister. She has Jerry's blue eyes and brown hair, but her skin is darker. Mary is eight, the first child born at Amarna, and Esther named her for me. An honor, I know, but I hope she won't have to be called Little Mary too many more years. Probably not. She's not a scholar like her brother, but she's extraordinarily adept with her hands. Now she's drawing cats on her gessoed slate, and for an eight-year-old, her drawings catch the lithe essence of catness amazingly well.

Next to Mary is her singing partner, Deborah, who has also begun scrawling on her slate. She's six, Miriam and Jerry's youngest, and Miriam's image, with her copper hair and fair skin. She's vivacious and flirtatious as I suspect Miriam might once have been. Or wanted to be. I suppose I encourage that in Deborah even at the risk of spoiling her.

The youngest of the children isn't here. She's only three, and hasn't yet become one of my children. Rebecca's child—the one whose birth killed her. Rebecca's last wish was that the child should be called Rachel. A fitting memorial, I think, to Rachel Morrow.

"All right, children, let's begin." I lean forward, pick up the damp rag in its plate in the center of the table, and hand it to Mary. "You and Deborah clean your slates. Now, today we'll start with numbers. Specifically, the number one million. I've talked about millions of things before, but do any of you really know what a million is?"

Jonathan responds, "It's a one with six zeros after it."

"Yes. How long do you think it would take to count to a million?"

"You mean by ones? Well, it'd take a long time. Maybe a couple of hours."

"Let's see if we can figure out exactly how long. First, we'll count up to a thousand and time it by the clock." I look at the Seth Thomas on the spool cabinet on the north wall as I rise and go to the blackboard to mark down the time. "Deborah, you start. Just count as high as you can, one number for every tick of the clock."

Deborah only gets to twenty, then Isaac continues the count, with a few corrections, to one hundred. Mary takes it to three hundred, and Stephen and Jonathan complete it, and by then the younger ones are showing signs of boredom and agree heartily that it takes a long time just to count to a thousand. About fifteen minutes, in fact.

Then comes the multiplication, and while the others watch, Jonathan makes the calculations on the blackboard and finally reveals that to count to one million would require nearly ten and a half days. They are all satisfactorily amazed and, I hope, have learned a little about calculation as well as measuring time.

And *million* is a concept vital to these children. Their world is as small and flat as the world of their ancient ancestors. It took more than thirty millennia for humankind to discover *million* and the even larger numbers it spawned, and they gave us the measure of the universe.

That measure must not be lost.

By the time the midday meal is finished, cumulus clouds are marching in over the horizon, but they offer no real threat of rain. I find

Stephen waiting for me on the deck, and once I've settled into my chair, he wastes no time on small talk. "Did you bring one of your diaries, Mary?"

His impatience pleases me. I reach into my skirt pocket for a diary—the third one—but again, it's only a prop and a prod to memory. "Of course I did. Now, where was I?"

He turns in his chair, his hooded eyes intent. "You were telling me about Armageddon here at Amarna."

I open the diary, study the erratic notations, and it requires a stringent mental bracing to return in memory to that time. It reminds me that spring days spent in quiet, satisfying endeavors are the obverse of dark days spent in terror, and the coin can flip so quickly, so casually. "Yes, when Rachel and I retreated into our cave."

"Your cave?"

"The basement. But it seemed like a cave to me. I felt like . . . like time had folded in on itself, and I was a Cro-Magnon woman huddled at the hearth in my cave, with the glacier wind and the Dire Wolves howling outside, and tens of thousands of years had been lost as if they'd never existed."

His eyes narrow thoughtfully, then he asks, "But why did you have to stay in the basement?"

"Because of the radiation from the bombs. FEMA—that was the Federal Emergency Management Agency—had published volumes on surviving a nuclear war. Surviving! They estimated it would take two weeks for the initial fallout to clear. So, Rachel and I stayed in our cave for two weeks without once even opening a window. We didn't know how bad the radiation was here. Actually, I don't think we got much initial fallout. That storm protected us. But we didn't know. Jim had a Geiger counter, but we didn't find it in the shelter or in their house, so we didn't know about the radiation. We didn't know *anything*. That was the worst part. We didn't know whether Jim's radio just wasn't working or couldn't pick up anything through the basement walls or whether there was no one out there broadcasting. The only thing we *did* know is that it was colder than usual for September. We just huddled there in our frigid cave for two endless weeks—wondering."

I pause, look up into the cloud-dappled, springtime sky. "The odd thing is, Stephen, that was a time of hope. I mean, a time when it was still *possible* to hope. I imagined the worst, yes, but sometimes I imagined the best, which was that we'd made a mistake, that there hadn't really been a war. Or I imagined that even if there had been a war, it wasn't extensive enough to destroy *all* civilization. And I imagined that when we left our cave, we'd find other survivors, pool our resources, and work ourselves out of the disaster. I imagined we'd find at least vestiges of a government to help us. Of course, I realized it might not be ours. We might have lost the war." I have to laugh as I speak those words. You can't say that without either laughing or crying.

Then I look around at Stephen. "But the two weeks finally ended. Rachel and I finally came out of our cave."

His obsidian eyes are fixed on me; he seems to have stopped breathing. "What did you find?"

"Nothing that I had imagined."

I close the diary. I need no prod for memory now. Sometimes I wish I *could* forget.

See, Winter comes to rule the varied year,
Sullen and sad. . . .
    Welcome, kindred gloom!
Congenial horrors, hail! . . .
Cruel as death, and hungry as the grave.
                    —JAMES THOMSON, *THE SEASONS.*
                                    WINTER (1726)

While the dogs barked insistently, Rachel stood on the landing at the top of the basement stairs, her hand on the doorknob, but she paused there, and Mary waited impatiently, pulse hammering. When Rachel at length opened the door, the dogs spilled out, claws scrabbling on the oak floor. But there in the chill, dim silence, their barking ceased, and Mary looked around the house with the daunting sense that she'd never been here before. She noted the open cabinet doors in the kitchen, the disarray left in their hurried evacuation. Only two weeks ago? It seemed like something remembered from her childhood.

She made her way into the living room. The drapes were closed. There was an emptiness under her ribs, and she wondered whether to call it hope or fear. She turned, saw Rachel behind her, then pushed the drapes aside and opened the sliding door. A rush of wind billowed the cloth as she went out onto the deck and into the outside world she'd been waiting so long to see.

September. She had to remind herself that this was September. Indian summer.

The wind, thick with stinging snow, pummeled her, the cold like a knife blade at the back of her neck. The deck was an untracked plane of snow, the lawn a rippled dune of snow, the beach, except for the dark band cleared by the waves, a swath of white and gray, snow and ice.

She had to remind herself that this was morning. Her mind balked at that as it did at Indian summer. Her mind recognized this somber light as winter dusk. The horizon was obliterated by sullen clouds and a fog of snow, and she could see only a few hundred feet past the breakers, where the northeast wind blew fans of riffles against the shoreward surge. And the sea was steaming. Whirlwinds of vapor rose from the roiling surface, danced ahead of the wind.

"Rachel . . ." The wind whipped the word away into the snow.

Rachel stood beside her, staring out at the sea, eyes shadowed with dread. "I've seen snow here. Only three times in twenty years, and only in December or January." She looked up at the oppressive clouds. "But I've never seen it so dark. I've never seen that color. . . ."

Mary saw the odd brazen cast of the clouds. Two words came unbid and clear into her mind. She didn't say them aloud, although she saw Rachel's lips move as if to form them.

Nuclear winter.

The implications in those words were stunning. They numbed her mind as the cold numbed her body. She said dully, "Rachel, we'll have to go down to Shiloh and see if anyone there can tell us what happened or what's going on now."

"If anyone there knows." She swept up a wad of snow from the railing with her gloved hand, then turned and crossed to the door.

"Before we go anywhere, we have to find out if any of the animals survived."

Mary started to protest the delay, but she couldn't bring herself to argue with Rachel. Not now. They went to the garage first, where, in that hour of frantic preparation that seemed so long ago, they had pushed the van out and moved the chickens and rabbits in. The air was sour with the smell of droppings, and their entrance set the chickens flapping and squawking, while the rabbits scrambled for cover, eyes gleaming in the beam of Rachel's flashlight. The living left in their wake scattered heaps of the dead.

For the living, the first problem was water; the water basins had frozen. Mary went into the house to fill a bucket at the kitchen sink, a task that took an inordinate length of time. The pipes hadn't entirely frozen, but only a gurgling trickle flowed out of the faucet. And while she waited for the water to slowly, slowly fill the bucket, she thought of Shiloh. They had to get to Shiloh, had to find out what had happened and what was being done.

Finally she took the bucket to the garage and broke the ice out of the basins, filled them with fresh water. Rachel had replenished the feeders and begun picking up the carcasses. Mary helped her carry the small, stiffened bodies to the chicken coop where predators couldn't reach them, and the cold would preserve them. She stared at the mound of dark feathers and fur turning white with snow, and all she could think of was Shiloh. All the answers were there. The only answers they could hope for.

But Rachel had already set out through the drifts toward the barn. Mary caught up with her. They passed the garden, a jumble of frozen leaves and stalks, and the snow-blanketed beehives near the orchard. Rachel said, "If any of the bees survived, they'll need extra honey."

"Won't they freeze to death?"

"They can keep the temperature in the hives around ninety-eight just with their body heat. But they can starve to death—if the radiation hasn't already killed them."

Mary didn't respond to that. She plodded on through the snow toward the barn. Shadow and Sparky were barking in play, leaping and rolling in flamboyant showers of white, and Rachel smiled. "Look at them. They're so happy to be outside."

Mary watched them with a feeling close to resentment.

Shiloh. She held on to that. The Apie station. Yes. Harry Berden would know what had happened, what to do.

As they neared the barn one question was answered: Pan was alive. They could hear his throaty bleating. When they went into his shed, they found the feeder empty, the water trough covered with an inch of cracked and refrozen ice. Rachel broke the ice with a shovel, and it was a measure of Pan's thirst that he began drinking immediately, putting aside his usual fastidious preference for impeccably clean water.

Then they went into the barn, where the other goats and Silver milled about them, complaining noisily, but they were all alive, even Josie's kids. Both Persephone and Josie had full udders. The kids had been weaned, but would turn to that source of sustenance and liquid again under these conditions. So would the other does. Rachel greeted them all like long-lost friends and called it a miracle.

Mary thought of Shiloh Beach.

Again, water was the first problem. It seemed warm in the barn—relative to outside—but a skim of ice covered the trough. Rachel cleared it, and Silver and the goats crowded in to drink. Mary climbed up to the loft and pushed three bales of hay down, and while Rachel dragged one out to Pan's shed, Mary impatiently forked hay into the feeders.

She knew Rachel would want to rake out the barn now, to milk the goats, to take honey to the bees, to check the reservoir, to build fires in the house, to waste time on the myriad chores she could find to do here, but Mary could tolerate no further delay. She plunged the pitchfork into the ground and strode out of the barn, met Rachel on her way back from Pan's shed. "Rachel, please, we have to go to Shiloh."

Rachel studied her a moment. "Mary, don't . . . well, just don't get your hopes too high."

Mary bit back an angry retort, but she couldn't stop the clenching of her hands. "We *have* to find out what happened."

"Yes. Well, the van won't start."

"Then we'll walk."

"Not in this weather. We'll ride. Silver can carry both of us, but we'd better get more clothes on before we go. And the guns."

They made a strange procession, Mary thought. A horse, two women, armed with rifles, riding bareback, two dogs trailing them. Mary rode behind Rachel, swaying with her in rhythm with Silver's steady gait, Rachel holding the reins in one hand, the other resting on the bundle of rope and burlap sacks slung over Silver's withers.

When they reached the Acres house, they should have had a clear view of Shiloh Beach. They didn't. The air was opaque with snow, the dusky clouds a burden on the mind. Along the white ribbon of the road, there were no cars, no tracks. Rachel fumbled under the cuff of her glove, then pulled her muffler down. When she spoke, her words formed puffs of white. "It's ten o'clock now. We'll have to watch the time, Mary. We can't stay out in this long."

Mary felt the cold seeping through her layers of protective clothing. "Just long enough to get to Shiloh."

"And back," Rachel reminded her.

Silver's hooves bit through the snow to the black asphalt. Mary looked back at the trail of the mare's tracks, braided with the dotted lines of the dogs' tracks. Even as she watched they faded, erased by the wind-harried snow. Houses materialized one after the other out of the haze. Lightless windows made black patterns on gray and white, and not one chimney showed a wisp of smoke.

They had traveled nearly five blocks in this dim, suffocatingly silent world when they came to the first burned house. It looked like a crude *sumi-e* painting, black strokes of charred studs against white drifts. From that point every house they passed was a gutted ruin. Mary couldn't make sense of those ruins, not until she realized that in the last two weeks there had been nothing and no one to stop fire, driven by the wind, from leaping from one house to the next.

The black and white piles were like markers in a graveyard, set at regular intervals, hinting maddeningly at knowledge held secret. Even the dogs seemed oppressed. They paced behind Silver, tails low, ears flicking constantly for a sound. Mary rocked with Silver's lulling amble while the chill air parched her lips and throat, the snow whirled into her eyes, and even though she could feel Rachel rocking with her, she had an irrational sense that she was alone, and with every moment hope waned within her.

The Apie station. They'd find someone there. Harry. He'd be there.

The shopping mall began to take shape ahead of them, and as they drew nearer emerged out of the murky atmosphere as a ruin, the long, low L of buildings reduced to a snow-shrouded slag heap of rubble. The parking lot was dotted with cars, some still aligned in angled formations, and of the fifty or more cars, at least a third were wrecked and burned, as if they'd been hit by artillery shells, as if—

Rachel said hoarsely, "They were blown up." She pointed to the nearest hulk. "Bullet holes. That means Rovers."

Mary felt a chill between her shoulder blades that was not the cold as she looked around the ruins, seeking any hint of movement. But nothing moved here except the wind.

The dogs were digging at a mound of snow near what had once been the supermarket entrance. Rachel shouted, "Shadow— Sparky, what are you into?" She slid off Silver's back, ran to the mound, and pulled the dogs away. Mary dismounted and followed her, stared numbly at the face in the snow. A Rover. A skull design in red and black still marked his face, but the design was marred by the frozen cascade of blood from his crushed forehead.

Rachel squinted into the shattered building. "Under those girders—that's the rear end of a pickup. They must've driven it into the store and blew it up. Bastards! Why destroy everything? Did they think that would help *them* live?"

Mary looked away, but she saw other similar mounds in the snow. "Rachel, we'd better get to the Apie station."

"It won't be there."

"How do you know? It *will* be there."

Rachel looked at her, eyes strangely opaque. Then she called the dogs and set off across the parking lot, with Silver following like another large, placid dog. Mary skirted the mounds, trying not to see the hands or knees or feet left uncovered by the snow, trying not to recognize the charred remains spilling out of one of the exploded cars. Two adults. Three children. It was like crossing a battlefield.

But if the Rovers had spent their nihilistic passion here, maybe the rest of the town had been spared—and the Apie station.

Highway 101 was strewn with motionless vehicles given a semblance of movement by windblown snow. Rachel and Mary trudged southward, passing one burned building after another, and finally Mary couldn't deny the bleak truth: nothing in the heart of Shiloh had escaped the fires. They skirted cars without looking into them. They drifted down a defile of blackened relics. And when they reached the Apie station, Mary gazed at its ruins with tears freezing on her cheeks. The riven steel of the antenna tower lay sprawled atop the rubble like the bones of a dinosaur.

So much for our link with the rest of the world, she thought. Harry Berden hadn't gone home to Boise soon enough. She told herself that his body was probably buried in that snow white, fire black ruin, but she felt nothing she recognized as grief—not for Harry, not for her mother, not for anyone. All she felt was a keening desolation. She stood trembling, heart stuttering, and the pain seemed past bearing.

So much for hope.

At length, she looked at Rachel, saw the same despair in her eyes, but it was caged behind a stubborn resolve. Mary nodded. "It's only been two weeks. The government, the army—someone will show up eventually. Besides, there *must* be survivors around here. *We* survived."

Rachel shivered. "Yes. We survived." Then she turned away and walked toward the ruins of the building that had housed Connie's clinic, and for the next half hour they searched among treacherous avalanches of fallen boards and brick. They were rewarded for their efforts with three large bottles of antibiotic capsules, two of aspirin, another of alcohol, four rolls of gauze, a package of tape sutures, an assortment of disposable syringes, a scalpel, a pair of scissors, and a box of ten twenty-cc vials of morphine. Rachel put it all in a burlap sack.

We're scavengers now, Mary thought, as they made their way through the debris to the highway where Silver and the dogs waited. This is how we'll live. *If* we live. Like jackals at a carcass, we'll live off the remains of a dead civilization. Her cold-numbed feet dragged, her fingers ached, and with every breath of chill air, she felt her internal temperature sink a fraction of a degree.

Rachel leaned wearily against Silver's flank. "Mary, we'd better get home. Let's head for the beach. The tide should be out, and it'll be easier going that way."

Mary wanted to object that they couldn't go home yet. They hadn't found any survivors. And there must be survivors in Shiloh. Somewhere. But she knew, as Rachel did, that if they didn't get out of this enervating cold, they might not be able to count themselves among the survivors much longer. Tomorrow, the next day, they would, they must try again.

With the aid of a car fender, they mounted Silver and at the next cross street turned west. Burned houses marked the way, and Mary was convinced that the somber sentinels would continue all the way to the sea. It was then that she saw, emerging out of the fog of snow, an open area surrounded by trees and shrubs untouched by fire. The deep green of azalea and rhododendron leaves under the snow was pathetically bright, and in the midst of this unravaged island stood a church: an old, white clapboard, picture-postcard church. Mary stared at it, expecting it to disappear, a phantom of her hope.

But it didn't disappear. It took on substance with Silver's every step forward.

"Rachel, do you see it?"

"I see it. That's the old Community Church."

At the back of the building a brick chimney rose above the ridge-pole. There was no smoke coming from it. And yet—Mary focused on the space above the chimney. Yes, a wavering of the tree branches behind it. Heat waves.

"The chimney! Rachel, there's heat—a stove, something! Someone's *in* there! *This* is where the survivors came!" She couldn't wait for Silver's slow gait to bring them closer. She slid off the mare's back and ran toward the church, shouting, the dogs running with her, barking as if they shared her joy.

"Mary! Mary, *wait!*"

Mary didn't hear Rachel, not until she caught up with her and grabbed her arm. "Mary, if there *is* anyone in there, we don't know who it might be!"

With an effort, Mary tore her gaze away from the church to look at Rachel. "What?"

"We don't know who's in there. It could be Rovers."

Mary took an aching breath. Rachel was right. She looked up at the chimney, at the wavering air above it. But someone *was* in there.

They walked slowly toward the church, Rachel ordering the dogs to heel, her rifle ready in her hands. Mary listened intently, but the only sound was the rasp of their breathing. They were thirty feet from the entrance when one of the double doors swung open.

Rachel snapped, "Mary, hold the dogs!" and stood with her rifle raised, aimed at the door.

Mary knelt and grasped Shadow and Sparky's collars, stared at the door, at what came out of it.

A dog. A big, tawny dog, German shepherd in his lineage.

He was carrying something in his mouth. He gazed at them with amber eyes, a ridge of hair rising on his shoulders, and for seconds the tension was borne out in silence.

Until Mary recognized what the shepherd held in his mouth.

A hand. A human hand.

And she screamed.

As if that sound were a cue, six more dogs scrambled, snarling, out of the door. The shepherd dropped his burden, baring a serrated arsenal of teeth as he led the attack, snow exploding under his paws. Sparky and Shadow barked and lunged against their collars, but Mary held on when her only impulse was to run. She flinched at the crash of the rifle. Rachel only fired into the air, but the shepherd stopped, then bolted into the trees south of the church, his pack at his heels. Neither Sparky nor Shadow stopped barking until the last dog had disappeared.

Rachel knelt by Mary and said shakily, "You can let go of them now."

Mary loosed her rigid hold on the dogs' collars. "It's like something out of a Russian folktale—the wolf pack chasing the troika."

Rachel stroked Sparky's head. "Dogs are only a few thousand years removed from wolves. They both survive by packing. Where's Silver?"

Silver had retreated to the street, and Rachel had to go retrieve her. The mare wasn't anxious to approach the church, nodding her head nervously and pulling at the reins. Mary waited for Rachel, then together they approached the door, but a few paces short of it stopped, and Mary stared at the hand in the snow. A cracked arm bone was attached to it, hung with black-red, frayed muscle. Meat. Mary felt a painful surge in her stomach.

Rachel only glanced at the hand. "The dogs were probably scavenging in the church. You won't find anyone alive in there."

"But the chimney, the heat . . ."

"Well, there's the basement. The door is around at the back. Fellowship Hall, one of the hottest gambling spots in town." Then when Mary looked at her blankly, she sighed. "Bingo. Mary, don't you think if anyone was alive in there—"

"No! Fellowship Hall. *That's* where they'll be!" And Mary turned away from the doubt in Rachel's eyes, set off around the side of the church, kicking through the drifted snow, only vaguely aware that Rachel was following her. At the back of the church under a portico, she found the entrance to Fellowship Hall. She pounded and yelled, jerked at the doorknob, and finally the ice that sealed the door gave way.

A landing, a short flight of stairs leading down into a pocket of dimness. "There's another door, Rachel. Come on!"

The survivors *would* be here. It made such perfect sense. A big

111

room, underground, where they'd be safe from radiation, where it would be easy to keep warm. They must have some sort of non-electric stove. Mary reached for the doorknob, but Rachel was shouting at her. "Can't you *smell* that?"

Mary couldn't even hear her. She flung the door open and was three steps into the room before the smell hit her, as palpable as a blow: the sticky, foul smell of death. She covered her mouth and nose with her hand, tried not to breathe, but her pounding heart demanded more air, forced her to inhale the hideous stink.

A cavernous room with a low, beamed ceiling, the only light a pale glow from a propane stove near the door. Rows of folding tables had been put to use as beds. This had been a makeshift hospital. And now it was a charnel house, the table beds occupied by corpses shrouded in bloody, vomit-stained blankets. Her eyes fixed on the bodies nearest the light, on tumid faces smeared with the blood of uncontrollable hemorrhages, on gray skin speckled with red petechiae. The light faded into darkness a short distance from its source, but it was enough to delineate this chamber of horrors. It was enough, as the heat from the stove was enough to maintain the temperature at a level that sustained the processes of decay.

"Lassa." Rachel's voice was muffled by her hand. "Oh, damn, they all died of Lassa. Mary, let's get *out* of here!"

Mary turned, lunged for the door, ran into Rachel, who had suddenly stopped, staring at the body of a man lying near the door where the glow of the stove lighted his bloated caricature of a face. He was fully dressed; he had apparently simply fallen there.

Rachel whispered, "Reverend Gillis. This was his church."

Somehow, it intensified the horror to know this corpse had had a name. Mary looked into his swollen face and saw a tiny, flickering movement in his eyelids. "Rachel, he—he's alive! Look at his eyes!"

Rachel was trying to pull Mary toward the door. "He's not alive. That's only maggots."

Mary staggered, felt darkness closing in like fetid water. She stumbled out the door and up the steps, fell and crashed against the risers, heard panting cries that didn't stop until she reached the outer door, until she sank to her knees and vomited in the snow.

When the spasms stopped, her ears were ringing, shadows hovered at the edges of her vision. She took a handful of snow and let it melt in her mouth, spat it out. Finally she looked around, saw Rachel sitting on her heels, back braced against one of the columns supporting the portico, Shadow and Sparky crouched on either side of her, panting out clouds of vapor, ears flat against their heads. Rachel was pale, her eyes haunted. She asked, "Are you all right?"

Mary nodded. She couldn't seem to form even the simple word *yes*. She clenched her teeth to stop their chattering.

Rachel rose. "I found the propane tank. The one that supplies the stove." She gestured toward a white mound near the door. The snow had been brushed off the top to reveal a silvery surface bisected by a riveted seam.

Rachel helped Mary to her feet, then took her arm and led her to the street. "Wait here," she said, and in a few minutes returned with Silver and the dogs. Mary didn't question her, didn't speak. Rachel handed her Silver's reins and a rope looped through both the dogs' collars. "Hold them for me. Mary? Do you understand?"

Mary didn't understand her purpose, but she could still understand the words. Rachel walked toward the church, and Mary gripped the reins and rope, shivering uncontrollably, saw Rachel stop when she had covered half the distance to the church, then raise her rifle and, after a moment, fire. The recoil rocked her back. Mary gasped at the shock of the report, held fast against the animals' lunging. The propane tank exploded with a dull thump. Orange flames billowed, attacked the white clapboards with a vicious crackling.

By the time Rachel returned, whorls of flame were fanning out from the center of the explosion, smoke boiling up into the turbid air until the wind caught it, whipped it seaward. The crackle became a roar, and within minutes the back wall of the church shimmered with flames.

Rachel nodded, her eyes closing. "Ashes to ashes . . ."

Mary Hope stared into the flames, mesmerized by their shapes. Like the waters of a stream flowing over boulders, they too flowed, always the same and never the same, giving form to processes. *Ashes to ashes.* Yes, it was fitting; fire was fitting as an end.

Rachel knelt by the stove and put a piece of wood on the fire as if it were an offering. Mary blinked. She wasn't looking into the flames of the church. The cast-iron Franklin stove. The basement. The cave.

She pulled the blanket around her, hands clenched in the rough wool. Her face was hot; the cold crept up her back. She felt the shift of the big, round hassock as Rachel sat down beside her. Rachel said nothing, and the weight of her silence drew Mary's eyes to her face. The fire gave it a glow of color that was illusory. The truth was in her eyes, where there was no light except the reflected glint of fire.

Mary turned away, watched the currents of the flames, felt the cold outside scratching at the windows. It infiltrated the earth and the walls of this cave, and only the fire kept it at bay. But the cold was patient; as patient as death.

Yet it wasn't cold that killed the people at the church. It was something hovering at the edge of life as it was defined: a virus, invisible as the cold and equally deadly.

Had anyone at the Federal Emergency Management Agency taken that invisible factor into their calculations when they considered the survivability of a nuclear exchange?

Mary gazed into the fire, and she had a vision of the heart of this continent: the vast plains where the wind swept unimpeded out of the Arctic. She saw the bombed cities, black cankers of ruin, and she saw the cities, towns, and villages that had *not* been struck by that terrible, swift lightning. How many were within the fallout plumes? That factor had been calculated. She remembered the maps FEMA had published. On those maps most of the eastern third of the country, from the Mississippi to the Atlantic, was blackened by overlapping plumes. How long does it take to die of radiation poisoning? She remembered the columns of figures expressing that horror statistically. That factor FEMA had calculated to the last decimal point. By now it was over for most of the people in the black plumes.

But in the heart of this continent there was a town that was in the white of the map. A town where tens of thousands of people had survived the war. But how would they survive the invisible armies of disease? Had FEMA calculated that?

There was a hospital in this town. No lights in its windows now, no electricity to run the miraculous machines, no fuel for the auxiliary generators, no medications after the first onslaught of sick and injured. And there never had been a medication that would cure Lassa.

And had FEMA calculated the factor of anarchy, of madness: the madness unleashed out of terror and despair, as explosive and as destructive as the bombs? Would that small plains town, untouched by the bombs, still be a burned-out ruin? Yes, she could see the blighted blocks of rubble. Not all of the town had burned. No. There had been a war in its streets, and someone had won. Road gangs, Klan, NRA, American Legion, National Guard, Army, Apies—the lines were vague now. And who would maintain law and order when all that weighed in the scales of justice was survival?

She saw the town under a dusky, frigid sky, desolately isolated. The communication system that had been the warp and woof of this nation had succumbed to EMP. Electromagnetic pulse, the nemesis FEMA had tried to deny as it had nuclear winter. A few radios were working. They buzzed with static and pleas for help.

No one in this town could answer those pleas. Burned buildings marked out the grid of vacant streets. No vehicles moved, no one walked in those streets, nothing lived in any of the places where people had gathered to seek help and comfort.

There were still some survivors crouching in storm cellars or basements. They had survived cold, disease, and anarchy. But they would not survive hunger—not when the last of their stored or scavenged food was gone, when they looked out of their caves and saw nothing but snow and ice for a thousand miles in every direction.

And Mary saw this town replicated ten-thousandfold around the world. A world enshrouded in death.

No. Perhaps not an entire world. The southern hemisphere might be spared some of the devastation. But no southern nation would survive without catastrophic disruptions in their climate, their food and energy supply systems, their economic and social structures. And would they survive Lassa? Mary remembered a newscaster coolly reporting at least a week before the End that two million people had died of Lassa in Australia and five million in South Africa.

I guess we deserved it. We treated this lovely planet so negligently, we treated each other so cruelly.

We deserved it.

"No, *we* didn't deserve it. There were billions of people who never did anything in their lives to *deserve* what happened to them."

Rachel's words roused Mary, bewildered her because she didn't realize she'd said anything aloud. She wondered how much of what she'd been thinking she had spoken. She said nothing more now.

Rachel sat hunched in her down jacket, hands spread in front of her to catch the heat. Shadow nuzzled her knee for reassurance, but she had none to offer. She said, "We'll have to move one of the wood stoves into the garage, or we'll lose *all* the rabbits and chickens."

Mary closed her eyes, and she was surprised that the first sound to emerge from her mouth was an approximation of a laugh.

"Of course, we're going to lose them, Rachel. Sooner or later we're going to lose . . ." *Everything. We're going to lose us. Sooner or later.*

The wind, the voice of the cold, echoed its dirge in the chimney. Eventually Rachel spoke again.

"Strange, isn't it? I left for Shiloh this morning with very little hope. I came home with very little hope. You left with a great deal of hope and came home with none."

Mary pressed her hands to her eyes, and for a moment she couldn't get enough breath.

"*Why?* Why should I still have any hope? Hope for what? This is what they call nuclear winter, the winter of our ultimate discontent. The *last* winter because it will never end! This is—so why . . . why . . . ?"

I want to cry, she thought as the words poured out like sand from a rusted cup. I want to cry, but I can't even do that. Dry. All dried up and shriveled inside, dead already. Brain dead. Soul dead.

Rachel was watching her. Mary could feel that, but she stared into the fire, and at this moment she felt detached from herself, from Rachel. She looked down, as if from a distance, on the two of them in a beleaguered island of warmth and light in the chill darkness. And Rachel said, "I've been thinking about what separates homo sapiens from its animal cousins."

Mary didn't attempt a response to that. She listened from far away to the sounds of the words.

Rachel said, "I've been told that animals can't imagine. Yet they dream. Isn't a dream imaginary? I've been told that animals can't imagine their own deaths, so they don't dread death. It's easier to believe that, I suppose, if you have to kill animals. Or if you take pleasure in killing them. But if that were true, the gazelle would just stand quietly while the lion breaks its neck. No, when it comes to death, what separates us from our cousins isn't the capacity to imagine and dread it. The difference is choice."

Mary looked around at her, returned to herself, willing eyes and mind into focus. Rachel was regarding her with a gaze shadowed with sorrow, but there was no recognition of defeat in it. "Choice is the measure of our humanity, Mary. Death is inevitable, but until it becomes imminent, we still have a choice. We can choose to die, or we can choose to live. I can't give you any reason why you should go on hoping or living, or why I should. The time may come when I'll know, one way or the other. But I'm not ready to surrender yet. And you're wrong about one thing: this winter *will* end. I've read the TTAPS report. I don't know what kind of spring will follow, or whether we can survive until spring comes. But I intend to find out. That's my *choice*."

She stopped then, as if there were no more to be said, and denial clamored in Mary's mind. She sat mute, trying to shape it into words, to forge her despair into arguments. The wind howled in the waiting darkness, while she shivered with cold.

But the arguments melted like snow in her hands.

Choice.

She became aware of the sensation of a smile, something she'd never expected to feel again. It was a fragile sensation besieged by grief, but she held on to it, called it hope. Her eyes were suddenly blurred, and at last the tears came, and she welcomed them. She reached out, embraced Rachel, and together they wept, together they acknowledged their grief and fear and hope.

How long they wept in each other's arms, Mary didn't know, but finally she drew away, said, "I promise you, Rachel, I won't surrender, either."

Rachel nodded, then cleared her throat and rose to tend the fire. "If you'll look on the shelves at the foot of the stairs, you'll find a case of bourbon. I think this is the time to open one of those bottles."

Mary came to her feet stiffly as if she hadn't moved in hours, and perhaps she hadn't. While Rachel added more wood to the fire, Mary searched for the bourbon with a flashlight. At length, they sat facing the renewed fire, each with a mug half-full of smoky-flavored whiskey. Sparky leapt up on the hassock behind them, while Shadow sat again at Rachel's knee, and now Rachel offered her the reassurance of her hand gentle on her head.

Mary sipped at the whiskey, savored the warmth of it. "Rachel, there must be other survivors somewhere."

"I'm sure there are. Somewhere."

"And there must be some vestiges of the government left. They'll find us, or we'll find them sooner or later."

Rachel shook her head. "A government, maybe. Not the old U.S. of A. That government was already foundering. It won't survive this."

Mary took another swallow of whiskey and grimaced. At the beginning of this day she wouldn't have recognized the truth in that, but she did now. "The Bill of Rights, the Constitution— damn, to lose them, to lose the *ideas* . . ."

"Maybe they won't all be lost. A great deal survived the last dark age. The Renaissance was built on it."

"But this time . . ." She couldn't yet assimilate the scope of this dark age.

Rachel said dully, "This time will be unimaginably worse—for humankind, for all the species of animals and plants that will be wiped out in this frozen holocaust." She closed her eyes. "But I can't deal with that now. I can only deal with our survival. Someday maybe I can deal with what's lost and what can be saved. Not yet."

Mary watched the flow of the flames, listened to the moan of the wind in the chimney. The seeds of a commitment had been planted, but had not yet germinated. She was only sure of two things: they had survived, and they had chosen to continue to survive.

No. They had chosen to *try* to survive.

When the last match goes out, O how shall we
Ever recall the proper flint and stone
To create bright and warming flame once more?
When the last match goes out, shall we see
If we are a multitude or alone? . . .

—DANA E. SCOTT, *"NIGHT SONG"*
(1986)

It's only four days short of May, and April seems determined to depart in clouds and rain. But the rain has stopped now—at least, temporarily—leaving only the clouds, and I revel in their soft, gray light, in the rich scents of wet earth and grass. Shadow runs ahead as I walk through the north pasture with my moccasin boots and wool skirt shaking rainwater off the grass, and the pasture is vividly green, powdered with pink clover blossoms, humming with bees.

At this time of day, just after midday meal, all the women are busy in the kitchen, except for Esther. She's at the firepit in the open shed behind the house tending the kettle of fat she's rendering for soap. The fitful wind occasionally brings the stink of it to me. I expected to help with the soap making, as I usually do, but I was told I wasn't needed.

Miriam made that pronouncement, of course.

I wonder if she thinks I believe she was concerned for my advanced years. She's simply trying to isolate me from the family. Since Stephen's whipping, she's done nothing to rock the familial boat, no doubt recognizing that our Elder is still too much my ally. Or, as Miriam would put it, too much under my evil influence. But she has other options open to her.

Yes, I must gird my loins for battle. Rachel used to say, "And the voice of unreason is heard in the land." That was before the End, when the voice was a roar heard all over the world. Now my world has shrunk to a few square miles, but the voice of unreason is still heard here. I'm getting too old to lose another battle. I've lost too many.

I stop and look up at the Knob, at the vault snugged into its slope. Perhaps I haven't lost all of them.

At length, I turn and continue toward the east fence. The chunk of axes biting into wood comes in an odd, syncopated rhythm from that direction. Just beyond the fence, Jerry, Stephen, and Jonathan are felling trees, which will not only clear a space to enlarge the pasture, but supply us with heat next winter.

Stephen and Jonathan see me and shout hellos, but they pause only briefly. They're chopping at small hemlocks, while Jerry notches a tall spruce. The long, two-man crosscut saw waits nearby, and I frown at that. The spruce is probably three centuries old, its branches as thick as the trunks of the trees the boys are cutting. If Jerry must be rid of it, he'd do better to cut the branches and leave it a snag that would cast no shade, rather than risk breaking the crosscut saw. We have a dozen smaller saws, but no replacement for the big one.

In so many ways we live off the past. Already, Jerry is using a bow and arrows for hunting. There's still some ammunition for the guns, but he's saving that. I'm not sure what for. For the same reason he's saving the dynamite, I suppose.

His arrowheads come from Rachel's collection of Indian artifacts.

Jerry props his ax against the spruce and walks to the fence to meet me; he smells of sweat and damp leather. "How are you, Mary?"

"Better than I have any right to be, probably. I'm sorry I didn't think to bring you some water."

He wipes his sleeve across his forehead. "Well, it's not that far to the creek. I . . . I'm glad to get a chance to talk to you."

Shadow lopes up to greet Jerry, but when she starts under the fence to see the boys, I call her back sharply. I don't want her getting in the way of their arcing blades. She sits, reluctantly, at my command.

"What is it you want to talk to me about, Jerry?"

He's not anxious to begin, whatever it is. He leans against the fence post, frowning. "Well, last night, when Miriam was on her way upstairs for a visitation, Jonathan—" Jerry looks around as if to be sure his son can't hear him. "Jonathan asked Miriam if . . . if she was going to *copulate* with me."

Jerry, who casually discusses the women's visitations, blushes at the word *copulate*, and I find that annoying. I say nothing, waiting for him to go on.

"Anyway, Miriam was upset. She asked him where he'd heard about such things, and he said—he said *you* taught him about . . . sex."

I'm past annoyance now, nearing anger. "Yes, I talked to him about sex, and I showed him a physiology text. Jerry, he's fourteen years old. He asked me about sex, and I answered him. I always answer the children's questions if I can."

He sighs. "I think this is one question you shouldn't answer."

"Then who *will* answer it? Don't make a taboo of sex, Jerry. It's a vital part of life. Besides, the children are fully aware of all aspects of the reproductive cycle. They see it every day in the animals."

"But that's not the *same*. Anyway, it's up to a boy's father to answer questions like that."

"What makes you more qualified than I to explain human reproduction to Jonathan? At this point *he* knows more about it than you do." I pull myself up short. Jerry is insulted and hurt, and that wasn't my intention. Still, I can't refrain from inquiring, "Are you going to explain the menarche to Little Mary and Deborah and Rachel when they're old enough to ask questions about that?"

He says stubbornly, "It's a mother's place to tell her daughters about . . . such things."

I take time for a deep breath. "Jerry, I just don't like to have *any* subject put out of the children's reach. I don't care what it is."

"I know, and as far as I'm concerned, it's not that important. But it *is* important to Miriam, and she said she'd bring it up in the family meeting next Sunday. It'd mean a lot of argument and bad feeling."

I don't believe his professed lack of concern. Besides, it's the principle here that's important, not the subject of sex—the principle that children should have their questions answered. But he's right about one thing: if Miriam brings this up at the weekly family meeting, it *will* mean argument and bad feelings, and we're too small a group to tolerate dissension.

"It's blackmail, Jerry, and that's a very dangerous game."

He looks at me blankly. "It's what?"

He doesn't know the word *blackmail* or its implications. "Never mind. All right, I'll give in on this point, but I do it with misgivings. Just don't ask me to limit my curriculum, such as it is, further."

He grins with relief. "Don't worry, Mary. Thanks. We *have* to keep peace in the family. You understand that."

"Yes, I understand, Jerry." And I understand something that wouldn't make sense to him if I pointed it out to him: Miriam is testing him, testing her power. Testing me.

And I realize wearily that I've lost this skirmish.

But there will be others.

"It's time for Stephen's lesson, isn't it?" Jerry glances at Stephen, who is hurling the ax blade into the trunk of a hemlock. "I'll send him to the house when he's finished with that tree."

Does Jerry think he's throwing me a bone with that? If he hadn't brought up Stephen's lesson, I would have. That's why I came here in the first place.

No, he just thinks he's keeping peace in the family.

The rain has resumed. I'm sitting at the table in the living room, a book of the poems of Emily Dickinson open before me as I look out at the gray sky, gray sea, gray silhouettes of trees. The rain collects on the roof and falls in streams like a glass-beaded curtain. I like the gray of this kind of day, this kind of gentle, nurturing rain, but such days make me think of hourglasses and clepsydras, and how we might build them, because our only clock—other than the Seth Thomas, which can't keep ticking indefinitely—is the sun, and it's hidden today.

But in fact the family gets along very well without knowing exactly what time it is. We count years, months, weeks, and days. We may talk about hours—and I use that term more than the others do—but it's a vague designation. Minutes and seconds have no place in our lives. And I remember once reading about a division of time called an attosecond; when it was written out, the decimal point was followed by seventeen zeros, followed by a one.

"Good day, Mary."

Stephen is standing beside me, his hands freshly scrubbed. I motion to the chair at the end of the table. "Sit down, Stephen. How are you?"

"I'm fine," he replies absently, eyeing the open book. "What's that you're reading?"

"Emily Dickinson. We haven't studied any of her poems in school yet, but we will." I offer him the book. "Would you like a preview?"

"Yes, I'd like that."

"Take it, then. Oh—I'll need it tomorrow. Mary wanted to know about Emily Dickinson. Maybe you could read it with her in the evening. She needs some extra help with her reading."

He seems pleased at that. "I'll help her anytime she wants. Why was she interested in this woman?"

"Because of our cat. I hadn't thought about the names of the animals as teaching aids. Now I'm waiting for someone to ask about Falstaff." Then I add: "But our Emily isn't the first of the pets here named after Emily Dickinson. Rachel and I named Shadow's first pup Emily."

He leans forward, arms folded on the table, and I am again gratified to see the glint of curiosity in his black eyes. "When did Shadow have her first litter?"

"In November, about two months after the End. She had a litter of five, but only three were born alive." The gray of the sky seems to turn melancholy with the memory. "One pup looked perfect, but it was born dead. The other was pitifully malformed—stubs of legs, not even slits over its eyes. I buried them next to Topaz. I took a flashlight and a shovel and went out into a howling night and dug through the snow into the frozen earth. And that wasn't the last grave I dug for the pups. Even our little Emily died that winter. None of the first litter survived."

"Oh." He lets his breath out in a sigh. "Can you . . . would you mind telling me about the Long Winter?"

The Long Winter. Luke called it that. I don't think Rachel and I had a name for it, other than nuclear winter. Or simply, with a little emphasis on the article, *the* winter.

I lean back, look out at the beaded curtains of warm, greening rain. "Yes, I'll tell you about it, Stephen. It's part of the Chronicle."

"When are you going to start writing it?"

I touch the small, black portfolio on the table. "I've already begun. At night, while you're sound asleep. Only a few pages so far." Too few. My time is getting short.

"Can I read it?"

"When I've finished, yes. I'm writing it for you, Stephen." I don't give him time to question that. "The Long Winter. Well, it was bitterly, miserably cold, a constant twilight in the daytime, starless and moonless black at night, and the air smelled like . . . rotten smoke. It was . . . ."

He waits for me to go on, then: "What, Mary?"

"Terrible. Terrifying." I reach for the diary on the table, but keep it closed for now. "We had to live in the basement. I still don't like to go down there, although Esther and Miriam have made it very pleasant. And we wouldn't have survived without it or without the extra provisions and supplies we'd bought. Or without scavenging. Looting. We went to the houses near us that hadn't been burned, and we looted them of food, tools, clothing, medicine—anything that might be useful. Of course, Rachel always took any books she found."

"That's not really looting," Stephen objects. I mean, you weren't stealing from people."

"No. There was no one to steal from. Not around here."

"What happened to them?"

"Some were killed in the fires and road gang attacks immediately after the End. Some died of the cold. And some of those who lived through the first weeks joined in groups in the hope that they could better survive together, like at the Greenly farm. It was about five miles up the Coho River. Rachel used to trade rabbits and honey for Aldo Greenly's hay. She said if anyone could survive, it would be Aldo Greenly. He'd made a career of hardy subsistence."

Stephen asks hesitantly, "But he . . . didn't survive?"

"No." I shake my head slowly. "Nor his wife, his two sons, and their wives and children. Nor the other two families that had moved in with them. One of them brought Lassa to the farm."

"It really *was* a plague, wasn't it?"

"Well, it certainly was here. Maybe there were places it hadn't reached before the End. I don't know. I'll *never* know. There's so *much* I'll never know."

"Maybe someday . . ." But he seems to recognize the unlikelihood of such a someday. "When did you and Rachel go to the Greenly farm?"

"Not until November. I wanted to go before that. I was sure we'd find survivors there, but a trek of ten miles round-trip had become an expedition. The weather was so hellish. The storms that came in off the ocean were vicious, half hurricanes, half blizzards. Some days we couldn't even get to the barn, not until we rigged guide ropes. Between storms, we went scavenging, but even on one of those trips, we nearly got lost when a storm came up suddenly. Both of us had frostbite."

"I think you and Rachel were brave to leave Amarna at all."

I shrug. "I guess we didn't think we had much choice. We were afraid the food and clothing, even the metal tools that would rust, might be ruined before we found them. And . . . we had to get out of that cave when we could, or we'd have gone insane."

He nods, although I doubt he understands how close we were to insanity then. "Did you have a hard time getting to the Greenly farm?"

"No. We were lucky with the weather that day. I mean, we weren't overtaken by a blizzard. But when we reached the farm . . . well, we found two bodies in the house and a graveyard near the barn. Twenty wooden markers with names painted on them." I close my eyes, remembering that little graveyard, remembering my tears. Someone had cared for the people buried under those snowy mounds, and one by one, day by day—all the markers had dates—there were fewer to care for the living or the dead. And I knew then that the world was full of such graveyards, where love and hope were buried in relentless grief until the last griever died.

I open my eyes to the gentle, gray rain. "We owe Aldo Greenly a great deal. We found a root cellar full of home-canned food. And three Saanen goats, some Plymouth Rock chickens, two sows, and a boar. Aldo raised quarter horses, too, but we didn't find any of them that first trip. But we found tack and saddles and tools—we're still using some of them—and seed and chicken feed. And hay. The loft of the barn was full. And the two-wheeled utility cart. It was designed to be pulled by a tractor, but we adjusted it for Silver. Oh—we found three half-starved kittens. Anyway, the first Greenly expedition was . . . well, I can't call it a success, not when I remember that graveyard."

I pause, look at Stephen, who listens sympathetically. Yet there is nothing in his experience that would make it possible for him to imagine the despair that haunted us in our search for other survivors, nor that perverse mix of hope and fear we felt when we approached a place where we thought we might find survivors: hope that we'd find people alive, that they might have some contact with the rest of the human race; fear that they might be less than benevolent or sane, that they might kill first and wonder about us later. We had a horse, wagon, guns; throughout history, people have been murdered for less.

And Stephen can't imagine the loneliness that accumulated around us every time our hopes were dashed. We didn't believe we were the only survivors in the world. If we had survived, others would. Somewhere. But not here, and we began to wonder if we'd ever see another living human being. That kind of loneliness is beyond imagining, and it seemed then beyond enduring.

Stephen says earnestly, "It's sad to have to live off other people's misfortune, but you and Rachel never harmed anybody."

I look into his guileless face, the color of bronze, smooth and unlined. "No, Stephen, but we didn't hesitate to take advantage of their misfortune. We had pledged ourselves to survive. But in the weeks that followed, the year turned to winter, and that only made that unnatural winter worse. We were always cold, always exhausted. Just keeping warm took hours every day, not only tending the fires, but sawing and splitting wood. After we used all our seasoned wood, we had to go out in that foul, dark cold and cut trees. At least, we still had chain saws that worked. And most of the time, we had water in the house, but only trickles. Bathing and laundry became almost too difficult to consider, but as long as we kept fires in the kitchen and bathroom and cleared the ice off the reservoir every day, we managed to keep the plumbing intact. And, as Rachel said, we could be grateful no one ever got around to making toilets electronic."

Stephen smiles at that, but it fades as I go on. "It was a terrible time, and I always had the feeling that the darkness was the shadow of death. Every night I dreamed of death, dreams that woke me up, left me shaking. I think we might've given up if we'd only had ourselves to consider. But we had the animals. We lost two goats and more chickens and rabbits, although we did get a wood stove set up in the garage. And we lost Cyrano, one of our male kittens, but the animals that lived depended on us."

"And you depended on each other," he says quietly.

"Yes, that above all. Neither of us could've survived alone, and that brought us together in a way I don't think anyone could understand unless they'd been through a similar ordeal. And finally, we had some hope."

His lips part expectantly. "What was it?"

"Well, it came on the winter solstice, which seemed fitting. I went out that night with the dogs so they could relieve themselves. Two feet of snow lay on the ground, and the wind was screaming out of the east. I looked up into the sky, expecting to see the same thing I'd seen every night for nearly a hundred nights: absolute darkness. But on that night I saw . . . the moon." I smile, remembering the wonder of it. "A full moon, Stephen. It was veiled in dirty clouds, but I could *see* it. I called Rachel to come out, and we wept and shouted and danced in the snow. Nothing I've ever seen in my life was as beautiful as that amber moon."

"It was like the rainbow, wasn't it? The rainbow God sent to Noah after the Flood."

I feel my smile fade. The god that sent the rainbow to Noah, according to the writers of the Pentateuch, sent it as a covenant that the world—their world which was little larger than mine is now—would never again be destroyed by flood. That god did not, it seems, make any promises about not destroying the world by nuclear fire and ice.

"Stephen, what the moon on the winter solstice meant was simply that hope was no longer unreasonable." I open the diary, and his eyes fix on it avidly. "The first entry in this diary is dated January first of the new year. It begins: 'Another blizzard today. We haven't seen the moon again nor even a break in the clouds since the winter solstice.' "

His shoulders slump, and I add: "There was no promise in the moon on the winter solstice. The Long Winter didn't end then. More of our animals died, including nearly all the hens. Of course, the hens that survived weren't laying; it was too dark. We were just lucky Josie kept giving milk through the worst of the winter. But it wasn't until March, I think . . ." I turn a few pages in the

129

diary. "Here it is. March first. We saw the sun. Briefly and dimly. About the same time we saw a few gulls and crows. I don't know where they went during the winter, those that lived. South, maybe. I have great respect for crows—even if I've cursed them over the years for eating the seeds right out of our garden—but seeing the gulls gave me real hope. I suppose I'm biased toward gulls because they're so beautiful. The essence of freedom and grace." Then I smile at Stephen. "That's rank romanticism. Gulls are hardheaded and birdbrained. But it wasn't their beauty that made them so welcome to us. The fact that they survived suggested that not all the birds in this part of the world had been destroyed. We lost the sandpipers, you know."

"What's a sandpiper?"

I try to explain it to him, my voice husky with memories of those doughty little birds flying over the surf like sparkling schools of fish, and when they fed in the sand, flurrying in and out with the waves like animate foam. I can only hope sandpipers survived on other beaches elsewhere in the world. What's a world without sandpipers?

I clear my throat and go on. "One reason we were so glad to see the gulls and crows was because they're such good scavengers. In January and February, we still had violent storms to sweep the beach clean, but by March, there weren't as many storms, and the debris collected above the high-tide line: dead fish, crabs, jellyfish, kelp by the ton, sea lions, even gray whales. The stink of it—our noses never got used to it."

He wrinkles his nose. "That must've been awful."

"Yes, it was. The flotsam and jetsam of death. And not just dead animals and seaweed. The storms drove in wrecked boats, broken lumber from houses, even furniture. And sometimes . . . human remains." I look down at the diary. "Anyway, the winter wasn't over for us, but it gradually eased off. In March it warmed up enough to rain instead of snow. But at times the rains were freezing rains, and that cost us some of the trees in the orchard." I turn more pages. "By late March we had an occasional *almost* clear day, but all that year the sky had an odd, opalescent cast, and there were always sundogs and halos. The light was reddish gold, the shadows blue green. The sunsets were spectacular. By the first of April, the frogs were singing, and some of the wild plants were showing signs of life, and our bees began foraging for pollen. The winter killed a lot of them, and Rachel consolidated the five hives into three and kept feeding them honey from the year before, but we thought it a miracle that any of them survived."

I close the book, keeping my place with one finger. "But nothing really flourished. We planted a garden in early May. Outside, I mean. Rachel had seedlings growing in the greenhouse before that. But the outside garden was a continual disaster. There were frosts in May, and we had to start all over. We sowed clover and orchard grass for the livestock, but not much of it took hold. In April we started letting the goats out in the north pasture. It wasn't fenced then, and we hobbled them so they wouldn't wander off, and that was a mistake. One day we came home from a scavenging foray in time to see a pack of feral dogs kill one of the kids. We knew then we couldn't leave them outside our fence without one of us on hand. We'd made our fence fairly dog-proof; added three lines of wire to make it higher. Power line. Makes good fencing, and there was plenty of it around. But we *had* to let the goats into the north pasture because there just wasn't enough forage inside our fence. We began taking turns on the scavenging trips, so one of us could serve as shepherd. I don't know whether it was worse going out alone into that ruined world, or staying home and waiting for Rachel to return, wondering if she would. We still found food in some of the houses, and we collected anything else that might be useful, even some furniture, but that was mostly for the hardwood. One of our projects was making soap—as a pesticide; we still had plenty of soap for our own use—and that took hardwood ashes."

He asks, "Couldn't you go up to the Coast Range for big leaf or vine maple like we do?"

"We did later when we had more time. Just keeping ourselves and the animals and the garden going took all our daylight hours then."

"Did you still live in the basement?"

I skim a few entries in the diary. "No, we moved upstairs in

April. We used the basement for storage. Mostly food, what there was of it. The dogs and cats had to learn to feed themselves, so they became good hunters. Except Shadow. I think she'd had her hunting instincts bred out of her. But she was a good shepherd. She picked that up with very little training. As long as one of us was nearby, we could leave the goats and pigs in the north pasture with her, and she'd keep them from wandering."

Stephen's eyebrows go up. "You let the pigs out in the pasture?"

"Only occasionally. We couldn't have fed them otherwise. Most of the time they stayed in the pigpen. We built the pigpen ourselves, and that was quite a project. It was jerry-built from scavenged lumber, and we weren't carpenters, but it lasted ten years."

"*Jerry* built the pigpen?" he asks, obviously confused.

I laugh at that. "No, I don't mean our Jerry. Our Jeremiah. It's just an idiom, Stephen. It means . . . well, carelessly made."

He nods, and I turn again to the diary. "The insects began swarming in April. There were so few birds to keep them in check, although the starlings helped. I'll have to give them credit. And we saw a few finches and sparrows and swallows. But the garden—the bugs nearly ate it to the ground. We sprayed with soap solution and used companion planting, but it didn't have a chance between the late frosts and the bugs and slugs and especially the UV, and if we'd had to depend on it for food for the next winter, we'd have starved. Still, we did have meat. At first, we had the animals that died in the cold, and later we had fresh rabbit. The chickens didn't do as well as the rabbits, and we didn't eat any of them, since we were trying to build up the flock. We shot deer occasionally. That wasn't so difficult in late spring and summer. The problem with meat, of course, was preserving it. The only advantage of the cold in the winter was that we could preserve meat by freezing it. After the thaw, the only solution was to dry or smoke it. So, we had to build a smokehouse."

"Didn't you salt any of your meat?"

"Yes. Neither of us liked it, but we tried it. At least we had a ready source of salt here—the ocean—not only for the meat, but for the livestock. We had to boil and filter the water and put it out in shallow pans to evaporate—just like we do now." I skim a few more pages. "In June . . . yes, I recorded that with exclamation marks. We caught one of Greenly's horses. We'd seen the horses around his farm earlier, but we couldn't get near them. This time we resorted to a subterfuge. We took Silver out to Greenly's when she was in heat. That brought an older stallion, but Ceph was in his entourage, and he was easy to rope. He wasn't even a yearling then."

Stephen leans back, folds his arms. "Why did you call him Ceph?"

"That was short for Bucephalus. Alexander the Great's horse. You remember reading about Alexander. Anyway, Ceph was beautiful, a roan with a blaze and white stockings. Of course, one reason we caught him so easily was that he was half-blind. That was what the Arkites called the Blind Summer."

"I've heard Enid talk about that. She said even some people went blind. She didn't know why."

"It was because of the increased ultraviolet radiation. The ozone layer was disturbed by the nuclear explosions, and that let in more UV. That's what gives you a sunburn."

"Does it sunburn your eyes?"

"Yes, you could say that. It burned the plants, too, and only the ones that grew in the deep forest thrived. Even some of the conifers on the edges of the forest died. We went scavenging for glass to build a sort of roof over the garden. It looked like a drunken architect's Crystal Palace. Glass filters out most of the UV, Stephen. We wore dark glasses, hats, and long sleeves to protect ourselves, but the worst of it was trying to protect our animals. We closed the hives and only let the bees out in the evening or on rainy days, but we still lost a lot of them. We covered the chicken coop and rabbit hutches, and kept the goats and horses inside the barn during the middle of the day. We fitted them with hats or cloth fringes to shade their eyes and covered the pigs with coats made of sheets. They sunburn so badly anyway. Still, we managed with most of our animals, but the saddest thing . . ." And for a moment, something in me balks. I don't want to relive all these memories. Once was enough.

Stephen leans forward, eyes shadowed with what he reads in my face. "What was the saddest thing, Mary?"

"The wild animals, Stephen, the innocent victims of our insanity. The birds—oh, it made me weep to see them. At first, they kept trying to fly, but finally they just went to ground and waited to die or be killed. The nocturnal animals—coons, bobcats, owls—and underground creatures, like moles and to some extent the gray-diggers, they survived. But the gulls, my beautiful gulls, they'd gather on the beach and just stand facing the wind until they died. The stronger ones cannibalized the weaker. But some of the youngest survived, the chicks that hatched latest and didn't have so much exposure to the UV. Still, by August, the beach was littered with dead again. The UV also eliminated most of the feral dogs. We found their starved bodies on our forays in August and September. We found dead coyotes, too. That was the first inkling we had that coyotes had moved into the coast forests."

Stephen nods. "I've heard them singing."

"Yes. They're far more adaptable than most predators. Not like the bears. I remember one day . . . Rachel had gone scavenging with Silver and Sparky, and I was cleaning the barn while the goats were out in the north pasture. I heard Shadow barking and ran out to the pasture with my rifle, and there was a brown bear blundering after one of the kids. I knew he could barely see. I fired the gun into the air to scare him off. I didn't want to kill him, but I suppose that was as close as he'd come to meat in weeks. Finally, he did knock the kid down and probably would've killed it. So I killed him. It took three bullets, and when the poor beast lay dead, I sat beside him and cried. I thought, *I've killed the last of his kind.* Maybe I did. At least, in this corner of the world. I've never seen a bear since."

A silence grows out of that story. At length Stephen says, "But the bear probably would've died anyway."

Stephen has never seen a bear, and I doubt he ever will. He knows them only as beasts pictured in books. "Yes, Stephen, I suppose he would've died anyway. And we made use of the carcass. It provided meat and oil and even a little fat for soap and bone-meal for the garden. We tanned the hide—our first attempt at tanning. Anyway, by the end of summer, the UV had let up, and some of the late crops weren't a total loss. We stored root vegetables both for us and the livestock for winter. We scythed grass and clover for hay. It wasn't enough, any of it."

I stare at the pages of the diary and the erratic tracks of my writing. "But we survived, and I should've been grateful. I was. And yet . . . I remember thinking sometimes that we had no *right* to survive. Not when so many people had died. That was one of the things that weighed most on our minds then. Grief. Grief for people we'd loved; grief for people we hadn't known, but whose work we knew; even a vague sort of grief for the nameless billions who died in the initial blasts or of radiation poisoning, disease, cold, starvation. And there were other kinds of grief. We grieved a beautiful planet ravaged. We grieved the thousands of species of plants and animals destroyed. We grieved a civilization lost."

My pain alarms Stephen, but I go on: "Rachel said civilization is the highest expression of the human mind. At least, it had the potential for that because it could free people of the drudgery of survival and provide the tools and knowledge that make compre-hension and creativity possible. The trouble is, homo sapiens bring a lot of primitive genetic baggage into the world along with our wonderful new cerebral cortexes. We're social animals with instinc-tive needs to establish dominance hierarchies. We're territorial and xenophobic and, like any organism, programmed to reproduce, and we did it compulsively and irrationally. And that's what destroyed the golden age, and with it all the art and poetry, all the discoveries and insights accumulated over the last ten thousand years."

Did Rachel really say that? Yes. Many times. But not in those words. The words are mine. Stephen's narrowed eyes tell me he's thinking about what I've said. He isn't sure what it means yet, and he silently waits for me to go on.

"Rachel knew even then that our civilization was lost. In this hemisphere, at least. But *I* still clung to the hope that remnants of it had survived. I was convinced that if we went east beyond the Coast Range, or north or south along Highway 101, we'd find people. Civilization. On the first anniversary of the End, we talked about a journey in search of survivors, but there was still too much to do to prepare for winter. Besides, we were exhausted, and I was afraid we'd end up sick. And at that time we couldn't have gone *south.* There were a lot of lightning storms that summer, and on September fifteenth we saw the smoke from a huge forest fire to the south. We watched it for days. The wind was from the north, so we weren't in its path, but the smoke covered half our sky. It rose in an immense cloud like a thunderhead, the color of opal where it was thickest. Strange, how many destructive things are so beautiful. Even the cloud of a nuclear bomb was beautiful."

Startled, Stephen asks, "Did you see such a cloud?"

"No, I never actually saw one. I saw pictures of them. Anyway, we decided we couldn't go south or any direction that fall. We had the winter to think about."

Stephen cups his chin in one hand. "Was the second winter as hard as the first?"

"No, or we wouldn't have survived it." I skim more pages in the diary. "But it wasn't an easy winter, and we were on short rations. We both lost a lot of weight. In December Shadow gave birth to another litter of puppies. And every evening Rachel spent at least an hour sorting and reading the books she'd scavenged, and I . . . well, I was always too busy or too tired for that. I think I even resented it, really, although I never said anything to her. I closed my mind to the books."

"You, Mary?" Stephen studies me dubiously. "But you love books so much. And you said—well, when you first saw Rachel's books, that's when you knew you'd found a kindred soul."

"Yes." I run my fingers over the cover of the Emily Dickinson. It was one of Rachel's books. "I had always loved books, Stephen. I learned that from my parents. But after the End . . . I didn't understand it till later, but it was as if the books didn't exist for me, and I didn't even wonder about that." Then I turn again to the diary. "At any rate, we did have snow that second winter, but it melted by the middle of January, and it was almost a normal spring for the coast. There were more birds. More insects, too, and many more slugs. But the garden thrived in spite of them. So did the livestock, and in May Silver gave birth to a colt, a bay filly. We called her Epona. The rabbits and chickens did well, and the bees recovered enough so that by late summer we took a good harvest of honey and wax. That's when we learned to make candles, although we still had some kerosene and whale oil." I close the diary and look out through the rain curtains at the gray sea.

"The most encouraging thing was to see the ocean rejuvenated. The tide pools filled with life again, and barnacles and mussels began colonizing the rocks. We saw a few salmon in the Coho and even whales spouting on their way north. Every sign of recovery was a miracle to us. Some of our crops and animals died, others lived. Two of Shadow's pups died, but two lived. And we lost another cat. That left only Mehitabel, a lone female."

And I remember how I sympathized with her. I thought a great deal that year about being a female without a male. For all I knew, our species was near extinction, and I could do nothing to save it. I had no doubt I was capable of it; my menstrual cycles continued with frustrating regularity. Sometimes I saw Rachel and me as two Eves in a precarious Eden born of Armageddon.

I'm reminded that I've lapsed into silence when Stephen asks, "Did you and Rachel ever go to look for other people?"

"Yes, but not until late summer. By then we'd harvested the crops and put up the hay, and the animals born that year were old enough to fend for themselves. Still, we decided we couldn't leave any of the animals for more than three weeks. We fortified the rabbit hutches and the chicken house and pigpen, and rigged water tanks and food bins that would hold enough to last that long." I leaf through the diary, seeking the entry marking the beginning of our trek, but pause before I reach it, distracted by another entry.

"I made a note on August twentieth, Stephen. We saw an odd, brown cloud in the east over the mountains. Actually, we'd seen similar clouds earlier, and at first we thought they were smoke from forest fires, except the color was wrong. We learned the answer to that puzzle on our trek—one of the many hard lessons we learned. Anyway, on . . . here it is. On the last day of August we set off on our odyssey: two women, two dogs, and two horses loaded with food and camping gear. I remember worrying about the animals we left behind, but once we turned east on the Portland highway, all I could think about was what lay beyond the Coast Range. Or what I hoped . . ." My throat closes on the words. Stephen watches me; he seems to be holding his breath.

Finally I say, "First, you have to understand what that land was like Before. The Willamette Valley. A huge trough running north and south, a hundred miles wide, bracketed by the Coast Range on the west and the Cascades on the east. Oh, Stephen, it was so beautiful. Gentle hills and dark earth, wheat and hay fields bright green in the spring, and in the summer dotted with bachelor's buttons, and at harvest time, they were like golden seas. Wild roses grew along the fences, and the orchards—some of them had thousands of fruit or filbert trees, and when they bloomed, they were glorious. You'd see hawks soaring over fields of strawberries and clover, and between the fields there were stands of firs and groves of oaks with their limbs frosted with moss. The rivers were wide and slow and deep green, and there'd be fishermen at almost any bend."

Stephen is rapt, and I might as well be describing Oz. It is, in fact, a fantasy now.

"The biggest cities in the state were in the Willamette Valley, Stephen. Portland, which was a major seaport, even if it was so far inland. The ships came up the Columbia River. And Salem, which was the capital of the state. And they were targets for those reasons."

He tilts his head, brows drawn. "Targets?"

"Targets for the bombs. I knew they would be, and I didn't expect anyone to have survived in the cities themselves. But I thought somewhere in the Valley we'd find . . . some remnant of civilization."

"But you didn't." It isn't a question.

"No. I hadn't counted on the firestorms from the bombs and the effects of the nuclear winter and the Blind Summer. What we found east of the divide of the Coast Range was a desert. A charred, dry wasteland. All the trees had burned. The river that flowed by the highway was brown. Every field was cracked and gouged with gullies. Only a few sprigs of grass and lupine tried to root there. It was a gray, silent place where no insects buzzed, and birds didn't live to sing, and the only thing that moved was whirlwinds of dust."

"What did you do?" he asks in a whisper.

I shrug. "We kept going east. I knew we wouldn't find anything alive within thirty miles of Portland, but I convinced myself that the burns just east of the Coast Range were the result of forest fires that began in the mountains. And I convinced myself that between the forest-fire burn and the blast zones, there'd be a green corridor where people could survive. Rachel wasn't convinced, but she knew I'd have to see for myself. So, we went on, following the highway, although at times it was buried under dunes. We passed small towns and farms, most of them burned out. On the fourth night we camped at a farm where the barn and house were still standing. We slept in the barn. The house was . . . occupied by the remains of the family that had lived there. That night we were wakened by the timbers of the barn groaning. The windmill outside was creaking madly, and when we opened the barn door, we ran into a wall of windblown dust. That's when we understood the brown clouds we'd seen from Amarna, Stephen. They were dust storms. This one went on for two days, while we huddled in the barn with the wind battering at it, and the dust sifting through all the cracks until we could hardly breathe."

Stephen laces his fingers tensely. "Weren't you afraid?"

"Terrified. And I had to face the fact that there'd be no green corridor in a place where dust storms of such magnitude could be generated, that the wasteland was a product of firestorms fanning out from the bombs that hit Portland and Salem. Of course, there might've been green corridors in the Cascades or in the south end of the Willamette Valley, but we weren't equipped for that long a trek—not through this new desert—and we couldn't stay away from Amarna that long. So the coast seemed our only hope. But we knew if we headed south on the coast, we'd hit that big forest-fire burn from the year before, so we decided to head north."

"That's too bad," he says, shaking his head. "If you'd gone south, you might've found the Ark."

I stare at him, and I have to control the caustic reply that comes first to my lips. He speaks out of ignorance and innocence, and I bring out a smile for him, then turn my attention to the diary.

"Once we crossed back over the summit of the Coast Range, we were in living forest again, and we bathed in a cold mountain stream and feasted on trout. I realized then that *we* lived in the green corridor. The only question was how far it extended. The road we took over the mountains joins Highway 101 about fifty miles north of here. There was a small town at the junction, but it was deserted, all the buildings in ruins. Well, it wasn't entirely deserted. We found a mother cat and her five half-grown kittens there. We managed to catch three of the kittens, and we were happy to discover that two were males. We made a cage of sticks and rope with a piece of plywood as a floor, and for the rest of the trip, the kittens rode in state on top of Silver's packs."

Stephen laughs at that picture, and I add, "I don't think the kittens were impressed with this lofty perch. Anyway, that night we built a big signal fire. We thought if there were any survivors in the area, they'd see it. But there was no answer to our signal. The next morning, we continued north, then after a few miles, the forest suddenly ended, and we were in another burn. Forest fire, not firestorm. It went on for miles, for days. Dead, black trees as far as we could see. Sometimes we'd cross patches of green forest, but they were small. Most of the towns we went through along the way had been burned, too. Even when we found houses intact, no one was living in them. We saw a lot of little graveyards with wooden markers. None of the dates were later than four months after the End."

I close my eyes, but open them again quickly. A montage of those poignant little graveyards waits in my mind's eye. Stephen remains patiently silent until I'm ready to continue.

"We kept going north on the coast highway, lighting signal fires every night, but there were no answering signals. Finally, we came to a junction with Highway 26. We'd been away from Amarna for nearly two weeks, and we couldn't stay much longer. Rachel got out her map and pointed to a cross mark just off Highway 26 about fifteen miles inland. Saddle Mountain. She'd been there Before— it was a state park—and she said there was a road to its base and a trail up to the summit. And Saddle Mountain is more than three thousand feet high. From the top we could see well over a hundred miles in every direction. We could see man-made smoke or fire, and *our* smoke or fire could be seen over all that distance. So we headed east, and when we got close to Saddle Mountain, we found it was in one of those islands the fires hadn't touched. The trail to the summit was passable, and at the top the old fire lookout cabin was still standing. That gave us some shelter. The wind was sometimes fierce, and nothing grew on the summit but stunted grass and salal."

"What did you see from up there?"

"The world, Stephen." I give that a laugh. "A small piece of it that seemed very large to us. To the south and east, we saw the burn we'd been traveling through, and above the haze on the eastern horizon, a few tiny, white cones—the high peaks of the Cascades. To the west we saw the ocean, and to the north, green forest and the Columbia River where it meets the sea at Astoria. Beyond the river lay more forest, but on the horizon we saw a strip of gray. We looked at it through the binoculars, and it was another burn. Then I turned the binoculars on Astoria. Most of the town was in ruins, but not all of it. Yet there was no sign of smoke—the kind produced by cooking fires, the smoke of civilization. That didn't discourage me. We planned to stay for a few days, and we'd have ample opportunity to look for smoke at every time of day and the lights of fires at every time of night. And sooner or later—so I told myself— someone would see our signal and answer it. From the beginning of our trek we were so desperate for a sign of human life, we'd put aside the old fear of strangers who might be killers. *We* were willing to take that chance, and I couldn't imagine that anyone out there wouldn't be willing to take that chance with *us*." I pause then, and

Stephen seems on the verge of a question, but he looks at me and says nothing.

And I go on. "So, we built a fire on top of Saddle Mountain and kept it burning day and night. We spent most of the daylight hours hauling wood up for the fire, but one of us always surveyed the countryside at least once every half hour. At night we went on shifts: two hours watching, two sleeping. The times weren't exact, but nearly so; Rachel's watch still worked. The first two days were clear, and the nights were dark—it was a new moon—but we didn't see any smoke or lights. Still, I kept thinking, one more day, one more night. *Someone* would answer our signal. On the third day the wind shifted to the south, and we could see clouds on the horizon, but we kept the fire going all day and into the night. And watched. Watched and hoped. And saw . . . nothing."

Stephen reaches for my hand where it lies on the open pages of the diary. "Oh, Mary, weren't you sad when nobody answered your signal?"

My gentle Stephen. I remember that last night. . . .

"Yes, Stephen. Yes, I was sad."

And this Star, that is toward the North, that we clepe the Lode Star,
appeareth not to them. For which cause, men may well perceive, that
the Land and the Sea be of round shape and form. . . . And if I had
Company and Shipping, I trow well, in certain, that we should have
seen the roundness of the Firmament all about.
          —JEHAN DE MANDEVILLE (SIR JOHN MANDEVILLE),
            THE TRAVELS OF SIR JOHN MANDEVILLE (c. 1371)

A shadow of cloud hid the stars on the western horizon, but the rest of the sky was icily clear. Mary Hope looked up at Polaris, the North Star, the Lode Star, and wondered how many miles of trackless wilderness, how many leagues of unmapped sea human beings had crossed over the millennia, all guided by that constant star. Yet only an accident of location placed it in line with Earth's axis at this point in the planet's history.

The wind blew chill out of the south, carrying the pungent scent of smoke from the fire behind her. It was too far away to provide any warmth, but she could hear the rush of flames. She sat on a ledge of rock with only a blanket to soften its cold hardness, sat cross-legged like a sadhu on a mountaintop, tranced in search of wisdom, and watched Cassiopeia and the Big Dipper swing around the fulcrum of Polaris. The Milky Way cast a veil of stars on the endless black of absence where silence echoed, and the accumulated light of all those distant suns served to make the sky lighter than the land only by the fine degree that was to her eyes discernible. She felt her eyes wide open, pupils large and dark, reaching into the dark of the land. The sky was full of suns, yet she denied them, sought one light, one small sun in the darkness below the myriad.

Where are you? You must be out there. Just one light, that's all I ask.

Behind her, behind the fire, the horses were tethered to forage on the sparse grass; Rachel and the dogs and kittens were asleep in the lookout cabin. Mary could hear no sound as evidence of their existence, and she was possessed by the conviction that they did not exist, that she was the only thing living in this fathomless darkness.

No, it was a sensation more than a conviction, but it was pervading. And it was new. Through three days and three nights of maintaining the fire and scanning the land for an answer, she had never doubted that she *would* see that wisp of smoke, that small sun of light.

Now, finally, doubt whispered its chill in the wind, and she began shivering and couldn't stop.

A sound behind her—loose rock displaced by light feet. Shadow came up beside her, nudged her elbow. Mary rubbed Shadow's back, wondering if Rachel was awake. It seemed too early for her shift. But a few minutes later Mary heard Rachel's footsteps on the stone along with the patter of Sparky's paws.

When Rachel sat down next to her, Mary asked, "Is it time?"

"Past time, actually. It's about twelve-thirty. Which makes it a new day." She paused, then, "Do you realize what day this is?"

"No, I . . . I guess I've lost track of the days."

"This is September fifteenth," Rachel said dully. "The second anniversary of the End."

The second anniversary. Two years. Mary looked out at the black world where nothing provided her any frame of reference for dimension. Or time. She made no response to Rachel's revelation.

At length, Rachel said, "Mary, we'll have to leave tomorrow. At this elevation and this time of year, that storm might mean snow."

Mary closed her eyes, breath stopped by a rush of panic. She blurted, "We can't leave, Rachel! Just one more day—they'll answer our signal by then."

A sigh in the wind. "They? If anyone were out there to see our signal, they'd have answered it by now."

"Maybe they're afraid to answer. They don't know who we are—"

"Mary, please. You know better."

Sparky whined and put his front paws on Mary's knees, and she stroked his head. Yes, she knew better. Her shoulders slumped with the release of unrecognized tension that left her muscles aching.

"Rachel, there *are* survivors out there."

"Yes, there are survivors. Probably millions in the southern hemisphere managing to adapt to this new Stone Age. There must be survivors all over the world in isolated pockets like ours. But not here, Mary. Not here."

Mary stared at Rachel but couldn't see her face, only the shape of her body limned by the firelight against the darkness. Her voice was quiet, nearly toneless, when it should have been strained with pain.

And Mary realized she was listening for her own pain.

She gazed out into the dark wilderness, and held back a cry. *Let me see a light. Just one tiny spark of light.*

Not here. Somewhere in the world, lights were burning on this night. Not here. The word that gagged in her throat was *loneliness*.

Human beings were social animals. They weren't made to live in solitude so absolute, so hopeless. They weren't made to live celibate, sterile lives, to die in a void.

"Rachel, if we could only go on farther, across the Columbia, maybe, or south into California . . ."

"Of course, we could go on, but we have to make up our minds whether we want to continue to be farmers, or to take another step backward and become nomads. You can't have both, Mary. We've been away from Amarna over two weeks, and we've covered less than two hundred miles. And even then, we may go home to find some of our animals dead, or something worse might've happened. The point is, if we choose to go searching over long distances for survivors, we'll have to forfeit Amarna, and I wonder how long we'd survive as nomads. Most of the land we'd be traveling through won't be exactly hospitable."

Is that all it comes to—survival?

And Mary knew the answer.

Without a whimper, the hope died and left within her an irrevocable silence.

She said, "It would've been easier—more merciful, anyway—if we hadn't lived through the winter."

The wind gusted colder in the wake of those words. At length, Rachel said, "Maybe. And maybe something will put us out of our misery eventually. Right now, I'd prefer to pursue other options."

"Other options?" Mary stared at Rachel's shadow shape. "What other options do we *have?*"

"Well, there's the problem of finding other survivors. Our trouble is there are only two of us. That forces us to choose between being farmers or nomads. But maybe somewhere—it'll have to be somewhere fairly near—others were luckier in terms of numbers, so some of them would be free to leave home to make the same kind of search we are now. They'd look for exactly what we're looking for. Maybe they couldn't actually see our fires, but they could see our smoke. There's hardly a day when we don't have a fire of some kind going. We can't find them, but they can find us—by our smoke."

The hope that had seemed dead stirred. "Yes, anyone following 101 is bound to see our smoke, and that's the only way to travel along the coast." Then the hope sighed into quiescence again. "So, all we can do is go home and wait and . . . survive."

Rachel leaned forward, rested her elbows on her knees. "There's something else we can do. We can prepare our legacy to the future."

Mary laughed, heard the acid edge in it. What kind of legacy could they leave? And to whom? To what future?

Rachel said levelly, "I've been thinking about it for a long time. There's nothing we can do about the hellish mess humankind has made of this living world, and there's nothing we can do about our lost civilization, except . . . Mary, when you try to define civilization, what you come up with has to include the factor of accumulation. The discoveries of each generation are its legacy to all those that follow."

Unseen in some indefinable distance, an owl cried. Mary said, "But the chain is broken now."

"Yes, but it's been broken before." Rachel's voice was as soft and as poignant as the owl's. "Not so totally. Usually it breaks in one culture, while it's maintained in another. A great deal is always lost in those breaks. We don't know how much was lost in the dark ages in Europe, but we know what was saved. Western civilization was built on it."

"And was that a good thing?"

There was a hint of annoyance in Rachel's reply, but it didn't last. "It depends, I suppose, on how you define *good*. A lot of extraordinary things happened, or were invented, discovered, or created in the context of Western civilization that I'd call good. I know far more about the universe than Solomon in all his wisdom, not because I'm so much wiser, but because of the two and a half millennia of civilization that occurred since he died. Every painting I did was a child of that civilization. And shards of that civilization *have* survived."

"What, Rachel? What could *possibly* have survived?"

"I don't know what might have survived elsewhere. I only know what has survived in our possession. The books, Mary."

Mary shuddered, folded her arms against her body, overtaken by a sensation of fear she could neither control nor understand.

Rachel meant the books at Amarna, her own and those she had scavenged the last two years. She had spent every hour she could purloin from their punishing schedule reading those books, sorting them by subject and author, separating out the duplicates. Mary had never taken part in that, had avoided looking at the books, much less reading them. She hadn't even recognized her denial of them, nor let herself wonder why she denied the written word, which had once been her craft, her art, her life.

Now, as she thought about the books, she found herself suddenly and silently weeping, and the ravening agony of grief doubled her over.

Now she understood.

It was fear of this knife-edged pain that had blinded her to what was so obvious to Rachel. For Mary, handling and reading those books was tantamount to touching and talking to the corpses of loved ones. They were reminders of what was lost. It was that loss she had wanted to deny as she wanted to deny the darkness before her now.

Yet now the grief, inch by inch, second by second, surrendered. She felt herself trembling, and it wasn't because of revived pain or even the cold wind. It was a manifestation of hope.

Our legacy to the future.

The *future.* That was where hope lived.

Rachel said, "We have over six thousand books at Amarna now. Of course, it's a pitiful fraction of human knowledge. But it's all we have. I don't believe they're the only books left in the world, just as I don't believe we're the only survivors, but I keep thinking maybe we have the only existing copies of some books. They *must* be preserved if it's remotely possible. Mary, what else can I do for humankind? You're young and still capable of bearing children—if other survivors do find us—but I'm past that. And maybe those books will make more difference in the long run."

Mary felt an encompassing calm, and she tried to remember when she had felt anything like it, when fear and doubt hadn't been foremost in her mind. Before the End, certainly. Yes, she could remember one moment in her life when she felt a similar calm: the night she finished the last page of the last revision of *October Flowers.* The calm arose from her realization that she had accomplished something worthwhile, and she had done it well.

She thought about that book, thought about *her* book being read in an unforeseeable future, and the idea was profoundly satisfying. She thought of the legions of writers—all dead now, probably, if they weren't before the End—who had written with the conviction that their words would be read by future generations they couldn't imagine.

She thought about the books at Amarna, the books she had denied for two years. She didn't know what Rachel had picked up in her scavenging, but she knew what had been there Before. The encyclopedias. At least, they offered summaries of knowledge. Books on science, especially earth sciences. On human history. On art. Yes, the children of the future would have some idea of what the Parthenon looked like, or the stricken gray figures of Kollwitz, the woodcuts of Hiroshige, the Sistine Chapel ceiling, the seething sunflowers of Van Gogh, the columns of Karnak. For a moment the grief revived. Was that all the children of the future would know of those astounding creations? A few pictures in a few books?

But they would know *something* of them. They would know what was possible for the human mind.

Fiction. There wasn't much fiction at Amarna. At least, there was a complete Shakespeare. And a volume of Sophocles' plays. Dickens, Kafka, Melville, Tolstoy, Cervantes, Austen, Conrad, Steinbeck . . .

Yes, and poetry. Dickinson, Eliot, Yeats, Dante, Wordsworth, Sappho, Auden, Whitman . . .

So little, such a minute fraction, but Rachel was right. It was all they had.

Mary said on a long exhalation of breath, "Yes. Oh, Rachel, *yes.*"

Rachel laughed. "Yes, we should do it?"

"Yes, we *must* do it." Then she hesitated. "But how? This climate is so damned hard on books."

"There's also the problem of acidification. Not many of our books are printed on paper that won't acidify. There are ways to stop it, but they're too technical for us. I think all we can do is seal the books as nearly airtight as possible, then hope that someday, someone will learn how to make paper and ink—or even a crude printing press—so they can copy the books before they disintegrate."

That seemed a remote possibility, and Mary was again aware of the chill in the wind, the acrid smell of the smoke from their signal fire.

Rachel seemed to sense her doubt. "Mary, we can't predict the future, and I know it's unreasonable to ask more of life than life, but I do, just as human beings always have. This is my *more*. Maybe nothing will come of it but a pile of rotten paper. But I have to try."

Mary pulled in a deep breath, felt it astringent in her throat. "No, Rachel. *We* have to try."

Two years ago, in the frigid shadow of the winter, they had made a choice to survive. Now they were making another choice in a silent, lightless wilderness.

A choice to live, not just survive; to live as human beings.

For as there are misanthropists, or haters of men, there are also misologists, or haters of ideas, and both spring from the same cause, which is ignorance of the world.

—PLATO (428–348 B.C.), PHAEDO

T he last lesson today was on geography. The globe on its wrought-iron stand is still by the table where the children were gathered around it a short while ago, naming continents and oceans. When we came to the end of our allotted time, and the other children made their hurried exits, Stephen stayed, studying the globe. "Mary, it looks like if you could cut out Africa and South America, they'd fit together."

It was a startling observation for a thirteen-year-old whose education, despite my best efforts, is so limited. Now I sit in my usual chair at the head of the table, and he stands beside me, tense with

151

concentration, his eyes fixed on the book open on the table. He's looking at a map of the megacontinent of Pangaea, a map of our world as it was 250 million years ago. For the last fifteen minutes, with the help of this historical geology text, I've been introducing him to plate tectonics.

He asks, "Is the land still moving, Mary?"

"Yes. That is, the continents are riding on top of the plates, and they're still moving. But very slowly. At best, a few inches a year."

He smiles, the fire of wonder in his eyes. But I see it quenched at the same moment I hear a sound behind me. Someone has come out of the kitchen.

I choose not to show that I'm aware of her. "Stephen, you can take this book and look through it. If there's anything you don't understand, I'll help you with it."

But he shakes his head, looking past me. "I've got to help Jonathan split wood."

I don't try to stop him. I watch him as he hurries out the back door. Then I say, "Hello, Miriam."

I hear a quick intake of breath. *Witch*, she is no doubt thinking. How did I know it was she standing behind me? She walks past me to the long side of the table, puts down a bowl and a basket of pea pods. I close the book, but only after she has given it an oblique scrutiny, and I see something in her eyes that surprises me.

Fear.

I've never seen Miriam afraid, not even for a fleeting moment as now. It is as unnerving as the opening of a door where I didn't know one existed. You can't hate someone who is capable of fear.

And do I *hate* her? I hadn't thought my feelings were so extreme. And they aren't. Not for Miriam. I don't hate her. I hate what she represents to me: the perpetuation and potential triumph of unreason. I hate her lack of fear, and above all, her lack of doubt.

Miriam has never in her life said, "I don't know."

Her hands move quickly about the task of emptying the pods; the peas rattle and ricochet against the glazed sides of the bowl. But she pauses, tosses her bright hair back from her shoulders.

"Why are you staring at me?"

I am for a moment embarrassed. "I didn't mean to stare, Miriam. I was only thinking . . . how much you remind me of Luke."

She resumes her work, facile hands moving ceaselessly. "I look more like my mother than Luke."

There's a cast of antagonism in that, and I don't know if it's for me or Luke. "Well, you're certainly prettier than he was," I reply lightly.

Her cheeks redden as she slits open a pod with her thumbnail and strips out the peas. "Beauty is only in the soul."

"No doubt. But it's your hair that reminds me so much of Luke."

Slit, strip, peas tumbling into the bowl. "Luke was only my physical father. My uncle, Brother Jonas, was my true father."

I hear the antagonism again, and I'm sure now it's for Luke. I wait to see if she'll say more, and finally she does.

"Some said my uncle was a hard man."

I respond cautiously, "Did they?"

"Well, maybe he was in some ways. Not like Luke. But Brother Jonas was a good man. He was a man of faith, and he loved God and always kept His Commandments. Always!"

And, of course, the children in that good man's household had no choice but to love Jonas's god and keep those patriarchal canons. For a while the only sounds are the cracks and rattles of her work. I remain silent, and finally Miriam stops, looks at me, then down at the book.

"What were you showing Stephen in that book?"

"I was telling him about plate tectonics."

When I don't elaborate, she looks at the cover of the book, takes some time to read its title, which is also its subject. I see again, only because I'm looking for it, that hint of fear in her eyes, but it is immediately masked by righteous contempt.

She says, "That's one of those books that goes against the Bible."

"Miriam, it has nothing to do with the Bible."

"Nor God!"

"No. It's not a philosophical treatise. You're welcome to read it before you condemn it." And I wince at my own words. That didn't need to be said. I know she won't read it. She *can't* read it. Her reading skills are minimal, and her voluminous quotes from the Bible at morning services come primarily from memory.

Her back is straight as steel. "I don't need to read it to know it's evil. It teaches our children to deny God!"

"No, Miriam, it does *not*." Then before my temper gets out of control I add, "God moves in mysterious ways, and no mere human can know all those ways nor claim to understand the dimensions of God."

"But God spoke to the prophets, and through them to me. I *know* God's Word and His Truth."

I don't rise to the bait, and after a moment she adds: "My children will learn to listen to God, and I don't want them taught evil."

I don't rise to that bait, either. All at once I'm weary of this, and I know it's a mistake to argue with her. It only feeds her conviction. And her willingness to argue with me feeds my anxiety. That willingness is due in part to the fact that we're alone, but it also suggests a burgeoning confidence in her. I hear a rush of rain on the roof. Just a squall; the light has gone gray.

"Miriam, I don't want to be your enemy. We can't let ourselves be enemies, not when our little community is so vulnerable to schism."

For a long time she studies me as if I am something inanimate, or rather a phenomenon to be cautiously observed. And I look back at her, seeing her in the same way: a phenomenon like the smoldering embers in a lightning-struck tree that are the seeds of a conflagration.

Finally she shakes her head, smiles faintly. "No, Mary, you aren't my enemy. You are the *Lord's* enemy."

I take a deep breath, let it out slowly.

Gird up your loins, old woman.

Yet what of that fleeting fear I read in her eyes when she looked at this book? Why would she feel anything but contempt for a book that describes the evolution of this planet as it occurred—not as it was written by the authors of the Pentateuch in an era when the world was still thought to be flat? Was she afraid of the truth in this book? Rather, the reality?

It finally comes home to me that Miriam fears this book as a body of arcane knowledge, magical knowledge: black magic. Here at Amarna, I am the possessor and fountainhead of that knowledge. A witch. And in the words of her god, "Thou shalt not suffer a witch to live."

In the same book of the Bible, her god prescribes ceremonies for animal sacrifices, decrees laws dealing with slavery, and advocates revenge in kind as a means of redressing wrongs.

I've been through all this before in another time, another generation. Generation unto generation . . .

The backdoor opens, and Esther, Grace, and Enid come in, wet and laughing with exhilaration from the rain. But Esther stops when she sees Miriam and me. "I'm sorry. Are we interrupting something?"

Miriam takes a pod out of the basket, slits it open. "No, Esther. I'm just getting these peas ready for midday meal."

Grace sits down by Miriam. "Here—I'll help you. Oh, the rain just came in buckets, so we had to leave the garden work for now."

I rise, take the book to the shelves on the south wall, then go into the living room to look out at the rain. There are streaks of blue sky in the west, but above Amarna clouds hang like shadows. I hear the children come in the backdoor, then Jeremiah, all creating a congenial cacophony. This small, fearfully isolated community is still united.

The squall drifts on within half an hour, and indoor work is put aside for outdoor. At this time of year the garden comes first. And the garden begins in the greenhouse.

I've always thought the greenhouse was one of the most agreeable rooms in the house. I suppose it's not precisely a room, although it's surrounded on three sides by the house, and I can never think of it as outside. The angled glass panels of the roof let me look up into the sky, but they stop the rain. The west wall is nearly all glass, even its door, and I can see the ocean, but I can't feel the sea wind. I walk on stone, but it must be swept with a broom like any inside floor. But half of this floor is earth, and that puts me outside again. So do the plants that grow in that earth: tomatoes, leaf lettuce, poppies, spinach, and, to distract whitefly from the others, nasturtiums. And for pleasure, sapphire blue lobelia.

The shelves along the walls are crowded with pots and trays filled with damp, dark earth in which green miracles are occurring. Year after year the miracles occur as they have for millions of years in different shapes and forms. The tart scent of the tomato plants, warmed by the sun, blends with Bernadette's herbs: parsley, sage, rosemary, and thyme—and how I wish I could remember all the words of that old song—chamomile, basil, borage, marjoram, peppermint, goldenseal, pennyroyal, hyssop, hepatica. And even a little cannabis.

This early in the year, the plants, except for the perennials, are miniatures of their once and future selves and charged with potential. But today many of the vegetable seedlings are leaving this sunny womb to survive—or not—in the true outside world in the garden. Bernadette is, aptly, midwife of this process.

Bernadette's hair—short and curly, entirely white now—flies wildly around her head. She has become even smaller with age, but she's still quick and impatient, still like an inquisitive squirrel with her sun-browned face, her gray, questing eyes, her small hands constantly busy. She is saying to Esther, "That flat there—yes, the cabbage. That goes. Then there's more broccoli and these two cauliflowers."

I'm at the worktable on the north wall stacking the slitted tar-paper squares that will go around the cabbage seedlings to discourage cutworms. The squares are much the worse for wear, and I'm not sure we have more tar paper in the storeroom. I look up at Stephen, who waits to carry one of the flats with its precious cargo. Esther places it in his hands, tells him, "Now, just watch where you put your feet on the way."

"Esther, I never have dropped one." He seldom calls her Mother, nor do Miriam's children call her Mother.

I put a stack of tar-paper squares under my left arm and take up my cane. "I'll walk up with you, Stephen."

He smiles at me, leads the way, then pauses while I open the sliding glass door. We walk past the deck and the north wing of the house, then up the gentle slope to the garden. The grass is starred with dandelions and tiny, white English daisies. Stephen concentrates on keeping his load balanced. He doesn't look up as he speaks. "Mary, I haven't finished *Treasure Island* yet."

He's slated to report on that book in school. "There's no hurry, Stephen. Besides, I've given you quite a lot to read lately."

His mouth tightens. "Miriam says I can't read at night. It wastes candles."

I am jarred by sudden anger at that. There are *always* enough candles for reading. I try to keep the anger out of my voice. "Well, you'll just have to finish it when you can. Do you like it?"

He glances up at me, grinning. "Yes. It's really exciting."

And what more can a teacher ask? Yet I wonder how much of the world of Jim Hawkins makes sense to Stephen, who would find the world that existed only thirty years before he was born incomprehensible. But so would Jim Hawkins.

A cascade of laughter distracts me. Little Mary and Jonathan are running toward us on their way to the greenhouse. Jonathan shouts in passing, "Hurry up, Stephen. They're waiting for more seedlings."

Stephen retorts, "I'll get there when I *get* there!"

When we reach the garden, *they* are indeed waiting; that is, Miriam, Grace, and Enid. Isaac has been detailed to hoe chopped kelp into the soil at the east end of the garden, and little Rachel is ostensibly helping him. She looks around at me and grins, and her small, fair face reminds me, as it always does, of Rebecca. But there's no pain in that reminder, perhaps because Rachel is so replete with life and laughter and the unaware innocence of all young things.

This end of the garden is—like the seedlings the women are planting in its plowed, hoed, fertilized, raked rows—beautiful in its potential, and already the carrots have put up lacy plumes, and the first umbrella leaves of squash are unfurled. Miriam stands near

157

the gate. She gives Stephen a cold look as she takes the flat. "About time."

I put in, "About time for the tar paper, too. Sorry to be so slow."

She shrugs. "Put them down. We'll take care of them later." Then she turns away, takes the flat along the row to Enid and Grace.

I prop the squares against a fence post, take a deep breath of the musty perfume of the earth, and remember the seasons I've spent here coaxing out the green miracles with hard work. This was Rachel's garden. This was my garden. Yet now I am unnecessary here.

I start down the slope toward the house. Stephen joins me, walks silently beside me for a while, then at length he speaks. "Miriam says you hate her, you know."

Startled, I stop, search his face. He said it so matter-of-factly, so indifferently, yet what I see in his hooded eyes is bewilderment.

"Stephen, did Miriam tell you that?"

"No, not me. I heard her talking to Grace yesterday in the garden."

Of course. If it can be said that we have a gossip in our community, it is Grace. And if one wishes to convey anything to the community without doing so personally, one has only to tell Grace.

I turn and continue toward the house. Miriam is experimenting in manipulation and propaganda. She isn't subtle, but here she doesn't need to be. *Damn* her.

"Mary?" Stephen kicks at dandelion heads as he walks.

"It's all right, Stephen. Don't worry."

"*Do* you hate her?"

And that's the question I asked myself only hours ago, but my feelings aren't as simple as an affirmative or negative would indicate.

"I wonder why Miriam would say that, Stephen. And how she feels about *me*."

We have no further opportunity to discuss the matter. Little Mary and Jonathan are coming around the corner from the house, each carefully balancing a flat of seedlings. Stephen says, "I'd better hurry and get another flat up to the garden."

"Yes, you go ahead." I watch him jog toward Mary and Jonathan, stop to exchange a few bantering words with them. They part laughing.

By early afternoon the last rain clouds have vanished, the sun is striking rainbows on every blade of rain-dewed grass, and the air is as clear as a drop of water. I've draped the chairs on the deck with blankets. The wood is still damp, but I don't want to sit inside now and waste this crystalline afternoon. Shadow curls napping at my feet, and Falstaff, the old yellow tabby, has taken up residence in my lap, purring while I stroke his broad, amber back. He seldom plays the lap cat, but apparently he finds my lap in this sunny place acceptable.

I listen to the omnipresent rumble of the surf, watch the foam-laced breakers curl and spill in white avalanches, but I'm thinking about Miriam, about rumors of hate, about candles for reading. There's so little time for the children to read, especially in spring and summer when the tasks necessary to survival take up most of the daylight hours. If Miriam won't let Stephen read at night by candlelight, he's left only a short time after evening services before he goes to bed.

And Miriam is well aware of that. She doesn't want him—or any of the children—to read. Except the Bible. For her that one book is the fount of all wisdom. It is all she will tolerate in the way of wisdom.

The other adults are more tolerant, but it is the tolerance of indifference. They follow Jerry's lead in that. He sees no harm in my teaching the children, nor is he particularly interested in what I teach them. He did, after all, give his word.

But if it ever comes to a choice between me and Miriam—rather, as Jerry will see it, between me and peace in the family—I wonder how tolerant he will be.

And the family peace is fraying. I felt it at midday meal. Uneasy pauses in the conversation, uncertain glances exchanged.

Or is that only a projection of my own tension? Certainly Jerry was his usual ebullient self, eating heartily of chicken stew, peas, and potato cakes thick with butter, while he talked about the cedars he found up the Styx, which will provide good lumber for the addition to the north wing.

Shadow lifts her head, looks northward, and I see Stephen and Isaac coming around the corner of the house. They don't bother to go to the steps at the south end of the deck, but climb over the railing. Stephen waits to offer Isaac a helping hand, then as they approach me he says, "Miriam said Isaac should rest for a while. Is it all right if he stays with us for the lesson?"

No doubt Miriam is making Isaac her innocent spy. "Of course, it's all right. Isaac, why don't you go in and get a chair."

He boosts himself onto the railing. "This'll be all right."

Stephen gestures toward the empty chair. "You sit there, Isaac."

Isaac shrugs, gets off the railing, stops to pet Falstaff. The cat rouses, annoyed, and leaves my lap, venting his choler with a swipe at Shadow's nose as he departs. Shadow only draws back and growls, then resumes her nap. Isaac laughs, and that brings on a spate of coughing, which he ignores as he settles in the chair.

Stephen winces at the dry hacking, then turns to me. I think he'd like to talk about Miriam, about my feelings for her, hers for me, but he is constrained by Isaac's presence. He asks, "Did you and Rachel ever go on another journey to look for survivors?"

I would also like to finish our discussion about Miriam. I don't like to leave it unresolved in Stephen's mind, but I'm equally constrained. "No, Stephen. That one trek was lesson enough. It taught us our limitations and forced us into certain decisions."

"You mean like preserving the books?"

"Yes. Our legacy."

Isaac asks, "What's a legacy, Mary?"

"Well, it's a sort of gift. A gift to future generations."

Stephen perches on the railing. "Jeremiah said when Grandpa Luke was on his deathbed he told him Rachel had a divine mission to save the books."

I nod, thinking how deceptions stick like burrs to your skirts. Luke held the secret so many years, but I encouraged Jeremiah to divulge it. It served my purposes.

"Rachel and I considered it the most important thing in our lives. Yet it was so slow. Time, that's what we were shortest on. And wax. The bees only produced so much every year, and we needed most of it for candles."

"Wax?" Stephen asks. "How did you use wax?"

"To seal the books. First we wrapped each one in aluminum foil—we had a lot of that from our scavenging—then we covered the foil with melted beeswax. We applied it with Rachel's bristle brushes, the same ones she used for her encaustic paintings."

"Oh, yes." Then he adds: "I don't think I really understand some of her pictures."

"You mean the abstracts. Maybe because they aren't pictures; they're paintings. I think what she was trying to say is that things aren't always what they seem, but they're all interrelated."

"I think the pictures are pretty," Isaac insists.

Stephen laughs at that, then: "Mary, what did you do after you covered the foil with wax?"

"Well, when the wax was a quarter of an inch thick, we wrapped each book in another layer of foil to protect the wax. Our packaging was at least watertight. We experimented with a couple of duplicates." I look north toward the vault. Its brick and stone and cedar seem so solid, so steadfast, but time and weather can destroy mountains.

Stephen asks, "Will you ever open the vault, Mary?"

"Me? No. It can't be opened until your children, or their children, rediscover how to make paper, so they can copy the books and learn from them and preserve the knowledge for *their* children."

Isaac pulls his legs up, sits cross-legged. "How many books *are* there in the vault?"

"Nearly ten thousand, Isaac."

His eyes go wide, and Stephen sighs. "It would take forever to copy that many books."

"A long time, at least, but the more people there are who can write, the sooner they'll be copied. Or even printed. A simple printing press wouldn't be so hard to build." Then I laugh wearily.

161

"Oh, Stephen, we can't predict the future. That's what Rachel said. We can only try. And hope."

He studies me, and sometimes his eyes seem as fathomless as a night sky. At length, he nods, as if I've answered a question for him.

I shift in my chair, seeking a more comfortable position. "Anyway, sealing the books was a long, slow process. Of course, at first we didn't have the vault, so we kept the sealed books in the basement. And one reason we were so slow is that we usually read, or at least skimmed, the books before we sealed them. With each book . . . it was like sending a baby out on a river in a reed basket, hoping a princess would find it."

"Like the baby Moses!" Isaac says eagerly.

"Yes, Isaac." I don't point out that Moses was only one of many infants in mythology sent out on such river voyages. "The hope kept us alive and . . . yes, I'd say happy. Surviving still meant hard work, and we were always learning new skills, but there was satisfaction in that. We took pride in our strength and resourcefulness. The old griefs never quite died for us, but we were surviving as human beings, not simply as organisms do, without cognizance, without a frame of reference. We didn't surrender our humanity."

Stephen nods, and there's a shadow of sadness in his eyes. "But how did you keep going when you were so . . . alone?"

"Well, we kept busy, Stephen. We had no choice about that. But it wasn't all work. Sometimes in the evenings we entertained ourselves with card games or Scrabble. That was Rachel's favorite game."

"I like Scrabble, too," Isaac puts in.

I use the Scrabble set as a teaching aid now. No one here is equal to a real game of Scrabble. "Yes, it's a good game, Isaac. But there was one entertainment we missed sorely. Music. It was a part of our humanity that was denied us. The records—oh, those silent disks. Rachel had hundreds of records, a sampling of the best music of five centuries, but even if we'd had electricity, our stereo had been destroyed by EMP. I wonder how many centuries it will take to reinvent the symphony orchestra, and if . . ." Both Stephen and

Isaac are gazing uneasily at me. They don't understand what I'm talking about. Or what they've lost.

Isaac smiles tentatively, and I want to touch the soft contours of his cheeks. But I only return his smile and go on. "At any rate, our life here at Amarna was quiet and even satisfying for eight years after our trek. We had problems and small disasters, but we managed to deal with them. We lived and worked from season to season, rather than from year to year. Now, when I look back, it seems those seasons passed quickly. Then one day—the first of April, in fact—nearly half a year after the tenth anniversary of the End, everything changed for us at Amarna."

Now Stephen smiles, too. He thinks he knows the nature of that change, thinks it was the change that Rachel and I had longed for, the answer to our hopes.

So did I, on that April Fool's Day.

Paul was the great Coryphaeus, and the first corrupter of the doctrines of Jesus.
—THOMAS JEFFERSON, *LETTER TO W. SHORT*, April 13, 1820

I seem stark mute, but inwardly I prate,
  I am, and am not, I freeze and yet am burned,
Since from myself my other self I turned.
—ELIZABETH I (1533–1603), FINIS, *ELIZA REGINA*,
ASHMOLEAN MUSEUM MANUSCRIPT

The last two weeks in March had been gray with cold rain that beat down the seedlings in the garden and made the pasture a swamp, but this, the first day of April, dawned clear, the sun drawing a mist of steam from the rooftops and fields.

When the morning chores were finished, Mary took a bucket and chisel and set out for the beach. The tide was unusually low, exposing the rocks—and the mussels growing on them—at the base of the Knob, and tonight they would feast on mussel chowder. Yorick followed her, and she didn't discourage him, although he had a tendency to wander. She took the silent whistle; he always responded to that. Yorick was the image of Sparky, one of the litter born to fey Ophelia last fall, the last litter Sparky had fathered. The last Ophelia had mothered.

At the foot of the path Mary climbed over the logjam of driftwood cast up by the winter storms, then paused to savor the sun on the sea. The wind blew out of the east, throwing rainbows of spindrift back from the massive avalanches of the breakers, and as she watched them she remembered music she hadn't heard, even in memory, for many years. Beethoven. One of the symphonies. Which one, she couldn't be sure.

Yorick ran out to the water's edge, chased a gull that casually lifted into the wind and hovered out of reach, while Mary struck out for the Knob, her shadow stretching before her. Lean and vigorous, that shadow figure, and it reflected the way she felt today: in tune with her world, blending with her surroundings, tan chino pants the color of the light sand, blue-gray jacket the color of the heavier, dark sand.

Abruptly Yorick stopped his dance with the gull, faced south, ears forward, and began barking. Mary turned, alert, but not yet alarmed. Something was moving on the beach about two hundred yards away. She wondered why she hadn't seen it before, but it was close to the piles of drift. Maybe it had been hidden there.

It. Why was she thinking *it?*

What she saw was a human being.

The chisel clattered against the bucket as the bale slipped out of her hand. She blinked, expecting the figure to resolve into a mirage, an accident of light and atmosphere. But it remained unmistakably human, despite the exaggerating effect of a backpack.

A human being.

She stood flailed by emotions, all conflicting—disbelief, hope, fear, joy—and the result was paralysis.

But that passed, gave way to caution. She called Yorick with the silent whistle, ran to the tumble of drift, and crouched behind a log, held Yorick with a hand around his muzzle to keep him from barking.

And watched the stranger draw nearer with every stumbling step.

165

He gave no indication that he was aware of her. Yes, it was *he*. She could see a red beard; a wide-brimmed, leather hat shadowed the rest of his face. He wore a sheepskin jacket, gray with soot and dirt, and pants of dark cloth stuffed into hiking boots. The boots had to come from Before. The backpack, too. He was tall and thin, with long legs that didn't seem to function properly, that gave him an odd, scarecrow aspect. A rifle was slung over his left shoulder.

He stopped. He was only a hundred feet from her now, and she wondered if he had seen her.

No. His eyes were fixed ahead on the Knob. He staggered, nearly fell, then got his balance again. He was *ill*. She almost cried out at that realization. When he was only a few yards away, she heard him shouting over the roar of the surf. No, he was singing. " '. . . the beautiful, the beautiful river . . . gather at the river . . . flows by the throne of God. . . .' "

But his legs couldn't keep pace with the song. Again, he staggered, his knees buckled, and he toppled like a felled tree.

Yorick slipped out of her arms, ran barking toward the man, but he didn't move. *He's dead*, Mary thought—might even have said it aloud as she ran after Yorick.

The stranger lay sprawled on his belly, face half-buried in the sand. She turned him on his side, his head lolling. He was alive, and she nearly wept with relief. But she could turn him no further until she got the backpack off, and her hands were shaking so badly, it took an inordinate amount of time to unbuckle the straps, and all the while he was straining for breath. His skin was wan as alabaster, damp with sweat, the sand clinging like a rough second skin. Mary hesitated, her mouth dry. It occurred to her that his disease might be contagious.

But even if it were, what was she to do? Leave him here to die—the first living human being she'd seen in ten years?

Finally she got the pack off, and he slumped over onto his back. Her breath catching at the feel of his skin hot against hers, she brushed the sand away from his eyes and mouth. His long, narrow head seemed skull-like, with jutting cheekbones, deep eye sockets—a face that at first seemed old, yet she realized he was younger than she. His hat had fallen off, revealing a cloth band that re-strained his long, tangled, copper red hair; words were embroidered on the band, but she didn't try to read them. Where had he come from? How did he get here?

It didn't matter. Not now. She ran for the ravine, Yorick barking at her heels. She was panting when she reached the top of the path, but she still had breath enough to shout for Rachel. All five dogs—even Shadow, limping with her arthritic joints—joined the ca-cophony, and Rachel came out of the greenhouse. "Mary, what's *wrong?*"

Mary worked the words through panting gasps. "A man . . . there's a man on the beach . . . he's *alive*, Rachel!"

Whether he would remain alive was moot. Mary and Rachel carried him up the mud-slick path, and once they got him to the house, they put him in Mary's bed and stripped off his clothes. They saw the scars then, the white weals across his back, and Rachel said tightly, "Man's inhumanity to man hasn't abated, I see."

His fever registered 103 degrees on Rachel's old mercury ther-mometer. Through the remainder of the morning and into the af-ternoon, they alternately bathed him with wet cloths, then when the chills struck, covered him with layers of blankets, and in the rare moments when he roused to semiconsciousness, plied him with water and willow-bark tea. They couldn't leave him alone at any time. In his fever he thrashed wildly, threw off the blankets, leaving him naked to the next chill.

But by late afternoon his fever had dropped two degrees, and he had quieted enough so that they could take turns with their min-istrations and the chores that couldn't be shirked. Rachel killed a chicken for supper, and while it baked, she simmered a pot of broth at the back of the stove. Finally, when they finished supper and the last of the evening chores, Rachel offered to take the first watch with the stranger. Mary went into Rachel's room and settled in her bed with Shadow lying at her back, two of the cats at the foot of the bed.

Sleep was a long time coming, and she was surprised it did come, surprised when Rachel opened the door, lighting her way with a candle in a pewter holder, and told her it was two in the morning. Mary had been dreaming. One of the old death dreams. She got out of bed and began dressing. "How's our patient?"

Rachel put the candle on the small table by the bed and sat down to rub Shadow's back. "Well, he's past the crisis. Fever's down to ninety-nine, and he woke up long enough to talk to me."

Mary sighed her relief as she pulled on a sweater. "What did he say?"

Rachel laughed. "That I was an angel of mercy. Maybe he thinks he's died and gone to heaven. He definitely believes heaven is a possibility. Did you notice that headband he was wearing?"

"What about it?"

"The words embroidered on it. 'Yea, though I walk through the valley of the shadow of death, I shall fear no evil.' "

Mary looked at Rachel, but her face was turned away from the light, and Mary couldn't be sure of the edge she felt in those words. "He sounds like a dyed-in-the-wool good Christian. What else did he say?"

Rachel shrugged. "He asked me my name. I asked his. It's Luke, by the way. No surname." For a moment she seemed distracted, as if she had more to say, then she looked up at Mary and offered a smile. "You'd better go see to our good Christian. I'm going to get some sleep."

When Mary entered her room, she felt a shiver of uncertainty that she blamed on the night chill. An oil lamp burned on the bedside table, and in its glow the stranger slept. She checked the fire in the blue-enameled stove, then sat down in the chair Rachel had drawn up by the bed. Rachel's book was on the table. Loren Eiseley. Mary leaned back and looked on the face of this stranger, a man named Luke, and tried to sort out her thoughts.

The short span of sleep had put a little space between her and the clamor of emotions she had endured throughout the day: the shock of seeing another human being, the added shock of finding him so ill, the constant fear that this, the only survivor they'd met in all these years, might die before uttering a coherent word.

Yea, though I walk through the valley of the shadow of death . . .

And he had indeed walked through that valley, but he was out of it now. He would live. And Mary knew her life would inevitably be changed by that fact.

She and Rachel had walked their own valley and had climbed out of the shadow; they had a purpose in living, a purpose that provided them satisfaction and even pleasure. No more than a third of the books had been sealed, but they had decided that this summer they'd begin building a permanent shelter for the books, their gift to humankind and the future. But this stranger embodied the potential of a different kind of gift. At the moment she brushed the sand from his face on the beach, the possibility stirred to life, but she hadn't put it into words then. Only now did she let the words shape the idea: *this man can father my children.*

She was thirty-four years old, and in all probability capable of bearing children. The clockwork regularity of her menstrual cycles had been a continuing source of annoyance. It had been so futile, her body's monthly preparation for something that could never happen.

But it *could* happen now.

Before the End she had considered bringing a child into that world unkind at the least and certainly irresponsible. Was it any kinder, any more responsible, to bring a child into *this* world?

Yet did she really have a choice? In a world where the continued existence of the human species might be in doubt, could she choose *not* to bear children if she were capable of it?

She looked at the stranger's face, his forehead, cheekbones, the aquiline prow of his nose etched in lamplight that glinted in his coppery hair and beard. The face that had on the beach struck her by its look of age, now seemed young, like a hungry child's. His eyes were closed, but she had seen them, knew them to be the color of the sky on a clear, spring day. She wondered if this stranger was someone she could love.

Or someone who could be a lover?

She smiled, the muscles of her abdomen tensing against the sensations unleashed by that thought. Was that the real explanation for her desire for motherhood?

No, her need—her obligation—to bear children was something she couldn't escape. But this man as a lover . . .

She wondered why she hadn't permitted herself to think of him as a lover before. Yes, she had been intensely aware of his maleness when they undressed him and bathed him to quell his fever. Even now that he was chastely covered, she was aware of his body, flat-muscled, long-boned, with sunburned skin evolved for northern climates. Today she had been too preoccupied with his illness to think of him as a lover.

Now . . . she thought about it, thought about making love. For ten years she had lived like a nun, had resigned herself to celibacy. She'd had no choice in that.

Now maybe she had a choice.

Then her smile slipped away. She was getting ahead of events. Wouldn't it be ironic if this stranger, whom she envisioned as the father of her children, as her lover, were sterile or if he simply rejected her?

And Rachel—where did she fit into this scenario?

Mary shivered and folded her arms against her body.

Changes. This stranger potentiated changes like a magician pulling chains of bright scarves out of his sleeve.

She reached for the Eiseley and found it as difficult to read as she had to sleep a few hours ago. Yet she did at length become engrossed in the words, and she had read two of Eiseley's essays when she was distracted by a change in the pace of the stranger's breathing. She watched while he opened his eyes and looked around the room. Finally his gaze fixed on her, and she felt a spasm of fear. His eyes had been open before, but he had never been fully conscious, and she had never fully recognized that there was within that sick body a unique mind, one entirely unknown to her.

He looked at her for what seemed a long time, then he frowned, cleared his throat.

"You're not Rachel."

Mary laughed. That wasn't at all what she might have anticipated as his first utterance. She closed the book and put it on the bedside table. "No, I'm not Rachel. She's sleeping now."

"Then she *is* here? There *is* somebody named Rachel here?"

"Yes, of course there is." Mary rose, picked up the glass on the table. "You'd better get some more water down you. With that fever, you'll be badly dehydrated." She helped him sit up and held the glass for him while he swallowed most of the water. She saw the scars on his back and again wondered about them. When he sank back and closed his eyes, she returned to her chair, expecting him to fall asleep.

But his eyes opened, focused inward now. "I had a vision. I was walking on the shore, and I was sick and sore afraid. Then suddenly there was a woman there before me, and she had dark eyes full of wisdom and kindness. She held out her hands to me and said, 'I'm Rachel Morrow.' Then . . . she was gone. But I knew she was sent by the Lord, and if I'd just keep going, I'd find what I'm seeking."

Mary felt as if a trapdoor had been tripped beneath her. But she reminded herself that she shouldn't expect lucidity when he was just recovering from a serious illness. It wasn't surprising that he was confused about the circumstances of his meeting with Rachel.

Mary said, "You met Rachel a few hours ago here in this room. Don't you remember?"

"No, I haven't seen Rachel yet," he replied levelly. "Not in the flesh."

Mary let that pass. "Well, you will tomorrow morning. Are you hungry? We have some broth for you."

"Yes, I'd like that. But first—what's your name?"

"Mary Hope. And you're Luke, right?"

His mouth sagged open. "How did you know that?"

"Never mind. Don't you have a last name?"

"My family name is Jason, but we don't—" He stopped abruptly.

But Mary caught that potent pronoun *we*. So there were *other* survivors.

He didn't give her a chance to ask about them. "I have to go outside."

171

"Outside! You're in no shape to go outside."

"I . . . have to go to the privy."

Mary rose. "Well, you don't have to go outside. We've managed to keep the plumbing in operation. Okay, let me help you."

He pushed the covers back, realized he was naked, and his face went red as he hurriedly pulled the covers up again. Mary went to the closet and returned with a plaid, woolen robe—a man's robe, one of the many articles of clothing they had scavenged. He reluctantly let her help him into it, then she lighted a candle in the flame of the oil lamp, put it in a holder, and offered her shoulder. She felt his resistance to that support, but he was too unsteady to walk without it. When they reached the hall, Cleo and Candide skittered away like small, striped ghosts, while Yorick and Agate roused with threatening growls. Luke held out his hand for them to smell, with that raising himself a few notches in Mary's estimation. Then she guided him into the bathroom, put the candle down by the sink, pointed out the clean towels for his use, and asked if he needed any help.

He withdrew from her, shocked. *"No."*

She shrugged and closed the door, returned to the bedroom for the lamp, then went to the kitchen to stoke up the banked fire in the cookstove, reminding herself that she must bank the coals again before the revived fire burned out. Rachel was expert at that, at maintaining that magic glow of fire. There were still some matches left, but they were too precious to use unnecessarily. The only alternatives now were a welder's sparker and a magnifying glass. Mary took the chicken broth out of the cooler, ladled some into a pan, and put it on the stove. Then she got a bowl out of the cupboard, changed her mind, and decided a mug would be easier for Luke to handle. Yes, there was still one left that wasn't chipped.

Then she picked up the lamp to return to her patient and found him leaning against the bathroom doorjamb. He smiled at her, and she realized it was the first time she'd seen him smile. It was an ingenuous, wistful smile, and she couldn't do less than return it. She offered her shoulder. "Come on, Luke, let's get you back to bed."

172

He seemed to accept her support more readily now. He said, "This is a very fine house."

Mary wondered what he was comparing it to, but didn't ask. In the bedroom he kept the robe on and sagged into the bed. She covered him, then left him long enough to go to the kitchen and fill the mug with warm broth. When she returned and offered it to him, he thanked her, then didn't say another word, concentrating on the broth like a starving man. When he finished it, he asked for another mugful, but this one he downed slowly, while Mary sat in the chair, watching him.

Finally she asked, "How long have you been traveling?"

"I think . . . well, it must be about nine months now."

"That's a long journey. Where do you come from?"

He glanced warily at her. "From a place to the south."

And he wasn't going to be more specific. Did he think she might be a threat to the *we* he'd left behind? Perhaps. She was as much an unknown quantity to him as he was to her.

He sipped at the broth, studying her. At length, he said, "You're a beautiful woman, Mary Hope."

Again, he had surprised her. And made her self-consciously aware of her sunburned skin, of her hair cut short with no attempt at style, of her callused hands with the broken nails always stained with dirt however often she scrubbed them.

"Luke, you haven't seen many women lately, have you?"

He looked down at his mug. "I . . . I was just thinking, your husband must be very proud of you."

A probe of sorts? Why didn't he just ask?

"I have no husband."

"Did he pass on?"

"I've never had a husband. Rachel and I are the only ones here."

That brought a frown of consternation. "All the others passed on?"

"There never were any others here, not since the End."

"The End? Oh. You mean Armageddon. How did you survive all these years with no men? I mean, with nobody to help you?"

Mary shrugged. "We managed very well, actually."

He considered that while he finished the broth. "It's a miracle."

"Our survival?"

"Yes, and . . . and my coming here." Then with a short laugh, "But I don't even know where I am, except I'm where I was meant to be."

Mary didn't ask him to explain that. She said, "You're just north of what used to be the town of Shiloh Beach."

"Shiloh? The first permanent tabernacle of the Hebrews was at a place called Shiloh."

"Well, this town was named after the place in Tennessee where one of the bloodiest battles of the Civil War was fought."

"The Civil War?"

"The American Civil War. You know, North and South, the Blue and the Gray. Would you like some more broth?"

He shook his head as he surrendered the mug to her. "No. That was wonderful. You're a good cook."

"Rachel cooked this, and she's a master with spices and herbs."

"Rachel . . ." He seemed to savor the name, smiling faintly. "Rachel the shepherdess, daughter of Laban, wife of Jacob, mother of Joseph and Benjamin. And you—Mary, the mother of Jesus."

And Mary again had that feeling that a trapdoor had disappeared from under her. She and Rachel had always considered the religious associations in their names ironic. Luke Jason obviously found them deeply meaningful.

She didn't attempt a reply to his biblical lesson, and after a short silence, he asked, "Are you Rachel's daughter?"

"No, we're not related. She took me in Before."

"Oh." He didn't seem to understand that, but his eyes were closing with weariness. Mary remained silent until she thought he was asleep, then she reached for the Eiseley.

But Luke wasn't asleep. He roused, asked, "What book is that?"

"It's a collection of essays by Loren Eiseley. Would you like me to read to you?"

"Who was Loren Eiseley?"

"Well, he was a poet and a scientist. He—"

174

She stopped, catching the look of alarm in Luke's eyes as he asked, "He was a . . . scientist?"

"Yes, he was a scientist," Mary said, finding herself annoyed at his suspicious tone. "Is that a problem for you?"

He didn't answer her question. "Where did you get such a book?"

"Here. It's one of Rachel's books."

"Rachel's?" That didn't seem to make sense to him. He looked across the room at the bookshelves. "Are those . . . scientists' books?"

Mary answered coolly, "Some of them."

"Yet God sent me here," he mumbled, and something more she couldn't understand. But her annoyance turned to chagrin when he was overtaken by a racking bout of coughing, and she was helplessly aware of his weakness, his vulnerability. When the coughing eased, he lay panting, his forehead wet with sweat, his eyes closed.

"Luke?" She took his hand, finding a stringent elegance in its form that surprised her as much as its strength when it closed on hers.

Dear stranger, stay with me.

She remembered the scars on his back and wondered what he had suffered in his lonely travels, wondered where he'd been, what he'd seen, why he left his home, why he left the *we* he was so reluctant to talk about.

He whispered, "I have a book. . . ." Then his eyes flashed open. "My pack, where—"

"It's over there in the corner. Do you want something out of it?"

He nodded. "In the top flap . . . my book . . ."

Mary went to the backpack, and among the crumpled clothing that had a musty, musky smell, she found a Bible, its black leather binding frayed at the edges. She opened it. King James translation. Of course.

She offered it to Luke, and he said hoarsely, "You said you'd read to me, Mary Hope. . . ."

She sat down with the Bible. "Okay, I'll read to you if you'll close your eyes and try to sleep. What do you want to hear?"

"Maybe . . . yes, Psalms. There's great comfort in Psalms."

She had to look in the table of contents. She turned the thin, brittle pages carefully and finally began, " 'Blessed is the man that walketh not in the counsel of the ungodly. . . .' " And she thought, *Luke, you've come to the wrong place.*

The Seth Thomas clanged six times as Mary pushed her damp hair back from her forehead and turned to the kitchen window, her face hot from stoking the fire in the cookstove. The sun was a long way from showing itself over the hills to the east, but the sky was suffused with pellucid light like fragile porcelain.

The dawn of a new day—in more than one sense—and she met it with an odd mix of exhilaration and anxiety. She wanted to cry, but she didn't know why.

She jumped as a small, yellow tiger of a cat leapt up on the counter. "Cleo, you know better." When she put the cat down on the floor, she saw that the kitchen was under siege: Cleo's twin, Tony; Candide, the gray tiger; Petrouchka, a placid, odd-eyed calico tom; Jet, whose leopard lines marked her as part Siamese.

Peacefully coexisting with the cats were Agate, Yorick, and Yorick's sister and brother, Sheba and Pip. All three looked more like Sparky than their mother, Ophelia, who had been in every way Shadow's daughter. Mary sighed, thinking of Shadow and her painful gait, the patchiness of her coat that had been so sable soft. She was still sleeping at the foot of Rachel's bed now, and when Rachel woke, she'd have to lift her off the bed. She was the last of the animals from Before.

"Okay, kids, I'll get your breakfast as soon as I put the kettle on."

She placed the gray enamel kettle on the stove, then lined up the dogs' and cats' bowls on the counter. Their staple breakfast was milk and boiled chicken—guts and gristle, everything but the bones—with leftover vegetables for the dogs. This was the only meal they'd be given for the day. They had to catch their own if they wanted more. Mary put the bowls on the floor, segregating dogs and cats, but left Shadow's bowl on the counter and added an egg from the cooler.

The kettle began to shrill, and she snatched it off the stove to silence it. She didn't want to wake Luke or Rachel. Usually Rachel would already be up and about, but Mary hadn't wakened her. Let her have a little extra rest.

Or perhaps, Mary realized, her motives were entirely selfish: she wanted to be alone. She was still trying to sort out her emotions, to understand the changes Luke Jason wrought in her once-ordered world.

She turned, the muscles in her jaw taut, and took two mugs out of the cupboard, spooned chamomile and mint from their canisters into the tea ball, put it into one mug and poured hot water over it, inhaling the dusty, pungent aroma, thinking—as she did every morning—that she'd give her eyeteeth for a cup of coffee. She left the kettle wheezing at the back of the stove and took the mug out to the deck, where land and sea were drawn in soft pastels, and the air was as astringently cool as perfume. Our exquisite island, she thought, a model of what a world had been and perhaps might be again. In four and a half billion years, this world had tolerated many disasters on a planetary scale. But every disaster left it irrevocably changed.

Change. That was what she feared.

The swish of the sliding door startled her. Rachel stood at the open door ushering dogs and cats out. "Come on, everybody outside. Leave poor Shadow alone with her breakfast. Pip! Come on, little one." When all the animals had trooped out, the dogs sallying forth to patrol their territory, the cats taking up stations on the deck to groom themselves, Rachel joined Mary at the railing, raised her mug before she took a sip. "Thanks for getting the tea ready— *and* feeding the menagerie." Then she eyed Mary with a whisper of a smile. "You washed your hair."

Mary ran her hand through her damp hair. "Well, Luke was asleep, so I thought I might as well take a bath and wash my hair. Maybe I can get it dry before bedtime for a change."

"And this early-morning urge for cleanliness had nothing to do with our young guest."

Mary felt her face go hot. "I just thought as long as I had to be awake anyway . . ."

"I know. But don't kid yourself. Or me. After all, he's a man in the prime of life, and you're a woman in the prime of life. I wish you well."

But she forgot to revive her smile, and that was a signal Mary had long ago learned to recognize. When Rachel was angry or anxious, she seldom expressed it in words. Her words were those to be expected under normal circumstances. But she forgot the smiles that should go with the words.

Mary took a swallow of tea, found it cool and flat. "I guess I'd better go see if Luke's awake."

"I looked in on him a few minutes ago. He was sleeping like a baby—if babies snore. Did he wake up during your shift?"

"Yes, and he stayed awake for quite a while." She told Rachel what had happened last night, surprised at the detail she demanded, equally surprised that she could remember with such clarity exactly what Luke had said.

Finally Rachel asked, "What do you think of him?"

"I . . . don't know. Except he is definitely a good Christian."

Rachel sighed as she looked out at the misted ocean. "Damn. After all these years, we finally encounter another survivor, and he turns out to be a rockbound, good Christian—and a literalist, undoubtedly."

"Did you expect a Buddhist? Or an atheist?"

Rachel looked sharply at her, then nodded. "Good point. The odds are against any survivor in this country being anything but a Christian."

"Why does that bother you? What difference does it make?"

Rachel took time for a sip of tea. "The only reason I'm bothered is that historically Christians have had a penchant for burning books."

That silenced Mary, sent a chill through her. The books—their justification for survival, their hope for the future of humankind.

And it hadn't occurred to her that humankind, as embodied in a good Christian named Luke Jason, might not revere the legacy of the books.

I have a book. Those were Luke's words. A book.

Rachel said, "Just remember the example set by Paul at Ephesus, and the good Christians who burned the Library of Alexandria and flayed Hypatia alive. And book burning by good Christians has continued ever since, right down to that insidious ass, the *Reverend* Fallon and his Moral Purification campaign. Remember the pyres of burning books in front of the Washington Monument? That was only a year before the End." She paused, studying Mary intently. "Face it, not many of our books would be included on a literalist's list of acceptable reading matter. But when it comes to books, I'm as much a zealot as any literalist. I'll protect ours with my life if I have to, and I think I might be capable of killing for them."

The mist was dissipating, and at the horizon waves glinted with the first sunlight. Mary said nothing, engrossed in flickering visions of burning books; visions of the fleshy, unctuous face of Reverend Fallon as she had seen it years ago on a television screen, Fallon in his nasal, rural accent urging his faithful to *purify* themselves and the world; visions of Rachel as a fated Hypatia, battling hordes of fleshy-faced zealots.

"Rachel, I can't believe it would come to that. I mean, I can't believe we'd have to die or . . . kill to protect the books from Luke."

Rachel gave a short laugh. "I hope not. The trouble is, we're not just dealing with Luke. There's that *we* he inadvertently mentioned."

"But we don't really know much about Luke—or his *we.*"

"No. And with Luke I think we have an opportunity to make him an ally, even a convert. He's given us an advantage: he thinks he was sent to me by his god. He saw me as—what was it? Full of wisdom. If he was searching for enlightenment when he embarked on his journey, he'll find it here. At least, enough to give him some respect for books. Mary, I'll play any role I must—even the role of god-sent ministering angel full of wisdom." She laughed ruefully. "Just don't blow my cover."

179

Mary mustered a smile. "Don't worry. I'll leave the enlightenment entirely in your hands."

"Well, I'd better check our supply of candles and oil. I'll be doing a lot of reading at night. And we *do* have a Bible or two and a couple of books on biblical history."

"Maybe he won't stay here long enough to get enlightened."

Rachel eyed Mary curiously. "I think he'll stay awhile. Unless he's taken a vow of celibacy."

Again, Mary felt the heat in her cheeks. She could think of no response, and after a moment Rachel said gently, "I meant it when I said I wish you well." But there was in her eyes an equivocal melancholy.

Mary looked up at the spruce trees where the sun lighted their green crowns. "We have livestock to feed and eggs to gather and goats to milk—and I'd damned sure like some breakfast before we start."

Rachel finished her tea. "And we have a patient to look after."

Luke Jason's temperature dropped to normal by the third day, and by the fourth Mary and Rachel found it impossible to keep him in bed. They could only manage to keep him in the house, which he explored thoroughly. He pored over the titles of the books that filled every shelf and stood in piles on the floor, but he didn't comment on them. He studied Rachel's drawings and paintings, awed by the representational ones, but oddly bewildered and suspicious of all of them. He made friends with the household menagerie. Except for Shadow. She declined his every overture. He asked many questions about Amarna and their history here, and they patiently answered him. They didn't question him about his history, and he volunteered nothing.

On the fourth evening he sat down with them to a supper of rabbit stew thickened with cattail-root flour, steamed asparagus—the first of the season—cheese, and a salad of oakleaf and miner's lettuce. Before they began eating, Luke folded his hands and bowed his head, then glanced up at Rachel. "Don't you say grace here?"

M. K. WREN

Rachel answered, "I always thought the god that could create this universe should be omniscient as well as omnipotent. That god would *know* I'm grateful for every mouthful of food. I wouldn't have to say so in words."

Mary tried not to smile. So the enlightenment had begun. Luke's eyebrows went up as he considered what was undoubtedly an entirely new concept to him. "Yes, God knows every man's thoughts. Still . . ."

"If you like to put it in words," Rachel said, "by all means, do so."

He did, while Rachel and Mary waited politely, then, his thanks said, he turned to the meal with an appetite that precluded all conversation except his enthusiastic comments on the cuisine. Rachel laughed, called up the old saw that hunger is the best sauce, adding, "Sickness seems to work as well, once you're over the worst of it."

He did consider himself over the worst, and after they concluded the meal with Gravenstein applesauce, canned last summer, he helped clear the table and declared that he would wash the dishes. "I'm still weak, but I'm good for woman's work."

The silence that followed sent a flush into his face, and he added with a sheepish smile, "But everything is woman's work here, isn't it?"

Mary gave him the laugh he was no doubt hoping for. "Yes, it is, but you're probably not as strong as you think you are. Go sit by the fire. Rachel and I will take care of this woman's work for now."

It was dark by the time the woman's work was finished and Rachel had replenished the living-room fire. Luke sat on the couch facing the fire with Pip snuggled against his thigh, while Aggie lay at his feet providing a pillow for Tony and Cleo. Rachel lifted Shadow onto the couch, then sat down beside her, and Mary sat cross-legged on the floor by Aggie, welcoming Trouchka into her lap.

Luke smiled at her. "They're like a family to you."

"Yes. They *are* our family. All good and true friends."

For a while the fire hissed and crackled in a comfortable silence. Rachel finally broke it. "Luke, do you have a family?"

Mary saw him tense defensively. It was the first time since the night of his arrival that either of them had asked him such a personal question.

He took a deep breath. "Yes, I have an uncle. My parents and all the rest died in the Long Winter."

Rachel said, "I'm sorry," then waited patiently. But he said nothing more. Rachel turned to Mary. "Maybe this is a good time to open a bottle of our mead to celebrate Luke's return to health."

Mary put Trouchka on the floor and rose, but stopped when Luke asked her, "What's mead?"

"Well, it's a kind of wine made with honey." She took one of the candles in their glass holders from the mantel and lighted it in the fire. "Actually, ours is more a fruit wine than a true mead."

"Wine? You mean spirits?"

Rachel gave that a gentle laugh. "Not spirits in the sense that it's distilled. We do have a small still out in the garage, though. Alcohol is such a good solvent and disinfectant. Do you object to drinking wine?"

He paused before he replied. "The Bible says we shouldn't drink spirits."

Rachel seemed surprised. "But wasn't it Saint Paul who said, 'Drink no longer water, but use a little wine for thy stomach's sake'?"

"I . . . I don't remember that." But he seemed reassured by it. He said to Mary, "I'd be pleased to have some . . . mead with you."

Mary took the candle with her into the kitchen, got a bottle of mead out of the cooler and three wineglasses from the cupboard, and put them on a tray. When she returned to the living room, she put the tray on the side table by the couch and filled the glasses. The mead had a pale pink hue and the tart scent of wild berries that always reminded her of summer. She handed a glass to Rachel, another to Luke, then resumed her place on the floor, watching Luke with a faint smile. He held the glass as if it would break if he moved too suddenly. It was cut crystal, its prismatic facets making rainbows of the firelight. He whispered, "How could such things be made by the hand of man?"

Rachel said, "With skill and art, Luke. They belonged to my great-great-grandmother. She brought them with her to Oregon."

"Where did she come from?"

"Ireland, originally. She was a child when her family left Ireland. They went to Tasmania first, and after she married, she and her husband sailed for Oregon."

"How far is it to . . . Tasmania?"

"Well, I don't know exactly. It must be over eight thousand miles. You know where it is, don't you?"

Luke averted his eyes and shrugged. "I'm not sure."

"I'll show it to you tomorrow on the globe." She took a moment to taste her mead. "I'm surprised you don't know geography, Luke. Someone taught you to read. Didn't they also teach you geography?"

"A little. But things of this world aren't important, you know. Not after Armageddon."

Mary saw the tightening of Rachel's mouth, but when she spoke, it was with consummate casualness. "But the world is still here, isn't it, Armageddon or not?"

Luke's attention was on his glass as he gingerly tasted the mead. He waited after the first swallow, as if he expected something to happen. A bolt of lightning, perhaps, Mary thought.

He said cautiously, "This tastes . . . good." Then he turned to Rachel. "Yes, the world is still here, but it's not like it was before Armageddon."

"No. At least, parts of it have been devastated. Still, that doesn't explain why you relegate an entire planet to a state of unimportance."

"Because nothing in *this* world is important. Saint Paul said, 'Set your affections on things above, not on things of the earth.' "

"But what did he mean by *things of the earth?* Was he talking about geography—which no one knew much about in his day, by the way—or was he talking about the mundane, selfish concerns that always commanded the affections of most people?"

Luke eyed Rachel speculatively while he took another sip of

mead. "I think you must be right. He *was* talking about selfish concerns."

"But this planet Earth—shouldn't we admire the creator of such a beautiful world, the creator of the whole magnificent universe?"

"We *do* admire the Creator."

"Then we should also admire the creation."

Luke wasn't entirely convinced. "But the creation isn't as important as the Creator."

"Luke, I was an artist and in a lesser sense a creator. I can assure you, I consider my creations more important than I. Besides, isn't understanding the creation one way to understand the creator?" She paused, then with an easy laugh, added, "But I didn't intend to launch into a theological debate. Aren't you tired?"

He shook his head. "No, and I enjoy a . . . a theological debate."

"Then maybe we'll continue another time." She stroked Shadow's head while she sipped her mead. "Poor lady, I wish I could give you some of this. It might help your aches and pains."

Luke started to pet Shadow, but withdrew his hand when she stiffened and growled. Rachel said, "Don't mind her, Luke. She's just getting a little crotchety."

"She must be very old."

"Yes, she's at least thirteen. I'm afraid this is one member of our family who won't be with us much longer."

Luke seemed stricken by that, or perhaps it was the sorrow he read in Rachel's eyes. "I'm sorry, Sister."

Rachel glanced up at him. "Sister? Is that how you address women where you come from?"

"Yes," he admitted, as if he'd been caught out. "We call each other Sister or Brother."

Rachel waited a few seconds, then, "Tell us about your home, Luke. I don't mean for you to tell us where it is. It's just that we'd like to know more about you."

He took another swallow of mead, then nodded decisively. "You have a right to know more, since you saved my life."

Mary met Rachel's eyes briefly, a glance that exchanged their recognition of a small step forward, while Luke pulled in a deep breath and said, "My home is about three miles from the ocean in a river valley. It's a small river, but the Doctor calls it the Jordan, and he calls our little valley Canaan. In the summer when the morning bell rings and the birds start singing, the mist comes up from the fields, and the hay smells so sweet . . . well, sometimes I think the Lord gave us a taste of heaven here on Earth."

Mary saw the shine of tears in his eyes, and she wanted to reach out and take his hand, so poignant was the silent cry of homesickness in his voice. She asked, "Can't you go back to your valley?"

"Yes, I can go back, and I will when I've done what I set out to do."

"What's that?"

The question seemed to put him on the defensive again. "I'll tell you about it . . . someday."

Rachel asked, "Is this a family farm where you live?"

"We're not all family, except we're all in the family of Christ."

"It's a religious commune?"

"I guess you could say that. We call our settlement the Ark, and just like Noah, the Doctor was warned by God in a vision."

"The Doctor? Who is he? Or is your doctor a woman?"

Luke laughed at that. "No, he's a man. He's my uncle. My father's brother. I was named for him."

"What kind of doctor is he?"

Luke seemed perplexed. "Well, he's a healer."

"Ah. Luke the beloved physician."

"Yes. He said it was his name that made him decide to be a doctor. He wanted to be a healer—to heal men's bodies first, then to heal their souls. He and my father grew up in Portland. The Doctor worked among the worst of sinners—drunkards and whores and thieves. He brought a lot of them around to Jesus. Until he had the vision."

Rachel asked without a hint of skepticism, "What kind of vision?"

"A vision from God. The Lord showed him Armageddon and told him it would come soon, said for him to take his loved ones and those who were truly reborn in Christ and find a place for them to live in His ways until Armageddon and until the Lord . . . comes to Earth again."

Mary was watching Luke's face, and with that last phrase she caught a shadow in his eyes that she might have called doubt if it had lasted longer.

Perhaps Rachel caught it, too. "Did the Doctor believe the second coming would follow the End—what he calls Armageddon?"

Luke bristled. "It says it will in the Book of Revelation." A hesitation while he eyed Rachel uncertainly. "You know that."

"I know the author of Revelation said that."

"Then it must be true."

"It depends on what you mean by *true*. Truth is not a simple thing. But you were telling us about the Ark. The Doctor found an ideal place for it, from the way you describe it."

Luke's angular features eased into a smile. "He did, and only the Lord could've led him to it. It was six years before Armageddon when the Flock came to Canaan Valley. I was nine then, and I remember the building of the Ark: cutting trees, sawing logs for the houses and barns, putting up the beams and walls, making the furniture—and all with our own hands and the tools we could use with them. We didn't use any machinery. The only things we had to buy were paint and nails, and we could've made the nails if we'd had the smithy finished."

Mary stared at him. "You have a smithy?"

"Well, we have the building and equipment, but Brother Peter died in the Long Winter, and he was the only one who knew blacksmithing. But two of the brothers are trying to learn it. It's in the Doctor's books."

Rachel asked, "Does the Doctor have many books?"

"Not nearly as many as you have here." He glanced uncomfortably into the shadows at the bookshelves.

"What kind of books does he have?"

"Books about healing and crops and livestock. And the teaching books for the children. They came from schools, mostly, from the city."

Rachel seemed on the verge of pursuing that further, then took a sip of mead. "You were telling us about the building of the Ark."

He regained his animation at that. "It was a wonderful thing to see, and they let us kids help where we could. Well, first we built the church with a tall steeple for the bell. The church is in the center, and the households are built in a big circle around it, all twelve of them."

"The Doctor has an eye for symbolic numbers," Rachel noted. "Does one family live in each household?"

"More or less, but the people who didn't have families, and later the Barrens, were divided up to live with the families. There were about eight to each household in the beginning."

"Then there were nearly a hundred people in the Flock?"

He nodded, staring into the fire. "There were ninety-five of us when we built the Ark, and a hundred and fourteen when Armageddon came. But after that . . ." He shook his head, and his eyes seemed to sink back in their deep sockets. "We didn't even know what had happened, not for two days afterward. I always thought . . . well, it seems like we should've *known.* But the day of Armageddon was just another sunny day, when we looked back on it. Hot for September, an east wind blowing. The smoke came on the wind and covered the whole sky. We thought it was just a bad forest fire, but the Doctor's radio went dead, so he and my father decided to go to . . . to the town south of us. They had the truck loaded up—"

Rachel cut in, a little startled, "The truck?"

"Yes. We just used it to go into town to trade vegetables and herbs for seed and lime and anything we couldn't make for ourselves. Anyway, it was two days after Armageddon when my father and the Doctor headed for town in the truck. When they got to the highway—"

Now it was Mary who interrupted him. "The truck started?"

Luke shrugged. "Sure it did. It was over twenty years old, but we kept it in good shape."

"Oh, then it was built before electronic ignitions." He gave her a puzzled look, but she didn't try to explain EMP, instead asked,

"What happened when your father and uncle reached the high-way?"

"Well, they didn't see any cars, but about a mile down the high-way they came onto a bunch of people—maybe twenty of them—walking south. The Doctor said they were like ghosts, all gray, their eyes dead, most of them sick or hurt. They told him they came from a place near Salem, and they'd seen the mushroom clouds over Salem and Portland before everything began burning. They said everywhere they'd been, they'd seen nothing but grief and death, and there were thousands of people like them, dying along the roads. Then one of them looked in the truck and saw the food, and they swarmed over it, clawing at each other like animals. That's when the Doctor and my father left the truck and headed for home. As soon as he got back, the Doctor called us to the church and told us Armageddon had come. I remember the way he shouted out the news. I've never seen such joy in a man's face. It was like he'd already looked on the countenance of God. And we thought . . ." Luke paused, frowning. "We thought we'd be leaving this world soon, that Jesus would come and lift us up to heaven. . . ."

In the ensuing silence Mary waited for Luke's conclusion, his explanation for what could only have been a monumental disap-pointment.

At length, he took a shaky breath. "But the Bible says a day is like a thousand years unto the Lord. The time that came after that—the Long Winter—the Doctor said it was another test God made of us."

"Is that what *you* think?" Rachel asked quietly.

He didn't look at her. "The Doctor said it was."

And Luke was not going to deny the Doctor. Yet Mary was sure now that what she read in his eyes *was* doubt, if not denial.

"It was a hard testing," he went on dully. "Turned bitter cold in just a week, and we lost all the crops still in the ground. Most of our livestock died, and there wasn't a single person in the Flock who wasn't sick at least once that winter. Mom was one of the first to go. The Doctor said she had pneumonia."

Mary looked at Rachel, remembering that dark and terrifying season. She said, "We had our own Long Winter here."

"Did you? Was it dark all the time, like dusk at noon?" Then at her nod, "I thought the darkness was . . . just at the Ark."

Mary managed not to laugh at the naiveté of that. "The darkness covered all the northern hemisphere and probably part of the southern."

Luke's jaw went slack. "How do you know that?"

"Because some scientists predicted the nuclear winter many years before the End."

"Scientists? They *predicted* . . . the Long Winter?"

Mary glanced at Rachel, but she remained silent. Mary said, "Yes, Luke, that's part of what science is about—understanding things well enough to predict what they'll do."

Luke seemed to consider that. But then he said, "So the Lord chose to further test everybody in the world."

"Just everybody in the northern hemisphere," Mary replied irritably. "At least, with nuclear winter. Economic and social collapse, along with Lassa and other epidemics—I guess you might call that a testing."

Luke nodded, recognizing none of her irony. "The Doctor said all the world would be destroyed at Armageddon."

"And yet we're still here—and so is the Ark."

"Yes. Those who survived are the chosen of Christ."

Mary was about to point out that the odds were high that most of the survivors in the world had never *heard* of Christ, but Rachel adroitly intervened. "Luke, how did the Flock survive the Long Winter?"

A frown settled in on his features again. "A lot of us didn't survive it. We made one of the households into a hospital, and it was always full. And with our fall crops and most of the livestock gone, we didn't have enough food. It was a time of dying, everybody wasting away, always too cold, too hungry, too sick, too burdened down with grieving. Before the thaw came, we buried seventy people. And five newborns. The babies—they were all born sick or dead, one of them so strange, its mother went crazy. Oh, Lord, I couldn't understand it! I couldn't understand *why*—" The sudden outburst was as suddenly cut off. He looked down at his hand clenched on the wineglass, relaxed it. "It was a hard testing, and if it wasn't for the Doctor leading us on through prayer and faith, *none* of us would be alive."

Mary rose and refilled his glass, as well as hers and Rachel's. She felt his grief, a leaden ache under her ribs, knew it as she did her own. Yet she was thinking how ironic it was, his grief and his gratitude for life, when he clearly believed in a better life after death, perhaps even believed in an imminent apotheosis. She sat down on the floor again, asked, "What about your father? Did he die in the Long Winter, too?"

Luke took a swallow of the mead. "This tastes like . . . when the women are making jam. No, my father didn't die that winter. It was in the Blind Summer. He and I were the only ones left of our family then. My sister and brother passed on in the winter, too. I thought it was over for us, the dying. Then one day my father was out plowing, and the horse got spooked. He went around to her head to talk to her, but she bolted. Trampled him to death."

Neither Rachel nor Mary broke the silence for a time. Finally Rachel said, "Blind Summer is an apt term. The scientists predicted that, too."

He turned, surprised. "They knew the sun would get hotter?"

"They knew the ultraviolet radiation would increase. The sun didn't change, Luke. Nothing happening on this little pebble whirling around it could affect the sun. Oh, Mary, remember the headgear we rigged for our animals? But the wild animals . . . when I think of the suffering humankind inflicted on those millions of creatures—we had no *right* to do that. We might choose to destroy ourselves, but we had no right to destroy so many other creatures."

Luke objected, "But Armageddon—it was the Lord who brought down the fire from heaven to punish the sins of men."

Rachel let her annoyance show. "Those fires didn't come from heaven. Human beings made those fires. I'd like to believe that any—that god is above all *just*. A just god wouldn't make the innocent suffer so hideously with the guilty." She waited, while Luke stared at her, doubt burning in his eyes, then she shook her head ruefully. "But I'm getting into theology again. Since you speak of the Ark in the present tense, I assume it survived. How many people live there now?"

His mental shift of gears was obvious. "How many? Well, there were fifty-three of us when I left."

Mary closed her eyes, and for a moment she felt dizzy. She was trying to imagine fifty-three human beings alive in one place. That was a *community*—a place where there was real hope for the future of humankind, a place where . . .

But Rachel seemed to take that revelation and its potentials in stride. "Then you've had some increase since the End."

"Yes. We took in eight people who found their way to the Ark during the Long Winter. The Doctor said we had to take them in, since they were good Christians, and the Lord had led them to the Ark."

Rachel nodded. "You said you lost seventy of your maximum of a hundred and fourteen in the winter, and I assume you've had some deaths since. How many *births* have you had in the last ten years?"

Luke didn't answer immediately, again on the defensive, and Mary wondered why it should bother him to admit what was obvious and inevitable, considering what these people had suffered.

Almost grudgingly, he said, "We've only had three babies live. The Doctor says the radiation made the women barren."

"And the men sterile," Rachel pointed out. "You said the day of the End was sunny with an east wind? You must've had more fallout from the Willamette Valley than we did. Well, at least some of your flock are still fertile. You seem to be multiplying and bearing fruit, even if it's slowly." She paused, as if waiting for Luke to comment on that, then when he didn't, she asked bluntly, "Are you one of the fertile males?"

His cheeks reddened, but he answered the question. "Yes, I am." He glanced fleetingly at Mary, and she felt within her an equivocal sensation that she identified as hope.

It is possible, and she wondered if that made it inevitable.

191

Rachel accepted Luke's disclosure with a nod. "In that case, I'm surprised you left the Ark. I'd think you'd be too valuable to the Flock."

Mary thought irritably that Rachel made him sound like a prize stud, but she said nothing, and at length Luke replied, "Yes, I guess I am . . . valuable, but I had to go."

"Why?"

"Well, to . . . to find out if there was anybody else left."

"Yes. We made a sojourn like that many years ago. We didn't find anyone. I understand the reason—the true reason—for *your* sojourn, Luke, but I'm surprised the Doctor or the elders let you leave the Ark."

"They let me go because—well, I had a vision. It came in a dream. The Lord told me to go out and find . . . other people. I told the Doctor and the—how did you know about the Elders?"

"You mean that the elders form a sort of ruling committee over which the Doctor presides?"

"Yes, that's true, but how did you know?"

Rachel might have told him that such a system of government was almost inevitable in the kind of community he described, but she only shrugged and asked, "Where did you go? And did you find anyone?"

"Yes," he said, smiling a little, fully aware of the power that single word wielded. "I'll tell you about my travels, if you'd like."

Mary looked up at Rachel, saw that she had apparently frozen with her glass only a few inches from her lips. *If you'd like.* How, after all these years, could they *not* like to hear about his travels if they included the discovery of other survivors. Mary asked perversely, "Aren't you getting awfully tired?"

He didn't expect that. "*No.* Really, I'm not."

For a moment he seemed as imploringly earnest as a child who didn't want to be put to bed. She rose to add more wood to the fire. "Yes, of *course* we'd like to hear about your travels."

He returned her smile, watching her as she sat down, drawing her knees up and folding her arms on them. Then he took a long breath, as if he were bracing himself, but not for an undesired ordeal. She had the feeling he'd been waiting a long time to tell this tale.

"Well, even after the Doctor and the Elders agreed that I should make the journey, it took a while to get ready, but the day finally came. I set out after morning service on the first of July with Amos, my mule, and headed south on the coast highway. I remember it was a clear day, and I . . . I'd never done anything before that seemed so right and good. There were times later I doubted that, but now . . ." He paused, blue eyes warm as he looked at Mary and Rachel. "Anyway, the first few days I passed a lot of little towns and didn't find a soul in any of them, but I wasn't discouraged. I knew the Lord was guiding me. Every evening I built a big beacon fire in case there was anybody around to see the smoke or the light."

Those words were a mnemonic snare, and Mary looked into the flames in the hearth and remembered another fire: the one that had burned in the fathomless darkness on Saddle Mountain.

Luke went on. "Sometimes I camped in empty houses along the highway, but most of the time I bedded down on the beach near my fire. In a couple of places the highway had slid out, and I couldn't walk on the beach for one reason or another, so I had to go around through the forest. I got myself good and lost once, but I just headed for the highest hill I could see and listened for the ocean."

Rachel asked, "Did you have maps?"

"The Doctor gave me some road maps. I still have one, but it's in tatters. Anyway, Amos and I kept going on down the coast, and one day I saw a sign on the road that said I was leaving Oregon. Gave me a funny feeling, like maybe I might never come back again. I stayed on Highway 101 to Crescent City, but it was in the middle of a big burn. You could hardly tell there'd ever been a town. So I headed on south for Eureka. I think—yes, it was along there I ran out of the burn and into the most beautiful forest and the biggest trees I've ever seen."

Rachel smiled at that. "The redwoods, no doubt."

He nodded eagerly. "Yes, that's right. I saw signs along the road that told about them. Well, I came out of those woods after a few days, passed through what was left of some towns along the way.

I wasn't too far north of Eureka when I thought I saw smoke in the hills to the east. I built a big fire that night, but a storm came in toward morning. Rain lasted three days. The fourth day I built another beacon fire, but I never saw even a breath of smoke." He paused, shook his head. "Maybe I didn't really see any smoke to begin with. Anyway, I went on to Eureka, and at first I couldn't figure out what happened to it. It was partly burned, but everything around the bay looked like it had been dynamited. Then I saw the mud. I guess there'd been a flood."

Rachel raised an eyebrow. "Of course there had. Nearly every town on the California coast was hit by tsunamis from the big quake."

"I don't know that word, soonaw . . . whatever."

She spelled it out for him. "It's a Japanese word. It refers to the waves triggered by earthquakes."

"Oh. When was this big quake?"

Mary blinked, and she was glad he was looking at Rachel, who was more successful at hiding her surprise as she responded. "The California quake? It was a few months before the End. April, wasn't it, Mary? It was the worst disaster in American history. The death toll was at least two million."

Luke was visibly staggered. "I don't remember anything about that," he said, nearly whispering.

Rachel studied him with a tolerant smile. "I think you've led a very insular life, Luke."

"Insular? There's another word I don't know."

"Well, it comes from the Latin for island. In this context, it means isolated, cut off."

"You know so many things. You're a very wise woman—just like my vision told me."

Rachel held her smile. "If I'm wise, it's because I've had wise teachers, the best from all the ages." Then at his puzzled frown: "The books, Luke. They're my teachers."

He nodded. "Like the Bible."

Rachel's smile slipped. "That's *one* book." Then she added:

"Other books are full of different kinds of wisdom. But I want to hear more about your journey."

He seemed distracted, as if he'd lost his place. Mary prompted, "You were talking about Eureka."

"Oh, yes. Well, I didn't find anybody there, so I kept going. South of Eureka, Highway 101 angled inland, and it was about there I counted off my first month. I had a walking stick, and I cut a notch in it every night. Didn't seem like I'd covered much ground for a month's travel, but it was slow going. I had to build my beacon fires, and that meant gathering wood, and I wasn't carrying much food, so I had to hunt or fish along the way. It wasn't long after I notched off that first month that I ran into another big burn, and as soon as I hit a main junction I decided to go east. I came to the end of the burn that way and found a lake. It was called Clear Lake, and it was beautiful with little houses on the shore. I was sure somebody must still live there, but I didn't see a sign of smoke. I stayed awhile to fish and hunt and dry the meat. Good thing, too." He gazed into the fire, but he was seeing something else that even in memory stunned him.

"Once, before Armageddon, the Doctor went to Sacramento. He told me about the huge farms and orchards. I figured when I headed east into the big valley, I was bound to find people. But that place . . . it had changed since the Doctor saw it. It had turned into a desert. To the north and east, that's all I could see: dry, brown desert. To the south there'd been fires. I went half a day south and never came out of the burn, so I figured there was no use going any farther that way."

Rachel asked, "How far were you from Sacramento?"

"As I remember, it was maybe fifty miles down I-5. That's how the highway was marked on my map."

"Sacramento had probably been bombed. You were close enough to be in the firestorm zone."

"Firestorm?"

"From the nuclear bombs."

"Is that what caused the desert?"

"No, that was probably caused by the nuclear winter—the cold would be far worse inland than it was on the coast—and what you call the Blind Summer. The plants were killed, Luke, and that left the land bare to erosion. Weren't there any plants at all?"

"Nothing but sagebrush and dried-up grass. There wasn't any water. Thank the Lord, I'd filled up my canteens at Clear Lake. It was days before Amos and I found a creek with a little muddy water in it." He stopped, staring again into bleak memory. "In that place, I could believe—I mean, there was no way to doubt what the Doctor said about Armageddon. The world had come to an end there."

"Yet you said there were plants," Rachel interjected. "Where there are plants, there'll be animals. You could say the world had *changed* there, but not that it had ended."

Luke didn't seem to know how to respond to that. Mary took a swallow of her mead, again prompted him. "What happened after you found the creek?"

"Well, I kept on north on the highway. Finally I came to Red Bluff. Just acres of ruins, the sand piling in the windows, but there was a river running though it, and along the banks there were big trees with their bark peeling off, but they were green and seemed healthy otherwise. There were willows and cattails, and even some ducks and rabbits. And fish in the river. I camped there, stocking up on meat, about four days. I saw a big, snowcapped mountain to the north with smoke coming out of one peak." He laughed bitterly. "At first I thought somebody was living up there, but there was too much smoke to be made by people. Besides, nobody could live on top of a mountain that high."

"That was probably Mount Lassen," Rachel said. "It's a volcano. It must've been going into an active phase. Did you see Shasta? It would be farther north."

He shrugged. "I remember a town called Mount Shasta. That was past Redding. All the towns along there were in ruins. But after that I ran into patches of forest, and it was easier going. At least, there was more water. I went through two more big burns going into the Siskyou Mountains, but when I finally got to the Oregon line, I was in green forest, and dear Lord, it was beautiful. Just over the line, I camped at a place called the Siskyou Summit.

There was still a sign there. I made another beacon fire. I was so tired, so discouraged, but I figured since there was live forest here, this would be a good place to find people. And I did. I mean, they found me."

Mary felt her heart take a double beat; she leaned toward Luke as if by getting closer she could have his answer sooner. "*Who* found you?"

In the strained set of his jaw was something on the edge of hatred, and when he spoke, it echoed coldly in his voice. "It was Amos hee-hawing that woke me up, and when I looked around, I saw maybe ten men, all carrying rifles or shotguns. They had beards and wore clothes with a funny pattern—different shades of green blotches."

Mary said absently, "Camouflage suits."

"Survivalists," Rachel added.

Luke sighed, his anger waning. "I never did find out what they called themselves. I guess one of them hit me on the head. When I woke up, I was in a little room that was mostly underground with nothing in it but a cot and a chamber pot and one small window high up. All I could see was a bare yard and a metal fence with barbed wire on top. People walked by once in a while, and I hollered at them, but they just went on like they didn't hear, except one old man. He squatted down by my window and talked to me. Told me there were a thousand people in the settlement—he called it a compound—but the next thing he said was they had ten tanks fueled up and ready to roll. There couldn't have been that many people in what I saw of the place later, and I sure never saw a tank. They had a lot of guns, though. I asked him if he believed in God and Jesus Christ, and he got mad, said *he* did, but he knew *I* didn't. Then he asked why I spoke American if I was a Russian. About then, two men came in and took me out into a big room. There was a table there with a man sitting behind it and an empty chair in front of it. That's where they made me sit. The man at the table was in charge. Tall man with white hair and a long beard. Looked like a prophet. The others called him *sir*, but none of them used names. He said I was a spy, and he wanted to know where I came

197

from. Well, I wasn't about to tell him. I figured he'd likely as not send men with guns—or tanks, for all I knew then—over to Canaan Valley. He kept asking me questions, but I wouldn't answer, and finally the other men . . . they started trying to beat the answers out of me."

Mary winced. "Is that how you got the scars on your back?"

"The scars . . ." He seemed surprised, then his eyes flicked down. "I . . . got a few scars from that place. Well, they put me back in my room, and I saw they'd boarded up the window. That was before the door closed. After that, I couldn't see anything. I don't know how many days I was there or how many times they brought me out to ask me questions. The only other thing that happened was now and then somebody came in with food and water."

His tone was flat, emotionless, yet Mary felt an intangible electric link spanning the small distance between them, felt her mind opened, if only briefly, to his mind and to endless hours of dark terror. She said, "I don't know how you kept your sanity."

Luke looked at her and caught his breath. Then he turned away. "Well, I prayed a lot. Talked to Jesus like He was right there in the room with me. Maybe He was. Finally one day the head man came in. I called him Prophet Lucifer. . . ." Luke stopped, frowning. "You know, the funny thing is, he looked a lot like the Doctor. Anyway, he said he'd decided maybe I wasn't a spy after all, and he was going to let me go. He led me outside, and that was the only chance I had to see the settlement. There were five big buildings, all half-underground, built of cement blocks. This was in a valley, and in the distance I could see barns and fields. Maybe thirty people were gathered, even a few women and a couple of children, and there were two or three big dogs. They looked kind of like Aggie."

Mary stroked Agate's shaggy back. "German shepherds, probably."

"I guess so. Then the prophet gave me my rifle and pointed to a backpack, said my things were in there, along with some pemmican and jerky. I asked about Amos, but he said, 'We need the mule.' I didn't argue. I just hope they took care of ol' Amos. The prophet led me to the main gate. There was a road leading up out of the valley, and I took off at a trot. I must've been a mile away before it came to me *why* he let me go. He figured I'd head for home, and he could track me and find out where I came from. I climbed a hill above the road, and sure enough, after a while I saw two men and a dog coming my way. I headed north into the woods, trying to figure out how to get free of them. About sundown, I made camp. Once, I heard the dog bark in the distance. The next day I kept going till evening, when I came to a little lake. Well, that's what I'd been looking for, that or a river. The dog couldn't track me into water. Late that night I swam across the lake. Used a log to float my pack. Cold!" He laughed ruefully. "Dear Lord, that water was cold. When I left the lake, I walked up a creek maybe a quarter of a mile so the dog couldn't pick up my scent where I came out of the lake, then I climbed up on the bank and rested till sunup. When I had enough light, I set off through the woods till I came to a highway and headed east on it. Must've been three days later when I came on another lake, and I was so tired and hungry by then, I had to stop. Caught some fish and lit a fire to cook them. First fire I made since I left that settlement. I found a limb for a new walking stick—the prophet kept my old one— and I cut my first notch in it. I wonder what happened to it. Must've dropped it while I was sick. Anyway, I guess I outfoxed those men. Never saw them or the dog again."

Mary sighed, looking at Luke in amazement. Then she realized that Rachel was watching her, and Mary found her knowing regard unnerving. She asked Luke, "Where were you by then?"

He took a swallow of mead. "I didn't find out till a couple of days later when I came to a junction with some road signs. I was on the west side of Upper Klamath Lake, according to my map. Most of the lake had dried up, but there was still some water and fish. I built my first beacon fire since I was captured, but I slept a good ways from it. Well, I knew if I was going over to the east side of the Cascades, I had to do it then. I didn't know how much time I'd lost, but the vine maples had turned, and it was cold at night.

So, I went north to Crater Lake. It was a wonderful, strange place. The color of the water . . . I couldn't describe it."

Rachel nodded. "You don't have to. I've been there. Crater Lake is one of the sacred places of the Earth. Was it . . . changed?"

"Well, I don't see how it *could* change."

Rachel smiled at that. "Where did you go from there?"

"East till I came down out of the Cascades, then north toward Bend." Again, his eyes were haunted by disquieting memories. "It was another desert. I guess it always was dry over there, but this was blowing dust and dead pine trees sticking up out of the dunes, and I nearly died for lack of water before I reached Bend. The town was burned out, but there was a river there. I stayed for a while to lay in food, and every night I burned a beacon fire, but I never saw any smoke. Didn't expect to, really. Finally I decided I'd better get back across the mountains before winter set in, so I headed west and came to what was left of a town called Sisters. There'd been forest fires through there and to the north, so I took the south fork of the road west of town. The ground was already covered with snow, but the weather stayed good, and I got over the pass. The highway followed a river, so I had fish and water for a while, but after a couple of days I ran into another burn. I never got out of it till after I left Eugene."

Rachel asked anxiously, "Was there anything left of Eugene? The university? The library?"

"Nothing in the whole city. Everything had been burned."

Rachel let her breath out wearily. "Probably firestorm from the bombs that hit Salem."

"Must've been. Anyway, I realized then that I had a better chance of finding somebody alive on the coast than anywhere inland. It was a long way round and a long time traveling for me to come to that."

Mary's eyes were burning. "Yes, we came to the same conclusion. But we didn't find anyone."

"I did."

She stared at him. "You found someone *else?*"

"Yes." He shifted, stretching one arm along the back of the

couch. "Two days west of Eugene, I stopped to camp, and I was laying out my bedroll when I saw two men standing by the fire. Lord help me, I had my rifle up ready to shoot before I even thought about it. That's what those people in the Siskyous taught me. But I didn't shoot. I went over to them and saw they were both old. At least, they looked old. I never did know how old any of them really were."

"Any of them?" Rachel asked sharply. "How many *were* there?"

"Six, altogether. Three couples, husbands and wives. They lived on a farm south of the road. Before Armageddon they lived near Eugene. They were neighbors, and they stayed together when they ran away after the fires came down on the city. There'd been sixteen to begin with. The three couples, eight children, and Martin's mother and aunt. All the children and the two elder sisters died in the Long Winter, and no babies had been born since. They were all weak and half-sick, and I think they'd given up caring about anything. They didn't even seem to care much about living. One of the women—her name was Ann, and I've never known a kinder woman—she said to me, 'To every thing there is a time.' Quoted me the verses from Ecclesiastes. She said that's the way it is with life. You have to take what comes. I asked her if she believed in God and Jesus Christ, and she said . . . it didn't make any difference." Luke shook his head, bewildered still. "They were so good to me, so peaceable. But I didn't understand their peace. Not one of them ever prayed; they never had services. Martin said once if God could let Armageddon happen, he didn't see any reason to praise Him."

Rachel asked, "How did you answer that?"

"Well, it was hard to answer. I mean, when I was with those people . . ." He pulled his shoulders up and back in an unconscious gesture Mary had noticed before. "I told Martin that Armageddon was part of God's plan, that it meant the Second Coming. But he just smiled and went on with his work. They asked me if I wanted to stay the winter. It was the middle of December, and walking day after day in rain or snow didn't sound so good. Besides, I knew they could use some help with the farm. So I stayed. For seventy-two days. I notched my stick every night. Two weeks before I left, Ann died. She . . . had a lot of pain. I helped dig her grave, and I was the only one who prayed for her, though I know the others grieved for her. I decided I had to leave; I had to keep searching. Martin told me he'd once seen smoke in the hills farther south, so I figured I'd better go see what I could find that way. Well, I wandered those hills for a couple of weeks and didn't find any sign of people, so finally I decided to head for the coast again. The rain set in about then, and it seemed like I could never get dry or warm. I reached the coast at a town called Reedsport, but it was just like all the other towns I'd come across—half-burned, all grown over with weeds. Nobody there. By then I wasn't feeling good, but I didn't stop. The Lord was still guiding me, but my body wasn't up to His guiding. I don't remember much of the last few days. I just knew I had to keep going north. I didn't know why." He smiled, first at Rachel, than at Mary. "I've been gone from the Ark for nine months and walked over a thousand miles, and I saw nothing but desolation. The only people I found—well, in their own ways, they were crazy. But now I understand: this was God's testing of me. He meant for me to finally come here."

The fire had burned down to flame-licked coals, and its gilded light drew them together in a span of warm silence. At length, Rachel said, "A remarkable journey, Luke. Thank you for sharing it with us. But I think it deserves sharing with others, too."

Luke stared at her. "What others?"

Rachel didn't answer that. She rose, went to the mantel for one of the candles, lighted it in the coals of the fire, and took it with her when she left the room. "I'll be right back."

The dogs and cats stretched themselves, and Mary started to rise, but her right leg responded with a spasm of cramping. "Damn, I've been sitting still too long." She looked up to find Luke standing above her, hands extended.

"Let me help you, Mary."

She surrendered her hands to his and let him pull her to her feet. And why, she wondered, should that leave her trembling like a silly adolescent? She flexed her leg to restore the circulation. "You must be exhausted, Luke."

He laughed. "Don't worry about me, Sister."

"I *won't* worry about you anymore—not after hearing that story."

"It's the story," Rachel said as she returned, "that you must get down in writing." She handed him one of her small, bound sketchbooks. He opened it, but couldn't seem to make sense of the blank pages.

"There's nothing *in* this book."

"Not yet. Luke, you must put your story in it. I have a good supply of India ink, and you can use my pens."

He still frowned at the book. "I . . . I wouldn't know what to say."

"You said it for Mary and me."

"Yes, but that was just talking."

"Then write it as if you were just talking."

"But why do you want me to write it down? If anybody wants to hear it, I can *tell* it to them."

"Not after you're dead," Rachel replied flatly. "Luke, your story is important to your people and your children and *their* children, to let them know what the part of the world you saw was like. If nothing else, it will warn them to stay away from the Siskyou Mountains."

He laughed at that, then, "Well . . . maybe I *could* write it, like you said, as if I was talking to somebody, but you'll have to help me."

She smiled. "Of course."

Luke turned, sought in the shadows for the books on the shelves. "Did anybody else ever write anything like this?"

Rachel took up the poker and began teasing the coals of the fire together. "Thousands of people have, Luke. I don't know offhand what I have here." She straightened. "Well, I do have a facsimile edition of the diary of William Clark. I'll find it tomorrow."

"Who's William Clark?"

"Half of Lewis and Clark." Then when he still looked blankly at her: "Lewis and Clark were nineteenth-century explorers." She finished banking the fire and turned the damper. "And now I'll say good night. Morning comes early. Come on, Shadow." She lifted the dog and put her down on the floor, then departed, the candle lighting her way, Shadow limping behind her.

Mary felt an uncertain tension, standing in the near darkness with Luke. She was sharply aware of the difference in his smell and hers or Rachel's. She had long ago learned to accept the natural odors of their bodies, and she didn't find Luke's offensive. Only different.

She turned and lighted two more candles, handed him one. "Here, you'll need some light."

"Thanks. Mary, I know I'm sleeping in your room. Let me sleep here on the couch tonight. I'm well enough now."

She smiled, but shook her head. "You still need another good night's sleep. Go on, now."

He shrugged, started to walk away, then looked back at her. The words came hesitantly: "Do you understand why I'm here? I mean, what I left the Ark to search for?"

She did, although it was only at this moment that she recognized it, and she chose not to acknowledge it. There were potentials there she couldn't deal with yet. "It's late, Luke. We'll talk about it another time."

He nodded, moved away in a circle of golden candlelight. "Good night, Mary Hope."

"Good night, Luke Jason. Sleep well."

When she heard the bedroom door close, Mary stood motionless in the dim silence, feeling the beat of her pulse, and again she wanted to cry and didn't know why. Changes. She was only now beginning to sense their dimensions.

She went to the greenhouse door and saw the light behind the glass door that opened into Rachel's room. She crossed the greenhouse in the silver-blue moonlight and slid the door open, saw Rachel in her narrow bed, propped up with pillows, a book open in her lap, an oil light burning on the table. Shadow lay beside her.

Mary sat down on the end of the bed. "That was quite a story."

Rachel nodded. "The stuff of epics. Think how quickly we've sunk back to a time when a journey of a thousand miles is an epic."

"Sometimes I wonder . . ."

"What, Mary?"

Mary shrugged, not sure what she was trying to say. "A thousand miles, and the only human beings he found were a few survivalists and a handful of dying victims." Luke called them all crazy, and she could accept that of the survivalists. But the others . . . They weren't crazy. They were only hopeless. Without hope. Without children.

Rachel said, "That thousand miles covered a very small fraction of the world."

"But that fraction *is* our world now. The rest is terra incognita for us and always will be."

Except for the Ark.

Mary felt her mind full of cobwebs, squeezed her eyes shut to look for a way through them. Finally she said, "Rachel, I know what Luke's mission is. The Ark is dying; not enough women are capable of bearing children, so he went out to find women like me—potentially fertile." She opened her eyes, but couldn't look at Rachel. "That's his mission, and he's made it . . . mine. He's made it possible. . . ." But the words got tangled in the cobwebs. She hadn't had time to think out the implications for her in the Ark, in fifty-three people living in a community.

She had recognized that she had an obligation, now that Luke made it possible, to bear children. Yet until he told them about the Ark, she hadn't faced the fact that to bear a child here at Amarna would be futile. Here that child would grow up in solitude, condemned to live a life of savage loneliness, to die leaving nothing behind but its bones.

If that child were to become something other than a sterile end in itself, it must have a community. *Community* was a concept integral to civilization and humanity. Whatever her doubts about the Ark, it was a community, and now she knew beyond a hope that it was the only one she would ever encounter.

Her throat ached with the words: "Rachel, if I go to the Ark, will you go with me?"

Rachel answered without hesitation. "No. Not until I've finished with the books. That's *my* part in humankind's future, Mary."

Mary saw the equivocal sadness behind Rachel's fragile smile and shivered as if a chill wind had brushed the skin at the back of her neck.

"Mary, the decision is yours," Rachel said. "I can't help you with it."

Yes, it was hers, and it had already been made. Yet it didn't seem a decision. There was no choice in it.

She watched the wavering candle flame. "Strange, isn't it? A man who insists Armageddon has already happened, that the second coming of Jesus—the end of life in this world for all good Christians—is *about* to happen, yet he worries about begetting a new generation. I don't think he really believes that Armageddon nonsense."

"The problem is, he thinks he *should* believe it."

Mary wasn't sure what Rachel meant by that, but she didn't want to talk about it now. What Luke believed, or thought he should, didn't matter. She had no choice.

She rose, leaned down to kiss Rachel's cheek. "Past our bedtime. By the way, that was a clever ploy, conning Luke into writing his memoirs. You'll make an author of him, and I've never met an author who didn't have a great respect for books."

"Well, it did occur to me that the act of writing might change his attitude a bit. And you're the one who should help him with it. You're the writer here."

Mary thought about that, tried to remember when she'd had that sure sense of herself as a writer. She couldn't recapture it. "Good night, Rachel." She crossed to the sliding door, opened it, and looked back to see Rachel in the amber light, and in Mary's eyes she suddenly seemed small and vulnerable.

"Good night, Mary."

No. Rachel was too resourceful ever to be lonely.

Ah, my Beloved, fill the Cup that clears
Today of past Regrets and future Fears. . . .
  —EDWARD FITZGERALD, *THE RUBAIYAT OF OMAR KHAYYAM*
                                                    (1879)

We may insist as often as we like that man's intellect is powerless in
comparison with his instinctual life and we may be right in this.
        —SIGMUND FREUD, *THE FUTURE OF AN ILLUSION* (1927)

And that spring, Luke *courted* me."
    Stephen looks at me curiously. All he knows of courtship
is garnered from books he's read. On this clear April afternoon,
we're outside on the deck, a limber-limbed boy sitting with his legs
drawn up, arms wrapped around one knee, and an old woman ab-
sorbing the warmth of the sun on ever-aching joints and talking
about her youth, about courtship.

Such an ancient ceremony, courtship. Homo sapiens was born
with the rituals encoded in its genes, rituals as old as bisexual reproduction. I laugh, imagining trilobites wooing their mates with

207

skittering minuets in the deeps of the sea; brontosauri circling one another in ponderous sarabands; smiladon yowling arias to show off his scimitar fangs.

Stephen asks, "What did Luke do to court you?"

I study him, wondering if his generation won't invent some sort of courtship rituals, even if their pairings are determined by necessity.

"Luke produced prodigies of labor that spring, Stephen. He looked at the pigpen and said, 'You and Rachel built this.' " And I try to imitate his indulgent tone. Stephen laughs, probably because to him I sound like Jerry. "I admitted as much, and Luke said, 'I'll build you a new one.' And so he did. The saws and axes needed sharpening? Our plow and harness needed repair? The roof of the barn was leaking? The gateposts had rotted? The apple trees needed pruning? And our smokehouse . . . had we also built that? He would take care of it. And so he did."

Still laughing, Stephen asks, "What did *you* do?"

"What *could* I do but . . . love him?"

In that halcyon spring Luke was easy to love. He was as powerful and graceful as a rutting buck, as solicitous as a bowerbird. He was easy to love because he tried in every way to please me. He couldn't, not in every way, not a man of his philosophical mold. But he tried. And he tried to please Rachel. He had to please her in order to please me, and he understood that. But he *wanted* to please Rachel, as a child wants to please its parents, a student its teacher, an acolyte its master.

Stephen rouses me from my memories. "Did Luke write the story of his journey?"

"Oh, yes. Jeremiah has it now. Maybe he'd let you read it. It was an arduous process, the writing of that story, but Luke took great pride in it. And Rachel inspired him to read books other than the Bible and to listen to ideas that were new to him. She told him a myth is the essence of an event. She told him to read between the lines and finally applied that principle to Genesis. She showed him glimpses of the universe."

Glimpses. That's all he'd open his eyes to see, but I thought he understood what little he saw, and I thought he understood the significance of the books and the importance of building a place to house and protect them.

"Mary, how long did the courting last?"

"About three months, actually. It was odd about that courtship. It was tacit. He couldn't seem to work up his courage to actually say he wanted me to go back to the Ark with him."

"Maybe he was afraid you wouldn't go with him."

My laugh at that has a bitter edge. "I wouldn't have refused him. I had no choice. And I kept wondering why he didn't understand that. Why he wouldn't *ask*." Then I shrug. "But I'd have done the asking if necessary. In fact, it made no difference whether I loved him or not. That only made it easier to accept what I had to do."

But I *did* love him.

Rather, I was *in* love with him, and I doubt Stephen will ever understand that. My happiness hung on Luke's smile. Yet at times I was angered almost past tolerance because he couldn't fulfill all my expectations. I spun dizzily on a silken filament, and he was at the center of the web always.

I pull in a deep breath. "But perhaps I did, unconsciously, restrain him from the asking. That was because I wanted one final proof of his intentions."

"What was that?"

"The vault, Stephen. I wanted the vault built."

Stephen looks north toward the Knob. "Was that for Rachel?"

A perceptive question. "Partly, yes. But it was for me, too, not only because I believed fervently that the vault must be built, but because it seemed the ultimate test of his love."

Stephen stretches his legs out, crosses his ankles. "I guess he must've passed the test."

"Yes. Rachel and I helped, but the vault was really Luke's project. Rachel drew the plans the last week of May, and we chose the site. The drainage is good on the Knob, and it's highly visible. It gets the brunt of the winter storms, but that slope also gets sun all year long. The actual building began on the first day of June. Luke dug an excavation into the hillside, then he scavenged brick and stone from Shiloh. He used the stone for the walls and lined them and the floor with brick. Fortunately we'd stockpiled some sacks of mortar. He felled a cedar tree and split it into beams and planks for the roof and inside walls. He made the door of cedar and found brass hinges and a stainless steel chain and lock. He covered the roof with composition shingles three layers thick, added another layer of cedar shingles. Oh, it's a work of art in its own way, Stephen. A labor of love. It took him most of the summer to construct this Taj Majal."

At that, Stephen tilts his head quizzically. "This what, Mary?"

"The Taj Majal was a very famous building Before." And I wonder if it's still standing. Is it a vine-smothered ruin that may someday be disinterred as Angkor Wat and Chichén Itzá were and might be again?

Stephen is waiting patiently for me to get on with my story. But what can I tell him about the culmination of Luke's courtship? He wouldn't understand it, and it's none of his business or anyone else's. It belongs to me alone now, the memory, and it will die with me.

I tell him simply, "It was in June, on the summer solstice, when Luke finally asked me to be his wife. I accepted."

In its essence, the delight of sexual love, the genetic spasm, is a sensation of resurrection, of renewing our life in another, for only in others can we renew our life and so perpetuate ourselves.
—MIGUEL DE UNAMUNO, *THE TRAGIC SENSE OF LIFE* (1913)

L uke reached the end of the path ahead of her, looked back, grinning exuberantly. The sky floated a skim of cloud as subtle as the interior of a shell, the summer-tamed waves frothed beyond the velvet sand, and Mary laughed as she ran with him toward the breakers, chisels rattling in their buckets, sand flying around their feet until they reached the dark, wet sand vacated by the tide. They walked north toward the Knob, laying strings of foot tracks over the convoluted tracks of flowing water, and Mary told him about a similar day not so long ago when she had started for the Knob with her chisel and bucket and found a stranger on the beach. Luke nodded and took her hand in his.

At the base of the cliffs on the seaward side of the Knob, the ebbing tide had exposed rock terraces paved with tiny barnacles, a brittle mosaic that wheezed under their boots. In sea-scoured hollows, small, mysterious worlds shimmered beneath aquamarine water—worlds of roseate brocades, peridot swatches, yellow-gold spikes, where sinuous green silks glowed iridescent blue when the light struck at the right angle, and sea anemones opened into exotic blossoms of pale green and pink. The terraces were transected by fissures carved by the knife of the sea, and on their honed faces, mussels crowded, tufted mats of hissing, shining blue-black shells. Mary and Luke filled their buckets with seawater and set to work, carefully prying the mussels off the rock with their chisels.

Within half an hour the tide began to turn, rising into the fissures, draining away, but returning again in the long, constant rhythms of the sea. Mary worked methodically back from the encroaching water, taking only a few mussels from any one area, always leaving the largest to live and breed. The memory of the time when these rocks were barren of life gave her a profound respect for this profusion.

When at length, the tidal surges served warning that the sea was reclaiming its own in earnest, Mary and Luke walked up the slope of the beach until they found a satin-backed log to rest on. Mary put her bucket down next to Luke's, assessing their harvest and calling it good, then sat beside him, while he delved into his shirt pocket and pulled out a cloth-wrapped package of venison jerky. He offered her a piece, but she shook her head. "I'm too thirsty for that. You didn't happen to bring a canteen, did you?"

He motioned southward. "It's down there—the creek."

For a while they didn't speak, and Mary cherished the tranquil silence as she watched the sea slowly flood the sand. Gulls wheeled restlessly, flying so high they were almost invisible. The weather would change soon.

Luke wrapped the remaining jerky and put it back in his pocket.

"Rachel always has a different way of looking at things, doesn't she?"

Mary felt the tranquillity shiver like the water in a tide pool ruffled by a wind. "Different from what?"

He shrugged. "Different from anything I've ever known."

"Did you expect her to look at things the way *you* were taught?"

That surprised him, and Mary felt an acid rush of annoyance. So much surprised him.

"No," he said hesitantly, "I guess I shouldn't expect her to look at things the way I do, but I've never known any other way."

Mary knew her annoyance was only another of the irrational emotional swings she'd been experiencing lately. But she didn't want to talk now. She simply wanted to sit here in the sun on this perfect day and watch the tide come in. With Luke. With Luke who was at his core kind and generous. With Luke whom she loved. She didn't want to probe the philosophical chasm that she knew would always exist between them.

He said, "I was thinking about what Rachel said last night, about the Book of Revelation."

Mary winced, stared fixedly at the breakers. So think about it. Fine. Just don't *talk* about it.

"Remember," Luke went on, inexorably, "what she said about the beast—the number of the beast—that maybe it was a code the first Christians used? I didn't know that."

There was so much he didn't know, even about the one book he considered the fount of wisdom. Mary watched the erratic circling of the gulls, held on to her silence, tension knotting hard under her ribs.

"And what she said," Luke added, "about prophesying the end of the world. Remember? She said to prophesy the end of a *human* world—the end of a civilization—was to prophesy the inevitable. But I still . . . I mean, it isn't the same, what Saint John was prophesying."

Mary had read the Book of Revelation last night out of curiosity, and above all she didn't want to talk about John the Divine's fren-

zied visions. She had sensed too much method in the saint's madness.

But Luke wanted to talk about it, and her silence didn't deter
him.

"It wasn't just the end of a civilization he was prophesying. It
was . . . well, it was more than that. The battle of light and dark,
good and evil. I think she's right: Saint John *was* writing in codes.
But he *saw* what was coming, way back then. The Lord showed
him Armageddon."

And Mary's patience snapped at the end of its tether.

"Luke, he didn't *see* anything! He wrote what he *wished* would
happen, what he knew the faithful *wanted* to hear."

Luke stared at her, aghast. "Don't *say* that!"

"Why not? It was a piece of fiction—nothing more!"

"No!" And his open hand cracked against her cheek, knocked
her off balance. She caught herself with her hands in the sand, her
face stinging, and it was a moment before she could make sense of
what had happened.

Stupid, she thought, and the appellation was directed at herself.
Why can't you learn patience?

And yet—

"Damn you, Luke!" Anger overwhelmed regret suddenly and
forcibly, and she felt her lips draw back from her teeth, saw him
kneeling in the sand before her, reaching out to her.

"Mary, I'm sorry! Lord help me, I didn't mean—"

"Let me go!" She tried to pull free, but his grip on her arms only
tightened with her struggles, and her frustration fed her anger, until
finally she began crying, and then she knew that was what she
wanted—tears to wash away the poisons of doubt and fear, and
Luke to hold her in the comforting cage of his arms against his
chest, where she might hear his heartbeat while he said softly, over
and over, "Mary, I didn't mean to hurt you. Mary, I love you . . .
I love you. . . ."

And what she wanted was his kiss; a kiss to taste her tears, one
for each closed eye, a kiss on her lips.

There was the catalyst, and out of it would come all the answers.

She opened her lips, her arms moving around the curve of his ribs, hands reaching down the long muscles of his back, and she reveled in the unleashed shivering of nerves in her own body.

Give me this covenant, this promise.

It didn't matter that he was impatient and inept, that the voracity of his ardor, once catalyzed, left no room for sensibility. He kissed her throat as if seeking the pulse of life there, opened her shirt to find her breasts with his lips, fumbled at her clothes and his as if they were insurmountable barriers, and perhaps he realized that she expected more than consenting rape, but he knew no art in this. And it didn't matter.

It didn't matter that he took her thoughtlessly, suddenly, that he left her nothing to savor but the sheer power of his body, that he forced himself into her against instinctive spasms of muscles and bludgeoned down that resistance by brute force. It didn't matter, because she wanted him, at any price, here within her body; she wanted that wordless covenant more than she had ever wanted anything in her life.

Mary lay with her head in the crook of Luke's arm, feeling the weight of his hand at rest on her breast, the cool wind playing a tactile fugue with the warmth of the sun on her naked skin. This she would want to remember, this warm, sated moment unshadowed by doubt.

At length, Luke stirred, propped himself on one elbow, leaned over her, kissed her, openmouthed, and when he drew away, she brushed at the sand caught in his sun-haloed beard, compared the color of his eyes to the blue of the sky behind him. He said, "Mary Hope, I love you," and she closed her eyes, believing him.

Then he sat up, laughing as he combed through his hair with both hands. "We'll never get rid of all this sand."

"Yes, we will—come on!" Mary rose and ran toward the ocean, feeling young and joyous. Luke followed her, and hand in hand they plunged into the breakers, laughing at the shock of the icy water, dancing like children in the white foam. Finally, shivering and exhilarated, they returned to the log, let the sun and wind dry their bodies, then dressed themselves and sat together in a pendant silence. Mary turned her face up to the sun and tried to hold on to this fragment of time.

Finally Luke said soberly, "Mary, I didn't leave the Ark just to find survivors. I went in search of . . . women who can bear children."

She felt her smile slipping away like the moment, like a golden nugget in a mountain creek, swept out of her hand by the swift current.

"I know, Luke. And you found me."

"The Lord led me to you. I didn't expect to find a woman I could care for. I only hoped to find . . ."

A brood mother, no doubt. He couldn't seem to finish that. She waited, and at length he said, "Mary, I want you to be my wife."

She nodded. "I *will* be your wife, Luke."

"But there are some . . . customs at the Ark you must understand."

She studied his face, watched him frowning over his choice of words. He said, "You have to understand that there aren't many of us who can . . . bear or father children."

"But you've fathered children, haven't you?"

"Yes. One. The Doctor keeps records of visitations, so he knows who fathers each child."

"What's a visitation? Intercourse?"

His fair skin reddened. "Yes."

"Were you married to the mother of the child you fathered? Was it one of the children who lived?"

He smiled fondly. "Yes, he lived. Jeremiah is his name, and he was born a month before I left the Ark. But I wasn't married to his mother. The child was fathered on a visitation. She's a widow. She lives in her uncle's household, and he serves as true father to the boy."

Mary pushed the toe of her boot into the sand. "Is *any* widowed or unmarried woman subject to these . . . visitations?"

"Yes, except the ones the Doctor knows are Barrens."

"What about married women?"

"If a woman's husband can't father children, yes." He looked at her anxiously. "But you'll never have visitations—not as *my* wife."

"But you'll be making visitations."

"Yes."

Mary shrugged. It was a highly adaptive arrangement. Still, she was relieved that she would be exempt from visitations by other men.

"Luke, how does the Flock resolve this mate-swapping with their religious beliefs? As I remember, Jesus had definite ideas about the sanctity of marriage."

He stiffened, then said levelly, "In Romans, Saint Paul wrote that we are dead to the law, and that we must bring forth fruit unto the Lord. The Doctor says if we're to bring forth fruit, we have to do it this way. He said we *must* bring new souls into the world for the Lord on Judgment Day."

So that was how the Arkites rationalized the need to procreate in the face of Armageddon. Yet Luke still doubted. She knew if she questioned him, he would deny his doubt, but she heard it in his voice.

He went on firmly, "Our ways are not the old ways before Armageddon, Mary. But there is neither love nor lust in a visitation, and the vows of marriage are still sacred."

That sounded like a direct quote.

Mary said softly, "Till death us do part."

"Yes. Till death us do part. Mary, we must talk to Rachel. She'll come with us. You'd never be happy without her, and she can't stay here alone."

Mary shook her head, and there was a chill in the wind now. "Rachel won't go to the Ark with us, Luke."

"But she *must*. I know the Flock will accept her. The Doctor will see her wisdom as I have. She'll be revered there, she'll be cared for. Mary, she's an old woman, and she can't—"

"She's *not* old, Luke! She's not . . . old."

Luke put his arm around her. "I know what you mean, but . . . well, she's not really young."

217

Mary let his arm rest on her shoulders without recognizing its existence. "You don't understand. Old or not, she *won't* go with us, not until she finishes the books. And *I* won't go until you finish the vault."

"I intend to finish it. Then you and Rachel can put the books in the vault, and we'll all—"

"You can't just *put* them in the vault. They'd rot away to nothing. They have to be sealed, each one. Oh, Luke, we explained that to you."

He took his arm away from her shoulder, leaned forward with his elbows on his knees. "That could take years, Mary. I don't understand why . . . why it's so important to her."

Mary stared at his hawklike profile against the pale sand, and she wondered why she'd thought he *did* understand. His willingness to labor mightily on the vault had nothing to do with the books.

But he *must* understand—somehow, on some level.

"Luke, you said you made your journey because you had a vision."

"Yes. I did."

"Rachel had a vision, too."

Luke straightened, sought in Mary's eyes verification of that assertion, and she made sure he found it.

"Her vision came in a dream, Luke, like yours. In her dream she found a book lying on the beach as if it had been washed up there. She said it was bound in white leather and had pages of gold and letters of light. The message told her that she'd been allowed to live and her books had survived for one reason—so that she could preserve the knowledge of the past for future generations. It said: *I have laid up a gift upon the shore from the children of yesterday for the children of tomorrow.*"

Luke was enthralled, and Mary felt her stomach churn in recognition of a betrayal. Rachel would never sink to mythmaking to justify her intentions.

Yet she had declared she would play any role, would kill or die for the books.

Luke said, "Then it was the Lord who commanded her to preserve the books. I . . . didn't realize. . . ."

"I know. But she—don't tell her I told you about her vision.
She considers it . . . a private matter."

"Between her and the Lord, yes." He sighed. "I understand why
she can't come to the Ark now. The Lord will watch over her until
her task is finished. But then, Mary, *then* she can come to the Ark."

Mary felt her eyes hot with tears. "Then she *must* come to the
Ark."

"Oh, Mary." He took her in his arms, held her gently like a
frightened child. "We'll come back to Amarna next spring to visit
her and make sure she's all right. The Doctor will understand. And
I'll tell her how to find the Ark. I checked my map, and it's only
about four days from here. Mary, everything will be all right. The
Lord is smiling on all of us. I *know* it."

And Mary yielded into his embrace. "I know it, too, Luke."

They walked back to Amarna on sand soaked by the surging and
ebbing waves, its surface transformed into an endless mirror reflecting the opalescent clouds, and it seemed they were walking on
the sky.

After supper, when the lowering sun cast a ruby light into the house,
Luke excused himself and went downstairs to the basement to his
makeshift bedroom. Rachel wished him good night with a smile
that faded as soon as he turned away, then she went out to the
deck to watch the sunset. Mary followed her, stood at the railing
beside her, blinking into the sun that hung above the horizon under
orange clouds whose reflections made the sea molten, gave the
breakers a blue cast. The wind had stopped, waiting to turn; the
air was sweet with the vital scents of summer.

Rachel said, "There might be a green flash."

They waited while the Earth moved, and the glowing disk of the
sun touched the horizon, slowly slipped beyond it, and finally vanished with a brief, pinpoint flare of blue-green light.

"Ah!" They spoke almost in unison, laughed at the concurrence
of their amazement, and in that moment Mary remembered all the
sunsets they had watched together, hoping for that rare *ah!*

Rachel went to one of the cedar plank chairs Luke had built for them, waited for Mary to sit down in the other, then said, "I assume Luke finally got around to declaring his honorable intentions."

Mary looked at her, saw her oblique smile. "Yes. Finally."

A brief silence, then: "How soon will you be leaving?"

"Not until the vault is finished. I don't know, exactly. Rachel . . ." Mary wanted to plead, to beg, but she only said, "You could go with us."

"No, I can't, Mary. You know that."

"But when you're finished with the books . . ."

"Maybe." Her eyes narrowed, accentuating the web of lines surrounding them. "I'm not sure I'd be welcome in a place like the Ark."

"But you would. Luke says you would."

"Does he? Well, meanwhile, I have work to do here."

Mary looked out at the horizon where the sun had vanished. "That was my work, too."

"But you believe you have other work to do now, don't you?"

"I must do it if I'm capable of it. What else can I do?"

"So, I don't see that there's a problem."

"The problem is . . ." The muscles of her jaw were tense to the point of pain. "I don't want to leave you here alone."

"Why not? Don't you think I can manage alone?"

"Of course, you can. Rachel, I . . . love you too much to leave you."

Rachel reached out and rested her hand on Mary's where it lay clenched on the arm of the chair. "But I must do what I believe is right, just as you must."

Mary put her other hand over Rachel's, felt the warmth and strength under the brown, parchment skin. "Luke said we can come back in the spring to see you. And it's only four days to the Ark. He'll tell you how to find it."

"Well, I'll be glad to know exactly where you are. But I'll be all right. I'm more worried about you. Childbirth is always a risky undertaking. I'm glad the Doctor is actually a physician."

Mary hadn't considered the risks to herself in her decision, and she couldn't muster a shred of fear now. She remembered lying naked to the sun in Luke's arms, wondering if by some stroke of luck she might have been impregnated. She had counted the days and knew it wasn't probable, only possible. But the day would come when it would not only be possible but inevitable.

I am doing what I must. I am doing the right thing.

"I'll be fine, Rachel. Don't worry about me."

At midnight Mary lay awake with bars of clouded moonlight crossing the sheet that covered her, and she listened to the murmur of the breakers and remembered the first time she had heard them at Amarna. *I am here . . . I am always here. . . .*

The door opened. She saw Luke framed in the shadows. At times she had doubted he would come, yet she wasn't surprised to see him now. She sat up, waited for him to take her outstretched hand.

He had questions, but again she didn't want to talk. She pulled him close until she could kiss his mouth, until she could whisper near his ear, "Make love to me, Luke." That was what she wanted, and what she had, the two of them in the moonlight on white, smooth sheets, smooth skin warm and damp and musky with effort as they panted toward culmination. Mary lay open-eyed, gorging on sensation, arching her back and whimpering on the razor's edge between pain and pleasure, while she watched the moon haloed in iridescent clouds, while she waited for his spasm of ejaculation, and laughed, holding at the center of her body and her being the potential of life.

The right thing. Yes. This is *right*.

But touch a solemn truth in collision with a dogma . . . and you will soon find you have disturbed a nest, and the hornets will swarm about your eyes and hand, and fly into your face and eyes.
—JOHN ADAMS, *THE LIFE AND WORKS OF JOHN ADAMS* (1851)

And on her lover's arm she leant,
And round her waist she felt it fold,
And far across the hills they went
In that new world which is the old.
—ALFRED, LORD TENNYSON,
THE DAYDREAM (1842)

Y esterday Little Mary brought a frog to school, which led eventually to the subject of cold- and warm-blooded animals, which led inevitably to the subject of the evolution of those diverse solutions to the problems of surviving extremes of heat and cold.

Evolution. That seminal, magnificent concept that always fired literalists with manic zeal. Or fear, really. I had often touched on the subject of evolution, and certainly yesterday wasn't the first time the children had heard the word.

But Miriam warned me two days ago that she would not let her children be taught "evil." And three days ago I surrendered on the issue of teaching human reproduction.

I knew better. But Jerry wanted to keep peace in the family.

Today I was aware even at breakfast that Miriam's children were quiet and uneasy, but I didn't know why. Until now. It is the appointed hour for school, but when I enter the dining room, I find only Stephen and Little Mary waiting for me. On the table near Stephen's right hand is a hapless garter snake imprisoned in a glass jar.

"I see you brought us another example of a cold-blooded creature, Stephen." He nods, but says nothing. Mary is atypically still, hands folded in her lap. "Where are the other children?" I ask.

Stephen looks up at me, and his reluctance at being the bearer of this news is obvious. "They're out in the garden."

I am abruptly consumed with anger, wrenchingly intense, and it must be apparent in my face. As if in defense of his schoolmates, Stephen adds: "Miriam told them they *had* to help in the garden."

Stephen knows that order has nothing to do with a need for help in the garden; fear is hidden in his eyes. His world has been shaken with a temblor he doesn't understand. Mary understands it even less, and her eyes, pale against her dark skin, shine with pent tears.

I manage a smile. "Wait for me. I'll be back in a few minutes."

I go out the backdoor without slamming it, walk up the grassy slope at a measured pace, and all the while my pulse is pounding, my chest tight. *Damn* her.

All the women except Bernadette are in the garden, and all Miriam's children are there. They stop their tasks—hoeing, watering, weeding—and watch me silently as I make my way to the gate, open it, and step inside.

Miriam stands near the gate, regal in triumphant self-righteousness. Deborah clings anxiously to her arm. A short distance away Isaac kneels in a row of broccoli, hands full of uprooted weeds, and looks guiltily from me to Miriam. Near him, Jonathan, sober and uncertain, leans on a hoe.

My voice is steady when I speak, and that surprises me.

"Jonathan, Isaac, Deborah . . . you're late for school."

They don't answer me. I don't expect them to. Miriam says coldly, "They aren't going to school—not today, not ever again!"

My voice is still steady. "Didn't Jeremiah tell you that one condition for your staying at Amarna was that I would teach the children?"

"*He* may have agreed to that," she retorts, her chin coming up, "but *I* didn't. I didn't agree to have my children taught blasphemy!"

Stalemate. For now, at any rate. I can't ask the children to make a choice between me and their mother.

But I smile and ask, "Blasphemy? Have your children asked you more questions you can't answer, Miriam?"

Her cheeks redden, but there is about her now an aura of power, and I recognize at this moment that it's quite possible her power is not illusory. She says, "We'll settle this Sunday evening at the family meeting."

Poor Jerry. So much for his longed-for peace in the family.

The gauntlet has been thrown down, and the family may not survive this rupture of its peace. Miriam is willing to risk that for the sake of her convictions.

But so am I. Stalemate, indeed.

I glance once at Esther, whose children are waiting for me in the house. No doubt they are there because their mother made a hard choice to stand up to Miriam, and I'm grateful. That's why I say nothing to her now. I don't want to remind Miriam of her mutiny.

I turn away and start back to the house. No one bids me goodbye.

In the afternoon, after a midday meal marked by uneasy silence— which Jerry seemed to find annoying, rather than ominous—the cloudy sky delivers a soaking rain, and I sit at the table in the living room and watch the rain marching in off the ocean, hanging its beaded curtain from the roof. Enid occupies the other chair. I'm waiting for Stephen, and she's taking time for a cup of tea before she goes to her loom. Her bony hands are tensely clasped around her mug. "Well, I'm sure we'll work everything out at the family meeting Sunday."

Sunday is the day after tomorrow. It seems a long time away.

"What an optimist you are, Enid."

She stares at me. "Of course, we'll work it out. We *have* to, Mary."

I don't argue the point. Gentle Enid, she doesn't smell disaster in the wind. She is as irrational in her beliefs as Miriam is, yet I tolerate that in Enid because she tolerates *my* beliefs, even if she doesn't understand them. Tolerance is a rare quality, and it is one with Enid's capacity to love without question. She loves the children, she loves the adults in this family, she loves me.

But I wonder, will she love me when I am called a heretic, a blasphemer, an abomination before the Lord? When everything that has given my life meaning lies broken at my feet?

"Sister Mary? Oh, dear—what's wrong?"

I'm taken off guard by the concern in her voice. "What?"

"You . . . you're crying."

And so I am. I wipe away the telltale tears. "Must be old age creeping up on me."

She tries to laugh at that, but she's distracted by Stephen. He approaches hesitantly, as if he isn't sure he should interrupt us. Enid smiles at him as she rises. "Well, I'd best get to work. Stephen, have you seen Little Mary?"

"She's waiting for you in the workroom."

"Oh, my, I really *must* get to work."

She hurries away, and Stephen sits down in the chair she has vacated. He looks out at the rain and finally asks, "What's going to happen, Mary? I mean, with school and . . . and Miriam."

"I don't know, Stephen."

He considers that. "Sometimes I think Miriam *does* hate you, but I don't know why. You've never done anything to her. Except maybe . . ."

His eyes are downcast, and I have to ask, "Maybe what?"

"Well, when you wouldn't let her finish the whipping."

Does he think all this is somehow his fault? Oh, my sweet child,

225

not-yet-man. I reach out and take his hand. "It goes much deeper than that. But don't worry. We'll resolve this one way or another."

He studies me intently, and perhaps he realizes how little real comfort there is in that assurance. Then he looks at the diary on the table. "Maybe you'd rather not have a lesson today."

"Why not?" I ask, surprised. And I wonder if Stephen and I will be allowed more of these lessons after the family meeting.

"No reason," he says, and means no reason he can explain. "Besides, maybe this is a good time for you to think about happy memories."

"*Happy* memories?"

"I meant . . . well, you and Luke that summer at Amarna."

"Oh. Yes, of course." I suppose my memories of that time *are* happy. Luke and I were in love. What an amazing state of mind that is. I think it's similar to Miriam's state of mind where religion is concerned. There is an extravagant exultation in being in love, living always at the extremes of emotion. The problem—which is never evident to the victim—is that this exultant state induces mental tunnel vision.

"Weren't you happy when Luke asked you to be his wife?"

I hear the *clack-clack* of Enid's loom, her patient instructions to Little Mary. "Yes, I was happy, Stephen."

"And Rachel? Wasn't she happy for you?"

"Yes, she was happy *for* me. And I thought . . . but, of course, she wasn't in love. She didn't suffer from tunnel vision."

He looks perplexed. "From what?"

"I just mean that I only saw what I wanted to see. I thought Rachel was as happy as Luke and I were. But in fact she had nothing to look forward to but hard labor eking out a living here, spending any remaining time and energy on the books—all in absolute solitude. In loneliness. But I was incapable of envisioning that future for her. And I was doing what I thought I had to do, what I thought was right."

"But *wasn't* it right? I mean, if you *could* have children . . ."

In his world, where there are so few people and new life is so precious, my doubts make no sense.

"That summer it seemed right, Stephen. And it *was* a happy time for me, and a busy one. Luke and I were determined to see that Rachel was well prepared for winter. The three of us harvested and stored most of the crops, split wood, cut and baled hay, and Luke shot two deer and smoked the meat. We canned vegetables and made jams and applesauce, harvested honey, made cheese. And Luke finished the vault. On *that* day I know Rachel was happy. It was the last day of August. We carried all the books we'd already sealed to the Knob and stacked them in the vault, then we opened a bottle of our mead and celebrated right there."

I don't add that we opened more than one bottle, and we were all a little drunk. We laughed and sang until the sun set and the shadow of dusk fell on the sea. The last song was "Auld Lang Syne."

"Well, after that, Luke felt his work at Amarna was finished. There were a few odds and ends to do to prepare Rachel for winter, but that only took a few days. On the sixth of September Luke and I left Amarna. We set out on foot, each of us carrying a backpack. Rachel offered us one of the horses, but Luke said there were plenty of horses at the Ark, and we wouldn't need much in the way of worldly goods. All we needed would be provided for us at the Ark. . . ."

Rachel walked with us as far as the east gate. I held her for a long time, and I remember feeling a sudden fear, a sense of loss as urgent as panic. But Luke called to me to come along, and the panic vanished. I was smiling when I turned and waved my last goodbye.

By then I was too far away to see if there were tears in Rachel's eyes.

The great question which, in all ages, has disturbed mankind, and brought on them the greatest part of their mischiefs . . . has been, not whether be power in the world, nor whence it came, but who should have it.

—JOHN LOCKE, *AN ESSAY CONCERNING HUMAN UNDERSTANDING* (1690)

T his had once been a state campground. A paved road, tufted with weeds, veined with blackberry vines, still wound through the trees. Luke led Mary to a campsite that was separated from the beach only by a sloping, salal-covered bank six feet high. To the south a creek tumbled over a rocky bed until it reached the sand, where it sprawled in a weave of shallowing channels toward the sea. Two spruce trees, bent by winds into a canopy, dappled the ground with shade. The concrete table and benches were intact, as well as the firepit.

Mary sagged down on one of the benches, backpack and all, her feet and legs aching. Luke had insisted on starting out this morning as soon as there was light enough to see. Yet now he insisted on stopping, and the sun was still thirty degrees above the horizon. He was standing by the stream, his back to her. When he turned, he smiled as if he were about to divulge a secret he could no longer keep.

"We're only about five miles from the Ark, Mary."

She felt a tingling at the back of her neck. "Then why are we stopping here?"

Without responding, he came over to the table, turned and rested his pack on it while he unbuckled the straps, then helped Mary out of her pack. "This is a nice place, isn't it? I've camped here when I was out with hunting parties. There's good fishing off those rocks to the south." He delved into his pack, found the collapsible fishing rod, and began putting it together. "And I'm not looking forward to jerky and pemmican for supper. I'll see if I can't catch something tastier."

She walked with him as far as the beach, then began searching above the high-tide line for driftwood, while he strode toward the small headland to the south, and she wondered why it had apparently always been the lot of women to gather firewood.

In the next hour she accumulated a substantial stack of wood and kindling; she laid a fire ready to be lighted; she gathered two cupfuls of wild huckleberries from the bushes growing along the road; and finally she sat down on the concrete bench with the sketchbook that had been Rachel's parting gift to her.

She opened it to an ink drawing of the Knob. Rachel had added a few strokes to suggest the vault. On another page, a magnificent stump lying on the beach, roots flung skyward. On the next page, a dark, textured arch: the base of the tree. Then a montage of cats; she recognized Trouchka with his odd spots. Then Shadow in various poses—Shadow whom she knew she would never see alive again.

She looked out at the ocean, squinting into the double glare of sun and reflected sun. Luke had offered to put Shadow out of her misery, as he put it. But Rachel had refused him. She would take care of Shadow to the end.

Mary could see Luke in minuscule silhouette on the headland. She wondered if the changes she felt in him in the last four days were real or only figments of her own anxiety. Sometimes she imagined the Ark as a magnet that wrought subtle alterations in his emotional and mental charge as it drew him into its field of influence.

From the first night, when they camped in an old burn where charred firs loomed over the new growth of alder, they slept in separate sleeping bags, although they might have zipped the bags together and, if nothing else, shared the warmth of their bodies in the chill September nights.

And at the end of the second day they unwrapped the last of the baked chicken they'd brought from Amarna, and Luke clasped his hands in prayer, as he always did before eating. But this time he spoke aloud, and when he came to the *amen*, he added, "Say it, Mary. Amen." And she was too startled not to.

That night, as they watched the campfire burn down to coals, he gently stroked her hair, and she closed her eyes, appreciating the affection she read into that gesture. Then he said, "You'll have to let your hair grow out. Women don't cut their hair."

Annoyed, she retorted, "If you're any example, *men* don't cut their hair, either, where you come from."

"It's unnatural for a man to cut his hair or beard."

She laughed. "Oh. The Samson syndrome."

He ignored that. "When we reach the Ark, you'll have to cover your hair. Do you have a scarf or bandanna?"

"What the hell's *wrong* with my hair?"

"Mary, don't say words like that!"

And they had gone to bed in silence, separately.

Last night, while the fire still burned bright, he took out his Bible and asked her to read aloud the passage he designated: Saint Paul outlining in rigorous detail the proper behavior for women.

And yet—she sighed in resignation. At other times he was still the Luke she loved, naive, but kind and gentle. She pressed her hands to her abdomen, wondering if one missed period could be taken seriously.

Then she rose and put the sketchbook in her pack. Luke had left the rocks and was walking up the beach. When he reached the campsite, he grinned proudly as he showed off his catch of iridescent black kelp fish, but across his right forearm was a scraped cut, and his shirt was torn at the shoulder, the ragged edges bloodstained.

"Luke, what happened to you?"

"Oh, I just slipped and went down on the barnacles."

"Well, let me clean those cuts."

"All right, but first I have to clean these *fish*."

"The fish can wait a few minutes." She went to her pack, found a handkerchief, then with her hand on Luke's arm, led him to the creek. "Take off your shirt."

He did, knelt with her on the bank while she dipped the handkerchief in the chill water and washed the cuts. They were only minor abrasions, except for the one at the swell of the deltoid. "Luke, you might have a new scar to add to the ones the survivalists gave you."

He looked at her, then turned away, eyes averted. "I didn't say that's where I got those scars."

Mary was bewildered, at first positive that he *had* said he'd acquired the scars at the hands of the survivalists. But maybe she'd only assumed . . .

"How *did* you get those scars?"

He rose, pulled on his shirt, ruefully noting the tear. "When we get to the Ark, you'll have to mend this for me."

Woman's work, no doubt, but she refused to be distracted. "Someone whipped you unmercifully. Who, Luke? And why?"

"I have to take care of the fish."

"Luke!"

Her importunate tone stopped him. He studied her, while she waited, a seed of fear growing in her mind. Then he said, "It was a long time ago, and it was a just punishment."

"Punishment! What did you do to deserve *that?*"

He took a deep breath. "I spoke blasphemy."

That explanation seemed so unlikely, she laughed. *"You?"*

"Yes, me!"

Abruptly she sobered. "Please . . . tell me what happened."

He folded his arms against his chest. "It was in the Blind Summer. I was sixteen then. It was such a hard time for us. There was so much grief and sickness and hunger, so much . . . disagreement. Lord help me, if I hadn't said it right out in church in front of the whole Flock—what was left of us—it wouldn't have been so bad."

"Said *what?*"

He seemed to find repeating it difficult. "I said—well, I said there wouldn't be any Second Coming. It'd been nearly a year since Armageddon. I said the Doctor was wrong about the Second Coming."

"And that was blasphemy?"

He frowned irritably. "Of course, it was!"

"Is it written in the Bible that the Last World War—or whatever it was called—was Armageddon? It was the Doctor who made that assumption. You didn't blaspheme. You only disagreed with him."

Luke shook his head. "No, you don't understand. The Doctor—he's a special man, chosen of God."

"A man who has *visions*," Mary said with cold irony.

"Yes! He's our rock, like Saint Peter was the rock of the new church of Jesus Christ."

"Was it this rock who punished you so terribly for disagreeing—"

"For *blasphemy*, Mary, before all the Flock!"

"Was he the one who whipped you?"

"No, the Doctor left it to my father to punish me, since he was Elder of our household. And afterward I went before the Flock in the church and . . . well, I don't remember much of that. The glory of the Lord came over me. They said I spoke in tongues. It was the first time for me." He sighed. "And the last."

Mary looked into his troubled face, and he seemed so achingly vulnerable, she couldn't hold on to her anger. Bringing to heel the defiant boy Luke had been was a necessity of survival for the Flock. They couldn't afford dissension or rebellion. But Luke paid a high price for their unity. She put her arms around him, closed her eyes when she felt his arms strong and needing around her.

Finally she drew away, waited until he could return her gaze. "You'd better take care of the fish. I'll get the fire started."

He kissed her forehead. "I knew you'd understand, Mary."

"Then why didn't you tell me about it sooner?"

He laughed self-consciously. "I guess because I was afraid you wouldn't understand."

"Oh, I understand, Luke." She understood far more than he did. "Come on, let's get supper ready. I'm hungry."

There was more to understand before the night was out.

After supper they sat together on one of the sleeping bags watching the fire, while the surf whispered constant assurances in the darkness, and Mary felt her equilibrium restored.

Until Luke rose, put more wood on the fire so that it flared harshly in her eyes, and she braced herself as he went to his backpack, returned with his Bible. He knelt, facing her. "Mary, the reason I didn't want to go on to the Ark today is that before you reach its gates, you must take Jesus into your heart as your personal savior."

She found his earnestness annoying. "I must *what?*" He started to repeat the formula, but she interrupted him. "What would happen if I weren't a Christian? If I were a Jew or Buddhist or Muslim or—heaven forfend!—an agnostic or—heaven forfend!—an atheist? Would I be denied entrance to the Ark?"

His face was slack with confusion. "Mary, the Ark is a place for Christians, for the blessed who have accepted Jesus—"

"Then if I'm not a Christian, they'll turn me away?"

"I . . . yes. We'd have to, because only—"

"Then you should be grateful Rachel and I didn't refuse to let *you* in at Amarna until we were sure your philosophy agreed with ours. You'd be *dead*, Luke, and swept out to sea with the crabs eating your carcass!"

He stared at her, then looked down at the Bible, contemplated it a moment, and his chin came up. "That was different. You're

233

not sick. You come to the Ark as my future wife; you'll be part of the Flock."

Mary finally shrugged, reminding herself that it didn't matter, all this literalist drivel. She had come this far because she had no choice. She was doing what she had to do. And if it would satisfy Luke . . .

"My mother made sure I was baptized properly in a proper Christian church, Luke. Isn't that enough?"

"You were baptized?" he asked eagerly. "The Lord be praised! Then you've been consecrated to Jesus. But you must make that commitment anew, you must be reborn into the love of God and His only-begotten Son. Mary, you must do it! Come—kneel here before me."

Something in her balked still, but she shifted position until she was on her knees facing him. Let him do his mumbo jumbo. It didn't matter.

"Pray with me, Sister! Pray with me!" He took both her hands in his and with his head tilted heavenward, eyes squeezed shut, he exhorted his god to accept this poor sinner who longed for his grace and his love and for eternal life in the wonder of his presence. He exhorted at length and in repetitious detail, while Mary knelt, staring at him, hands numbed in his tightening grip as he droned on and on, and there was in his voice a hypnotic cadence enhanced by the flickering light of the fire. The flames blinded her, surrounded Luke with darkness in which nothing could be seen to exist, and at some point—she didn't know how she reached it—she found herself weeping, heard her voice responding with Luke's, and she didn't know what she was saying, what he was saying, and her knees ached, every muscle in her body ached, and she cried, "Yes, yes, yes!" And finally Luke's voice rang out with a last "Amen!"

In the sudden silence Mary heard the murmur of the sea. *I am here . . . I am always here. . . .* And she sought in the darkness the pale light of the surf, but her fire-dazzled eyes recorded only illusions of flame.

Then Luke's arms closed around her, and she turned into his embrace. He said, "Mary, oh, my sweet Mary, I love you."

She lifted her face to his, whispered, "Then make love to me, Luke. Tonight. Make love to me if you love me."

He pulled away from her, gently but uncompromisingly.

"The Doctor will marry us when we get to the Ark."

Mary felt those softly spoken words as she had his slap on her face that June day at Amarna. She got to her feet, stared down at him.

"I suppose now it's *fornication!*"

He fixed his gaze on the ground. "It's just not right. . . ."

"Why was it right at Amarna? Not once, but many times it was right!"

"Mary, that was different," he mumbled.

She walked out of the firelight to her sleeping bag, unlaced her boots with shaking hands, then got inside the bag, jerked the zipper closed, bitter words on her lips crying to be spoken. But she held them back. She heard Luke getting into his sleeping bag, the zipper buzzing.

She lay facing away from him, toward the sea, and pressed a hand to her body, wondering again if that useless organ within was becoming a womb.

If not, would she have to wait for a sanctioned visitation from her sanctioned husband? The thought brought a sardonic, silent laugh.

"I can't hear it."

Mary pushed the bandanna away from her ears and looked back along the dirt road cut through a stand of second-growth Douglas fir. Alders, vines, and grass encroached on the road. The morning sun fell in misted shafts through the trees. The only sound she heard was the chromatic warble of a bird she and Rachel had identified only by its call and named the mad bird for the manic edge in its repetitive song.

"You can't hear what?" Luke asked.

235

"I can't hear the ocean." The words were like the closing of a door.

"No, it's at least two miles behind us." With one hand on her cheek, he turned her face toward him. "You'll miss the ocean, won't you?"

She looked up at him, reveling in his solicitude. Yet she recognized behind it the anticipation he couldn't contain. Luke was coming home. After a year, two months, and ten days, he was coming home, and from the moment he woke her this morning with a gentle kiss, he had been so full of joy for his homecoming that she had warmed to it, held on to it, hoping to make his homecoming her own.

"Come on, Mary, just a little farther, then there's a view of the Ark."

And he set off down the road with long strides. She hurried to catch up with him, and when they reached the viewpoint, he stopped, the tears in his eyes at odds with his smile. "There it is, Mary. There's Canaan Valley. Oh, Lord, praised be Thy name!"

They stood at the top of a steep slope shorn of trees in an old clear-cut. Caught somewhere between fear and hope, Mary looked southeast into a valley cradled between two low, forested ridges. The valley had an east-west alignment, with the river Luke called the Jordan trailing along the south boundary, the sun flashing on its dark waters between the barred shadows of the trees on the far bank. At the center of the valley, arranged in a circle perhaps four hundred feet in diameter, stood the twelve households Luke had described, all built of peeled logs, roofed with hand-split shakes. Each household had three small, shuttered windows on its long back wall and a brick chimney against one of the shorter end walls. The air was veiled with their smoke. Rock-lined paths led from the households to the center of the circle like twelve spokes toward the hub of a wheel. At the hub stood the church. It was also built of logs and shakes, the entrance facing west beneath a steeple that thrust high above everything around it and pointed a long shadow toward Mary and Luke.

But Luke hadn't told her about the palisades of vertical logs that connected the households at their outside corners, that made a fort of the circle, and she wondered what enemies those walls were built to exclude.

All of the valley was fenced. Barbed wire, perhaps; she could only see the evenly spaced fence posts from here. A road emerged from the forest in the northwest at an angle toward the southeast, passed a gate on the fence line, then continued at that angle until it reached the median of the valley, where it turned east toward the open gate of the Ark. South of the road lay a huge garden and a greenhouse. Across the road on the north was another garden, and east of that, an orchard, and farther east, a cemetery. Near the river, a barn presided over a corral and a cluster of smaller buildings. In the pasture at the northeast end of the valley, cattle, horses, sheep, and goats grazed. The southeast end was fenced off for a hay field; pyramids of curing hay dotted the pale stubble. And apparently the Flock was successful at growing grain of some sort this far inland. The tawny field at the west end of the valley was ready for harvest.

Mary released her pent breath in a sigh of satisfaction. The orderly arrangement of fields and fences and buildings seemed inevitable and right. She found Luke's hand in hers, and knew the future hung suspended for them on a golden thread, and there was beauty in it.

And there were people.

At first she didn't recognize the tiny, dark objects moving about in the gardens and fields, and she wasn't prepared for the exhilaration galvanized by that recognition.

There were more than fifty *people* down there—feeling, talking, thinking, laughing, crying, living human beings.

She whispered, "Luke, there are so many people."

"Yes, Mary. You'll never be lonely again." He pulled her bandanna down a little over her forehead, tightened the knot at the back of her neck, then cupped her face in his hands. "They'll be surprised to see a woman in pants, but that can be remedied. I want them to see how strong and proud you are, Mary Hope. I want them all to love you as I do." He leaned down to kiss her, lingering long over it.

Mary couldn't doubt it now. This was her homecoming, too. Of course, these people would have different beliefs and standards, but she would adapt, she would make herself acceptable, she would do anything necessary to become a part of this living community, to make her children part of humankind.

They were only a few yards from the fence-line gate when the church bell began ringing. Mary wondered, and laughed at the thought, if the bell was tolling for them in a way John Donne hadn't intended.

Luke lengthened his stride. "The noon bell. Everybody'll be going back to the Ark for midday meal." He reached the gate and un-hooked the chain, called out to the four men leaving the west field. They stopped, staring at him, while he pushed through the gate, fumbling at the straps of his pack. The men approached cautiously, and Luke flung off the pack and ran toward them, and when they recognized him, they also began running, and they met with em-braces and jubilant cries. Men and women were streaming out of the gardens now. Shouts brought more out of the Ark, and Luke walked up the road to meet the continually swelling throng.

Mary didn't take exception to being left behind. She unbuckled her pack, put it down by Luke's, and closed the gate, then watched the milling crowd in which he had lost himself. So much joy there, both for Luke and his friends. She caught a glimpse of Luke holding a baby. Was it his? She realized then how few children there were—no more than seven under the age of fifteen—and how few old people.

All the men were bearded with long hair confined by headbands. Many of them wore knit sweaters of undyed wool; others wore col-larless, long-sleeved shirts of the same ivory color. Their loose pants were a deep maroon, stuffed into the tops of boots, some of which were leftovers from Before, while others were a kind of moccasin boot laced nearly to the knee.

The women were similarly clothed, except they wore long, dark skirts and white scarves tied at the back of the neck, as Luke had tied her bandanna. But it was red, and Mary was acutely aware of how strange she'd look to these people—a woman with a red head covering, a woman wearing pants.

There was a man walking at a brisk pace down the road from the Ark, and Mary felt every muscle tighten. This was the Doctor. She could tell little about him at this distance except that he was tall and lean to the edge of emaciation; that he had long, gray hair fine enough to blow back from his face with his vigorous strides; that his beard fell nearly to his waist. What convinced her that he was the Doctor was the reaction of the Flock. They moved as one toward him, but didn't envelop him as they had Luke. They left him a little space, and in that space he and Luke met and embraced.

They talked for a while, and finally Luke, then the Doctor, then the rest of the Flock, turned to look at Mary. Soon they all began moving in her direction, the Doctor, with Luke at his side, in the lead. She stood fast, her heart pounding, until Luke motioned her to come forward.

She did, and when she was about twenty feet away, the Doctor stopped. Luke and the Flock took their cue from him and also stopped. They were silent. Over fifty people, and the only sound she heard was the fretful crying of the baby. She was the focal point of every eye, and she read in them a spectrum of hope, suspicion, doubt, amazement, and curiosity. But it was the Doctor who held her attention as she approached him. And to see the Doctor and Luke side by side was to see Luke in the present and in the future. The long, narrow faces were cast of the same mold, the deep-set eyes were of the same color, and there was in the Doctor's gray hair and beard a sandy cast that hinted that he had once been as copper-haired as Luke was now.

Yet Mary doubted Luke would ever attain the penetrating light in the Doctor's eyes, the stunning aura of potent vitality. A man of visions, she reminded herself, the kind of visions that might once have classified him as less than sane. But how many of the movers and makers of history had been certifiably sane?

On his headband, in red letters on white, were the words HE WAS A BURNING AND A SHINING LIGHT.

She stopped a few paces from him, meeting his intent gaze in part because she was fascinated by it. Mesmerized? Perhaps. His voice, deep and resonant, matched the power of his presence. "Mary Hope, have you taken Jesus Christ into your heart as your personal savior? Have you been reborn in Him?"

The questions were like a dash of cold water in her face. But why hadn't she expected them? She looked at Luke, found him gazing hopefully at her. Was he worried about what she might say?

She faced the Doctor. "Yes, sir, I *have* taken Jesus into my heart as my savior." Then she lowered her eyes submissively and heard a murmur of comment from the Flock. There seemed to be no hostility in it. She couldn't know yet whether the Doctor was pleased.

That resonant voice again. She looked up attentively while he asked, "And do you, Mary Hope, know in your heart that Armageddon has come, that Jesus will soon descend to Earth to seek out the righteous and carry them in His bosom to heaven?"

With that question, it was harder to meet his gaze. She replied, "Jesus spoke through Saint John the Divine and said, 'Surely I come . . . quickly.' " And how had she remembered that quotation, except that at the time she read it—three months ago, at least—it had seemed so sadly futile?

But her often wayward memory served her well. The Doctor *was* pleased. He smiled, and Mary wanted to weep with relief. Then he took a step toward her, held out his strong, callused hand, and waited until she put her hand in his. "Welcome to the Ark, Mary Hope." And as the Flock murmured its reflected pleasure he held out his other hand to Luke and said, "Luke tells me the two of you wish to be married."

"Yes, sir, we do." She looked at Luke, wishing she could match the blush that reddened his cheeks.

The Doctor laughed. "By the way, you needn't call me *sir*. At the Ark we call each other Sister and Brother. Luke, you have returned with your Ruth, and you must be her Boaz. Sister Mary, this is for you the first day. On the third day you and Luke will be married."

The murmurs of the crowd turned to shouts, and Mary and Luke were swept toward the Ark by the jubilant Flock. The church bell began ringing as they passed through the gate, and this time Mary knew the bells were tolling for them, tolling not for death, but for hope.

Luke was an Elder.

Mary lay under a smother of quilts in the middle of a double bed in darkness as dense as a womb, and she couldn't keep her eyes closed, even though there was nothing for them to register. The images were all out of her memory, and she was trying to put them in order, to make sense of this her first day at the Ark.

Luke was an Elder by the Doctor's decree, apparently. An honor, she was given to understand, for a man so young.

She turned on her side and drew her knees up, a sigh escaping her. She wanted Luke with her in this bed now, not two nights hence; she wanted him to hold her, to kiss her, to taste her nipples; she wanted him inside her, wanted that affirmation, that covenant. She stared into the darkness and listened to the silence, the absence of the sea.

This was Luke's household now. This bed, this room would be theirs once they were properly married. An oppressively small room with one tiny, shuttered window. A chest, pegs driven into the wall for a closet. A chamber pot. The privies were beyond the smithy, far enough away that chamber pots were a necessity, not a convenience. There was no mirror. She hadn't seen a mirror anywhere at the Ark.

This bedroom was one of four such cubicles that together occupied two-thirds of the rectangular building. The remaining third was left to a kitchen–dining room. She wondered how these households could have contained nine or ten people as they had before the End. Now most of them housed four or five. There would be six in this one now that Luke had come home with his bride-to-be.

Tonight Luke also slept alone, and she wondered if he found sleep as elusive as she did.

The other four members of the household were doubled up in the remaining two bedrooms. She became aware of a rhythmic murmur that at first made her wonder if an odd turn of wind had brought her the sound of the sea. But it was only snoring from the next room, the room shared tonight by Nehemiah and his nephew Adam. Old Nehemiah, he was called, and he didn't seem to take exception to it. He and Adam, a boy of fourteen, were the only survivors of a family that had once numbered eight people.

Mary had been immediately drawn to Adam. He was small for his age, with fine features and shining black hair. Quiet and shy, he seemed satisfied to sit on the margins of activity, listening avidly. That he admired Luke to the point of worship was obvious.

The other members of this household, Enid and Bernadette, were no more than thirty years old, yet they were classified as Barrens. That had been determined by the Doctor after years of childless marriages and fruitless visitations. When Enid spoke the word *Barren*, her large, hazel eyes filled with grief and something akin to shame.

Luke called Enid his big sister. She had come to the Ark when she was nineteen after her family was evicted from their farm in the Willamette Valley, and she was assigned to Luke's father's household. She and Luke were the only survivors of that household. Enid seemed quite willing to extend her sisterly affection to Luke's bride, for which Mary was grateful. She recognized Enid as the true center of this household, and Mary couldn't assume the role—she wasn't yet sure what it entailed—of the Elder's wife without Enid's cooperation.

But Enid wasn't even aware that she was the center here. She considered her real work to be weaving—not cooking, cleaning, and organizing the household. She was one of fifteen women expert at spinning and weaving the wool shorn from the Ark's sheep.

And Mary was also grateful that Enid was virtually incapable of silence. Mary learned a great deal about the Ark by saying nothing and letting Enid fill the vacuum.

It was Enid who told her about Bernadette, the other Barren in this household. She was absent from the Ark when Mary and Luke arrived. Enid explained that Bernadette was sometimes away from home—alone—for days at a time. Enid clearly thought such behavior odd. Not even the men who went out hunting traveled in the forest alone. When Mary asked why Bernadette embarked on such expeditions, Enid said, "Healing herbs and roots. She's a nurse and one of the Doctor's students at medicine." Not only did she venture alone into the forest, but space had been set aside in the greenhouse for her to grow cultivated medicinal herbs.

Bernadette hadn't put in an appearance until the evening meal. She wasn't wearing the de rigueur scarf when she arrived, and her blonde hair curled wildly around her small, squirrel-curious face. She was minimally polite to Mary, but she greeted Luke with a fondness that bore witness to long friendship. She wanted to know about his travels, but he put her off. He was going to tell all the Flock about his journey at evening service. She showed little overt interest in Mary until she brought out the seeds and bulbs Rachel had sent with her. Bernadette examined them, then eyed Mary curiously. "Where do you come from that you have all these plants?"

Luke had again put her off. "Later, Sister. I'll tell you and everybody else about that later."

Mary turned over, seeking a more comfortable position on the soft mattress. Then she stiffened, surprised by a sound. The creak of floorboards, footsteps moving down the hall toward the kitchen.

Was it Luke? Perhaps he couldn't sleep, either. She waited, wondering whether it would stretch the bounds of propriety here if she and Luke were to simply talk together, even if they were alone.

She threw the covers back, shivering in the chill air despite the long granny gown Enid had given her. Pajamas, apparently, were not appropriate for a woman. She felt on the floor for her slippers. At least, they were hers, like the robe she pulled on. She made her way to the door, then out into the hall, and saw a dim, golden light ahead: a fire in the hearth. When she reached the kitchen door, she paused.

Someone was sitting in front of the fireplace on the far wall, but it wasn't Luke. She sighed her disappointment, absently looking around at the varnished cabinets gleaming in reflected firelight; the cookstove, its cast iron densely black; the sink that had no faucets; the garlands of drying leaves, flowers, and roots hung from the roof beams.

It was Old Nehemiah who occupied the chair facing the fireplace. He turned. His face was in shadow, but his voice was welcoming. "Come in, Sister Mary. Warm yourself up. Gets kind of cold these fall nights."

Mary felt somehow caught out, but she didn't want to return to the solitude of her room. Nehemiah rose and dragged a chair near the fire for her. She sat down in it, smiled at him. "Thank you. I wasn't really cold. Just couldn't seem to get to sleep."

He nodded. "Always hard in a strange bed." Then he gazed into the fire, quite content to have her here, it seemed, and just as content not to talk. The fire wheezed and muttered to itself, a small fire in the big, brick hearth designed for cooking as well as heating; wrought-iron pot hooks were folded against the side walls.

Nehemiah was not, like Enid, a compulsive talker. He had said very little during the evening meal when all the household gathered at the kitchen table. He seemed as tough and hard as weathered wood, and he had undoubtedly been a man of great physical strength in his youth, but now the squared angles were rounded, his wide shoulders tended to hunch forward, his right hand was misshapen with arthritis.

He had no left hand. His arm ended just above the elbow. He was wearing a wool robe now, and the left sleeve hung loose. The absence of half his left arm had been more apparent earlier when his shirtsleeve was folded and safety-pinned at the end of his truncated limb.

She studied his gray-bearded face, in profile to her, assessing the calm steadfastness in it, and finally spoke. "Brother Nehemiah, would it offend you if I asked what happened to your arm?"

"Offend me? Of course not, Sister." He lifted the stub of an arm. "It's a miracle, this. A miracle that I'm still alive."

"What happened?"

"Well, it was three years ago. I was east in the mountains with a hunting party. We'd shot a big buck, and I was boning it out. Done it a hundred times, you know, and never slipped once. This time the knife caught on a tendon, and when it let go, it ran up my left hand, laid it open down to the bones." He frowned uneasily. "Sorry to be so . . . well, I know women sometimes get upset at that sort of talk."

Mary shook her head. "If I was flinching, it's only because I've boned out a few deer myself, and it always made me very nervous."

"Had to bone out your own game, did you? Well, I admire that in a woman—doing whatever you have to."

"Are you . . . unique in that sort of admiration?"

He gave her an oblique smile, then shrugged. "I suppose some of the Flock were surprised to see a woman here with pants on. And maybe I should tell you, there's some would think it odd for a woman to be talking to a man without anything on her head."

Mary self-consciously ran a hand through her hair. "I didn't re-alize that. I mean, I saw Bernadette—"

"Oh, Bernadette's sort of . . . well, people look the other way with her. But she's the best there is for a nurse or midwife."

A midwife? Mary wondered how much experience Bernadette could have acquired at that. "You were telling me about your arm. . . ."

Nehemiah settled back in his chair. "Well, the trouble was, when I cut my hand so bad we were five days away from home. The Brothers with me did what they could, but it got infected. By the time we got back, I couldn't walk, couldn't even hold myself up on a horse. My arm was all swollen up and turning dark. Hurt like hell, too. Excuse the language, but I can't believe Satan's got much worse to offer. The Doctor said gangrene had set in. The only way he could save me was to amputate, and he wasn't real sure I'd live through it. But I did, and it was a miracle. The Doctor took off the arm, and I didn't feel a thing. Well, I did afterward while it was healing up, but I didn't mind that."

245

Mary stared at him. "You mean the Doctor used an anesthetic?"

"Yes. Not the kind they had in hospitals before Armageddon. The Doctor kept a supply of medicines like that, but he said most of them didn't last. But he had the poppy. We grow them in the greenhouse. The Doctor says the poppy was put on Earth to ease suffering, but sinners made it the scourge of generations. Well, I can testify that the way the Doctor used it was God's way. He saved my life." A long sigh, then: "He's a saint, the Doctor. He's our rock, just like the Apostle Peter."

Luke had described the Doctor in nearly the same words.

Mary disciplined her features to betray none of her skepticism. A saint? Certainly a man of dazzling presence, a man to command attention, and perhaps awe.

The evening prayer service had been, more than anything else she experienced today, revealing. All the Flock had crowded into the candlelit sanctuary, and the air was charged with the array of their odors and the astringent tang of the cedar logs of which the church was built. Mary wondered why the Doctor asked Luke to speak before, rather than after, the service. She listened to Luke tell the story of his journey and was only surprised that he said so little about Amarna. "A farm where I was taken in when I was sick and nursed to health by Sister Mary and the old woman who worked the farm with her." That was all. *Old woman.* Damn him. Yet Mary was relieved that he didn't try to explain Rachel to these people. Nor did he mention the books.

When Luke concluded his story, the Doctor ascended to the pulpit, and the service began in earnest. First, the music, with Sister Judith at the pump organ, the Flock singing like a trained chorus fifty voices strong in three-part harmony. Some of the hymns were familiar, like "Bringing in the Sheaves," but most she had never heard. She didn't care. It had been so long since she'd heard music, she didn't notice the words, only the melodies, the harmonies, the rhythms.

When she was nearly limp with the power of the music, the Doctor began his sermon, taking his text from the Book of Ruth in honor of Luke's return with his bride-to-be. That the story wasn't particularly appropriate didn't seem to concern him. He built on it a lesson in faith, and for a solid hour urged the Flock to feats of faith for the sake of eloquently vague glory, threatened them as a consequence of failure of faith with an equally eloquent—and intensely specific—hell. His resonant voice boomed in the shadowed confines of the church, and the climax was wringing. All it lacked was a thunder of applause. Instead, he took his accolades in the form of a final exultant hymn, "Give to the Winds Thy Fears."

It was only then that Mary understood why the Doctor had let Luke speak first. It was pure theatre. *He* intended to provide the climax of the evening's "entertainment."

Nehemiah rose to put a piece of wood on the fire. The flames probed around the wedge of fir, seeking a foothold.

Mary asked, "Is he really a saint?"

"The Doctor?" Nehemiah sank stiffly into his chair. "Well, I don't know. He's not . . . perfect. Far as I know, there's only been one perfect man to walk this Earth: the Lord Jesus."

"But he wasn't just a man, was he?"

"I guess that's why He was perfect. The Doctor's a man. He's not perfect. But I've never met a man quite like him."

"Neither have I." Mary stared into the flames and remembered fires in the hearth at Amarna, wondered if Rachel were at this moment gazing into another fire.

No. Don't dwell on that, on Rachel.

"Brother Nehemiah, didn't Enid say you were one of the charter members of the Ark?"

He beamed proudly. "I sure was. I knew the Doctor when he was in Portland. Went to the same church, so to speak—his little church on skid road. I was working for the Social Services Division. Gave that up when I saw I could do more good working with the Doctor and the Lord than for the government. Me and my wife and my sister and her husband all came to Canaan Valley with the Doctor and helped build the Ark. Both Adam senior and I were chosen as Elders."

"You're an Elder?"

"Yes. I mean, I *was* an Elder—one of the only three original Elders to live through the Long Winter."

247

Mary hesitated, puzzled. "Then you . . . you were Elder of *this* household before Luke came home."

"Well, yes, I was."

"Does it bother you to have Luke step into your place like that?"

Nehemiah laughed softly. "No, it doesn't bother me. Told the Doctor that today. Luke, too. Besides, there's not a lot for the Elders to do anymore. Everybody here pretty much knows what has to be done and when. And if they don't—well, the Doctor can usually handle it."

As he *handled* the replacement of an Elder, Mary thought. That had been done today with no more than a word from the Doctor.

Nehemiah pulled in a deep breath. "Yes, I'm stepping down now, and like the Doctor says, it's time. And only right. Luke's going to take the Doctor's place, probably, sooner or later. We all know that."

Luke take the Doctor's place? Mary tried to imagine Luke in the pulpit urging the Flock to righteousness, threatening them with an agonizing hell. She tried to imagine Luke in the role of a saint.

She said, "But that's bound to be a long time in the future."

"Maybe. We never know what the Lord has in store for us. The Doctor's had some trouble with his heart lately. Bernadette's always boiling up foxglove for him. Not that he can't work with the best of us, long and hard. Still, you never know. Got to look to the future."

Mary wondered how much future Nehemiah foresaw if he, like the Doctor, believed the second coming of Christ was imminent. But she hadn't decided how to word that delicate question, when Nehemiah stretched and came to his feet. "Well, I'd best get back to bed. The cows'll be waiting early on for milking."

She looked up at him. "I enjoyed talking to you, Brother Nehemiah."

"I enjoyed it, too. You'll be a blessing for Luke and for the Flock. Good night, Sister Mary." And with that he lumbered away down the hall. She heard the latch on his door click.

Mary looked around into the silent shadows and knew she should go to bed, too, should try to sleep. But she couldn't face that empty bed yet. She put another piece of wood on the fire and watched the flames whorling around it, listened to their rush and crackle, and thought about saints.

The wedge of wood was charred black, checkered in squares with incandescent edges, when she heard the creak of footsteps behind her. She turned, only to be disappointed again. It wasn't Luke.

Bernadette. She wore a robe of berry-dyed wool, and her pale hair was even wilder than before. "Sister Mary." The words signaled recognition, more than greeting. She went to the chair Nehemiah had vacated. Mary waited, wondering if she would prefer to be alone, and at length Bernadette looked at her with her steel bright, gray eyes and said, "Tell me about the woman who worked the farm with you."

"I'd rather not." That slipped out before she thought about it. She added, "I miss her very much. Talking about her doesn't help."

Bernadette pursed her lips. "Was she your mother?"

"No."

"Your sister?"

"No. She's my friend."

Bernadette considered that, finally nodded. "Rare things, friends." Then she reached into the pocket of her robe, but Mary couldn't see what she brought out. She rose, got a piece of kindling from the wood box, held one end into the fire, then as she sank back into the chair, raised the flaming stick and casually lighted a leaf-wrapped cigarette.

Mary stared at her, while Bernadette tossed the kindling into the fire and puffed at the cigarette. When Mary got a whiff of the sweet scent of the smoke, she nearly laughed aloud. "I can't believe it. That's—"

"Cannabis," Bernadette pronounced calmly. "Cannabis is soothing to the nerves and a good analgesic to a point. It eases gastric restlessness and promotes sleep. Here . . ." And she offered the cigarette to Mary.

But Mary didn't take it. One reason was that she still harbored the hope that she was pregnant. The other reason she verbalized by asking, "Is this some sort of test? Am I being tempted by the Lord's advocate?"

Bernadette laughed. "You're not being tempted, Sister, and you passed *my* test when you didn't go all righteous on me. Some people here frown on cannabis as a soporific. Why don't you take a puff?"

"I . . . have my reasons."

"Which are none of my business." She nodded, then: "You're going to have a hard time here, Sister. You're not made in their mold."

Mary contrasted those words with Nehemiah's blithe assurance that she would be a blessing for Luke and the Flock. She asked, "Are *you* made in their mold?"

"Yes. I was raised in the mold. It's just . . . well, the mold seems to have bent a little for me. Everybody thinks I'm a little strange. But they never go outside the Ark. You learn a lot out there in the forest or along the seashore." She took another puff, savored the smoke. "Thing is, nobody worries about how strange I am. I'm a nurse, and I know medicines—the kinds we use—as well as the Doctor. I'm good at what I do, and what I do is important here. If people need you, they'll put up with a little strangeness—if you don't carry it too far."

Mary restrained a smile. "Thanks for the advice."

"Advice? I don't give advice. Nothing but trouble in that."

"That's probably good advice, too. Sister Bernadette, would you consider teaching me medicine and nursing? I'd like to have a reason to go into the forest or along the seashore occasionally."

"Would you, now?" Bernadette studied her through a veil of smoke. "Don't know that I'd want the company. Of course, it's not up to me. That'll be for the Doctor to decide. Besides, you've got another way to make yourself needed here."

"What do you mean?"

"Lord, woman, *you* know what I mean. All you have to do is get pregnant and have a live, sound baby. Can you do it?"

"Well, there's no reason to think I can't. My periods have always been regular, and I'm perfectly healthy."

"Those are good signs. How old are you?"

"Thirty-four."

Bernadette raised an eyebrow. "Don't look it. Well, as long as you're in good health, being a little past ideal childbearing age shouldn't cause any problems. You give Luke a baby. They'll love you like one of their own."

Mary hadn't thought about having a baby as a means of making herself acceptable here. It still seemed ironic—and incredible—that these people were so desperate for children in the imagined shadow of Armageddon and the second coming. She considered asking Bernadette the same question she'd wanted to ask Nehemiah, but she wasn't sure how to phrase it. Finally she put it as a statement.

"The Doctor believes that Armageddon has already happened, and Jesus will come to Earth soon."

Bernadette smiled benignly. "Yes, that's what he tells us."

Mary waited, refusing to say more, and Bernadette sighed. "You want to know if *I* believe that? Well, the truth is, I just don't know, and I figure I may never know. Meanwhile, though, you have to keep on living, and that means you have to keep on planning for some sort of future, even if it's just planting seeds in spring for fall harvest."

"Do other people in the Flock feel that way?"

"I couldn't say." Bernadette paused, eyed her coolly. "But whatever people think in their hearts, you have to understand one thing: they'll never go against the Doctor. That's the way it has to be."

Mary shivered. The cold was gathering at her back as the fire died. After a moment she rose. She was ready for sleep. At least, for solitude.

"Good night, Bernadette. I'll see you in the morning."

"Probably. By the way, I know where there's wild aster and pearly everlasting blooming. I'll bring you some—for your wedding bouquet."

Mary was too moved to speak. Then at length, she said, "I'd love that. Thank you."

Bernadette nodded without looking away from the embers.

I stood
Among them, but not of them; in a shroud
Of thoughts which were not their thoughts.
               —GEORGE NOEL GORDON, LORD BYRON,
                   CHILDE HAROLD'S PILGRIMAGE (1812)

To love and bear; to hope till Hope creates
From its own wreck the thing it
    contemplates . . .
               —PERCY BYSSHE SHELLEY, *PROMETHEUS*
                   UNBOUND (1818–1819)

May Day was once a minor holiday celebrated mostly by schoolchildren, a pagan festival emasculated, as so many pagan celebrations were, like Easter and Christmas. At Amarna the family doesn't recognize May Day. I do, but my celebration is simply a few minutes of prayerless gratitude for the imminent arrival of another summer.

Stephen and I are having our lesson on the beach today, sitting on the wave-smoothed trunk of a redwood. This is the kind of day on which the beach is most alluring. There's no wind to drive the sand in stinging veils, no clouds to come between me and the warmth of the sun. The sea is chatoyant blue green, the breakers turning lazily with no power behind them. It's as if the world has slowed down to a contemplative stroll. Shadow is chasing gulls through the shallows, and her hectic movements seem out of synchronization with her context.

And on this May Day the allure of the beach for me is simply that it takes me away from the house, from the family.

Yet when I look back on the morning, I can't pinpoint any particular words or actions that made me seek the solace of the sea. Of course, Miriam's children weren't in school, and after midday meal, Deborah returned the copy of *Winnie-the-Pooh* I loaned her last week. The child whose vivacity I treasure was subdued and near tears. But Miriam was almost cheerful today. Still, neither she nor anyone else mentioned the family meeting tomorrow night, and it hangs over us like an invisible shadow. The children show the tension more than the adults. They respond to it, as the adults do, by not talking about it, but the children are silent because they don't know what questions to ask. The adults know, but *won't* ask.

I haven't brought a diary to the beach with me today. I wrote nothing while I was at the Ark, but the memories are acid-etched. I've been trying to tell Stephen about my wedding, which is difficult, since he doesn't entirely understand the concept of marriage. But he understands religious ceremonies. He endures enough of them.

"It was a lovely, clear, fall day, Stephen, although I don't suppose even a drenching rain would've dampened my spirits."

He's sitting sideways on the log, one leg propped up to support his elbow. On this sunny day he wears pants cut above his knees, and he's taken off his moccasins. "It might've dampened *you*," he says, laughing.

"So it would. Anyway, just after noon, Enid and a gaggle of women came to my room to dress me. The way the bride dressed was part of the wedding tradition. Brides always wore white. The women decked me out in a long skirt, a blouse with full sleeves gathered at the wrists, and a scarf that fell to my waist, all made of fine, white wool. Then Bernadette presented me a bouquet of

253

lavender asters and white pearly everlasting, and Nehemiah came to take me to the church. He was to give me away, and he seemed as proud as if I really were his daughter."

"He was to give . . . *you* away?"

"A bride was traditionally given to the groom by her father. Nehemiah served as my surrogate father. Oh, those were ancient and densely patriarchal traditions, Stephen." I give him an oblique smile, but his answering smile is tentative. "Then with Nehemiah at my side, surrounded by those chirping women, I walked to the church, and everyone told me how beautiful I was. Well, I wasn't beautiful then and never had been. Yet later, when I met Luke at the altar, I looked into his eyes and . . ."

And saw there all my hope, all my future, and he looked back as if he saw his hope and future in me.

"I saw that I *was*, at that moment, beautiful. At least, to Luke. I remember Sister Leah—she was Rebecca's mother—sang 'Amazing Grace,' then Luke and I exchanged our vows of love and faith and obedience. Till death us do part. And Luke gave me his mother's gold wedding band." I look down at my left hand, wrinkled, disfigured with arthritis, and remember the hand, still smooth and straight, on which Luke placed that gold band. "And the Doctor smiled on Luke and me like a lesser sun and prayed that the lord should also smile on us, that out of our love would come the fruit of the lord's mercy and wisdom."

Stephen doesn't seem to hear the hollowness in that. He says wistfully, "It must've been wonderful. I wish . . ."

"What, Stephen?"

He turns seaward. "We'll never have weddings here, I guess."

"Probably not unless other people come here. Maybe then there'll be weddings." And I hope there will be weddings and not wars.

He only nods, and I go on. "After the wedding there was a feast on tables set up outside the church. No music or dancing or spirits, of course, but there was a great deal of conviviality. The array of food was astounding. It was as if every woman were entering her dish in a contest. And there were gifts for Luke and me. Handwoven cloth, baby clothes, a crib, a down quilt. At dusk the tables were put away, and we went to the church for evening service, which, as I remember, was mercifully short. Then Luke and I walked together to our household. *Our* household, finally . . ."

And the air was crackling with the first frost, the stars so clear, it was dizzying. By candlelight Luke led me to the room where I had slept alone for two long nights, and he ceremoniously divested me of my white scarf and blouse and skirt and made love to me with sweet, furious vigor, and it was a homecoming we celebrated until dawn.

"It was a golden autumn, Stephen, warm days and frosty nights, and the harvest was good. Halcyon days, that September and October."

He studies me a moment. "What does *halcyon* mean?"

"Oh, peaceful and happy. Not that those were *easy* days. They were working days, from dawn to dusk. I was astounded at how much the Flock accomplished, and it all seemed to happen without conscious organization. At least, that's what I thought, until I realized the organizational decisions emanated from the church— from that room behind the altar where the Doctor lived. He not only lived behind the church, but he'd set up his clinic there. Well, it was only an examination room and another room with three beds in it. But it seemed fitting that he should live and work there at the center of the Ark."

"Did you get to be Bernadette's apprentice at nursing?"

"No. I didn't have the nerve to ask. I knew that before I asked any favors, I had to prove myself as a working member of the Flock." I give that a short laugh. "And I was indeed a *working* member."

"What kind of work did you do?"

"Almost anything, Stephen. Fall was an especially busy time of year—just as it is here. There's so much to do to prepare for winter. At the Ark we had grain to scythe, thresh, and winnow, and our methods weren't far removed from those used in the Fertile Crescent five thousand years ago, even though the barley was a space-age hybrid adapted to cool climates. Unfortunately it wasn't adaptable enough to grow here on the ocean front. And there were fruits and vegetables to can, animals to butcher, meat to salt or smoke, wood to cut, split, and stack. Plus the usual chores of laundry, ironing, mending, cooking, soap making, candle making, and cleaning, not only the household, but the privies, the bathhouse, even—or es-pecially—the church."

And I offered myself for any task, drove myself to the limits of endurance under the goad of my compulsion to prove myself. Luke was solicitous and proud, and that was my reward. He was with me, morning and evening, at the church services, and that made them bearable. I never ceased to be enthralled by the music nor appalled at the sermons, at the Doctor's brutal eloquence, at the sheer nonsense of his messages. His recurrent themes were sin—and its consequences, told in Dantean detail—and the second com-ing of Christ. He hammered at those themes day after day, and I could understand why after all these years the Flock still expected Jesus to come and waft them to the heaven described by John the Divine, with its abundance of worldly treasures, where a man-shaped god sat on a throne as grand as any mortal king's.

Stephen breaks my reverie. "It must've been hard for you at the Ark."

"What? Oh. Yes, the work was exhausting, but that wasn't the hardest part of my adjustment to the Ark."

"What was the hardest?"

I look into his night-deep eyes. "The Doctor," I answer. "Rather, his philosophy. The trouble was, I couldn't agree with it, but neither could I express my disagreement, not if I hoped to stay at the Ark, and that was the only hope for any children I might bear. I wasn't raised in his kind of religion, Stephen, and I think you have to be to accept it."

That brings a long, thoughtful pause. "What kind of religion were you raised in?" he asks finally.

I doubt Stephen is ready to accept even agnosticism, and certainly nothing beyond that. Not yet. So I hedge. "My mother belonged to another Christian denomination. I was raised in the philosophy that people should decide for themselves what to believe, that no mere human being should tell them what to believe. And I was raised in the philosophy that the concept of god can't be made in the image of man."

"But it was the other way around," he objects.

"Was it, Stephen?"

He tilts his head, his heavy-lidded eyes half-closed. And at that moment Shadow comes bounding across the sand and greets him as if she'd been away on a long journey, and he laughs and ruffles her fur. I say no more about the image of god. Let him think about it awhile.

When Shadow settles herself at his feet, Stephen looks up at me and says, "I wish I could remember more about the Ark."

"You were only three when you left it. Do you remember anything at all?"

"Only a room with log walls and a big fireplace. It must've been the kitchen of our household. And I think I remember Brother Luke. He had a long beard. It was nearly white."

I'm trying to picture a white-bearded Luke when Stephen asks, "What else happened that fall?"

"Other than the long days of work, the hours spent listening to the Doctor's sermons—well, there wasn't time for much else."

Except for making love. It was my salvation then. Night after night Luke and I coupled joyously in the encumbered warmth of that bed. I might exhaust myself physically with the day's work, but I was never too spent to prove myself against his body. There were nights when he was absent from our bed on visitations—by decree of the Doctor, who kept a record of every woman's menstrual cycles and calculated her days of maximum fertility. I didn't begrudge those nights, nor did I feel any jealousy, only a piercing loneliness as I lay waiting for sleep.

Stephen rouses me with, "Do you remember Jeremiah when he was a baby?"

"Yes, I do. At that time Luke had fathered two children. One was Peter, who was born while Luke was away on his trek, and the other was Jeremiah. He was about fourteen months old. He had Luke's blue eyes, and I hoped our child would be as fortunate."

"*Your* child?"

"By late October I was fairly sure I was pregnant. The Doctor hadn't included me in his record keeping—maybe he was giving Luke and me a grace period to conceive a child without his advice—and I didn't tell the Doctor or even Luke that I thought I might be pregnant.

Stephen straddles the log, facing me. "Why not?"

"I didn't know much about pregnancy, but I'd heard of false pregnancies. Sometimes women have all the symptoms of pregnancy—and I think I had most of them, including some of the more unpleasant ones—but there's no baby. I just wasn't sure. I was afraid I might not really be pregnant, and basically I was afraid I might not be *capable* of pregnancy. Yet it was odd . . . I was so intensely happy then. It was as if the hope was enough. It was my secret, and I thought when I was certain—well, I imagined how surprised and happy Luke would be, how the Doctor and the Flock would take me into their hearts."

Stephen hesitates, finally asks, "When did you find out?"

"In November. The fifth day of November, in fact." I lean down, run my fingers through Shadow's silky fur. "For about two weeks before that, Luke had met privately with the Doctor a number of times after evening services, but he wouldn't tell me what they talked about at those meetings. I just assumed it was Ark business, *men's* business, and no concern of mine. And I . . . I loved Luke too much to doubt him."

I straighten and look out at the slow cataracts of the breakers. "Sixty-six days. I don't know why I remember that number so well. I'd been at the Ark for sixty-six days, and in that time I hadn't read or even seen a book except the Bible or a hymnal. I hadn't thought about anything except Luke and proving myself. And my child. I'd already privately named it Luke. Or Rachel, if it was a girl. Yes, I thought about Rachel, but only when I was alone, and that was rare. And when I did think about her, it was to count the months until spring, when Luke had promised we could go back to Amarna to visit her."

I turn to face Stephen, and he asks, almost whispering, "What happened on November fifth?"

"I learned the truth, Stephen. More of it than I wanted to know. After evening service that night, the Doctor asked Luke and me to come to his room. Just for a little talk, he said. Yet my first reaction was fear, and that surprised me. I mean, I should've been flattered to be granted an audience with the Doctor."

Fear, I learned too late, was the truer response.

It is piously spoken that the Scriptures cannot lie. But none will deny that they are frequently abstruse and their true meaning is difficult to discover, and more than the bare words signify.
—GALILEO GALILEI, (1564–1642) *THE AUTHORITY OF SCRIPTURE IN PHILOSOPHICAL CONTROVERSIES*

M ary had never seen the Doctor's sanctum sanctorum. She had, more than once, been detailed to clean the adjoining examination room, but the door to the Doctor's room had always been closed.

Tonight they entered by the other door, the one in the church to the right of the altar. The Doctor, carrying a three-branched candelabra, led the way into a small room with a low, plank ceiling. He crossed to the fireplace on the opposite wall and put the candelabra on the mantel. "We'll need a fire. Getting a bit cold at night, especially with this rain."

Luke went to the wood box. "I'll take care of the fire, Brother."

Mary stood uncertainly just inside the door, while Luke worked at starting a fire, and the Doctor at lighting an oil lamp. The rain sizzled against the window on the wall to her right. She drew her wool shawl up over her shoulders and looked around the room, feeling oddly like a voyeur. Yet there was little to see. Across the room, next to the fireplace, was the door that opened into the examination room. On the left wall was a narrow bed, and at its foot, a wooden chest; on the wall backed to the church, a small table. No doubt the Doctor took his meals there, the meals the women daily left in the church like offerings. There were two straight chairs flanking the table, and in front of the fireplace, a wooden rocker.

"Ah, that's wonderful, Luke." That was for the fire as it began to flare. The Doctor put the lamp on the mantel, blew out the candles, then sat down in the rocker. "Sister Mary, pull up a chair to the fire."

She brought a chair from the table and seated herself on his right, then rubbed her stocking-clad calves. It had been a long, warm Indian summer, and her body didn't seem ready for the cold yet. But she sat up and folded her hands in her lap at the Doctor's cool stare. No doubt he found it unseemly for her thus to call attention to her legs. Or, as he would say, with Victorian primness, her *limbs*. She watched the shadowed curve of Luke's back as he added another wedge of alder to the fire. Then he rose, brought up the other chair, and sat on the Doctor's left, and a silence took shape, augmented by the sputtering fire, the hissing rain on the windows, the creak of the Doctor's chair as he rocked gently.

"I asked you to come here tonight because there's something I must talk to both of you about. Particularly you, Sister Mary."

Mary glanced at Luke, but his gaze was fixed on the floor at the Doctor's feet. What would the Doctor want to talk about particularly with her? Had he guessed she was—might be—pregnant?

He said, "I've been talking to Luke lately about his travels, especially about the woman Rachel."

Mary stared at him. Those words were stunning not only because

they were totally unexpected, but because there was something ominous in the way he said the *woman* Rachel. Mary looked again at
Luke, but he was still staring at the floor. She faced the Doctor,
waiting for him to go on.

"Sister Mary, tell me about . . . Rachel."

"What do you want to know about her?"

"Well, how did you come to live with her at this farm?"

"Didn't Luke tell you that story?" Luke's head came up, then he
seemed to find the fire a magnet for his gaze.

The Doctor said, "Why don't *you* tell me about it?"

Mary shrugged. "I was on my way from Portland to Shiloh Beach
when my bus was attacked by a road gang. I managed to escape,
but I was shot in the leg. I ran into the woods and finally came to
a road, but I was too weak to go on. If Rachel hadn't found me,
if she hadn't taken me into her home and gotten medical help for
me, I probably would've died. She saved my life, just as she saved
Luke's."

That at least garnered a direct look from Luke and even a nod
before he turned to stare into the fire again.

The Doctor rocked back and forth monotonously. "Sister Mary,
how long did you . . . *live* with Rachel?"

The inflections in that aroused the first hint of anger, but it was
little more than annoyance sharpened by apprehension. "You say
that as if you thought we were doing more than simply sharing a
house."

"Is that what you think I meant?" When Mary didn't fall into
the trap of defending her assumption, but remained silent, he said,
"You didn't answer my question."

"How long was I at Amarna? Well, about eleven years. I'd been
there less than a year when the—when Armageddon came."

"You must have been very fond of Rachel."

"I *am* fond of her. We went through a lot together, and she's an
extraordinary human being."

"Ah. How was she extraordinary?"

What was he after? Mary found it difficult to keep her voice
under control. "Rachel is the kindest, wisest person I've ever

261

known; the most knowledgeable, the most . . . wonder-full." Then to be sure he understood that, "I mean, full of wonder."

"What did she wonder at?"

"At everything. At all of creation."

"Did she wonder about . . . God?"

He stopped the movement of the rocker, leaned toward Mary. She hesitated only for a split second. "Of course. We all wonder about god."

"Those of us who believe in Him do, certainly."

A chill hovered at her back as annoyance gave way to anger edged with fear. "Do you think Rachel doesn't believe in god?"

"I want to discover the truth of that."

She looked past the Doctor. "Luke? What did you *tell* him to make him doubt that?"

Luke looked up at her. "I didn't . . . I only told him the truth."

The Doctor cut in. "And what he told me I find very disturbing, Sister. For instance, he told me there's a *tree* she worships."

No more testing feints, Mary thought, yet she still couldn't understand his motive for this attack on Rachel. She brought out a derisive laugh. "That's ridiculous. Luke, you couldn't have said that."

"Well, what I meant—what I said was that place, the tree, it was . . . like a church to her."

The Doctor ignored that. "The woman Rachel also showed Luke *books* filled with pictures of idols made by *heathens!*"

Books. This was a thrust to the heart.

"Rachel is an artist and a student of art. Because she has pictures of idols doesn't mean she *believes* in them. She is a god-fearing, god-loving woman, and in her every act and thought a good Christian!"

Rachel would be appalled at that, but Mary was ready to lie like a trouper for her.

She didn't understand the motive behind the Doctor's hostility, but she was beginning to understand what it could mean to Rachel. It could mean he wouldn't accept her at the Ark.

"God-fearing Christian? Yet one night she told Luke that the light from some of the stars took a million years to reach the Earth!"

At least, he said nothing more about the books. Did that mean Luke hadn't told him about the even more damning books on geology and evolution? Still, starlight a million years old was damning enough to a man who believed the universe was created in seven terrestrial days only six thousand years ago.

"Rachel likes poetry," Mary said, trying to keep her tone light. "Sometimes—well, she takes a bit of poetic license with what she says."

"The truth," the Doctor pronounced, "needs no poetic license." And with that he rose, crossed to the chest at the foot of the bed. The empty chair still rocked, its shadow rising and falling on the wall. When he returned, he was carrying a small, black-bound book.

Rachel's sketchbook.

Mary's impulse was to snatch it out of his hands. He had no right to touch it. But the anger and pain knotted under her ribs was paralyzing: the anger of realization, the pain of betrayal. Her world, which had assumed a semblance of order based ultimately on the keystone of Luke, began to shiver toward collapse. The keystone had cracked.

She spoke finally, the words hissing like the rain on the windows. "Luke, you took that sketchbook without asking me. You *stole* it from me!"

Luke's eyes were wide in blank confusion, but he didn't have a chance to answer her accusation. The Doctor said flatly, "Luke didn't steal this book. I asked him to bring it to me."

"Does that make it right, just because he stole it at your request?"

"Sister Mary!" The whip crack in his voice brought her up short and reminded her that she existed in this community at his whim. He could exile her with a word—and her child. *If* there was a child.

But now he was willing to be placating. He sat down again, crossed one long leg over the other. "Sister Mary, at the Ark no one *owns* anything, so it's not possible to *steal* anything."

She eased open her fisted hands. "That sketchbook was Rachel's because she made the drawings. It's mine because she gave it to me, and it's precious to me for the same reasons. Luke was wrong to take it from me without asking. If he'd only *asked* . . ." She saw the misery in Luke's always legible features, and she couldn't go on.

He hadn't intentionally betrayed her; it had never occurred to him that by taking that sketchbook he was betraying her.

She had misjudged her keystone. It was made of friable clay.

Mary ordered her mind into calm, but anger lurked like a shark under the surface of her thoughts. She asked the Doctor, "Why did you want to see that sketchbook?"

The firelight turned golden the gray of his hair and beard, glowed in the glacier blue of his eyes. "You find the contents of this book *precious*, Sister Mary? You say the woman Rachel was an artist?"

"Yes, I do, and yes, she is an artist."

He opened the sketchbook, riffled through the pages. "And *this*—this is her handiwork?"

"Of course, it is."

"And you approve of this, even admire it?"

"Brother, what game are you playing?"

She heard Luke's quick intake of breath, but the Doctor wasn't distracted. There was a timbre of triumph in his voice. "The Second Commandment says, 'Thou shalt not make unto thee any *graven image*, or any *likeness* of any thing that is in heaven above, or that is in the earth beneath, or that is in the water under the earth.' "

For a moment Mary could only stare at him, staggered. All the art of humankind from its exquisite beginnings in Lascaux and Altamira, all the striving of genius over the millennia to create visual images that expressed the yearnings and insights of the human mind—all that with a few words rendered *sinful*, and thus to be despised, and now, for the first time, she realized that she had never seen an object of art at the Ark, not even a representation of the gods of the Flock.

But she had read the Ten Commandments in the last two months, although she'd had little time for reading even the Bible.

She said, "Go on, Brother. Quote the *next* verse."

Whatever riposte he expected, it wasn't that. His eyes narrowed

264

to slits as he quoted, " 'Thou shalt not bow down to them, nor serve them: for I the Lord—' "

"Yes!" Mary cut in. " 'Thou shalt not *bow down to them, nor serve them.*' That passage is about *idols.* That's what it meant by graven images. Those drawings aren't idols to be worshiped. They're only Rachel's way of understanding what she saw, of making a record of it."

The Doctor surged to his feet, loomed monolithically above her. "You're twisting words, Sister! The Bible says thou shalt not make *any* likeness of *any* thing—"

"To bow down to! To worship! You can't interpret that passage—"

"*Interpret?*" The whip crack was in his voice again. "You can't interpret the *truth!*"

But she wasn't brought to heel. "Tell me what Christ's last words were!"

That stopped him; he couldn't seem to make sense of it, and Mary rushed into the gap. "In the four gospels, there are *three* different versions of Jesus' dying words. Don't tell me finding the truth in that doesn't take some interpretation. *Truth is not a simple thing!*"

At that moment Luke nodded anxiously and said, "Yes, Brother, *that's* a truth. Rachel said that, I remember."

The Doctor glared at Luke as if he'd struck him, and Mary rode a surge of gratitude for Luke's simple affirmation, but she was too caught up in what she read in the Doctor's face to respond to it.

Now she understood. The Doctor's motivation for his attack on Rachel was manifest in his face, in the flush of rage underlain by stark fear. The combined assault left him speechless.

Mary asked, "Luke, did you tell him Rachel might come here to live?"

Luke seemed in the throes of realization of his unintentional act of defiance. He scowled absently, then nodded. "Yes, of course."

Now she understood. The Doctor had been for all these years, through pestilence and starvation and terror, the sole arbiter of truth at the Ark. That was the source of his power. Then Luke had gone out into the ravaged world and found another potential arbiter whose interpretation of truth was at odds with the Doctor's.

Luke would never think of Rachel in those terms, yet she had obviously influenced him, the Doctor's only living relative, his heir apparent, and if she could influence Luke . . .

The Doctor turned on Mary, and he was totally the prophet now, larger than life in his overpowering wrath. "You're venturing dangerously close to blasphemy, Sister!"

"Blasphemy!" The shark of anger lashed to the surface. "Because I know you're *afraid* of Rachel? You're afraid the Flock might listen to her, afraid they might find out *your* idea of truth isn't the only one!"

Luke pleaded, "Mary, please!"

"*God* is the truth," the Doctor crowed, "and you will answer to Him on the Day of Judgment that draws nearer—"

"But I won't answer to *you!*" She rose, still forced to look up at him, but at a smaller angle. "Haven't I proved myself here? Haven't I worked as hard as any other member of the Flock? Have I ever done anything that anyone could take exception to? No! Not until tonight, until you showed me something you had *stolen* from me—"

"*Silence*, Sister! It is not your place to question me, and if you persist in questioning the truth, you will no longer be welcome at the Ark among the righteous!"

"Then maybe I should go back to the *woman* Rachel and raise my child at Amarna!"

And suddenly panic snared her. It was a hollow threat, and if she hadn't given in to her anger and the heady pleasure of unleashing it, she'd never have made it.

Raise her child at Amarna? She was here because she had recognized the futility, even cruelty, of raising a child to live and die in sterile solitude. And the threat rang even more brazenly hollow when she reminded herself that she wasn't even sure there *was* a child.

Luke came to his feet, took a step toward her, indecision and hope struggling in his eyes. "Mary . . . are you . . ."

But her attention was fixed apprehensively on the Doctor. She saw a flash of hope break through the angry skepticism like a shaft of sunlight through an iron gray overcast, but it was gone in a moment, leaving nothing but hostile doubt.

"Your *child*? Are you saying you're pregnant?" He reached out, gripped her arm with bruising force. "Are you *sure*?"

Mary winced, and she couldn't stop her trembling. "I'm sure I've missed three periods."

"But it could be a false pregnancy."

"I'm well aware of that."

"You don't think I can test your claim now, do you?"

"I don't know or care—"

"Well, you're wrong!" And he grabbed the lamp from the mantel and strode toward the examination-room door, dragging her with him. "Come on, Sister. We'll find out if you're pregnant!"

Mary balked, but the last of her anger succumbed to fear when he exerted himself—and it seemed such a small exertion—to pull her into the examination room and slam the door. There, he released her, turned his back on her while he lighted a smaller oil lamp with a round, mirrored reflector. Then he filled a basin with water from a covered pail and began soaping his hands. "Take off your clothes, Sister."

She gazed numbly around the room: enameled cabinets, shelves of bottles and boxes, some marked with brand names from Before, and in the center of the room, the narrow, sheet-draped table with the metal stirrups at one end. The smell of alcohol was sharp in the chill air; the steel speculum glittered on a tray by the basin.

"Sister, I said take off your clothes. For the Lord's sake, I'm a doctor. Or is there some reason you don't want me to examine you?"

She could think of many reasons, but she crossed to the chair in one corner and began undressing. In the days Before, a nurse would have provided one of those silly paper smocks to maintain the illusions of modesty, but the Doctor was too impatient to offer a substitute.

"Get on the table."

And too impatient to offer a helping hand or notice that she was shivering with the cold.

"Lie back."

She had never felt so vulnerable in nakedness. She clenched her teeth when she felt his fingers pressing into her lower abdomen. A physician's touch had always seemed quite impersonal to her, but this seemed an invasion. And now he was feeling her breasts. She closed her eyes, trying not to flinch. Then she heard him move to the end of the table.

"Slide down this way." Two metallic clicks. "*Farther.* Yes. Feet in the stirrups." He guided her heels into the stirrups and pushed her knees apart, and she caught her breath, hands locked on the edges of the table. He put the lamp with the reflector in a mount that had undoubtedly been designed for an electric light. She could feel the warmth on the insides of her thighs. She waited, bracing herself for what had to be done, staring up at the grotesque shadow he made on the plank ceiling. The sudden insertion of the icy speculum shocked her into a cry.

"Be still, woman," he snapped. "Keep your legs apart."

She disciplined her body to stillness while the speculum penetrated slowly, expanding with small ratcheting sounds, and discomfort edged toward pain. Why was he so damnably slow about it? She raised her head, saw him bending between the silhouetted angle of her thighs, saw his face behind the lamp's glare. "Some women *like* this," he said contemptuously.

Those words were so dense with implications, she was stunned. But she couldn't deal with that now; she was too frightened, too preoccupied with what had ceased to be mere discomfort.

"Well, *I* don't like it!" she spat out. "Get on with it!"

He let her know through the speculum that she was not in a position for rebellion. Eyes squeezed shut, she thought of Luke waiting in the next room, thought of screaming loud enough to bring him in here. He wouldn't believe the Doctor was purposely humiliating her, hurting her, but his presence might stop the humiliation and hurt.

She fought against her own reflexes, felt small shifts of pressure in the speculum, heard the Doctor occasionally change position.

No. She wouldn't call Luke. That would simply delay this game. She could only lie here and endure until the Doctor determined the truth.

But would he admit it if she were pregnant?

He'd have to. The truth would be evident to everyone at the Ark in a few months. Unless he exiled her. And if she *weren't* pregnant?

She'd never have another chance at it.

She felt, through the instrument impaling her, a stiffening, heard the Doctor muttering to himself as the heat of the lamp shifted. Then abruptly he withdrew the speculum, threw it clattering into the basin. She lay gasping for air, only now aware that she'd been holding her breath.

"The Lord be praised!"

Mary found herself an incredulous witness to a metamorphosis, a transformation from anger and skepticism to joy verging on exaltation, a restoration of the Doctor as the revered patriarch, radiating benign strength. He offered his hands and pulled her up into a sitting position.

"Sister, forgive me for doubting you. Yes, you *are* pregnant. The Lord be praised, you are with child!"

Mary pressed her hands to her mouth to stop a cry of relief, of triumph for the life within her. She *was* pregnant, and that revelation put everything in perspective.

That the Doctor was capable of sadism didn't matter. *He* didn't matter. Nothing mattered except the transcendent truth of this child's existence. This child would outlive the Doctor, this child would prevail over his memory, prevail over the destruction of a civilization and the potential demise of humankind—this child and its children and its children's children.

She began weeping and found in the tears a resolution. The Doctor was courteously solicitous. She should get dressed. She mustn't get chilled. He'd go tell Luke about the baby. Was that all right? Or would she rather tell him herself?

No, she didn't care who told him. The Doctor left the room, and Mary pulled her clothes on, still shivering, still crying. When she got dressed, she stumbled to the door, and Luke was there to hold her, to laugh and cry with her. Then the three of them knelt, and the Doctor prayed for the child, whom the Almighty in His wisdom had sent to join the righteous and to await the Lord's coming and the sure ascent into His golden realm.

The Doctor didn't object, nor even seem to notice, that Mary took Rachel's sketchbook with her when she and Luke departed.

When at length Mary lay in their bed warm in Luke's arms, the euphoria faded. She stared into the darkness, listening for the sound of the sea, hearing nothing but a ringing silence. The rain had stopped.

"Luke . . ."

He stirred, kissed her forehead. "Yes, Mary?"

"Will the Doctor forgive what I said tonight? I mean, before . . . before he found out I'm pregnant."

Luke laughed sleepily. "Of course, he will. He told me when women are pregnant . . . well, it's the hormones, he said. Sometimes pregnant women act a little strange."

She found herself bristling at that, yet relieved. And she remembered the Doctor's abrupt transformation, his patent joy. Hormones. Yes, that could explain her reaction to his examination. She'd probably imagined his antagonism, the purposeful infliction of pain and humiliation.

Some women like this.

Had she imagined that?

It didn't matter.

But one thing she couldn't dismiss so easily.

"Luke, what about Rachel?"

He propped himself up on one elbow. "I don't know why he said such hard things about Rachel. He just didn't understand. But he will. Let me talk to him."

She sighed, vaguely aware of Luke's hand moving under the covers, sliding up her thigh, pushing her nightgown with it.

"Luke, did you tell him about Rachel's books—about the vault?"

"No. I . . . well, I just never got around to that."

It simply wasn't important to him. Mary shook her head, wondering if she should leave it at that. No. She had to be sure.

"I want you to promise me something."

He leaned down to kiss her ear. "Anything you ask, little mother."

"I want you to swear to me by everything you hold sacred that you will never tell anyone about the books and the vault—not even the Doctor." Above all, not the Doctor.

"But . . . why not, Mary?"

"Please, just do this for me. *Please*, Luke."

"If you ask it, I'll do it. I swear by the holy blood of Jesus, who died for my sins, I will never tell anybody about Rachel's books or about the vault. I swear it, Mary, on the life of our child."

She didn't doubt that he would keep his word. However friable the clay of her keystone, he wouldn't knowingly break a promise to her.

And the Doctor wouldn't live forever. Luke would take his place one day. And this child . . .

"Oh, Mary . . ." His arms encompassed her, making her feel small and safe. He kissed her, mouth open to hers, finally whispered, "This child is blessed, Mary. This child was conceived in love, as it should be. The Lord can only smile on such a child."

She laughed, overwhelmed by sudden exuberance, imagining—feeling—the child within her. She stretched herself against Luke's body, and he whispered, "Mary, can we . . . I mean, with the baby . . ."

"Yes, we can." She reached down the taut length of his belly, feeling the coppery hair soft under her hand, heard his groaning sigh. We can. Tonight we must.

He was gentle and thoughtful, even playful, and she reveled in it, found delay sweet, teased herself and him through long slow minutes to delicious impatience, to the shivering edge of the euphoria she sought, until at last she lay panting and ready under him. Yet at the invasion of steel-rigid flesh, she recoiled in panic.

He didn't understand, and she didn't want to think about the explanation. She wanted him, wanted the euphoria again. She heard his husky whisper in her ear. "Mary . . . what's wrong? Did I—"

"Nothing's wrong." She buried her face in the curve of his neck against the warm mat of his beard. "Don't stop, Luke . . . don't. . . ."

Nothing's wrong. *Nothing.*

I am persuaded that diverse of you, who lead the people, have labored to build yourselves in these things; wherein you have censured others and established yourselves "upon the Word of God." Is it therefore infallibly agreeable to the Word of God, all that you say? I beseech you, in the bowels of Christ, think it possible you may be mistaken.

—OLIVER CROMWELL, *TO THE GENERAL ASSEMBLY OF THE KIRK OF SCOTLAND,* August 3, 1650

T he Seth Thomas clangs eight times. The curtains are drawn on all the windows, and the children have been put to bed. Seven candles in an assortment of holders are aligned in the center of the dining-room table to light our deliberations. My joints ache unremittingly tonight. I sit trapped in my fragile, pain-ridden body, gazing at the stack of books at the far end of the table: Miriam's exhibits in the case for the prosecution.

At these family meetings Jerry always sits at the west end—the head—of the table, but otherwise there's no customary seating order. Tonight I chose to sit at the foot of the table. At my right is Bernadette, gray eyes revealing only dispassionate curiosity. Next

273

is Enid, clasping and unclasping her hands anxiously. Then Esther, as motionless as the Benin sculpture she always calls to mind. Miriam has placed herself at Jerry's right hand. I'm sure she considers that fitting. And Grace sits at Miriam's right hand. Grace hasn't once looked directly at me.

Jerry slumps in his chair, tugging at his beard, his brooding frown exposing his uncertainty. Finally he pulls in a deep breath. "We have a problem to settle tonight."

Miriam rises, and in the golden candlelight she is as beautiful as a tigress and as single-minded and incapable of mercy: she recognizes no alternative to her actions.

She says, "The problem we have to settle tonight, Jeremiah, is our children's souls. We've trusted this woman to teach our children, and she is teaching them *blasphemy*."

Jerry grimaces. "Miriam, I don't think Mary means to—"

"Who knows what she *means* to do? Look at this." Exhibit A, a historical geology textbook. She paws through it, stops at a time chart. "See what it says here: life begins—three and a half million years ago!"

"That's billion, Miriam," I say, "not million."

She glares at me, pushes the book to the center of the table, picks up another, the physiology text I'd given Jonathan to explain human reproduction. "Look at these pictures—men and women naked, showing bodily parts that God decreed in the Garden of Eden should be covered." That book thumps on top of the other, and I wince.

The next exhibit is another geology text. "Look at these pictures. Satan's monsters! And this—" The geology book is tossed on top of the others, slides against a candlestick, and jars a spatter of wax onto the offending illustration of a stegosaurus. The book whose pages she is creasing in her haste is on twentieth-century art. "Look at these devil's scrawls! Who but a worshiper of Satan could draw people like that?" *Les Demoiselles d'Avignon* is exposed for the family's scrutiny as Miriam throws that book down, and if her carelessness is calculated to blind me with outrage, it is approaching success.

274

The last book is folio size, bound in gold-stamped linen, filled with color reproductions on thick, satiny paper. She opens it, roughly thumbs through it. "Heathen idols! Every page full of heathen idols!"

And I say coldly, "Mythology, Miriam, the study of ancient religions and legends, and you will put that book down—carefully— *now*."

Her eyes, narrowed as if to contain the flaring resentment in them, fix on me. She grabs a handful of pages, and the ripping sound is accompanied by the scrape of my chair as I lunge to my feet, by shocked cries from the other women, by Jerry's, "Stop it, Miriam!"

She responds to his command, if reluctantly, and I gaze at the beautiful book, its bent, torn pages like the wings of an injured bird. "Was it Jesus who taught you maliciousness, Miriam?"

"It was Jesus who taught me to hate evil, and these books are *full* of evil!"

"*You* say there's evil in them, but evil is in the minds of men— and women. There's no *evil* in those books!"

Jerry cuts in. "Be quiet, both of you. You'll wake up the children."

I sink back into my chair, pulse ringing in my ears. Yes, the children, and for them I should be able to keep my temper.

Miriam is still on her feet, and she's also thinking of the children. "The Lord gave me my children so I could bring them up to be God-fearing. I won't have them taught to deny there *is* a God!"

I respond, as levelly as I can, "Don't be ridiculous. Where in those books does it say anything to dispute the existence of god?"

"Where?" She is triumphant now. "Wherever it says that fiendish creatures walked the Earth, that men came from monkeys!"

"You'll never find that in any of these books. Homo sapiens did not evolve from monkeys."

That makes her pause, but only briefly. "These books deny the Bible!"

"Only two of them have anything to do with the evolution of life on Earth, if that's what you mean, and they're—"

275

"Whatever denies the Bible denies *God!* The Bible is God's truth, God's word, and the only truth there is!"

I take a long breath, keep my voice steady when I want to rage. "You can teach the children what *you* call truth, but *I* will teach them to recognize reality as best they can."

"Truth and reality are the same thing!"

"*No!* Reality will not change to conform to your idea of the truth. Reality will not bend, Miriam—not for you or me or anyone else." I rise, cross to the old spool cabinet on the north wall, and when I return, I place what seems to be a piece of stone in front of Miriam, then go back to stand at the foot of the table. "What is that, Miriam?"

At first, she seems loath to take her eyes off me, but finally she picks up the stone that is obviously more than it seems. It is a tusklike tooth five inches long, curving to a blunt point, composed of opaque, blue-black agate with the texture of the enamel perfectly delineated.

The silence is as heavy as the tooth in Miriam's hand. It is Jerry who breaks it. "Let me see that." Miriam hands it to him, and he examines it. "Looks like a horn. Or a sea lion's tooth, except bigger. What is it, Mary?"

I don't answer him. "Miriam, what do you say it is?"

She replies impatiently, "A tooth, I suppose. What difference—"

"Yes, a tooth. But is that the material of teeth? No. It is stone. That's a fossil, Miriam, the canine tooth of a saber-toothed cat. And it's approximately thirty million years old."

She laughs harshly. "There! She denies God herself—"

"Have you ever heard me deny god? You are denying *reality*, Miriam, and that's my point. How do you explain this stone tooth?"

"Somebody carved it out of stone, and it was probably you."

"Why? Simply to confound you? And with these hands?" I smile bitterly as I hold up my swollen, misshapen hands. "But what about all the millions of fossils found all over the world—found and cataloged and photographed. Did I carve *all* of them?"

"I've heard of rocks like that," she says truculently. "Seashells made of rock. God put them in the high places to test our faith in Him."

"Does your god lie?"

"What? No, of course not, but that—"

"Of course not! It says in the Bible: *God that cannot lie.* The shells in the mountains aren't tricks or shams. They are a testament to the process of creation. You don't even know enough to identify that tooth, yet you think you know enough to understand the mind of God!" She tries to interrupt me, but I raise my voice, indifferent to whether it will wake the children. "You live in a state of abysmal ignorance, Miriam! You can barely read, you don't understand a fraction of what you see, yet you think you can tell other people what to believe! You call up Genesis and say—"

"I say anybody who doesn't believe in Genesis doesn't believe in God!"

"What kind of god would ask—"

She pounds her fist on the table in cadence with her words: "If there was no Garden of Eden, there was no fall from grace, and if there was no fall from grace, there was no atonement, there was no redemption, and there was no resurrection!"

With the candlelight glittering hectically in her eyes, she waits for me to answer her pronouncement. Instead, I ease myself down into my chair, and my response is addressed not to her, but to Jerry.

"I don't understand why Miriam has such a niggardly vision of God, why she thinks the generous, loving, and merciful god of whom Jesus spoke would be so grudging and petty."

"I never said God was—"

"You don't have to *say* it! Your idea of god is part of your mean little scheme of things, and anything that doesn't fit into it is evil. You don't know your god, because you don't know the incredible dimensions and richness of the universe you say you believe your god created. That's what I want the children to understand! You're worried about their souls? I'm worried about their *minds.* Human beings have been given astounding capacities to create, to understand, to love, and if we don't use them, if we lock ourselves in cages of dogma, then we are no longer human, we are nothing more than talking animals capable of cruelty. I want to teach the children so they won't become caged and vicious animals. I want to teach them because I love them. You don't love anything that doesn't fit into your myopic, colorless concept of the world. The children deserve more, and they will *have* more!"

She is—for the moment—silenced. Like Jerry and the other women, she stares at me, amazed. Perhaps she didn't think the old woman had it in her, all that passion, all those words.

Again, I address myself to Jerry. "Your father sent you to Amarna, to me, and didn't you promise—swear by all you hold sacred—to let me teach the children?"

He frowns, uncertainty still written large in his face. "Yes, I . . . made that promise."

Miriam stands trembling, her hands still in fists. "You didn't promise to let her teach the children blasphemy! Jeremiah, you can't be held by any oath you swore to *her*!"

He only seems annoyed by the distraction. "Be quiet, Miriam."

"I *won't* be quiet, and I won't let you give in to this—this *witch*!"

He ignores that, looks down the length of the table at me, then his frown deepens as his gaze shifts to the books. He hasn't made up his mind yet. "Mary, I *did* promise you could teach the children, but—"

"*No!*" Miriam looms over him, her face contorted into ugliness. "The Lord help us, she has you trained like that *dog* of hers! All she has to do is blow on that silver whistle, and you come running. And you call yourself Elder of this family!"

Jerry rises so abruptly his chair tips over behind him, and Enid gives a strangled cry of alarm, a startled cat skitters out of the room. Yet with Jerry's every muscle straining against his rage, Miriam can't seem to stop.

"Jeremiah, if you give in to her, we'll *all* know what kind of Elder you are! You never *did* have any backbone. Even when we were children, you couldn't—"

"Miriam!" His hand comes up in a shaking fist, but he doesn't strike her. He says between clenched teeth, *"Sit down!"*

She sags into her chair, finally aware of the depth of his anger. The husky tautness in his voice sends a shiver up my back.

"Miriam, you've gone too far! I am Elder, and I will decide whether Mary is a fit teacher for the children. I gave my sacred oath, and I will not break it. *That* is my decision. School will go on tomorrow morning as usual, and Jonathan, Isaac, and Deborah *will* be there!"

So. I have won this battle.

Yet I feel neither the elation of triumph nor even relief. Jerry made his decision for the wrong reason. Nothing is resolved.

And Miriam hasn't surrendered yet.

She says coldly, "School may go on as usual, Jeremiah, but *my* children won't be there!"

"Two of your children are also mine, and all of them will be there!"

"Or *what?*" she demands. "What if I choose to protect *our* children from what that woman teaches them?"

He picks up his chair, slumps into it, doubt slackening his features. At length, the doubt turns into bleak conviction, and he says, "There is no place in this family for anybody who defies the Elder."

Those words create a palpable silence, and the moment seems to expand, holding all of us motionless, all staring at Jerry, while he looks down at the double fist of his hands resting before him on the table.

No place in this family.

That means exile.

Jerry, you fool. No, it's Miriam who is the fool. She forced him into this. She turned her philosophical disagreement with me into a challenge to Jerry's authority. She gave him no choice but to unsheathe this, his ultimate weapon—the threat of exile.

Grace bursts out, "Jeremiah, you couldn't do that to Miriam!"

And Esther: "It would leave her children motherless."

And Enid, "But where would she *go?*"

"I don't care," Jerry says dully. "South, I suppose, to find the other survivors from the Ark."

Miriam is silent, staring at her half-brother as if he were a stranger who had just slipped a knife between her ribs. Jerry doesn't waver, but neither does he look at her. He says to the rest of us, "This meeting is over. Let us pray." And he raises his locked hands, bends his head over them. "Almighty God, we pray that you will guide us in the ways of your love, that you will help us find understanding, one with another, that you will succor us in this our time of need. Amen."

That is undoubtedly the briefest prayer he has ever spoken, and the women are caught short with their *amens*. He doesn't seem to notice. He looks up and repeats, "This meeting is *over*."

It is still a few seconds before that pronouncement has any effect. Bernadette rises first, reaching for one of the candlesticks. She hasn't said a word throughout this confrontation, but the dispassionate curiosity that typically glints in her eyes has gone dull. She glances at me, shakes her head wearily, then: "Come on, Enid. Let's go to bed."

Enid is dazed and at first seems deaf. Finally, as if she were weighted with invisible chains, she pulls herself to her feet and picks up a candle.

Grace, still indignant, starts to say something to Jerry, apparently thinks better of it, and gives me a look no doubt meant to be withering. "Miriam, you're not alone, Sister." With that she joins Enid and Bernadette, who are already on their way out the backdoor.

Esther comes to her feet, silver tears streaking her bronze cheeks. Without a word, she picks up a candle and goes to the basement door. I hear her footsteps on the stairs as Miriam silently rises.

She takes a candle, turns to leave, and Jerry speaks. She stops.

"Miriam, *I* will conduct morning service tomorrow."

That is not only foolish, it is inexcusable. He wasn't driven to that.

Miriam's only visible response is the marble pallor of her face. Her voice is uninflected, pitched low as she turns to Jerry. "I'll pray for you, Jeremiah." She goes to the basement door, closes it softly behind her, leaving Jerry and me sitting at either end of the long table in the flickering light of the two remaining candles.

"Jerry, I beg of you, don't take the morning service away from her."

He looks at me questioningly, some of the tension in his features dissolving. "You're kind and forgiving to ask that, Mary, but I must—"

"Kind and forgiving has nothing to do with it! She's been forced to her knees. It isn't necessary to add a beating."

"*I* consider it necessary, and I'm Elder here. Mary, why are you standing up for her?"

"I'm trying to avoid a worse schism than we already have. Do you think she's just going to bow her head and meekly do your bidding from now on?"

"Yes! That's exactly what she's going to do." He rises, frowning. "I don't understand you. I'd think you'd be more . . ."

"Grateful?" I take a deep breath, remembering how young he is, how little experience he's actually had with people. "Yes, Jerry, I'm grateful to you for defending me. But you did it for the wrong reason. You *had* to defend me, because Miriam made her attack on me an attack on you and your authority as Elder."

"I did what I thought was right! What else could I do but defend my own mother?"

I'm too bewildered to respond to that, and he seems annoyed at himself. He comes to my end of the table, sits down in the chair nearest me. "I realize you wanted it kept secret, Mary, but I know all about it."

I feel dizzied, as if I suddenly found myself on stage in the middle of a play and didn't know my lines or have an inkling of the plot.

"Jerry, what are you talking about?"

"I know, that's what I'm talking about. I know you're my mother."

I'm too stunned to do anything but ask, "How could you *know* that, Jerry? Did . . . Luke tell you I was your mother?"

"Not in so many words, but he told me you bore his child. It was conceived in love, he said. He took me into his household after the woman who called herself my mother died, and sometimes at night I'd find him by the fire in the kitchen, and he'd be . . . crying. And he'd talk about you. He never talked about you to anybody else, and I knew then that I was the child conceived in love."

"But no one actually told you I was your mother, did they?"

"No. People at the Ark didn't talk about you. But I knew."

He looks at me with a trusting smile, looks at me with Luke's eyes, and I'm tempted to let him go on believing what he wants to believe. And I wonder if it wasn't in the depths of grief for his mother that he decided to be the child conceived in love whom his father loved.

So, what do I tell him now? I've never lied to him, to any of these people, unless it seemed absolutely necessary. When you speak to a child, you speak as a child. But I can't bring myself to lie to Jerry about this, however childlike he seems now.

I take his strong, muscular hand in my weak, ugly one. "Oh, Jerry, I wish . . . I wish you *were* my son. I look at you and see Luke in you, and I wish I were a part of you. But I'm not. Jerry, you . . . you're not my son. You were over a year old when I came to the Ark."

He looks at me with the incredulous denial of a man told he is about to die. His head moves back and forth slowly, and finally, with a muffled cry, he pulls his hand away from mine, lurches to his feet, and in his eyes doubt turns to accusation. "But . . . why didn't you *tell* me?"

And I recoil from his accusing gaze with the hurt welling from deep within me, and it takes the shape of anger. I didn't want the childish assumptions and expectations he created for me.

"How *could* I tell you? I didn't know you thought I was your mother. And what difference does it make? Are you different because I'm not your mother? Is your life different than it would've been? Aren't I the same person you've known all these years?"

He retreats from me, shakes his head again in mute response to emotions he can't verbalize, until at length, he forces out, "It *does* make a difference! I—I've been a fool. And you . . . I *loved* you, Mary."

"You weren't a fool to think I was your mother. That was just a misunderstanding. But you *are* a fool if you think love depends on sharing common genes."

He's too full of his disappointment and pain to hear me. But I have disappointment and pain of my own to deal with. I told him he had defended me for the wrong reason, but I didn't know there was another reason beyond Miriam's challenge to his authority. He thought he was defending his mother. And both reasons are so petty in light of the principle involved in that confrontation that I feel sick with disgust.

"Jerry, you need to do some thinking. Some soul-searching. You have a lot to learn about people, about life, and especially about love."

He opens his mouth as if to speak, but he doesn't. He picks up a candlestick, nearly quenching the flame in his haste, then stalks away toward his room. I hear his door slam. For a while I sit in the light of the last candle, listening to the silence, remembering the years of silence I spent here before Jerry and the others came. No, not utter silence. I always had the sea. *I am here. . . .*

Shadow comes out of the darkness, nudges my arm, and asks to be petted. I oblige her, sighing for the simplicity of her affection. I have in my life often been as alone and vulnerable as I am now, but never so bone-weary.

But there will be no rest for these weary bones.

I am a slightly ridiculous, sad, old, distaff Quixote going out to do battle. For the future, because I am a human being, and my species discovered the future, and I can't free myself of its hold on me.

Miriam hasn't surrendered, and neither have I.

Jerry gave a moving sermon at the morning service, so Enid told me. His text was from the Beatitudes: *Blessed are the peacemakers.*

On the morning after the confrontation at the family meeting, the adult members of the family are assiduously behaving as if nothing has happened. We make conversation over breakfast about the weather—no rain, but the barometer is falling—about the livestock, the garden, the tasks that need to be done today. Miriam is the exception to the business-as-usual attitude. She remains silent, unless directly addressed, watching the rest of us with eyes that seem dead, as if the fires of anger had been so thoroughly banked, not even an ember glows.

She is playing a game with us today. Having been stripped of part of her power, she has abdicated the rest of it. She gives no orders, tells no one what should be done. This forces the other women to ask her for instructions, but, with a show of humility, she tells them to ask Jerry. At first, Jerry doesn't recognize the game and tries to make decisions on matters he knows little about, which leaves him looking inept.

But on the surface, all is well, which is to say there are no overt disagreements, no reminders of what happened last night. The surface harmony is for the children. At least, if I asked the adults, that would be their answer. But the children aren't deceived.

I remember there were times when Rachel and I had disagreements, when resentment accumulated until it became explosive. Our answer—one never verbalized—was to maintain surface appearances, going about our daily chores as if nothing was wrong, until our tempers cooled, until finally the time came around right, and we would talk out the sources of dissension and embrace in renewed love. Something similar is going on in the family now, but it won't work.

Miriam won't let it work.

She will pry at the cracks in the familial foundations until they collapse. But she won't be blamed. I will. Already, I can see open animosity for me in Grace's eyes, and in Enid's eyes, a profound doubt. Esther is still bewildered, more than doubtful. And Jerry? His resentment for Miriam and for me seems equal, and it is underlain with confusion that prevents me from feeling the same resentment for him.

After breakfast I go out into the greenhouse. The tomatoes are doing well this year, and Bernadette's arcane garden is flourishing, including the thick-leafed aloe that is a scion of the plant Rachel had growing here when I first came to Amarna. The poppies are beginning to bloom, unfurling crumpled silk petals of burning red around charcoal centers. They grow remarkably well in this artificial environment.

"Pretty things, aren't they?" Bernadette comes into the greenhouse from the north door. "I wonder sometimes if they aren't trying to tell the world they're full of miracles. Full of sleep for the sleepless, comfort for those in pain. Full of death."

She doesn't wait for a reply or expect one, but goes to the worktable, takes up a small pestle, and begins grinding dried leaves in a bisque porcelain bowl. I approach the table and ask, "What's that, Bernadette?"

"Comfrey. Can't you smell it?" She hands me a dusty-scented leaf. "Good for vitamin B_{12}. I'll fix you some comfrey tea later. You're looking sort of peaked, Mary."

"Am I? Well, I'll take your expert word for that. Besides, I rather like your comfrey tea."

"Little honey in it. That helps."

She continues grinding, and the soft growl of the pestle seems to follow me as I cross the greenhouse to the sliding door on the south wall that opens into my room. I'm at the door before she speaks again.

"Mary . . ." I turn, find her studying me intently. She says, "Be careful, Sister. You're an old woman. Old women are apt to die."

Those words strike with a chill incongruous in this tropical pocket of space with its sun-drenched banks of foliage.

Yes. This old woman's death would certainly solve Miriam's problems. I hadn't considered this alternative. It hadn't occurred to me that Miriam might rid herself and the family of my evil influence by the simple expedient of ridding herself and the family of me. But it has occurred to Bernadette, and I trust her judgment.

"Thank you, Bernadette." I go into my room to get the books I'd set aside for school. It's almost time.

Miriam's children seem glad to be back in school, but I find it difficult to concentrate. We practice addition and subtraction, recite multiplication tables, and Jonathan demonstrates some simple algebra. We study history; we're up to the dark ages in Europe. We read poetry. "My life closed twice before its close. . . ." We gather around the globe for a game of Where-in-the-World. We talk about crustaceans; Stephen brought a hermit crab from the tide pools. And at the end of our allotted time, I'm not sure what I've said or the children have learned.

Afterward, Shadow and I set out for the beach, and when I reach the foot of the path, I realize the tide is nearly high. I should've known it would be. I pick my way over sea-smoothed cobbles, then walk north on the margin of sand still above the reach of the waves. The surf has a throbbing rumble that I don't so much hear as feel. The breakers have whipped the foam to a creamy froth, and Shadow spatters through the scallops of incoming waves until she's belly-deep in foam, making small blizzards as her headlong gallop shatters the ivory mounds.

And I consider my own murder.

Is Miriam capable of murder? Probably. It wouldn't be murder in her eyes. She'd be ridding the world—her world, small as it is—of a source of evil, a purveyor of blasphemy, a corruptor of children's souls.

And my death would be her ultimate justification.

At least, it would be if it seemed an accident. An act of god. For Miriam's purposes, my death must be an act of god.

I look out at the roiling ocean. Old women are apt to drown—if they are so foolish as to walk alone near high tide.

"Shadow!" But she doesn't hear me. I reach under my collar for the silent whistle and give it a long blast. She looks back at me, then when I blow again, she returns to me, taking her time about it. I lean down to stroke her head. "Good girl. Come on, we're going back."

She follows me, reluctantly, and I feel a cast of anger in the apprehension that has taken firm root in my mind. How long, I wonder, am I to be denied the pleasure of walking alone on the beach or visiting the tree? Or climbing up to the Knob? Yes, old women are certainly apt to slip at the edge of a three-hundred-foot cliff.

Damn her.

But I don't intend to make it easy for her.

The midday meal is another test of our Thespian skills, but we get through it without ruffling the surface calm. Afterward, I go to the deck and stand at the railing. The wind is out of the north with a blunted edge of chill in it, but I prefer it to the chill inside the house.

Finally I hear the sliding door open. Stephen has a smile for me, but behind it is the anxiety, cloaked in silence, that haunts all the children today. We sit down, then I wait, giving him a little time. I know he has questions. I don't know if I'll have the answers.

He sits with one leg pulled up, heel caught on the edge of the seat, and at length, he asks, "What happened at the family meeting last night?"

No, I don't have the answers. I can only say, "Well, Jeremiah heard our arguments—Miriam's and mine—as to whether I should be allowed to continue teaching."

"Yes, we could hear some of the arguing."

I smile briefly. "I'm sorry if we kept you awake."

He shrugs. "So, Jeremiah decided you *could* keep teaching us."

"Yes, he did."

He watches me, as if he's waiting for me to go on. Then, "Why doesn't Miriam want you to teach us?"

"Because she doesn't agree with what I teach."

"I wish she . . ." But he doesn't finish that, instead asks, "Why did Jeremiah preach at morning service?"

"That was his decision. You'll have to ask him about it."

"I don't think he'll talk to me about it. Well, I'm glad he said you could keep teaching us." But his anxiety hasn't been alleviated. I don't know what I can say—and be truthful—that would allay his fears. Not when I am so steeped in fear myself.

"Yes, Stephen, I'm glad, too." Then I change the subject with, "You know, we're coming to the end of the Chronicle. A few more sessions, then we'll get on to more orthodox lessons."

"When will you be finished writing it?"

"I don't know." The question now, perhaps, is not when, but will I be able to finish it at all.

He says, "If you can't finish it, *I* will—as best I can."

I'm startled at that. I didn't mean to reveal so much of my fear. And I'm deeply moved. "Thank you, Stephen. Yes, if I can't finish it for any reason, you must. I keep it in the bottom drawer in the chest in my room." He nods soberly, and I bring out a smile. "So, where were we?"

"You'd just found out you really were pregnant. Mary, what . . ." He hesitates, and I know the question he asks isn't the one he started. "What did the Doctor do after that? I mean, was he still angry?"

Stephen is thinking of my argument with the Doctor about Rachel. I didn't tell him about the examination. "No, he didn't seem to be angry. In fact, he was as kind and concerned as a doting grandfather. He treated me like a prodigal daughter returned. All the Flock did. And in December they had more good news. Sister Hannah was pregnant, too. She was Miriam's mother, and it was Miriam she was carrying."

Now it seems darkly ironic that Miriam was taking the shape of life while I was at the Ark.

Stephen asks, "Were you happy then?"

And I remember that winter, a mild winter of gentle rains and few storms. I wasn't clairvoyant. I didn't even see the present clearly.

"Yes, I was happy. Luke was proud and loving, and everything seemed good. I was so consumed with my child, I didn't think past its birth. I was full of energy and self-satisfaction, and I couldn't imagine anything that would unravel the golden skein of my world."

He hesitates, his night-dark eyes hooded. "But something did . . . unravel it?"

"It didn't so much unravel, really, as disintegrate." I watch a solitary gull soaring low over the breakers. "That was late in February. I was seven months pregnant then. I always think of February as the real beginning of spring. The smell in the air is different, and the first daffodils are blooming. . . ."

But that year it wasn't a beginning.

*The gods can either take away evil from the world and will not, or,
being willing to do so cannot; or they neither can nor will, or lastly,
they are able and willing.*

*If they have the will to remove evil and cannot, then they are not
omnipotent. If they can but will not, then they are not benevolent. If
they are neither able nor willing, they are neither omnipotent nor
benevolent.*

*Lastly, if they are both able and willing to annihilate evil, why
does it exist?*

—EPICURUS (341–270 B.C.), *APHORISMS*

*I saw Eternity the other night,
Like a great ring of pure and endless light,
    All calm as it was bright;
And round beneath it, Time in hours, days, years,
    Driv'n by the spheres,
Like a vast shadow mov'd: in which the world
And all her train were hurled.*

—HENRY VAUGHN, *"THE WORLD"* (1678)

The Jordan ran high with the first spring runoff, and even from
the north garden, Mary could hear its murmur. To the east,
the orchard was on the fine verge of exploding into bloom. Just
outside the garden fence, a black Nubian doe, shadowed by her
new kid, browsed in the green grass growing up through last year's
rain-beaten straw. Mary leaned on her hoe and arched her back
against the dull ache at the base of her spine. She watched the kid
maneuvering on wobbly legs, bleating adamantly when the doe
moved too far away, and she pressed her hand to the swelling curve

of her belly, thinking to the child there: *Only two more months, and you'll be free.*

She often spoke to the child that way, and sometimes forgot and spoke aloud. The people who heard her laughed and asked, "Has it begun to talk back to you, Sister?"

In its way, it did. She felt it moving at times and was always awed by the sensation, savoring the private joy of knowing that however commonplace it might be in the grand scheme of things, she harbored a miracle.

"Sister Mary, aren't you getting too tired?"

Mary looked around at Naomi, one of the Barrens, who had also paused to lean on her hoe. The garden was full of people taking advantage of the sunny day to prepare the soil for planting. The raised beds in this garden couldn't be plowed, and in each of the long beds two men spaded kelp, ground eggshells, and manure into the earth, while two women followed with hoes to break the clods, then two more with rakes to smooth the nourished soil.

Mary shook her head. "No, I'm not tired."

Naomi sighed. "You really shouldn't be doing this kind of work."

"Yes, I should, Sister Naomi." Mary began cutting into the dark clods with her hoe; the fecund smell of the earth was pleasantly sour.

Another sigh from Naomi, but she didn't argue. All the women had argued with Mary too often, too fruitlessly. They wanted her to do nothing but rest, and she understood their concern. They had seen too many of the few women who became pregnant lose their babies. But she would not become an invalid, would not sit placidly while her muscles turned flaccid. Her hope was in her good health and strength, and she didn't intend to forfeit them to fear.

Two months. After the baby was born was time enough to sit and rest. No. Time to indulge herself in the pleasure of nurturing the child. She thought of it as a friend as well as a miracle.

And as soon as possible after the child was born she and Luke and the baby would go to Amarna. Luke had promised he'd talk to the Doctor about the trip, about Rachel. Mary would have to remind him again. She cleaved the lumps of dirt, feeling the rhythmic impacts through the hoe. Luke was so hesitant, almost timid, when it came to the Doctor, yet these last four months, the Doctor had been unfailingly solicitous and full of good humor.

"Mary, would you like some water?"

She looked up to see Bernadette offering a canteen. Mary took it and tipped it up to let the cool water wash down her throat, then returned it with her thanks.

Bernadette nodded absently. "Where's Luke today?"

"He's in the west field helping with the plowing."

Bernadette looked toward the dust clouds rising behind the two teams of horses. Then she glanced up at the sky. "Getting on toward evening. I gathered some fern fiddleheads for supper. You need the vitamin C. Did you drink some extra milk this afternoon?"

Mary smiled at her stern expression. "Yes, I did. Thank you."

"For what?"

"For your concern."

She responded testily, "It's my job, looking after you and Sister Hannah." Then her eyes narrowed; she raised a hand to shade her eyes as she stared westward. "God in heaven, what is *that?*"

Mary turned, and at first she saw nothing unusual, until a movement fixed her attention on the road where it emerged from the forest.

A rider on a dark horse, a bay nearly black in the shadows of the trees, moving at an unhurried walk toward the main gate. A dog trotted ahead of the horse.

"A stranger!"

The words ricocheted around her with cries of surprise and alarm, and people began moving toward the garden's west gate. Mary dropped her hoe and joined them.

A stranger.

It was a staggering event here, and she felt her heart pounding. From the south garden, from the west fields, she heard shouts and questions, and near her someone cried, "It must be the Lord!"

The rider had reached the gate on the road and stopped.

The lord? Mary laughed. Would Jesus come on horseback with full packs behind the saddle and the barrel of a rifle clearly visible?

Would Jesus be so small, bent over in the saddle like a tired child? Would Jesus be led by a black dog with white paws and . . .

Yorick.

And the horse—it was Epona. Of course, it was.

Mary pushed her way through the small crowd at the garden gate. *The rider—the stranger—was Rachel.*

Someone tried to hold her back. Bernadette. Mary pulled away from her, laughing, shouting, "It's Rachel! Go find Luke—tell him it's *Rachel!*" And she broke away and ran toward the main gate.

Rachel had come to the Ark, and Mary didn't stop to wonder why. She ran through the tangles of winter grass underlain with spring green, and the pent loneliness burst loose within her, and she wondered how she had borne it.

But now Rachel was here—she was here at the Ark.

When Mary was still fifty feet from the gate, Yorick wriggled under it and scuttled to meet her. She scooped him up, whirled around while he licked at her face ecstatically, then she put him down, and together they ran to the gate, where Epona stretched her neck over the top wire, soft lips pushed out in a nicker of greeting.

But Mary stood suddenly immobilized, jubilation overshadowed by a pall of apprehension.

Rachel's hair had grown to her shoulders, hung gray and lank, and her eyes shone feverishly out of shadowed hollows. She looked at Mary as if she didn't recognize her, asked plaintively, "Mary . . . ?"

Mary fumbled at the chain, pulled the gate open, and at that moment Epona turned, and Mary saw Rachel's right leg, the lower half of the pants cut away, the leg wrapped from the ankle to just below the knee in bandages soaked with pale, brownish patches.

Mary reached up for Rachel's hand. "Rachel, what happened?"

She enclosed Mary's hand in both of hers, but there was no strength in them. "I cut myself with that damn machete trying to clear some bamboo. Mary, I'm so glad to see you. Are you pregnant, or is it just those clothes?"

"It's not the clothes. Rachel, don't cry."

"Why not?" She managed a wry laugh. "*You're* crying."

"Never mind." Mary reached for Epona's reins and led her through the gate. "The Doctor has to look at that leg. When did it happen?"

"I think . . . five, six days ago."

Mary stopped, looked up at her with an emptiness born of fear taking shape under her ribs. She stared at the stained bandage, and now she became aware of a faint odor she couldn't name.

"Rachel, how bad is it?"

She grimaced. "It's bad, Mary."

"*How* bad?"

"Gangrene has set in."

She said it as matter-of-factly as she might comment on the weather. Mary stood dazed, trying to assimilate the word *gangrene*. A killer and a cruel one, and in this new Stone Age without antibiotics . . .

Mary sagged against Epona's neck, hands clenched in her mane, and turned her face away so Rachel couldn't see her fear.

And yet . . .

Nehemiah. The Doctor had saved the old man's life when his injured hand became gangrenous.

Yes, the Doctor had saved his life—by amputating his arm. Mary swallowed at the bitter, metallic taste in her mouth. But if there was no other alternative—

At least, she was sure the Doctor could do it.

"Look at the people," Rachel said. "It's hard to believe, Mary—so many people."

Mary roused herself, looked around to see all the Flock gathering a short distance away. She grabbed Epona's reins and urged her forward, shouting, "Somebody get the Doctor! Hurry! Bernadette, where's Luke?"

Bernadette was hurrying toward her. "He's coming. I told him—"

What stopped her was a flurry of movement in the crowd. The Doctor, with Luke in his wake, strode through the aisle provided him by the Flock. Mary's breath sighed out in relief. "Brother, thank the lord you're . . ."

But her voice failed her, she pulled back on Epona's reins.

She didn't understand what she saw in the Doctor's face. In the four months since he had learned of her pregnancy, he'd shown her nothing but beatific solicitude, and that was what she anticipated now.

What she found revived with chill clarity the memory of a night in November when rain hissed at the windows of his barren room, when he had condemned Rachel with the evidence of her art.

Mary had forgotten that night. No, she hadn't forgotten it, only put it aside as something to worry about later, after the baby was born.

The Doctor had not forgotten, nor forgiven.

Mary ordered Yorick to heel. He did, growling softly while the Doctor marched forward, the prophet, the messenger of righteous wrath.

Luke. She focused her attention, her hopes, on him. Luke would bring the Doctor around. He wouldn't let any harm come to Rachel. When the Doctor stopped a few paces away, Luke continued toward Mary and Rachel.

The Doctor's whip crack "Brother Luke!" checked him midstride.

It was then that Rachel said quietly, "Hello, Luke."

He looked at her, seemed to sway toward her, then turned his pleading gaze on Mary, and she couldn't make sense of his silence.

Finally he spoke, but not to Rachel. To Mary: "She shouldn't have come here!"

Now Mary couldn't make sense of his words. "Can't you see she's hurt, Luke? You *told* her to come here, you promised her help if she needed it."

The Doctor rested a hand on Luke's shoulder and spoke in the moving-of-mountains timbre of his sermons. "Brother Luke had no right to make that promise."

Mary faced the Doctor and found in his pale eyes a wall of ice. "Brother, whether he had a right to or not, Luke *did* make that promise."

The Doctor ignored that. "Is this the witch Rachel?"

Witch?

The word staggered Mary; she couldn't believe it, and without thinking, she laughed. "What *is* this—Salem in the seventeenth century?"

"What do you find to laugh about, Sister Mary?"

"I . . . I just couldn't believe you'd make such an accusation of someone who comes to you in her need."

"She has come to the wrong place! God said to Moses, 'Thou shalt not suffer a witch to live.' And I'll not suffer a witch to enter this, the abode of the righteous!"

All around them, the Flock stood silent, accepting that grotesque statement without so much as a murmur.

And Luke remained equally silent.

Mary cried, "Luke! This is Rachel—the woman who nursed you through your sickness and treated you like a son! Can you face her, can you face your god and call *Rachel* a witch?"

Luke let his head fall back, eyes closed, before he turned to the Doctor. "Brother, I owe her my life. How can you say—"

"You owe this daughter of darkness nothing! I say she is a witch, and I say she will not set foot in the Ark!"

"I can't believe she's evil. You don't know her, you can't know—"

"I *do* know her! I see the mark of Cain on her when nobody else can." He looked around at the Flock, then turned to Luke, pronounced with ringing contempt, "Or do you think you know better, Brother Luke? Do you think you can lead my Flock? Do you think you can lead them in the paths of righteousness? Because if you do, then I will step down, my Godly mission fulfilled, and *you*, Brother Luke, can take my place!"

Mary watched the transparent transition of emotion in Luke's face: shock, uncertainty, fear, and finally defeated compliance. He slumped, staring at the ground, and Mary remembered the scars on his back. Yet she felt not a trace of sympathy for him, for the pain so patent in his face. She looked at him and despised him; she wanted to spit on him. She shook with the intensity of her loathing and cried, "Luke, you coward! You pitiful, heartless *coward!*"

Luke stood mute, and it was the Doctor who answered with a sharp, "Silence, Sister! Or I'll know you've been tainted with her evil. I've given my judgment. She will go back to whatever hellish place she came from! You—you will turn your eyes away from me and *go*!"

That was for Rachel. She was watching the Doctor with a dispassionate gaze that did not waver for his vituperations. She didn't speak; she only looked at him out of her pain-wearied eyes and silently manifested her recognition and acceptance of a sentence of agonizing death.

But if Rachel was willing to accept her fate in silence, Mary was not. The denial rose from every cell in her body, a flood of fear and grief that drove her forward, bore her to her knees at the Doctor's feet. "In the name of your god, I beg of you—*help* her!"

"Sister, don't ask *me* to—"

"Who else can help her? Remember the parable of the Good Samaritan! Jesus wouldn't turn her away! You can't—"

"Get away from me!" He lashed out, his hand striking the side of her head, knocking her to the ground. She tasted the earth on her lips, heard Yorick barking, as the Doctor pronounced, "*I have given my judgment!*"

And there was no appeal.

Someone was helping her to her feet. She got her balance, looked around at him, at Luke, and while his eyes brimmed with baffled love, she waited, panting with rage, until he retreated from her.

And the Doctor stood like a figure carved in stone, and she knew that if she beat on him with her fists—and that was her impulse— she would only bloody her hands. At this moment she recognized something about him that she had always known but found expedient to ignore. This man was insane. He survived because these frightened survivors of the ultimate holocaust sustained his delusions as his delusions sustained theirs. A closed loop of insanity. That was the way the world ended, not with a bang nor a whimper, but with a meaningless paroxysm of madness.

Mary spoke into the pendant silence, spoke loud enough for everyone in the Flock to hear. "He has given his *judgment*. And Jesus said, 'Judge not that ye be not judged.' Look at him! He's *afraid*!"

"Be *quiet*, Sister!" He balled his hands into fists, his face livid with frustrated anger.

But she only raised her voice. "Wasn't Jesus the lord of mercy, who took in anyone who asked for help?"

"Damn you, I said—"

"But this man has condemned a woman all of you would call a saint if you knew her. He is *afraid* of Rachel because Luke called her a woman of wisdom, and he—"

"To the church!" His face nearly purple now, he flung out his arms, pivoted toward the Flock. "All of you—*go to the church!*"

Perhaps that's what they'd been waiting for: a direct order. They knew how to deal with that. Mary stood silent as one by one they began walking up the road toward the Ark. There was Nehemiah, shuffling along like a man of ninety. And Adam, looking back at her in bewilderment. Enid, Hannah, Naomi, Leah, Esther, and the other women who had dressed her for her wedding. And Bernadette, who had provided her bouquet of wild asters and pearly everlasting.

Mary turned her back on them and went to Rachel, again reached for her hand, seeking its strength, finding only heartbreaking fragility. And there was nothing she could say. The language of this despair was unknown to her.

"Luke's right," Rachel said softly. "I shouldn't have come here. It was a faint hope at best, and I knew it when I left Amarna. I'll go now."

Mary nodded. "You won't go alone." She looked around for Yorick, found him pacing anxiously beside her, then she took Epona's reins and started toward the gate.

"*Sister Mary!*"

She turned, saw the Doctor and Luke standing where she had left them, while behind them the Flock paused in their retreat.

The Doctor said, "Sister Mary, you will *not* go with that daughter of Satan. Come here!"

"Brother, I *will* go with her."

He took a step forward, pale eyes stark in his reddened face. "You carry our child! You can't leave the Ark!"

The despair fed the new rage that pounded with her pulse in her head. She shouted, "This is not your child and never will be!"

Luke cried, "No! Mary, you can't—"

"Brother Luke," the Doctor cut in, "control your wife. Bring her to the church!"

Luke looked at him, hesitated, then started toward Mary. "I can't let you go, Mary. You'll have to come with me."

Mary didn't answer that. She reached for the rifle behind Rachel's saddle, jerked it out of its sheath, snapped off the safety, and looked down the gleaming barrel into Luke's stunned face.

He seemed to freeze, and in his eyes she read elemental fear. A sudden calm possessed her. The shaking of her taut muscles abated, she felt the stock smooth against her cheek, the trigger waiting under her finger. *And if any mischief follow, then thou shalt give life for life.*

Luke pleaded, "Mary . . . please, Mary . . ."

"Why?" She didn't recognize her own voice, it was so guttural and cold. "Why should I show you any mercy? You want to live by the Doctor's rules, by the old Mosaic code? This is part of it— along with slavery, polygamy, and animal sacrifice. An eye for an eye, Luke!"

"But, Mary . . . I love you!"

Her hands flexed on the rifle, and she heard a voice—Rachel's voice—pleading with her not to kill, not to kill Luke, but the voice barely reached her consciousness. She stood with her finger tight on the trigger and laughed until she knew she was on the brink of tears, and she became acutely aware of herself, of Luke, of Rachel, of the Doctor, of the Flock waiting and paralyzed with fear. She saw the entire tableau as if she were outside it, no longer a part of it.

Eye for eye. Life for life.

But it didn't work and never had in the thousands of years since that philosophy was invented. She despised it as she did the Doctor's arrogance, as she did Luke's cowardice, yet she had nearly succumbed to it, just as she had years ago. Why was it so sweet in its promise of satisfaction, that ancient philosophy of revenge? As sweet as ignorance that wraps its nakedness in the shining trappings of faith.

Mary didn't lower the gun. She didn't move. "Luke, I won't kill you for the sake of revenge, but neither will I go back to the Ark. If you try to take me by force, I *will* kill you. So, go on, Luke. Go to the church with your prophet. And wait for the day of judgment."

In the silence that followed, she could hear the distant bleating of goats, the soft clangor of cowbells, the murmuring of the Jordan in the cool shadows of firs. None of the human occupants of this pleasant landscape moved or made a sound until finally the Doctor shouted, "Let her go! Let her go with her witch sister!"

But Luke stood gazing at Mary, his eyes flooded with tears. "Mary, you can't take our child. You can't . . . leave me. . . ."

She tried to remember why she had loved him and found no answer within her.

"Luke, if you love me—" Her mouth seemed to balk at the words.

"Oh, Mary, of course, I do. You know I—"

"If you love me, you'll bring me some food, blankets, bandages, and any medication that might help Rachel."

His mouth sagged open, and he glanced over his shoulder. The Doctor like a good shepherd watched this wayward lamb to see that it didn't stray too far. The rest of his Flock waited.

Luke gasped, "Mary, I can't do that. The Doctor wouldn't— Mary, you have to *understand*. He's held us together through all these years of tribulation. He *is* the Ark. And the Ark is our only hope!"

"Then you have no hope." She lowered the rifle, caught the glint of gold on her left hand, and slipped the ring off her finger, tossed it at Luke's feet. He stared down at it, but made no move to pick it up.

She turned and looked up at Rachel, but neither of them spoke. Mary whistled for Yorick and led Epona out the gate. When she closed it, Luke was still standing there, watching her. She looked past him, past the Doctor, past the Flock, to the Ark.

Now she understood why it was built as a fortress.

She took Epona's reins and started down the road, and it was only then that she realized she hadn't once in the six months since she entered this gate set foot outside it.

She pressed a hand to her body, waited for some movement there, but felt nothing.

Why had she brought Rachel here?

Mary only asked herself that question after she had a fire burning and two of the pots from the nesting camp set steaming on the grate, one filled with water, the other with the meat of the rabbit she had shot at the side of the road.

She put another piece of driftwood on the fire. The chill of evening had already set in. She was wearing Rachel's jacket, grateful for its warmth over the wool blouse that had seemed too hot only hours ago. But her head was bare. She had taken off the scarf as soon as they left Canaan Valley. Now she looked west toward the sun poised blinding orange a few degrees above the horizon. This was one reason she'd brought Rachel here: the sea, seemingly infinite, shining with a filigree of reflected gold. The quiet surf braided ephemeral strands of foam to cast upon the sand. *I am here . . . I am always here. . . .*

This was the campground where she and Luke had spent their last night before they reached the Ark. The wind in the black lace of the spruce trees that canopied this site whispered with ghosts of memories.

But she had brought Rachel here for practical reasons. There was no place along the road inland to the Ark with enough open space to camp, and no place where she could find water. The creek south of this site bubbled noisily, cold and fresh. Mary could hear Epona stolidly cropping the grass on the bank.

She squinted into the sun. "Rachel, there might be a green flash." And as soon as the words were out, she almost wept.

She had to discipline her thoughts to keep them out of certain byways of memory. She had to hold on to the mantle of numbness that had enveloped her since they left the Ark, that enabled her to resist the rage and grief and guilt that would paralyze her if she recognized it.

Rachel was oblivious to the possibility of a green flash. She seemed asleep, although her breathing was labored. At the foot of one of the spruces, Mary had prepared a bed of sword fern to cushion the sleeping bag, and over that laid the bearskin. But Rachel's bandaged leg was uncovered, pillowed by a fold of the bearskin. She couldn't tolerate any weight on it. Yorick lay motionless and awake beside her.

Mary didn't wait for the green flash. She went to the picnic table where she had opened Rachel's packs. Rachel had brought only the essentials for camping, including a few matches wrapped in foil and some jerky and smoked fish. And the first-aid box. In it Mary found scissors, tape and tape sutures, an antiseptic spray that had no doubt lost its efficacy long ago, a bar of soap, strips of sheeting for bandages, and an aloe leaf. A braided cloth cord was coiled in one corner between a twenty-cc vial of morphine and a single twenty-cc disposable syringe.

Why had Rachel brought only one syringe, and why such a large one? They had plenty of these disposables, of all sizes, at Amarna.

Mary knew the answer, but she channeled her thoughts away from it. She looked around at Rachel, felt the numbness shiver, ready to fall away. No. Hold on. Hold on to that. She hadn't looked at the leg yet, and only now did she face the real reason for her reluctance.

She had given up hope.

Mary silently castigated herself for that lapse. She could kill Rachel with pessimism.

Maybe the wound wasn't as bad as she feared. Maybe with care and nursing, it might heal. It *was* possible. She had to believe it was possible.

There was no alternative but to try.

She took the first-aid box and the pot of hot water to Rachel's erstwhile sickbed. Yorick raised his head, watching her. She knelt beside Rachel, saw her lips tremble in a grimace of pain. Even in sleep she still felt the pain. Mary pressed her palm to Rachel's forehead. The skin was hot. Her pulse, when Mary found it, was weak and erratic.

"Rachel?"

Her breath caught, sighed out when she opened her eyes. And Mary saw in her eyes, sunk deep in bruised sockets, something that lashed her with fear. The last time she spoke to her father before he died in that ticking cubicle in the hospital, she saw in his eyes the same indefinable shadow she saw now in Rachel's.

No. You have to try. You have to *try.*

Rachel said, "A fire going and supper cooking . . . all the comforts of home."

"I'll have supper—such as it is—ready in about half an hour."

"I'm . . . not really hungry."

"Well, you'll have to eat something. Rachel, you have to keep up your strength—or build it up again."

Rachel studied her for a moment, absently stroking Yorick's head. "I know, Mary. You have to try."

Mary was startled at that. She had almost forgotten the nearly telepathic communication that had developed between them over the years; they knew each other's minds so well.

"Yes, Rachel. I have to try."

"It's hopeless, you know, without amputation."

"No!" Mary shook her head. "No, it's *not* hopeless."

Rachel's gaze fell on the first-aid kit. "Help me sit up so I can see what you're doing." Then when Mary had assisted her into a sitting position, she said levelly, "You'll have to cut the old bandage away. I haven't . . . been up to changing it for a couple of days. You have hot water? That's the only thing I know to clean it with. I've been putting aloe on it and that antiseptic spray—not that either one of them does a damn bit of good. I just didn't know what else to do."

Mary didn't know, either, but she started by easing off the ankle-high hiking boot, then the wool stocking. She tried not to show her dismay when she saw Rachel's swollen, discolored foot. In the yellow light of the fire and the sunset sky, the skin had the look of dark, age-patinaed bronze. Mary began cutting the bandages, staying to the inside of the leg, away from the brownish patches. And as she cut through tape, cloth, and gauze, the foully sweet odor made her light-headed. She glanced up at Rachel's face, saw her lips compressed against pain, eyes haunted with dread. Yet she managed a smile. "Malodorous little beastie, clostridia."

Mary stopped cutting. "What?"

"Clostridia," Rachel repeated with grim nonchalance. "It's the little beastie that causes gangrene. Of course, it's a camp follower, so to speak. The real soldiers are staphylococcus and streptococcus. Blood poisoning, septicemia, cellulitis. It all comes to the same thing in the end. The microcosm constantly breaks down the macrocosm."

Mary's throat was too dry for her to speak. Trust Rachel to re-search her killer thoroughly.

No! Not her killer. Not this time. The microscopic legions would not be triumphant this time.

Mary finished the cut to the top of the bandage. The brownish exudate was too liquid to form scabs that would glue the gauze to the wound, but viscous enough so that she had to ease the gauze off, constantly aware of Rachel's hands locked on her knee to com-bat the compelling reflex to withdraw from pain. The wound was thus revealed slowly, inch by inch.

The machete had cut into the leg just above the ankle, baring the shinbone, then curved upward around the calf, ending at a point a handsbreadth below the angle of the knee. Rachel had tried to close the wound with tape sutures, but the swelling had pulled the edges apart, and the tapes hung like broken bridges across a riven canyon. The skin was dusky, and surrounding the wound, mottled, purplish blisters gleamed moistly. Shadowy tentacles of red reached toward the knee.

Mary got her trembling under control, ordered the muscles of her face into an expression of calm. "Rachel, you did a hell of a job on this."

Rachel laughed, although her forehead and upper lip were beaded with sweat. "Like they say, if you're going to do something, do it right."

Mary cut off a piece of the cloth bandage, dipped it in the water—still hot, but not scalding—and began gingerly cleaning the wound. The smell was dizzying, but she closed her mind to it and to Rachel's clenched hands, her muffled gasps of pain.

But finally Mary could close her mind no longer.

"Rachel, let me give you some of the morphine."

She went rigid. "No. I won't use the morphine until I have to. And promise me you won't use it on me unless I ask for it. There's not that much of it, considering it's probably lost some of its strength by now. Morphine is very stable, but this is at least ten years old. Mary, promise me—not until I *ask* for it."

Mary recognized the answer to the question she'd refused to face earlier. Rachel didn't intend to use the morphine as an analgesic, but as a poison.

But it wouldn't come to that. This wound *could* be healed. Somehow.

"All right, Rachel, I promise." And Mary told herself she could keep that promise because Rachel wouldn't *need* the morphine as a last resort.

Mary applied fresh tape sutures and used the antiseptic spray, knowing its only effect was to cool the skin. Next the aloe, squeezed from the gelid leaf, and she knew it was equally useless against an infection like this. What *would* be effective—other than the antibiotics now lost in history? Other than amputation under sterile conditions with the proper instruments and an anesthetic, however primitive.

The Doctor could've done it.

She found herself shaking and put the Doctor and what might have been out of her mind, smothered those thoughts and the raw hatred they engendered under her mantle of numbness.

There had to be some other answer.

"Sphagnum moss! Rachel, I remember reading something about sphagnum being used on wounds in the First World War."

"Yes. Maybe it harbors some sort of penicillinlike mold."

"There's plenty of sphagnum in the woods inland." Mary started to rise, driven by this new hope, then realized the sky had gone black; only a band of orange at the horizon marked the departed day. "It's too dark to find any now. Damn!"

Rachel caught her arm. "Tomorrow morning. That'll be time enough."

There was an unspoken plea in that. Rachel was near the limits of her capacity to tolerate Mary's ministrations. Mary nodded, began winding gauze around the leg, but before she finished, the exudate soaked through.

"Rachel, are any of these little beasties anaerobic?"

"Yes. Clostridia is. What we need is a hyperbaric chamber. All the best hospitals have them."

"Well, I'll just call an ambulance from the nearest phone booth. But it might help to leave the wound exposed to the air for a while."

There was no sign of hope in Rachel's eyes at that suggestion. "I guess anything's worth a try at this point, but if I'm going to lie here with that thing exposed, you'll have to do something to keep the flies off it. I don't want to give the maggots a chance at me *before* I die."

Mary shuddered. "Rachel, *don't* . . ."

"I'm sorry. Gallows humor, no doubt." She closed her eyes. "Tomorrow. We'll try that tomorrow."

Mary swallowed hard, focused her attention on wrapping the leg with cloth bandages, and even when she completed that task she didn't feel sure enough of her voice to speak. She gathered up the old bandages and took them to the fire, then searched in Rachel's packs until she found a pair of clean socks. She returned to Rachel and carefully slipped one of them on her foot. Rachel was still sitting up, propping herself with both arms. She said weakly, "Mary, you're a good nurse. I think it feels better."

"I hope so. And now I'll see how that meat is doing. Yorick would probably like some, too." Yorick responded to his name with a slight lift of his ears. When Mary knelt to ease Rachel down onto the sleeping bag, Rachel embraced her, unexpectedly, silently, almost shyly.

Mary held her, and she seemed little more than a child in her arms, but without a child's supple strength. There was so much that needed to be said now, but Mary still couldn't find the words. Perhaps tears were the only language that would encompass what she felt, and she held on desperately to stop them. Rachel didn't need that.

At length, Rachel drew away, looked into Mary's face, and finally nodded, as if all the words had been said. Then her breath whispered out, and she sank back, eyes closed. "Let me . . . rest for a while. . . ."

Mary tucked the sleeping bag around Rachel's shoulders, then took the soap and went to the creek to wash her hands in the frigid water. Then she crossed to the firepit and stirred the simmering rabbit meat, added more water, and built up the fire, reminding herself that she'd have to gather more wood off the beach tomorrow. There was a good stack by the firepit, but it would be a long night, and she had to keep Rachel warm.

At length, she speared a chunk of rabbit meat, put it in one of the cups from the camp set, then cut it into small pieces and covered it with broth. She woke Rachel and helped her sit up, offered the cup and a spoon. Rachel emptied the cup, slowly, as if she were taking a distasteful medicine. Finally she said, "There, I've cleaned my plate. Have you eaten?"

"Not yet."

"Then get at it. After all, you're eating for two." She seemed to want to say more, but she was too spent. She sank back onto the sleeping bag, murmuring words Mary couldn't understand, except for one word: *hope*. Mary covered her, waited until she fell into restless sleep. The uncertain pace of her breathing marked a counterpoint against the constant rush of the sea, while Mary sat huddled in an island of yellow light in the center of infinite darkness, profoundly alone and mortally afraid of her aloneness.

The baby moved, and she closed her eyes, concentrating on the sensation. *Our* child, the Doctor had said.

She felt rage within her as tangible as the child that stirred again, perhaps in response to it, and she pressed her hands to her belly. *You don't belong to the Ark, little one, nor to the Doctor, nor even to*

Luke. You are mine, but only for a while. One day you'll be entirely your own.

And entirely alone?

Mary clenched her jaws to stop a cry. Her muscles ached with the effort.

Entirely alone, this child who had been the focus of all her hope.

She had wanted to perpetuate the species. She had wanted to perpetuate her own humanity. For a chimera of instinct and ego, she had betrayed Rachel—betrayed her as surely as Luke had—and she had betrayed this child.

She felt the child within her, heard the wind sighing above her, and desperately sought her mantle of numbness and some relic of hope.

The child won't *grow up* alone.

She would live to see this child into adulthood. Then it must go out and seek other people, but until that time, it will be loved, it will be taught to read, to think, to sing, to make images and ideas.

And this child will have Rachel, too. Mary felt her teeth chattering and clamped them tight. Rachel *would* live. She would teach this child to be a human being, and perhaps ultimately it would in a sense be more Rachel's child than anyone else's.

Mary looked into Rachel's lined, pallid face, listened for her breathing, heard it, shallow and too fast, and she held on to the hope, held on to her encompassing numbness. Rachel would *live*.

Finally she rose. The fire had gone down. She added more wood, ate some of the rabbit meat and broth, fed some to Yorick. Then she whistled for Epona, and when the mare ambled into the firelight, Mary took her to the next campsite and tied her there. The rope was long enough for her to reach the creek and the grass along the road.

Then Mary lay down next to Rachel under the bearskin, surrounded by its musty odor, but sleep eluded her while she tried to lead her thoughts out of the paths of rage and pain. Rachel repeatedly woke, moaning and frightened, and Mary could only offer the reassurance of her presence. Each time Rachel sank back into restive sleep, Mary rose and replenished the fire. The moon was full tonight. It surprised her when she first saw it through the trees. She had lost track of the moon phases.

She had lost track of too much in the last six months.

The sky was bright with diffuse light, but the sun hadn't yet risen far enough to cast shadows when Mary woke from a sleep of formless, ominous dreams. A bird was singing. The mad bird.

She sat up, dazed with the sudden influx of memories. Rachel. Mary reached out to press her hand to Rachel's forehead, and she was convinced it wasn't as hot as it had been yesterday, and her breathing seemed easier.

Mary rose stiffly and ran her fingers through her tangled hair, then she frowned, distracted, when she saw Yorick lying in the grass near the road. He was gnawing on something, and she walked over to him to see what it was. He gave her a warning growl, but when she spoke his name sharply, he surrendered his prize.

A doughnut-shaped bone. A shank bone, in fact, from a cow. And it had been cleanly cut with a meat saw.

Mary let Yorick have the bone, and her first reaction was enervating fear.

"What's wrong?" Rachel was trying to sit up, leaning on one elbow.

"I'm not sure, but someone was here last night. They muzzled our trusty watchdog with a piece of shank meat." Mary was looking around the camp as she spoke. It was on the table: a blanket-wrapped bundle.

She went to the table, cautiously unfolded the blanket. Inside, she found drawstring bags of various sizes made, like the blanket itself, of handwoven wool. They came from the Ark.

Of course, they did. Where else would they come from?

Yet this parcel was so unexpected, she might as easily believe it came from the moon that shone so brightly last night. She opened a small bag and found it filled with ground bark, and on a torn scrap of paper, written in ink in tiny, precise letters, the words,

"Make into tea for fever." In another bag filled with dried rose hips, the assurance, "Good for vit. C." Another bag filled with crushed leaves was designated, "Comfrey, B$_{12}$." On the lid of a jar of yellow ointment, "Poultice for wound."

And there was a small, brown bottle with a dropper in the cap. The slip of paper was tied around it with a string: "Laudanum— three drops in cup of water." And Mary began to laugh, even though her eyes were blurred with tears.

Laudanum. Something to ease Rachel's pain.

Another bag was filled with strips of cloth for bandages, another with dried apple slices, another with a plucked and dismembered chicken, and the last with barley. And the leather cosmetic case— Mary had brought it with her to the Ark. She opened it, found her brush and comb, toothbrushes, soap, cuticle scissors, a jar of aloe and oil.

Finally there was Rachel's sketchbook. The paper for the admonitory identifications had come from the back of it, but Bernadette had been careful to tear out a blank page.

And it had to be Bernadette who had come in the night with this gift. Who else would have access to the medicines? Who else could get Mary's cosmetic case and the sketchbook from the household? Who else would leave the Ark at night, fearlessly traveling by moonlight a road as familiar to her as the forests around it, knowing exactly where Mary would go to camp because there was no better place nearer?

"Mary, please—*who* is Bernadette?"

Mary didn't realize she'd been speaking aloud. She took the bottle to Rachel. "Bernadette lives in our household. Look at this, Rachel. Laudanum. Now you can get some rest from the pain. And she brought herbal medicines—she's a nurse at the Ark—and bandages and a chicken and . . ." She couldn't stop laughing, and she didn't try, because Rachel was laughing with her, and there was hope in it.

The laughter died finally, and there were things to do—the first was giving Rachel a dose of laudanum—and nothing could dim the revived hope that was Bernadette's real gift. Even when Mary removed the bandages from Rachel's leg, the wound didn't seem to look as bad as it had yesterday evening. At least, she told herself, it looked no worse. She didn't bandage the wound, but cleaned it, applied some of the yellow ointment, and left it open to the air. She constructed a gauze tent with supports of sticks bound by tape, and placed it over the leg. Then she heated the leftover rabbit meat. Rachel ate only a cupful of broth, but she found Bernadette's herb teas easier to get down.

Despite her lack of appetite, despite her fever, Rachel seemed encouraged. She wanted to sit up, and Mary rolled the bearskin to put behind her against the trunk of the spruce, then helped her wash her face and brush her teeth, and combed and brushed her hair. Rachel spoke only occasionally, and sometimes she repeated the same question or forgot what Mary had said. She didn't seem to understand why Mary was determined to find some sphagnum moss. But that mental vagueness, Mary was sure, could be attributed to the laudanum.

Mary judged from the position of the sun that the morning was nearly half-gone when she was finally ready to leave in search of sphagnum. The fire was newly replenished, and she had tethered Epona on the bank of the creek where there was plenty of grass. Rachel lay quiet, and beside her, within easy reach, were a canteen, a cup, and the laudanum. Yorick refused to leave her.

Mary knelt at her side. "I won't be gone long."

Rachel's eyes were heavy-lidded, but she brought forth a smile. "I'll be fine. Good luck." And her eyes closed.

Mary set off at a brisk walk, but before she had covered more than fifty feet, she stopped abruptly. She looked back at the camp, saw Rachel propped against the spruce, motionless. Mary felt a chill she couldn't explain, but she shrugged it off. Rachel was only asleep. She needed that healing sleep.

Rachel was going to be all right, she was going to live.

Mary smiled in the warmth of that conviction and walked along the creek until it disappeared in an echoing culvert under the highway. She crossed the eroded asphalt, then again followed the creek into the forest. In places, salal and elderberry grew so thick she couldn't push through them, and she had to make her way upstream on the rocks in the creek. But within a quarter of a mile the forest canopy thickened, the undergrowth thinned, and she was deep in cool, green rain forest. She angled away from the creek, but didn't stray so far from it that she couldn't hear it. In this forest it would be all too easy to get lost.

She was traversing a slope luxuriant with sword fern, when her foot caught in a hidden snare of roots. With a startled cry, she fought for balance, lost it, plunged into ferns over her head, and tumbled down the slope, futilely grasping fronds that ripped out of the soft ground.

Her descent ended as suddenly as it had begun, and she lay dazed in a tangled mass of crushed fern, nostrils filled with the heavy, dank scent of the earth.

And she was looking into the face of death.

A deer's skull. It lay shrouded in broken fern only inches from her head. A pale spider crawled out from between the crenellated teeth. The bone was gray and rotten, stained with green moss, yet there was in the exquisite curves of its empty eye sockets a ghost of sentience that terrified her, and she didn't understand the terror, didn't understand the shivering of her muscles as she recoiled from that relic of life, didn't understand why she was sobbing uncontrollably. On her hands and knees, she backed away from the skull, staggered to her feet, stumbled toward the sound of the creek, and when she reached its bank, looked up at the sky through dusky plumes of fir and spruce, and a cry of anguish tore out of her throat.

But sky and trees absorbed the sound, made silence of it. She felt the burning in her throat, felt the reverberations in her head, but the sound didn't seem to exist here.

She didn't seem to exist here.

Hold on. Damn it, hold on. You can't let go now.

She sank down on a boulder warmed by the sun, sagged forward across her folded arms. She felt no physical pain, except for the aches that would turn to bruises later, but she couldn't stop trembling. She might have hurt her baby, she might have disabled herself, and what would happen to Rachel then?

Hold on. . . .

She took deep breaths and let them out slowly, and finally she felt the mantle of numbness, dark and weighted, settle into place again.

Yet she had lost something in that spasm of panic. She wasn't sure what it was until she remembered her mission here: sphagnum moss. Until she thought, *It won't help.*

What she had lost was hope.

Or perhaps she had only lost the illusion of hope.

"No! Rachel will not *die!*"

She listened to the words, teeth clenched, then rose and set off into the forest again. Sphagnum moss. She found it growing on the flank of a nurse log in a silent glade that reminded her of the forest around the tree at Amarna. She cut enough to fill one of the cloth bags, and on the way back downstream, she gathered fern fiddle-heads for the chicken stew. Barley to give it substance, and fid-dleheads—added at the last moment—for their piquant flavor and color.

She held on doggedly to the remnants of hope.

But when she reached the camp, even those eroded remnants began to slip out of her hands.

She heard Yorick's whining bark as soon as she crossed the high-way. Heart pounding, Mary ran to Rachel, found her uncovered, sprawled with one arm over her face, the gauze tent knocked aside. She had vomited into the litter of needles by the sleeping bag. Mary knelt beside her, pulled her arm away from her face. She was weep-ing, tears glistening in the dry furrows of her skin. She said in a panting whisper, "Mary, don't let me die alone . . . stay with me. . . ."

Mary gathered her into her arms, felt the shuddering tremors of her body, felt her cheek hot against her own, and it was a long time before the trembling abated, until finally, with a sigh, Rachel relaxed, and Mary eased her down, looked into her dark, sunken eyes, and still could find no words. Rachel touched Mary's cheek with fingers as tremulous as butterflies. "I'm all right now. Must've been a nightmare."

Mary nearly gave in to the waiting tears. No nightmare could be worse than what Rachel faced waking. The pain was wearing her down like the sea constantly battering its shores. Mary opened the canteen, filled the cup, and added three drops of laudanum. Such a small bottle, so little of the precious fluid left.

Rachel grimaced at the bitter taste, but downed it eagerly, and Mary rose, dug a depression into the soil with her boot heel, and kicked the vomitus into it, then knelt to right the gauze tent over the leg. Had the red shadow tentacles extended so close to the knee earlier this morning? She straightened the sleeping bag and said, "I found some sphagnum, so maybe we'd better try the World War One remedy."

Rachel winced. "Maybe we'd better just let it be." Then she studied Mary, finally nodded. "All right. Try it. After that, there's nothing left but the ax."

Mary turned away as if she'd been struck, and Rachel sighed. "I'm sorry. Just more gallows humor. I don't *want* to die. I want more than anything to live. And I don't want to die like this."

"You're not going to *die!*"

Rachel laughed briefly. "That would be a very unnatural state of affairs. You didn't get converted at the Ark, did you?"

Mary rose. "I have to take care of your leg. The sphagnum—I don't know whether I should try to sterilize it, or if that would—"

"Mary, please . . ."

The aching appeal reached through to Mary, and she sank to her knees. She didn't try to speak.

Rachel said, "If the sphagnum or your friend's herbal remedies help, no one will be more grateful than I. But I've had to face the fact that nothing is likely to help, that I'm dying, and you must face that, too. I have some things to say to you, and I want to say them now while I'm still clearheaded."

Mary pulled in a deep breath, shifted position until she was sitting cross-legged. "All right, Rachel."

"First, when you see your friend Bernadette, thank her for the laudanum. That was an act of mercy."

"But I won't ever see Bernadette again."

313

"Yes, you will, you must. Mary, you must go back to the Ark."

"What?" Mary stared at her. "No, Rachel. Never!"

"Just until your baby is born. I'm sure the good Doctor will take you back if you put on a show of penitence. You can't deliver this baby alone. If I thought I'd forced you into that, into something that could cause you untold pain, that might . . . kill you . . ."

"You didn't force me into anything, and women *have* been known to deliver their own babies successfully."

Rachel shook her head impatiently. "But it's too much of a risk!"

"If I go back to the Ark, I might never be allowed to leave it."

"I can't believe you couldn't outsmart that man, that you couldn't manage to escape with your baby. But if you die because of me—Mary, please, *promise* me you'll go back to the Ark."

Mary rested her hands on the curve of her belly, felt a tentative movement there, and wondered if there was any way to make Rachel understand that she would willingly face death—for herself and this child—rather than go back to the Ark. Yet she couldn't let Rachel suffer even this small additional anxiety. She said, "I promise you, I'll go back." A false promise, but that didn't matter. Rachel was satisfied.

"Thank you." She took a deep breath and for a moment seemed to be gathering her strength. "There's something else I must talk to you about. Mary, I always had the advantage in this relationship—what exists between you and me. I'm twice your age, and the odds have always been in my favor that I'd die before you did."

Mary laced her hands tightly. "Where's the advantage in that?"

"Only that it was never likely that I'd have to grieve for you. It was always likely that you'd have to grieve for me."

"I never should've left you." Her eyes squeezed shut against the pain that threatened to escape the dark mantle. "If I'd stayed at Amarna . . ."

She felt Rachel's hand on her clenched fists. "That's exactly what I must talk to you about. I can't stop you from grieving for me—that's a part of love—but I don't want you to add the salt of guilt to the grief."

Mary shook her head, but she couldn't speak. She wanted to say, to shout, *You're not going to die.* But she could no longer believe that any more than Rachel did.

"Mary, what if Luke had never come to Amarna? I still could've cut myself badly, and you'd be with me, but what could you do? There's no medicine available at Amarna to cure blood poisoning or gangrene, and for you to try an amputation would be futile. Whether you were with me or not, the outcome would be the same. And these last ten years have been a bonus of sorts. We kept each other alive. And living. I'm grateful for those years. I've had good company and even accomplished something for posterity. What more can a human being ask?"

Mary accepted the forgiveness she saw in Rachel's eyes as she had promised to return to the Ark. She accepted it for Rachel's sake, because it was an extraordinary gift, and to refuse it would be to deny the love Mary felt for her and to burden her with more pain.

"That's all I have to say, Mary." Rachel let her eyes close. The laudanum was beginning to slur her words, slow her breathing. "So, now . . . you'd better try the sphagnum. And fix me some herb tea. I'll try to keep down some food later."

Mary rose, looked around dazedly. Things to do. Yes, she had things to do. The sphagnum for Rachel's leg, the fire—it was down to embers—and tea and the stew. Oh, yes, things to do . . .

In the long reaches of the night Mary was wakened by Rachel's nightmare. Another dose of laudanum let her return to quiet sleep, and Mary added more wood to the fire, huddled over it to warm herself, then went to the bank to look out at the moon-silvered sea.

I have even accomplished something for posterity.

The books.

Rachel hadn't mentioned them. Perhaps she didn't consider it necessary.

She couldn't have finished the Herculean task of sealing and storing all the remaining books in the last six months, but enough to make her feel she could die satisfied with her contribution to posterity.

Mary thought of the books with a kind of hunger, a longing for words and their boundless range of expression. And she remembered how in another era she had ached and sweated over words, how she had hammered at them, molded them, cast them into harmonies that would ring in a reader's mind like a struck bell.

Mary Hope had been a writer.

She had forgotten that, and it should not be forgotten.

Rachel Morrow had been an artist. She had shaped insight into images, and that should not be forgotten. That it was possible for a gifted human being to perform such metamorphoses should not be forgotten. That it was possible for any human being to reach for the potential within the mind, to reach for understanding, for a new metaphor, a new image, a new harmony, to reach for the spectrum of emotion and conviction called love—that should not be forgotten.

Grief is a part of love.

Mary watched the ghosts of breakers tumbling onto the sand and felt the impatient stirrings of life within her.

This child would remember.

The day began in fog that obliterated the sea, yet when Mary looked straight up, the fog had a blue cast from the sky beyond. She knew that if she were standing a hundred feet higher, she'd be in full sunlight, looking down on clouds snugged into the contours of the shoreline. But she found an equivocal satisfaction in being submerged in the silent fog that made watercolor-wash patterns of the trees, that drew the limits of her world close and centered them on a crackling fire.

And on Rachel.

This was the last day.

Mary knew that as she busied herself warming the stew and boiling the dried apples into a sauce for Rachel—if she could keep it down. Mary put a pot of water on the grate to make herb tea, for fever, for vitamin C, for B_{12}. She fed Yorick and wished she could do more for Epona, who hung about the campsite, no doubt hoping for hay. Mary ate heartily—for two—and couldn't remember minutes later whether she had eaten or not. She was intensely aware of her surroundings, of every nuance of sensation, of her pain. Yet it seemed her nerves only functioned on the surface. Beyond a certain level was that impermeable mantle of numbness.

When at length Rachel woke, panting and crying out with pain, Mary offered her a cup of water laced with laudanum and waited until it took effect before tending her leg.

She hoped for a miracle still, but didn't find it. The sphagnum that she had yesterday bound loosely against the wound with strips of gauze had had no effect, nor had exposure to air, not on clostridia entrenched in its airless pockets beneath the skin. Today the red tentacles reached above the knee. The lower leg and foot were nearly black. Mary simply covered the leg with clean bandages as quickly as possible. Rachel couldn't face the broth or applesauce. Only a little tea.

The fog burned off by midmorning. Mary stood on the bank and watched the breakers emerge, the rocky point to the south, the cape in the distance to the north, finally the horizon. The vanishing fog seemed to take with it some of her protective numbness. She returned to Rachel, spread the blanket next to her, sat cross-legged on it, waiting. Yorick held vigil with her. Occasionally he went sniffing out his surroundings, but he always returned after a few minutes to lie close to Rachel, head on his front paws, eyes shifting from her to Mary.

Sometimes when Rachel woke she was lucid, although her conversation was disjointed, following her skipping thoughts with no transitions. "Can't overcome instincts with persuasion. Draconian measures. China. They tried, at least. You know, they killed millions of swallows because they thought they ate grain. The pope went to Africa and told the faithful to multiply and be fruitful. Damn fool . . ."

At other awakenings she was confused and vague. She thought Mary was her mother or Connie Acres. Once she woke complaining

317

that she had lost the right color of blue. "Cobalt won't do. No blue can take the place of ultramarine. Lapis lazuli . . ." Mary assured her she'd find her lost ultramarine, held her hand until she sank into sleep.

Sometimes she woke weeping in pain. At such times, when she came fully awake, she was most lucid. She would try to put off taking more laudanum, asking Mary to support her so she could see the ocean, commenting on every detail as if she were memorizing it. Yet the pain always overwhelmed her finally. Panting, her pulse fast and erratic, yet so faint, Mary could barely feel it, Rachel would finally surrender to another cupful of water made bitter by the few drops of laudanum.

In the afternoon Mary went to the beach and gathered wood while Rachel slept. She kept a small fire burning all day. And she watched the sun moving in the sky with a solid sense of the Earth moving under her. She watched the shadows of the spruce trees move across hummocks of scaled roots, through drifts of fallen needles, red brown, the color of dried blood. Time was inexorable. It did not exist in static form, yet it was integral to the universe and life. She considered time and whether she would, if it were possible, stop time on this vernal afternoon. But perception depended on time. It came to her that death and the cessation of time were one and the same. And the Earth turned, and the shadows moved, and the tide that was at low ebb at noon moved up the beach, each wave leaving its serpentine mark in the sand.

High clouds began sweeping over the horizon late in the afternoon, and when the sun sank behind them, they caught fire, but it was the red fire of embers, barred with radiating shadows of gray. The wet sand burned with reflections, the water was dappled with the red and pale blue green of the sky. Mary knelt by Rachel, supporting her so she could see this phenomenon of light. She watched until the colors faded, but as the fire in the sky waned, so did her strength. She was shivering violently when Mary tucked the sleeping bag around her, and pain tripped up every breath. She asked, "Is there more laudanum?"

Mary shook her head, the word catching in her throat. "No."

Rachel nodded. "Then it's nearly time. I want to see the stars first. I can wait that long, I think. Shadow? Where are you, love?" Yorick nuzzled her hand. "No, not my Shadow. She's dead, Mary, mercifully at my hand. So hard, mercy . . . for the merciful."

Mary didn't try to answer that.

When Rachel closed her eyes, Mary rose and built up the fire again. Its flames shimmered and blurred. Then she whistled for Epona, waited until the mare appeared, took her to another campsite, and tied her there. She stroked the massive, silken curve of her neck, her fingers finding the exquisite folds under her jaw, while Epona nervously rubbed her head against Mary's shoulder.

She returned to their campsite, where the fire flickered in an echo of the fires that had faded from the sky, leaving only a glow on the horizon. Rachel still lay with her eyes closed, but she wasn't asleep. Every breath ended in a soft moan, and the firelight glinted on the perspiration sheening her face. Mary sat down beside her, held her hand, while the night closed in like a tide around the island of firelight.

Finally Mary looked up through the branches, lace-patterned black on black, and saw stars shining out of the dark web.

The last day dwindled to the last minutes.

She felt Rachel's hand tighten on hers, heard her say, "There . . . that ancient light. I lived in a golden age, Mary, when we began to learn the real dimensions of the universe. I hope it doesn't shrink again in the human mind until those stars are only holes in a dome. What a small, cramped world it was. . . ." The words sighed into shallow panting, then: "It's time. Bring the first-aid box. The morphine."

Mary couldn't move. She stared into Rachel's pain-ravaged face, and she had no intention of denying her the relief she sought, that in sound mind she asked for now. The paralysis was both physical and mental, and it was total. Only when Rachel repeated in an anguished whisper, "It's time," did the paralysis release her. Mary forced herself to rise, made her way to the table, and returned with the first-aid box.

Rachel had managed to brace herself on one elbow, and the fire shone full on her face. In her eyes, past the pain, was a transcendent light that Mary didn't understand and knew she wouldn't until she stood at the same point looking over the rim of time to timelessness.

Mary knelt and opened the box, found the morphine. A golden age, and this was an artifact of it. Mercy in amber glass. There was more of it at Amarna, she knew. She wondered if it would still be viable when the time for mercy came for her. She offered Rachel the vial and syringe.

Rachel reached for them, but her trembling muscles betrayed her. The vial and syringe clattered together, then slipped out of her grasp. With a groan, she fell back against the bearskin. When she didn't speak, but lay staring hopelessly up at the stars, the transcendent light quenched, Mary said, "I'll do it, Rachel."

"No . . . oh, Mary, I can't . . . ask that. . . ."

"You didn't ask."

Rachel caught her hand, looked fixedly into Mary's eyes for what seemed a long time. Then her frail hand slipped away from Mary's. "It has to be given intravenously. It'll take . . . all of it. The full vial."

No doubt this had also been thoroughly researched. Mary picked up the vial and syringe, felt her equilibrium shifting dangerously, and realized the calm that surrounded her now was a fragile thing.

"Fill the syringe first. . . ."

Mary peeled the metal cap off the vial to expose the rubber seal, then broke off the plastic cap on the syringe, slipped it out of its sheath, pulled off the smaller sheath that protected the needle. She stabbed through the seal with the steel point, drew the plunger back against the pull of vacuum, holding the syringe so that the firelight was behind it, and she could see the liquid fill the tube. It was as benignly clear as water. She emptied the vial into the syringe.

Rachel began fumbling at her sleeve. "That cord in the box . . . use that as a tourniquet." Mary propped the syringe against the side of the first-aid box, then unbuttoned Rachel's sleeve, rolled it above her elbow.

The braided cord—she looked in the box and at first couldn't see it. She paused to get herself under control. And found the cord.

Rachel nodded. "Tie it around my arm . . . yes, that's right. . . ."

Mary followed Rachel's instructions without allowing herself to think past them, only aware of the monumental effort behind those quiet commands. "Tighten the cord. . . ." Rachel squeezed her hand into a fist, an effort that quickened her panting breaths. "Can you see the vein?" It was there, a small, blue wheal. "All right . . . the syringe . . ."

Mary picked up the syringe, held it tightly when she wanted to throw it, to do anything to rid herself of it.

But Rachel was waiting.

Mary angled the needle nearly parallel with the blue wheal. A moment's resistance, then the needle slid under the skin, into the vein.

"Now . . ." Rachel loosened the tourniquet with her free hand. And Mary pressed the plunger slowly, steadily, inexorably. She emptied the water-clear liquid into Rachel's vein, and never once trembled or faltered until the syringe was empty, and she tossed it away from her, a silent cry shrieking in her mind, as tangible as the pain that bore her down, gasping for air, into Rachel's arms.

Rachel whispered, "Oh, my Mary, my friend, don't ever regret this . . . no greater love . . ."

Mary lay shivering with her head on Rachel's shoulder, holding on to her and the vanishing moments, while the stars faded in the light of the rising moon.

And the sea sang softly, endlessly, *I am here.* . . .

Mary had all the long night to weep.

She didn't have to constrain herself now for Rachel's sake. There was no one to hear her sobbing, no one to know her anguish.

For most of the night she huddled by the fire, maintaining that pitiful island of light and warmth because darkness was intolerable. Yorick came to her with his ears back, his liquid brown eyes crescented with white, and she welcomed him in her arms, watched the moon move across the sky through gossamer clouds.

Yorick was at her side when she stood on the bank and watched the moon sink golden into the mass of clouds at the horizon. He was at her side when the last stars disappeared and the sky began to shed a soft, vague light.

And he remained at her side when she went to the beach and began gathering driftwood. The tide was high at dawn, and she had to stack the wood near the bank. As the tide ebbed she stacked it farther down the sand, and at midmorning she brought Epona to the beach and, with her help and the rope, pulled small logs to the place she had chosen well below the high-tide line and arranged them in a rectangle five by eight feet. On this foundation she laid the smaller pieces of wood she had gathered, building them to a height of a yard. She stopped then to rest, to get a drink and wash her tear-swollen face in the creek. Then she searched the woods for dead pine and spruce branches, cut armloads of dead fern fronds. When this tinder was added to the stacked wood, she returned to the campsite. The sun was at zenith, the tide at full ebb.

She knelt by Rachel's body and touched her hand.

This husk that had once been Rachel Morrow—how small it was, not a hint of beauty in it. It didn't make sense.

Mary zipped the sleeping bag around the body, then dragged it to the beach. It took a long time, but she didn't count the passage of time in any way now except in the change of the tide and the incremental return of the sea across the sand.

When at length she had placed the body on the mound of wood, she picked up a pine branch crusted with pitch from an old scar, used a match to light it, and when it was burning well, walked slowly around the pyre, igniting the dry tinder. The fitful wind combed through the crackling flames.

She looked down at her hands and was surprised that they weren't as translucent as the opaline smoke that billowed up from the pyre; she was surprised that her flesh didn't waver like the air above the flames. Her hands remained solid, opaque, and she pressed them to her body.

Rachel would never see this child that would be her heir.

Mary looked out at the sea, at the tourmaline green light behind the breakers, at the creamy froth cast up with every wave. *She's yours now.*

Finally she reached down to stroke Yorick's head.

"Come on, Yorick. Let's go home."

I acknowledge the Furies.

I believe in them, I have heard the disastrous beating of their wings.

—THEODORE DREISER, *LETTER TO GRANT RICHARDS* (1911)

Perhaps my dynamite plants will put an end to war sooner than your congresses. On the day two army corps can annihilate each other in one second, all civilized nations will recoil in horror.

—ALFRED NOBEL TO BERTHA VON SUTTNER, PEACE CONGRESS SWITZERLAND, 1892

Today the wind veers south, the clouds are thickening, but the storm front seems stalled. I imagine it as a trailing spiral on a weather satellite picture on television. Once we took such miracles for granted.

The possibility of becoming a victim of murder, *or* divine justice, makes me exceedingly wary. Yet when I consider Miriam's options—and I spent long hours of a restless night considering them— they seem few. At least, they are fewer now that I'm aware of the possibility and intend to avoid being alone in dangerous places.

I've considered the option of poison. Bernadette grows a number of plants that are poisonous as well as medicinal, but how would Miriam administer a poison to me? We eat out of communal dishes, and she's never been so solicitous as to offer me a cup of tea or anything of that sort, and forewarned as I am now, I'd never accept such an offering.

Of course, I sleep alone. She could easily slip out of the basement after the children and Esther are asleep. The children sleep the sound sleep of all children, and Miriam has often teased Esther about her deep, snoring sleep. "The house could fall down, and you'd never know it." There are no locks on the doors to my room. Miriam might smother an old woman with a pillow and claim she died of natural causes. Except that this old woman may be a bit stiff and slow, but still quite capable of struggling and making noise, and Jerry's bedroom is only a few feet away. Besides, Shadow always sleeps at the foot of my bed. She would certainly raise an alarm.

Yet I'm not comforted by these considerations. I've seen the way Miriam looks at me. The banked fire still burns behind her eyes. She hasn't surrendered.

She can't. She has made fallacies the basis of her perception of the world, and if their falseness is demonstrated, her system of perception will shatter like a house built of fine threads of glass. I am the one who stands outside her fragile temple of dark, spiderweb glass with a hammer in hand.

For the family, this day—Tuesday, the fourth of May—is again business as usual, although the tension is stultifying. The children are irritable, the younger ones prone to fits of temper or tears. The adults find inanimate objects on which to vent their frustration: the threads that break, the pot that boils over, the saw that sticks in the cut. I go about my business as usual, too, trying to avoid the adults yet remain close enough so that a cry for help could be heard.

But as the day grinds on I wonder if I *could* look to the others for help if I needed it. Today it is even more obvious that they blame me for this schism. Especially Jerry. Only pride stops him from backing down on his decision to let me continue teaching the children.

After the midday meal I go out on the deck to wait for Stephen,

325

grateful that the impending rain hasn't yet arrived. The wind blows erratically, but it's not so strong that the sun can't overcome its chill. I don't know where the various members of the family are, or what they're doing. Usually we discuss such matters during meals. We didn't today.

When Stephen finally arrives, Diamond and Pepper have inveigled Shadow into a game of tag. We watch them for a while, and I savor the pleasure of finding something to laugh about. But Stephen seems to curb his laughter as if he thinks it wouldn't be appropriate. At length, the dogs take a break to lie panting in the grass, and Stephen settles back in his chair with the faint frown that has become habitual lately.

I ask, "How are you, Stephen?"

I think he knows I'm asking about more than his physical state, but he doesn't want to, or can't, go beyond that. "I'm fine, Mary." He calls up a smile that at first is automatic, but when I hold his gaze with a questioning look, the smile leaves his mouth, finally manifests itself in his eyes. "Are you all right, Mary? I mean . . . well, it's been . . ."

"It's been tense, to say the least. I'm fine, too. I worked on the Chronicle last night. I only wish my poor hands could write as fast as my mind remembers." As I speak I reach into my pocket and take out one of the diaries, but I don't open it.

Stephen watches me, then he draws one knee up, clasps his hands around it. "What did you do after . . . after Rachel passed on?"

Those damned euphemisms. He learned them from the adults, who live entrenched in euphemisms. But I see in his eyes a cast of grief and take satisfaction in it. Not for making him grieve—and it isn't personal grief, not intense enough to cause him real pain—but because it is a response to Rachel's death. If her death has affected him, it is because her life has meaning for him.

I look out at the sea, slubbed with whitecaps. "After Rachel died . . . well, I came home. I don't remember anything about the trip. I just remember one day I was standing at the east gate. When I went in, the dogs and goats came out to greet me. They were all healthy, and I was amazed at that. But Rachel had only been gone about ten days. *I* was the one who'd been gone so long. Of course, Shadow wasn't here. I knew she wouldn't be, and it seemed so strange that nothing else had changed. I kept expecting . . ."

He finishes that for me, nearly whispering: "Rachel."

"Yes. I wandered around, checking the barn, the garden, the orchard. And finally the house. It took an act of will to enter this house. In every room I met Rachel's absence, even in the trail of blood on the floor from the backdoor to the bathroom."

"That must've been a hard time for you."

Hard? I want to laugh at the pitiful inadequacy of that word. But he doesn't know a better way to express it. Nor do I. "Stephen, did I ever tell you the story of the Buddha and the mustard seed?"

He shakes his head, eyeing me curiously. He has some idea who the Buddha was, although he knows very little about Buddhism. Not yet.

I begin, "Well, it seems a woman came to Siddartha, the Buddha, and told him her child had died and begged him to restore the child to life. The Buddha said he would—*if* she brought him a mustard seed from a house where no one had died or grieved a death. Of course, she couldn't find such a house, and that was his point. Grief is inescapable."

Stephen ponders that. "But Jesus raised Lazarus from the dead."

"Oh, indeed. After poor Lazarus was four days dead. At least, Jesus raised Lazarus according to John. Odd that none of the other gospels mention this astounding event."

His eyes go to black slits. "Are you sure?"

"Yes. But you can check it yourself." No doubt Miriam won't balk at his wasting candles in order to read the Bible.

"That's . . . strange." Then with a sigh: "But how did you stand it? The grief, I mean, when you were all alone here."

I hesitate, finally shrug. "I don't know how, but for the first month I think what kept me going was my baby. I had to consider its future, which meant *my* future, and that meant planting the garden and taking care of the animals, all the things necessary to living. And I decided the first night that I couldn't *avoid* memories of Rachel. This place is still steeped in her. I had to face the memories. I began by studying every object she had used or loved. I went to her favorite places, like the tree or the tide pools at the foot of the Knob. I looked at her paintings and drawings. And I started a notebook. I wrote down everything I could remember her saying. I mean, everything I thought significant. It was particularly painful, the notebook, but a strange thing happened after about a month. I found I was writing *my* thoughts, too. They all melded into one, and I couldn't be sure where her ideas left off and mine began. It was a revelation and a catharsis. And about that time I sealed the first book since my return. Rachel had worked on the books while I was gone, but there were still over two thousand left. When I finished sealing that first book, I felt . . . almost whole again."

"Do you still have your notebook?"

"It's in the vault, Stephen. Maybe to future generations I'll be famous as Rachel's Boswell."

"Her what?"

I laugh. "He was a famous biographer. We'll get to Boswell and Dr. Johnson later."

He pauses, then asks, "Would you mind telling me about your baby?"

The question is a natural one, and having gone this far with my story, I can't stop now. Yet I don't want to live through the answer to this question again. I've always spoken freely to these people about Rachel, but I've never talked about the baby. I'm not sure why. Perhaps if I had, Jerry wouldn't feel so betrayed now.

I look at Stephen, whose smooth, young brow is lined with concern, and I tell him, "The child came prematurely, a month short of term."

He pulls in a deep breath, his eyes focused inward on a point in memory. "Like Rebecca. But she was so sick before her baby came. Were you sick?"

"No. I don't know what happened, Stephen. I only know that one afternoon I started feeling—well, just crampy and uncomfortable, but I didn't think much about it, not till the contractions started. I was milking the goats, and the pain doubled me over.

But it didn't last long, and I finished the milking and carried the pails to the house. That was when the next contraction hit."

"What did you do?"

I shake my head at that, because I can remember my state of mind, remember I didn't *know* what to do. I'd read the books available at Amarna on first aid and physiology, but I still had a rather vague idea of what was supposed to happen in childbirth.

"Well, I wandered around the house talking to myself like a madwoman. I kept hoping it was a false labor. But finally . . ." And I remember that moment of fatalistic calm. "I knew this was the real thing, and it was coming too soon. That frightened me, but I had no choice in the matter, so I prepared for the birth. I bathed myself, built a fire in my room and laid in plenty of wood, put a kettle of water on the stove, and brought in a basin to wash the baby in and a sharp knife to cut the umbilical. I covered the bed and the floor at the foot of the bed with clean sheets, and I brought in enough candles to light me through the night. All this between contractions, of course. And I filled a syringe with morphine and put it on the table by the bed."

His breath catches at the word *morphine*, but he says nothing, and I go on. "Actually it was an easy labor and only lasted about eight hours. Toward the end I squatted on the floor as women have since—well, probably since before we were homo sapiens. All through my labor, I kept telling myself a child born only a month prematurely *could* live. I knew it would be touch and go, but . . ."

I remember with mordant clarity the culmination of labor, remember squatting naked in that warm room in candlelight, remember the overwhelming urge to bear down, to force the baby into the world, whatever the cost in pain, remember the exultant emotional surge that accompanied it. And finally the baby's head appeared, then its body came out into my hands. . . .

It was perfect, my child, gauzed with a creamy coating, still covered with fine, silky hair. It would have lost that in the last month. Incomplete, yet still perfect. And so small. It couldn't have weighed more than four pounds, and it filled my two hands easily. The umbilical cord was twisted like a slick rope around its right arm, and the tiny hand seemed to grasp it. The tiny, perfect, *lifeless* hand.

Poor little creature, what agonies did you endure? And your mother was oblivious, never guessing your death throes, helpless to offer succor even if she had known you were dying. . . .

"It never occurred to me, Stephen, even at the beginning of my labor, that the child . . . was already dead."

His eyes close, but he isn't surprised. Unlike Jerry, he had no reason to believe my child had lived.

But at the time of its birth I had no reason to believe it had died.

And I remember holding that mote of failed life and crying out with the clawing agony of this new grief, remember my cries echoing on nothing. That was what was left to me. *Nothing.* I had at that moment tested the depths of desolation, and I would never sink deeper.

Stephen's voice reaches through to me. "Oh, Mary, I'm so sorry."

My eyes are hot with tears, and it takes me a moment to realize I've been remembering a grief thirty years old. "Thank you, Stephen."

"The baby—was it a boy or a girl?"

Why is that always the first question asked about a newborn child? But what else can one ask? What is more essential to its identity at that point—except, is it alive or dead?

"It was a boy."

"Oh." That comes out on a sigh, as if the fact that the child was male made its death even more of a loss. But Stephen is the product of a patriarchal society, although his attitudes, shaped by the necessities of his isolated life, are less rigid than those of his predecessors. I've often wondered what human history might have been if men had never discovered the connection between copulation and conception.

For a long time Stephen is silent, studying me, and at length he says, "I don't know how you kept going after that."

I look seaward, remember the second pyre I built, a smaller one for the child I never named. "I'm not sure how I did, either, Stephen, and a great deal of the next year is lost to me. But ultimately

. . . I suppose I felt a duty to go on living. For one thing, there were the animals to consider. Mostly, there were the books. I had to finish what Rachel had begun. And time does heal grief. Finally. At least, it covers the raw wound with scar tissue. So, I went on living, with all the work and disappointment and even occasional joy that entails. And I worked on the books. But I was in no hurry about that, and I read most of them before I sealed them. In fact, it took nearly twelve years to finish the job. I remember the day when I put the last books in the vault and snapped the padlock shut. I had such mixed feelings at that moment. There was an emptiness, as if I'd used up all the purpose in my life. Then there was the conviction that Rachel and I had created nothing more than a crypt, that we'd buried the books like so many embalmed corpses, and they'd never be discovered and resurrected. But at the same time I felt . . . a link with the future and the past, as if I held the broken ends of a singing cord, one in each hand." Stephen is rapt, and what I see in his eyes gives me hope. He's beginning to understand.

Then I shrug. "Other than that, I simply lived, and I was lucky— I stayed healthy, except for occasional colds and a few teeth I had to extract myself. And, of course, the menopause. The design of the reproductive system in the human female leaves a lot to be desired. Sometimes I looked in the mirror and saw how old I was getting, and I began to have a little arthritis and other symptoms of the decline of various systems. The winters were the hardest times—the nights are so long at this latitude—but I think I held on to my sanity, and I accomplished what I had to do."

He looks at me with amazement, perhaps even admiration. "Did you ever wonder if anybody might come here someday?"

"I fantasized about that occasionally. After all, there *are* other survivors in our corner of the world. Luke found some, and Jerry told me a family came to the Ark from California."

"But . . . didn't you ever wonder if somebody from the Ark might come here?"

"I wondered, yes." I don't add that I was *afraid* someone from the Ark might come here, that I preferred my profound loneliness to their company.

But perhaps age had mellowed me by the time these survivors of the Ark arrived. And things had changed there. These people had endured grief and despair that had forcibly opened their minds to some degree. At least, most of them.

Stephen asks, "Weren't you surprised to see us down on the beach that day?"

I have to laugh at that. "Surprised? That's putting it mildly. Do you remember that?"

"No, not really. Except I think I remember seeing all the cats and dogs in the house. I liked that."

"They certainly weren't allowed in the households at the Ark." I open the diary, turn a few pages. "Well, you arrived on the second of February. That was about two months short of the twentieth anniversary of Luke's arrival at Amarna. I remember it was around noon, and I was in the house, when I heard the dogs barking. I came out to the deck and saw all those animals and people on the beach. And I hadn't seen another human being for nineteen years. Yes, Stephen, I was a bit surprised."

He laughs. "I wish I'd been old enough then to remember."

"It must've been quite a journey. Jerry told me it took you eight days to travel from the Ark to Amarna. I can understand that, with the animals to herd along. There were goats, sheep, hogs, cows, a couple of bulls, a small flock of chickens in a wooden cage, and five horses carrying loaded packs. Enid even brought her loom, dismantled into a Chinese puzzle. Anyway, I got out my binoculars, and I knew you were from the Ark by your clothing. I even recognized Bernadette and Enid, in spite of the changes inevitable in nineteen years."

And in a way, I recognized Miriam. It was her red hair, so exactly the color of Luke's. And I recognized—no, I simply saw something else: her imperious posture, her forceful manner with the other women and the children. But I had no premonitions about her. I wonder if it would have changed anything if I had. Probably not. Because of the children.

332

It was the children—Stephen, three years old; Jonathan, four years old; and Isaac, only a baby—who made me decide even at that point that I would have to take these people in at Amarna.

"Mary?"

Stephen is looking at me inquiringly, and I'm sure he's been talking to me, and I haven't heard him. "Yes, Stephen?"

"I was saying Jeremiah told us that you knew who he was before he said a word."

No doubt Jerry considered that amazing and probably a sign of maternal recognition. "It was only an informed guess, Stephen. I knew he came from the Ark, and when he reached the top of the path, I thought I was hallucinating. It might as well have been Luke coming toward me, except for the color of his hair. He had to be Luke's son, and his age made it likely that he was the boy I'd last seen at the Ark. Of course, Luke might've had other sons only a few years younger, and this might've been one of them. But I guessed Jeremiah, and I was right."

Stephen laughs, then: "Why did you decide to let us stay here?"

"Well, one reason was Jeremiah's responses to my questions."

"What did you ask him?"

"I asked if he thought the nuclear holocaust was the Armageddon Saint John imagined, and if the second coming of Jesus was at hand."

Stephen's lips part. He pauses before he asks, "What did he say?"

"He said that Luke had preached that the *true* Armageddon hadn't yet occurred, and that Jesus wouldn't take so long to find the righteous if he had in fact come again to Earth."

Stephen nods almost imperceptibly, then, "What else did you ask?"

"I asked if he believed the universe was created in seven ordinary days."

"How did he answer that?"

"He said, 'I don't know.' Profound words, Stephen. When you can say 'I don't know,' you've freed yourself to find the answer."

"That's why you decided to let us stay here?"

"Yes. And you—the children. I struck a bargain with Jeremiah then. His band of refugees could make their home at Amarna, if I would be allowed to teach their children."

Stephen doesn't respond to that, and perhaps he's thinking about the present dissension in this family that seems to be the ultimate result of that bargain. And I'm aware, as I wasn't when the bargain was struck—and my failure to recognize it was hubris—that it wasn't so much a bargain as a concession on Jerry's part. I couldn't have stopped him and his entourage from living here, although if I hadn't wanted them, they'd have had to take Amarna over my dead body. I doubt that was considered an option. Not then.

Stephen says, "There was a letter, wasn't there? From Brother Luke?" And when I frown absently at him, he adds: "Jeremiah told me about it. I asked him if I could read Brother Luke's journal—"

"Oh, yes. Is he going to let you read it?"

"Well, he said I could, but that was before . . ." His shoulders rise in an uneasy shrug. "Anyway, while we were talking about that, Jeremiah said you had something else Brother Luke had written. He said he carried a letter from the Ark and gave it to you that first day."

"So he did." I'm a little surprised that Jerry mentioned the letter. At the time he gave it to me, he didn't ask to read it, nor has he spoken of it in all these years. Perhaps it is in his mind sacrosanct. And I've never offered to let him read it. It was a very private communication, and I wasn't sure Luke would want anyone else to see it.

But perhaps the time has come for Luke's last words to be heard.

Time for his son to hear them.

"I'll read the letter, Stephen, but not today. I want Jeremiah to hear it, too. Tomorrow. I'll talk to him about it later."

"And will that be the end of the Chronicle?"

"Yes. I suppose it will be a fitting epilogue." I study him, trying to read behind his dark eyes. "What do you think of the story, Stephen?"

He clasps his long hands in his lap, staring at them, then looks up at me. "I'm glad you told me the story. I don't know if I understand everything about it yet, but . . . maybe I will. Someday."

That's all I asked and hoped for. Then I lean forward, push myself to my feet. "We've both had lessons enough for today. Let's go down to the beach. I need a little time with the sea."

And do I need the protection of his company?

Damn her. She's closed me in an invisible cage, and I despise it.

Just before supper I go out to the breezeway to get wood to fill the wood boxes in the house. The wind funnels through the narrow space, carrying the smell of rain. I balance my load—only five small pieces; I can't carry more at a time—on one arm, but pause when I hear voices. Jonathan and Stephen are running toward the back-door. They've been helping Jerry cut trees again; both of them are carrying axes.

"I think we should blow up the big stump," Jonathan says.

Stephen scoffs. "Sure. What're you going to blow it up with?"

"Dynamite. There's still some left. I remember when Jeremiah blew out the pond in the north pasture. Bet you don't remember. You were too little."

I don't hear Stephen's response. They pile into the house, slamming the door behind them, and the wood falls from my suddenly lifeless arm and thuds on the concrete.

Dynamite.

The image springs whole out of memory: a fountain of black earth, a billowing cloud of dust. And what an incredible thing the human mind is. The mind leaps chasms, plunges into nothingness, and comes up with a trapeze.

One thing I'm sure of at this moment: it was an error to think that Miriam must kill me to negate my influence. She has only to destroy what is most vital to me.

The books. The vault.

It hadn't occurred to me before. I suppose I didn't think it was possible. But it is. Nobel's legacy to the world may yet destroy mine.

"Oh—Mary, I didn't know you were here."

Esther has come out the backdoor. She sees the wedges of wood on the concrete and hurries toward me. "Did you hurt yourself?"

"No, Esther." She starts picking up the wood, and I tell her, "Here, I'll take that."

"Maybe you had too big a load." She is solicitous as always, yet she seems to be having trouble meeting my eye. She balances three pieces in the crook of my arm. "That's enough, I think."

I don't argue with her, but take my light load into the house and deposit it in the wood box by the living-room fireplace. When I go back for more, I find that Esther has detailed Stephen and Jonathan to assist me. I leave the job to them, go out on the deck, and feel the damp wind in my face. I'm shaking badly, but I can't seem to stop it.

Again, I consider Miriam's options.

If she *has* decided to negate me by destroying the vault, it must still seem an act of god. Would a dynamite blast fill that bill? Yes. *If* Miriam can't be connected with it. I can imagine it. In the middle of the night the silence is broken by a rumbling explosion, and the family starts from their beds, and Miriam, snug in hers, wakes from a sound sleep and asks in convincing innocence, "What happened?"

She could manage that—slip out in the deep of night, take a lantern to light her way, place the dynamite and leave a long fuse, long enough for her to run back to the house, get into bed, and seem to be sleeping when her god strikes the vault and its evil contents a thundering blow.

But doesn't she think I, at least, will call that explosion an act of man? Rather, of woman. Doesn't she think I will remind the others of the dynamite?

Perhaps she hasn't thought that far. Perhaps she's too obsessed to look past that act of god—the act of a vengeful, jealous god.

Or perhaps she knows this family better than I do. She knows their mood now, knows they aren't likely to examine closely her act of god. They'll accept the destruction of the vault as an act of god just as they accept the destruction of the temple in Jerusalem as an act of god because Jesus predicted it. That the prediction was recorded years after the temple was in rubble doesn't matter to them.

They are ready to have me repudiated by a higher authority. Then they can in good conscience join Miriam in repudiating me. *Join.* That's the key. This family lives too near the edge of survival to tolerate schism.

I leave the deck and walk across the wind-rippled grass to the head of the path, look down at the beach where ships of foam scud across the sand. I'm not afraid to stand in such a dangerous place now. Miriam won't bother to push me into the ravine. She doesn't need to.

"Mary?" I turn and see Isaac running toward me with his swaying, graceless gait, and his smile is a beatitude. When he reaches me, I put my arm around his frail shoulders.

"What is it, Isaac?"

"It's time for supper. We're having pea soup!" Pea soup is one of his favorites; he likes the green color.

I laugh. "Then we'd better get at it."

After another quiet meal in an atmosphere heavy with tension, I busy myself building fires in the living room and bathroom, then carry a bucket of water into the bathroom and put it on top of the stove to heat. This is the children's bath night. Every night is someone's bath night, but we're lucky if each of us gets a bath once a week.

But first, evening service, and I wait impatiently until the family leaves the house for the church. I go to the kitchen, take one of the oil lanterns out of the cupboard, light the wick with a strip of kindling dipped into the stove's firebox. More pots of water squat on the stove top in preparation for the baths. I go out the back-door, hear a hymn raggedly sweet in the twilight: "Nearer My God to Thee." The yellow glow of the lantern precedes me along the east wall of the new wing and around to the north side. The wind, heavy with moisture not yet resolved into rain, whips around the corner. Inside the storeroom, the air smells of dust and rust, and the floor-to-ceiling shelves are filled with crates, jumbles of tools, loops of rope and chain and electric wire, empty cans, buckets, glass jars, pipes and plumbing fixtures, house paint and turpentine, stacks of lumber, nails and screws, nuts and bolts. The lantern casts dense shadows as I search for that small, wooden box. Perhaps I remember it so clearly—and everything about the dynamite—because I didn't want it here. It was a bitter symbol of humankind's violent history. I can even remember that Jerry brought exactly twenty sticks to Amarna. He used five to blow out the spring.

The light falls on a box marked in stenciled letters: DYNAMITE. The box has been recently moved; there are clean areas in the dust on the shelf. I open the lid, my pulse rushing in my ears. The sticks seem innocuous, perhaps an inch in diameter and eight inches long, wrapped in thick, oily, yellow-brown paper. There is no hint of their lethal potential, except the word printed in faded black: DANGER.

I count five sticks. Ten are missing.

I replace the lid, turn the lantern on the hand-lettered message on the smaller box next to the dynamite: BLASTING CAPS—FUSE. I don't bother to look inside. I've seen enough. Too much.

When I return to the house, I put away the lantern and go into the living room, where Shadow is sleeping on the couch. I build up the fire, then sit down beside her, stare into the flames, and remember evenings with Rachel here while we were still alone, then her casual "lessons" with Luke at this same fire. And in the last ten years there were many evenings when the family gathered here to talk or sing. I'm not sure when we stopped having those evening gatherings. Their cessation was a gradual thing. It began with Rebecca's death three years ago.

I take a deep breath, let it out in a sigh, and consider my options.

At least, now that I'm sure of Miriam's intentions, I can stop her. I can tell Jerry and the others that the dynamite is missing and demand a search. I wonder where she's hidden it.

I hear myself sighing again. I can't look to Jerry and the family to help me. *But, Mary, why would any of us steal the dynamite?* And if I explain why, they won't believe me.

Still, they might if Miriam succeeds. Which will be too late.

And even if I can stop her from destroying the books now, she has an advantage over me: an advantage of nearly forty years. I am constantly reminded that I'm an old woman. I'm lucky to have lived this long, and I can't count on living much longer. There is in Miriam's eyes that banked fire that tells me she is impatient to do something *now*. But if I stop her now, she has only to learn patience, to wait until I die. I wonder how long it will be after my death before all the family joins her in a Pauline frenzy of book burning.

No, I can't simply stop her. I must negate her influence, just as she must negate mine. And perhaps age has an advantage. You learn deviousness when you can no longer, physically, solve problems in a more direct fashion.

I hear rain slapping at the windows, a hard rain that will undoubtedly last all night, and I smile. I won't have to worry about her dynamiting the vault tonight. A storm might make her act of god more plausible—she could say god struck the vault with lightning—but it has its drawbacks. For one thing, it would be difficult to light a fuse in a driving rain. For another, she couldn't avoid getting soaked. None of the waterproof coats and boots are left. Now we arm ourselves against the rain with wool and leather, which once wet take hours to dry. It wouldn't make her story that she was asleep before the blast credible if she or any of her clothing were wet with rain.

No, she'll have to make her attempt on a clear night. That means I can sleep tonight. And I'll need it. There'll be no rest for the wicked for many nights to come.

Now that I truly understand the threat facing me, I feel a deep calm, a mental clarity. On this fifth day of May I wake ready to take up the gauntlet and capable of being amiable and almost garrulous at breakfast—much to the confoundment of the adults, especially Miriam. School is again an invigorating experience, although I have to curb my tendency to lecture on general principles as if this were my last lesson.

By noon, the clouds from last night's storm are breaking up to let the sun make shining spangles on the gray-green sea. After midday meal I manage to corner Jerry in private long enough to ask him to join Stephen and me for our lesson. He is irritable and almost eager to turn me down until I tell him I'm going to read his father's letter. For a moment he seems stunned, then he squares his shoulders and nods.

I go to my room and open the bottom drawer of the chest on the east wall. My souvenir drawer. I sift through it like an archaeologist on a midden, unearth letters my father wrote to me; a bottle of L'Interdit perfume; my college diploma; the sketchbook Rachel gave me when I left with Luke for the Ark; the sole copy of *October Flowers*; the handcuffs awarded to Jim Acres by the Shiloh Apies garrison—the key is still attached by a string; a blue silk scarf that was a gift from my mother on my sixteenth birthday; the first piece of fossil wood I found on the beach here; Topaz and the first Shadow's collars.

There. In a flat, wooden box, Luke's letter. The paper—ordinary typing paper, a relic from Before—rustles like dead leaves. The letter was written in ink with a blunt nib; the handwriting is large and childlike, and page after page becomes more erratic, and by the last page almost illegible. Jerry told me Luke worked at it a few minutes at a time while he fought the nameless fever that had already killed over half his Flock.

I close the drawer and pull myself to my feet. When I reach the deck, I find both Jerry and Stephen leaning against the railing, Jerry watching me as I approach, Stephen looking seaward. When Stephen turns, finally, and looks at me, I feel an inexplicable chill. It's what I saw in his eyes in the split second when he first focused on me that engendered the chill.

Doubt. Was that it? But why? And I remember that he was oddly withdrawn in school this morning. I attributed it to the familial tension of which he and all the children are so intensely, so silently aware.

No, this is something more, something new, but I'm distracted when Jerry asks, "Is that the letter?" He looks at it fixedly.

I sink into one of the chairs, gesture toward the other. "Yes, this is the letter. Have a seat, Jerry."

He shrugs, nods at Stephen, who sits down beside me, while Jerry remains standing, arms folded in an attitude of mixed suspicion and uncertainty. Stephen is again looking out at the sea, as if he has no interest in the letter.

I unfold it carefully. "It begins, 'My dear Mary . . . I waited too long to find my courage. Now I can't come to you, I can't speak to you face-to-face, because there's so little time left for me in this world. I am sending this letter with my son Jeremiah. He is my only son still living. I told him to find you, because I know how much he can learn from you. You were good and true, and I was blind to the truth, but the scales have fallen from my eyes, and I know I betrayed you and Rachel. I've known it for many years. Finally, before I die, I must tell you. I pray the Lord to give me the strength to finish this.' "

I hear a muffled sound, look up to see Jerry's lips compressed, grief straining at his taut self-control. I turn the first page over.

" 'Mary, I wanted to go to Amarna many times, but never had the courage to face you. I think of you, and you are in my prayers every day. I see you as you were when we first met. In my mind you've never gotten old like I have. I see Rachel, too, and hope she lived in spite of her injury. When I count the years, I know she can't be living still, but I hope she died in peace. I wonder about our child. . . .' " And I hesitate, refusing to look at Jerry, but aware of his gaze on me. " 'A child conceived in love, and I know it sustained him. Tell him his father was a foolish man, but he loved his mother.' " I slide the sheet under the last one, swallowing against the tightness in my throat. I think Luke stopped there, too. The writing changes, becomes more erratic.

" 'That last day—I'll never forget it. You said if the Ark was our only hope, we had no hope. You spoke the truth like a prophetess. The Doctor kept saying Rachel was a witch, and I saw then that the Lord's grace had left him. She was a good woman, a woman of wisdom. But I didn't stand against him. He sinned by his lies, and I sinned by my silence. The night after you and Rachel left, he had a stroke. Some thought it was a judgment. Others said it was a witch's curse. I had to take over as preacher for a while.' "

I turn the second, dryly rustling sheet, glance up at Jerry. His face is expressionless now, but the muscles of his arms flex intermittently. I study the page, read, " 'It was a bad time for us, but we came through it finally. The Doctor got over his stroke, except his left hand and leg were never strong again, and it was like all the power had gone out of him. Sometimes you could still feel the strength and love in him, but other times he was hard to be with. And sometimes he just couldn't manage like he used to, and the Elders had to step in. But those were still good years. There were more babies. Mary, I had four children once, and three grandchildren.' "

I put the second sheet behind the others, and I'm sure there's been another lapse of time. The writing is getting difficult to read, the spelling degenerating.

" 'Night again. Bernadette wants to take my paper and pen away. Doesn't understand. Have to finish this. Brother Adam died today. He never believed you were evil. I was telling about the good years. Sixteen years, my sweet Mary, good crops and good years. But God sent a storm one night. Lightning hit the church, went down the steeple. You said we should have a lightning rod on that steeple, out in the open like it was, tallest thing around. A prophetess, yes. The church burned. Doctor was asleep in his room.' " I turn the page over, remember the first time I read these words. " 'He got burned so bad you couldn't recognize him, but it wasn't till the next day that he passed on.' "

And I remember I felt at that moment a resurgence of the old desire for revenge, and it seemed at first satisfied by the Doctor's painful death. I hoped that during the long hours he survived with burns so severe he was unrecognizable, he thought just once of Rachel, of the anguish *she* suffered, and finally understood what he had done. But I knew he did not. His death, even in agony, changed nothing.

Jerry says, "Please, Mary . . . go on."

I focus again on the page. There's been another time lapse; I can barely decipher the words. " 'Sun's up. Been sleeping like Berna-dette says. She'll come down with fever, too. Has to rest. After the Doctor's passing, we built a new church. Miss the bell. Half-melted, never rang true. We had two peaceful years. Seventy-eight souls here Christmas. Five came from near Eureka last October. Told you I saw smoke there. Good Christian people. Said there was fever where they came from, but they never had it. Maybe they brought this fever. Maybe God sent it. Only thirty-seven left.' " I look up at Jerry, see his eyes unfocused, haunted. He remembers.

He says dully, "Brother Luke called it a judgment. Those were nearly his last words."

I don't try to answer that, but turn to the next page. " 'I told the Flock to leave the Ark before they *all* died. Start new someplace else. No hope left at the Ark. Getting hard to write. Told Jeremiah how to find you. Others going south. Told him to redeem me to you. Teach him what I never could. And his children. Mary, forgive me. Pray for me.' " My voice has become as erratic as Luke's writing, and I clear my throat before I add, "It's signed simply 'Luke.' "

Jerry is looking south into the wind. At length, he says huskily, "My father was a good Elder, a good shepherd to the Flock, but it seemed like nothing he did helped when so much grief came down on us. I don't understand it, why we had to suffer so much at the Ark."

"Jeremiah, the Ark was a great success."

His head comes around abruptly. "It's deserted—dead! How can you call it a success?"

"You didn't live through the years right after the End. Rachel and I searched for survivors and found nothing but death and des-olation. Luke found only a few survivors and even more desolation. Yet at the Ark people lived. You're the second generation, and your children are the third. That two more generations came out of the Ark is a miracle."

His face is as transparent in its revelation of emotions as Luke's was. I watch him run the gamut from grief to skepticism to amaze-ment. He says softly, "Maybe we were driven out of the Ark for a purpose."

"Maybe. But purpose is a human invention. We need purpose, but we impose it on ourselves."

He ponders that, but makes no comment on it. He says, almost formally, "Thank you for reading the letter to me."

And I wonder if he regrets as much as I do that I didn't read it to him sooner. "Jerry, I keep it in a drawer in my room. When I die, I want you to find it. It will be yours then."

He nods. "I'll take good care of it." He seems to want to say or ask more, but when he speaks, it's only to say, "I have to get out to the north pasture." He glances at Stephen, as if he's forgotten why the boy is here, then departs without another word. I watch him until he disappears beyond the corner of the house.

Luke, at least you gave your son something to think about—if he's willing to face it.

I fold the letter and slip it into my skirt pocket, then look at Stephen. He stares at my hands as if they still held the letter, a muscle tensing spasmodically in his jaw. I say, "Stephen, the story is ended now. There's no more I can tell you."

"Isn't there?"

That question is so curt, so coldly adult, I am for a moment shocked and even angry. Stephen seems to realize, too late, the cold charge in his words. He turns away, holding himself rigid.

And I chide myself for my anger. I don't know what's preying on his mind, but it's serious, and I must understand it. I study his profile, the tight, sculpted contours of his full lips, and I wait for him to speak, but he seems willing to outwait me. At length, I ask, "You don't think the story is finished?"

He rises, goes to the railing, keeping his back to me, and again I wait, for the first time afraid. When at last he turns, his eyes fix on me with a gaze so full of fear and doubt I'm hard-pressed not to look away.

"Miriam told me something after morning service."

Miriam. Of course.

"What did she tell you?"

"She said Rachel was an unbeliever."

Rage is my first response to that, and I feel the chill of pallor in my face. How did Miriam know that? Has she been reading my diaries?

I almost laugh at that explanation, at the thought of Miriam purloining my diaries, poring over them in secret, trying to decipher my writing, laboriously spelling out each word.

No, the explanation is undoubtedly far more straightforward: to call Rachel an unbeliever was simply the worst thing Miriam could think of to say against her. She didn't care about the truth or falsity of her accusation.

And it is immaterial why she chose that particular blade to cut the bonds between Stephen and me. She chose her weapon well, however inadvertently. In these people's lexicon, unbelief and evil are synonymous. I needed time to prepare him for this, to teach him that there are many answers to the question of the existence of a god. But Miriam has forced the issue, and the damage she's done may be irrevocable. I can't lie to Stephen. Not now, with his dark, seeking eyes fixed on me. He would recognize a lie.

I ask, "Did you wonder why Miriam told you that?"

"Yes. But it doesn't matter, does it? I mean, if it's not true."

"It matters. But not as much as what you feel about it. Obviously it bothers you a great deal. Does it frighten you?"

He starts to answer negatively, then pauses to think about it and says, "Yes, I guess it does."

"Why?"

"Because I thought Rachel—I mean, everything you told me about her made me think she was good and wise and brave, but now . . ." The chagrin in his voice almost overwhelms his words. "It isn't true, is it? Rachel *wasn't* an unbeliever."

He seems to be begging for a comforting lie. No, he is begging for a comforting truth, and I can't offer it to him. I rise, take a step toward him, then stop, feeling his tension. He doesn't want me to touch him.

"Everything I told you about Rachel was true, Stephen. She *was* good and wise and brave. But there was one thing I didn't tell you. I didn't think you were capable of dealing with it yet. And I was right."

He stiffens, perhaps stung by that. "Then what Miriam said—it's true, isn't it? Rachel was . . . an unbeliever."

And finally I must answer, "Yes."

He is stunned by that syllable, staring at me as if I'd betrayed him, just as Jerry stared at me with incredulous accusation only a few days ago. But I can feel no anger for Stephen as I did for Jerry. I can only feel myself betrayed.

"Stephen, what you believe about god is your concern. It is your right as a human being to believe anything that makes sense to you. And it was Rachel's right to believe what made sense to *her*. If her beliefs don't agree with yours, does that negate her goodness, her wisdom, or her courage?"

He is as close to weeping as I am, but he won't give in to tears. He stands facing me, rigid and trembling, his voice thick. "But if she didn't believe in God . . ."

"What? Does it follow inevitably that she was evil? That's the way Miriam thinks, the way she wants everyone else to think."

"And you—what do *you* think? Are you . . ."

He can't speak the words. He wants to know if I'm an unbeliever, too. Oh, Miriam, how unerringly your blade has gone to the jugular.

"Stephen, what difference does it make what *I* believe? I've never asked you to believe the way I do, any more than Rachel asked me to believe the way *she* did. I just want you to . . ."

But he is past hearing what I want, what I hope for him. He stares at me as if he had never seen me before, and I know I've lost him.

My scholar, my hope for humankind. My heir. As much my son as the infant who died in my womb. I've lost him.

"I have to go help Jeremiah," he says coldly.

And I stand helpless, wordless, while he walks away from me.

In the vacuum he leaves, I clutch the railing for support, and the pain I feel now is shaped like grief and is of the same substance.

There have been times in my life when I knew that if dying were easy, if I had only to let go and slip into that sleep past dreams, I would do it. This is such a time, and age has eroded my will; I feel no resilience in body or mind. I am too brittle and fragile to withstand the shearing stress of this grief, of this defeat.

But dying is seldom easy, and even at the nadirs of despair, I always had a compelling rationale to hold on to life. My aching hands grasp the railing, and behind my closed eyes I seek the rationale that will give me a hold on life, on hope, at this moment.

What I find, finally, is stubborn pride. Will I spend my last years in defeated despair, or will I risk them for the shreds of hope?

Will I surrender to Miriam?

I straighten, look out at the sun-spangled sea, and I laugh, bitterly, on the edge of weeping.

Miriam, you've won another battle, but I still will not surrender.

That means I must begin my preparations for the next battle. My eyes are dry as I leave the deck and go to my room. I replace Luke's letter in its box in my souvenir drawer. My pulse beats hard and slow in my ears, and I feel a hint of the familiar constriction in my chest.

When I emerge into the greenhouse again, Bernadette is at her worktable transplanting seedlings into pots. She turns and studies me with narrowed eyes. "Stephen's lesson over so soon?"

I only shrug. "I'm going for a walk on the beach."

She presses dirt around a seedling with her small, strong fingers, nodding absently. "Take care, Mary."

When I leave the greenhouse, I call Shadow, then make my way down to the beach, with Shadow trotting ahead of me. I go south, but only as far as the old beach access where the bank is low, and I can make my way easily up to North Front Road. I follow it past the ruins of the Acres house back toward Amarna. Once I leave the remains of the asphalt, there isn't much left of the road into Amarna. The gravel is buried in moss; alders and bracken fern encroach on the margins, leaving only the tracks of our wagon wheels. I pass the gate at Amarna quickly, hoping no one there sees me, and walk up the quarry road until I come to the trail that leads to the tree. It seems fitting that my preparations should begin there.

At length, I reach the tree and sit down on the bench. I feel

Stephen's absence here, and I lock my hands together, accepting the pain to focus my thoughts away from him. I look up at the granitic column of the tree, savoring its monumental silence, gathering strength out of my memories.

Finally I call Shadow from her explorations. She comes to me panting, plumed tail waving.

"Shadow, speak!"

She knows that command and responds with three sharp barks. They seem brazenly loud in this domain of quiet. I lean down to pet her. "Good girl, Shadow, good girl."

Next I pull the silent whistle out from under my collar. It wheezes softly as I blow on it, but what Shadow hears makes her dance with confused excitement. The whistle means *come here*, but she's already *here*. I blow on the whistle again and say, "Speak, Shadow!"

For the next two hours—what I judge to be two hours by the movement of the shadows around me—I continue the lesson, working with her for a few minutes, then letting her go to explore or find water at the Styx, which murmurs unseen in the jungle of elderberry and fern. Then I whistle her back, repeat the lesson, and before this training session is over, she not only comes for the whistle, as she always did, but I usually hear her bark before she appears. But she isn't consistent, and I must have consistency in this. My life may depend on Shadow.

At supper I sense a different pitch in the tension that makes all but the most necessary or banal conversation impossible. Stephen is distracted and quiet, his gaze seldom lifted above his plate. He hasn't had a word for me, but neither has he spoken, except when questioned, to anyone else, and the questions haven't gone beyond whether he wants another helping of chicken. No one has asked about our truncated lesson this afternoon; no one seems interested in that small change in schedule. We've all withdrawn into ourselves, and I can almost hear the hum of thought, but none of it is expressed aloud.

348

And Miriam watches me, the cold fire in her eyes glowing perceptibly brighter this evening.

After supper, the skim of high, curdled altocumulus clouds in the west colors splendidly, but I enjoy that display alone. The family is at evening service. I wonder what text Jerry has chosen for his sermon tonight. *Before the cock crows, thou shalt deny me thrice?*

When the color fades from the sky, I go to my room and undress, put on my nightgown and robe, then take a book and my magnifying glass to the living room. I sit in the big armchair at the south end of the couch, ostensibly for the light from the oil lamp on the side table between the couch and the chair. But from this position, I have only to lean a little to the right to see the far corner of the dining room. The basement door is on the south wall of that corner, the backdoor on the east wall.

When the family comes in from evening service, they aren't surprised to find me here. I often read here by the fire and often stay up after the others have gone to sleep. Bernadette brings me my nightly cup of willow bark tea and sits down long enough to drink a cup of comfrey tea herself. She is never talkative, and tonight her terse conversation centers on Deborah, her apprentice. "Well, you were right, Mary. She does have a way with plants. Asks too many questions, though." But when she rises to leave, she adds: "Maybe I'll take her with me next time I go out for wild herbs."

When at last everyone has gone to bed, I stoke up the fire and settle down with Shadow sharing my chair, Diamond lying at my feet, the two black cats, Dante and Beatrice, curled on the couch. I'm reading *Alice in Wonderland.* My excuse is that I plan to use it in school. The ironies will be lost on the children, but they'll enjoy the fantasy.

My reading late isn't unusual, but I seldom stay at it past ten o'clock. Tonight I remain at my post, rising occasionally to revive the fire, to let a cat or dog in or out, or simply to limber my stiff limbs, until long after the Seth Thomas clangs out midnight. I am relishing the courtroom scene in *Alice* when Shadow, who is again nestled beside me in the big chair, raises her head, ears tilting after a sound. A soft tread on the basement steps, no doubt. A moment later the door opens.

Little light from the lamp reaches the basement door, yet Miriam's white nightgown augments the light, makes a ghost of her. But ghosts aren't pictured wearing moccasin boots. I watch her as she reaches for the knob of the outside door, then hesitates, turns toward me.

She remains motionless, and I am for a time—it seems a long time—paralyzed with fear.

Will she kill me now?

No, of course not. So says my rational mind as she slowly approaches me. Shadow growls, white, curved canines glinting. I rest my hand at the back of her neck, and the growling ceases.

Miriam stops perhaps two yards away, the golden light caught in her bright hair, lighting her blue eyes where the banked fire glows.

She says softly, "You're up late tonight, Mary."

"Am I? Well, I don't feel sleepy."

She smiles, only the lifting of the corners of her mouth. Then she walks back to the basement door, pauses there, speaks to me out of the shadows. "You'll get sleepy, Mary. Sooner or later you'll get sleepy." She opens the door and disappears beyond it. The door closes quietly.

My breath comes out in a tremulous sigh, and my heart is beating too fast.

Yes, Miriam, I *will* get sleepy, probably sooner than later. I can't keep up a vigil every night indefinitely. Miriam will be patient now. She will wait, and that's all I can hope for.

I stay at my post through the night until the clock strikes five, when I go out on the deck, see the gibbous moon hanging like a worn piece of ivory filmed with rose mist. The sky is deep blue; birds are already singing. Jerry will wake soon. His inner clock is amazingly attuned to the sun and always sounds an alarm in his head about half an hour before sunrise. Miriam knows that as well as I do, and that means I can safely leave my post now. I go to my room to sleep for an hour. I'm already feeling the lack of sleep.

And this is only the first night.

The day is much like the last three, although the pervading tension seems to have eased to some small degree, as if everyone decided that since nothing disastrous has happened thus far, they could relax, if only slightly. There is, of course, no relaxation of the tension that exists between Miriam and me.

Nor between Stephen and me.

Throughout the three hours of school, he is silent, and sometimes I find him looking at me with a questioning gaze I find hard to meet. The other children sense that strain, especially Isaac, who is bewildered at the strange silence of the surrogate brother he loves as much as his true brother. And I am tired and irritable, and it slips out, despite my efforts to control it.

After midday meal, while I'm clearing the table, I hear Stephen volunteer to help Jonathan rake out the barn and pigpens. Jonathan looks at me, startled, and he is about to ask why Stephen isn't having his lesson with me. I shake my head slightly, and Jonathan takes his cue and says to Stephen, "I'd never turn down help shoveling manure. Come on." And he leads the way out the backdoor. Stephen follows without once looking at me.

Enid and Esther have come into the dining room in time to hear that exchange. They stare at me, ready to ask the same question Jonathan almost did. I tell them flatly, "Stephen and I aren't having a lesson today," then retreat to my room before they can say a word.

A short while later I'm following Shadow down the path to the beach. Again, I walk south, loop back to the trail to the tree, and finally reach that haven of green solitude. There I devote the next two hours to reinforcing Shadow's training so that she'll not only come when she hears the whistle, but bark as well, and today I begin the next step. I've brought Topaz's collar from my souvenir drawer and a rope to serve as a leash, and Shadow, after some initial balkiness, accepts them. I walk her a short distance down the path, tie her to a moss-sleeved branch, then return to the bench and sound the whistle. I hear her barking long after I stop blowing. I go to her, praise her generously, then repeat the exercise again and again, each time moving her a little farther away. She is an apt pupil, and she doesn't question my sanity.

Perhaps she should.

That night I stay up again to read. Before the family retires, Esther and Bernadette express concern about my health, but are satisfied with my explanation that I'm simply not sleepy yet. No one else inquires, and Miriam watches me with that chill, knowing smile.

I don't actually see her during this night's vigil, but about midnight the basement door opens slightly, and I know she's behind it, looking out to see if I'm here. At three the door opens again. Closes again. She knows I'll be here, and she wants me to know that she's still waiting.

You'll get sleepy, Mary. Sooner or later, you'll get sleepy.

I'm already sleepy, exhausted, and I can't read. My eyes won't stay focused. I doze off occasionally, but I never let myself lapse into sleep except when Shadow is beside me, under my hand. She'll wake to the opening of the door, and her stiffening, her growl, will wake me.

I go to bed again at dawn and don't rise for breakfast. Bernadette comes in before breakfast to see me, frowns irritably when I tell her I didn't sleep well again last night, and declares that she will prepare one of her potions for me tonight. Then she informs me that she has fed the cats and dogs and asks if I want to be called later. I tell her to call me in two hours, in time for school. When she leaves, I wonder how much Bernadette has grasped of this game Miriam and I are playing. The medicine she offered to prepare for me tonight is not a soporific. I asked her specifically, and I've never known her to lie.

Today school is an ordeal exacerbated by Stephen's silence. There is an accusation in it, and my defenses are failing. I find myself repeatedly on the verge of tears, incapable of concentration, and in my burning eyes the shapes of my familiar world become alien and vaguely frightening. Today I feel Miriam behind me constantly, staring at me with that knowing smile. Yet when I look around, she is seldom there.

After midday meal I start for the beach path with Shadow, but I see Bernadette in the patch of elephant garlic at the southwest corner of the house. She motions to me to come over, then leans on her hoe amid the furled flower heads, already a yard high, bobbing in the wind on their long stalks. "I heard an interesting thing this morning, Mary."

"What, and who did you hear it from?"

"Grace. Silly old fool. No sense at all. She said she'd heard that something terrible was going to happen soon."

I feel myself stiffening, try to mask it with a smile. "Wasn't she more specific?"

Bernadette bends toward me, her tone mockingly ominous. "God is going to punish the wicked."

"Really? Well, that's good news." So Miriam is preparing for her act of god with a bit of prophesying.

Bernadette's bright eyes glint. "Good news. So it is. I never noticed that God was very quick to punish the wicked in the past." And she returns to her weeding, dismissing me, apparently, from her mind.

As I walk down the path to the beach I wonder if I'll ever understand Bernadette's religion or philosophy or whatever she calls it. In spite of that vein of cynicism that occasionally surfaces, she goes through all the motions of a believing Christian, and I don't think she'd bother if they weren't meaningful to her.

Today I *am* going to the beach—and staying there. I walk south with Shadow, who generally moves at a full run. It's refreshing to watch her, refreshing to feel the astringent wind at my back, to feel the heat of the sun, its reflection in the water-slick sand preceding me, dazzling my eyes.

I walk for about half a mile; far enough so that no one at Amarna can see what I'm doing. The first task today is to test Shadow near the ocean to see how far away she can be from me and still hear the whistle over the surf. I tether her to a log, then walk farther south, hide myself in the drift, and blow on the whistle. And I can hear her barking. When I've increased the distance to a thousand feet—I judge the distance by counting the ruined houses on the bank; they were built on hundred-foot lots—I add a new element to the exercise.

After I tie the leash to another log, I loosen the collar so it will slip over her head if she pulls at it. I order her to stay, walk down the beach past ten lots, then hide behind the scrolled screen of a derelict tree's roots. When I blow on the whistle, I hear Shadow barking, faintly at this distance, and I keep blowing. And hoping.

She doesn't disappoint me. Finally I see her running toward me. I don't show myself, but she doesn't need to see me as long as she can hear the whistle. When she has covered half the distance, I stop blowing. She hesitates, barks disconsolately, then begins weaving along the sand, nose down, until she picks up my scent, and when that leads her to me, she dances and barks, while I hug her and offer enthusiastic praise. I repeat this test four times, increasing the distance until I reach two thousand feet, and every trial is a success.

Satisfied, and exhausted with all my tramping up and down the beach, I make my way back to Amarna in stages, resting now and then, even napping in the dry, pale sand near the bank with my back against a burnished log, the sun hot on my aching joints. I'm in no hurry to return to Amarna. Yet I must finally. Shadow trots ahead of me, sniffing at the flotsam thrown up by the last tide. As I approach the path to the house a numbing anger grows within me that I should feel reluctant to return to my own home. It seems a long climb.

Through the evening meal, I am even more acutely aware of the tension underlying every word, of the veiled, accusing looks directed at me. I want to shout, "This is not *my* fault!" But I say nothing. After supper, while the family is at evening service, I take a bath, then stoke up the fire in the living room and settle in for another vigil.

This is the worst night. My body defies my intentions; my mind shimmers toward dreams, toward hallucination. The flickering light of the fire vibrates, and phantom shapes emerge from the dark. I slip in and out of sleep, and again I keep Shadow beside me, under my hand.

And again the basement door opens, once soon after midnight, the second time after four. I'm almost convinced that I hear soft laughter.

At five I go out to the deck. Another clear day. The moon hangs in the pastel wash of mist and sky, so nearly a perfect disk, my old eyes can't discern the slight flaw in perfection. But it isn't full yet.

Tomorrow night it will be full.

I don't bother to go to bed. I'm afraid to, afraid I might sleep through breakfast, and I am determined to make an appearance today at the morning meal. I let it be known then that I don't feel well, and the family's faces are mirrors attesting to the fact that I don't *look* well. For the first time since our final lesson I see something in Stephen's eyes other than accusing doubt.

And Miriam watches me, smiling that knowing smile. I wonder if no one else sees it.

Half an hour after school begins, I collapse, fall out of my chair amid the children's cries of alarm. They are convinced, and so are the adults when they come in response to the children's shouts. Jerry carries me to my room, then Bernadette takes over, sends everyone away. She's brought her medical case, and she listens with the stethoscope to my heart, checks my blood pressure with the old sphygmomanometer. She asks if I hurt anywhere. I shake my head. Then she prepares one of her teas—swearing irritably that it's only a combination of willow bark and foxglove, that there is nothing remotely resembling a soporific in it. Obviously I don't need a soporific now. I just need sleep.

And sleep I have—a day of sleep, sweet sleep to knit up my raveled sleave. This is also part of my preparation.

The cast of the light in the windows serves as my clock, and I know it's evening when Bernadette comes in with a tray: a bowl of chicken broth and a cup of tea. She checks my vital signs, frowning absently, then props pillows behind me and puts the tray on my knees.

I ask, "What time is it?"

"Suppertime. So, have some of that broth. No—the tea first."

I drink the tea, knowing I need the medicines that give it such a bitter, earthy taste. I take a few spoonfuls of the broth, and I am in fact ravenous, but I drop the spoon, let it clatter against the bowl, let my head fall back, my eyes close. "I'm . . . not hungry. . . ."

"Eat it anyway," she retorts, then with a sigh, "All right. I'll leave it so you can have some later. Cold."

She puts the bowl on the bedside table, removes the tray, then sits down beside me, presses her fingers to my wrist. "Pulse still a little fast. Thought you might be having a heart attack this morning. You could, you know. Blood pressure runs high. You've got poor Jeremiah going like a weather vane. Doesn't know what he should think."

An astute observation, but I neither speak nor move, and she asks, "Is there anything you haven't told me? Anything hurting you?"

"No. Nothing you can do anything about."

She snorts at that. "Well, maybe a few days' rest will do something about it." The bed shifts as she rises, and I open my eyes.

"Bernadette . . . where's Shadow?" I can only hope I haven't let too much anxiety come through in my voice.

"You want her in here?"

"Yes. Please."

"I'll find her."

The door opens, closes. I lie waiting for what seems an hour, but no doubt is only minutes. I must have Shadow in this room with me.

And finally the door opens again. I shut my eyes, and I'm drowsily grateful when Shadow jumps up on the bed and nudges at my hand with her nose. I pet her perfunctorily, then seem to sink back into sleep. I hear the door close.

I'm not asleep. I watch the light fade into dusk, listen to sounds from the house: the family at supper; then the clatter of pots and dishes; then, finally, the house is quiet. I hear singing from the church.

I have no light to read by, so my mind flows free, casting up

356

memories like flotsam. I remember my last phone call to my mother. I remember boys and men I loved, or thought I did. I remember making love. I remember deaths I've grieved. I remember walking with my parents on the beach, finding a shell so eroded in the tumbler of the waves that its outer wall was gone, exposing the spiral structure within. Dad said, "It looks like Mozart sounds," and Mother laughed and sang a Mozart melody. She sang beautifully then, but she stopped singing after Dad died. But at that moment the nacreous spiral of the shell and Mozart made sense in relation to one another. And years later Rachel told me, "Painting works on the same level in the mind that music does. People think they're responding to the subject matter. They aren't. Not if the painting is good."

I can't see the paintings on my walls in this dim light. I don't have to. I know them all, know their sources and the music in them. And I think about the books in the vault, remember the days before they were buried there, when Rachel pored over them, always frustrated by the shortage of time and light. It wasn't only the knowledge in them she sought; that was subject matter. She sought the music—the music that sings in the mind in response to relationships sensed in time, in cause and effect, in the *becoming* of transitions. She hungered for that music and reveled in the realization that her appetite was insatiable.

Evening service is over, and Bernadette comes in to check on me one last time before she goes to bed. I ask her to leave a candle, otherwise scarcely speaking or opening my eyes, except when she starts to take the bowl of cold broth. "Just leave it. I might wake up hungry."

She shrugs, then goes to the door, pauses for a Parthian shot. "Be careful, Sister. We're not as tough anymore as we think we are." Then she makes her exit, leaving me to wonder what she meant by that.

I wait until I hear no sound at all in the house, then wait a few minutes longer. Finally I push the covers back. I'm still dressed, except for my boots. When I was put to bed, Bernadette simply loosened my already loose clothing. I cross the worn carpet in stocking feet and, when I reach the sliding glass door, look cautiously out into the greenhouse. I see no lights in the north wing. I go to the door into the hallway, open it a few inches. No light under Jerry's door.

I return to the bed, sit down to pull on my boots. Shadow is awake, watching me. I don't offer her any encouragement. Next I go to the closet for the dark shawl, then to my souvenir drawer. I find Jim Acres's handcuffs, break the string on the key, and put them in my skirt pocket. My cane is on the back of a chair. The silent whistle is on the bedside table. I slip the chain over my head, hold the whistle against my heart for a moment as if it were a talisman. Shadow follows me around, tail wagging tentatively.

I pick up the bowl of broth, down a couple of spoonsful, then put it on the floor, and when Shadow begins lapping at it, I blow out the candle and retreat to the glass door, ease it open, step out into the greenhouse, ease the door closed again.

With my cane probing ahead for anything unexpected in my path, I make my way through the greenhouse, then open the outside door cautiously. I'm not so much worried about waking the family now as alarming the dogs, and outside the door I'm met by all five of them, but they know me too well to bark at me. They have in my absence been summarily put out of the house. I put them back in—at least, in the greenhouse. I walk past the deck to the corner of the house. There's no light in the windows of the new wing where Bernadette, Enid, and Grace are sleeping. I stand still for a while to let my eyes adjust to the darkness. The moon hasn't yet topped the hills to the east, but its light dims the stars. I hear nothing except the frogs in the pond in the pasture. And the murmur of the surf. Rachel used to say it sounded like a distant freight train; a train that has no end.

At length, I strike out north into a world of deep grays and blacks, sending my cane ahead of me at every step. I pass the gate into the north pasture, and the grass whispers with my passage, seed heads thrumming against my boots. The tart fragrance rises like a cloud around me, and there isn't a breath of wind to blow it away.

Ahead of me, above me, I see my objective: the Knob. The moon-light has already reached the top of it.

The light moves down the slope as I move up, and as the slope steepens, my panting is added to the night sounds. Rocks surface in the grass, and I must pick my way carefully. Now I'm in full moonlight, and I pause to look east. The moon is blurred in my eyes, yet I take pleasure in the resplendent white of it, remember that human beings, not so different from me, once set foot there. I've seen photographs of what they saw, the Earth rising, a lapis lazuli sphere in a fathomless night, over a lifeless ridge of ancient rock.

I told Jerry once about men walking on the moon, and he smiled tolerantly and said he had heard about that. But I know he didn't believe it. Yet he believes there is a god that manages human affairs.

Finally I reach the vault. I stop there to catch my breath, then climb past it to the top of the Knob. I can't see the horizon; the sea goes on infinitely. Beneath me, it churns up whorls of foam as it meets the rock bastions of the land in their age-old battle. The rock stands fast, even though its defeat is inevitable. It stands fast.

I go back to the vault, to the cedar door, run my fingers over it, feeling the grain etched by years of sun and storm. I tug at the padlock. It scrapes against the hasp, which doesn't give a fraction of an inch. Luke fastened it with long screws that have by now rusted into solidity. I take the handcuffs out of my pocket, slip one loop into the hasp, close it with a ratcheting sound and a click. The other loop I leave open.

I stand for a while, leaning on my cane. The night is sweet as silk, and I've discovered a magic pocket of time and place here: I've never stood at the top of the Knob on a warm, windless May night under a full moon. The beauty of it brings tears to my eyes.

A fine night for dying.

I shiver, look down at the house. The moonlight lies frost white on the angles of its roof. In this new Stone Age I'm an old woman. My pulse whines in my ears, my chest is tight and aching. And if my heart doesn't fail me, one good bout of pneumonia will kill me. Old women are indeed apt to die, yet I don't want to die tonight.

But tonight that is a distinct possibility.

I turn, press my palms to the door, in my mind's eye see the wax-and-foil-wrapped bundles stacked in their thousands within these thick walls. Such a pitifully small remnant of the treasure of knowledge. Still, it's all Rachel and I have to offer the future.

It's worth an old woman's life.

It occurs to me then that perhaps all my fear, all my mustering of courage, is in vain. Tonight at least. Miriam may not come tonight.

No. She'll come. Miriam is not by nature patient. She won't ignore this golden opportunity I've presented her.

Miriam will come.

I ease myself down onto the stone plinth, my back to the door, and contemplate the moon and the exquisite, indifferent night.

The moon is perhaps thirty degrees above the black contour of the hills when I see a yellow star of a light east of the house.

A lantern. It moves as if of its own volition toward the barn. I watch it as I might a natural phenomenon I can't explain. The light winks out. Miriam has gone inside the barn. That, no doubt, is where she hid the dynamite. Within minutes the light reappears, bobs toward the fence, flickers behind the trees. A pause: the gate. The light twinkles across the pasture, then slows as it moves up the slope.

And finally I can see Miriam. At least, I can see a ghostly shape reflecting the moonlight. On this balmy night she wears nothing but her long, white nightgown. She carries the lantern in her right hand, and under her left arm is a dark bundle. Her hair glows like an amber halo in the moonlight.

She is still at least fifty yards away. I raise the shawl over my head to cover my white hair, then twist around to reach the handcuffs, slip my left hand through the open loop, and stop to wait out a wave of panic that leaves me panting. Then with my right hand, I close the loop around my wrist, hear the ratcheting click,

360

and loose my breath in a sigh. Finally I bunch the shawl with my right hand to hold it up over the lower half of my face, at the same time grasping the whistle between my thumb and forefinger. Miriam is still moving through the moonlight like a mythical creature made whole of that mystic light.

I press back against the door, my hand hanging in the cold bracelet a little above the level of my head. I remain as still as the stones that protect this keep, this treasure house, this life of mine, of Rachel's.

Miriam is only twenty yards away, but she hasn't seen me yet. Faintly against the whisper of the surf, I hear her singing as she climbs the slope, singing like a child at play on a sunny afternoon— a child who thinks she is alone.

Now she stops, looks at me. She is less than thirty feet away.

And I begin blowing on the whistle as hard as I can, hearing nothing but its faint wheezing, wishing I could hear that high-frequency sound, wishing I could be sure—

"Who's there?"

I almost laugh. As if she didn't know. I keep blowing, and in the distance I hear—think I hear—the sound of barking.

Miriam stumbles toward me, the lantern drawing streaks in my eyes. Six feet away she stops again, puts her bundle down. It's wrapped in dark cloth.

I'm still blowing on the whistle, and now I'm sure I hear barking. All the dogs are barking. But the family—certainly awake by now— will have to get out of their beds, will have to discover that Miriam is not in hers, nor I in mine, will have to, above all, let Shadow out of the house so she can lead them to me, and now, with Miriam looming over me, I understand that the plan was foolish. It can't succeed.

She closes the distance between us, the lantern glaring in my face, hisses, "What are you doing here?"

I lower the shawl and whistle. "I've been waiting for you, Miriam."

Her face in the light reflected from mine is so fixed, so masklike,

I can't believe it is capable of change even as I watch it wrench into a grimace of frustration.

"You unholy *witch*! You're sick! You're old and tired and sick!"

"But I'm *here*, Miriam! I'm here to defend what I hold sacred, and I'm willing to die for it, if you're willing to *kill* for it."

She doesn't understand that yet. Her gaze shifts to my upraised arm, to the handcuffs. She pulls at the loop connected to the hasp, and I raise the shawl, blow desperately on the whistle. The distant barking gets louder, but there are no lights in the house.

"What *is* this?"

The handcuffs belong to a world unknown to her. I keep blowing on the whistle, while she puts the lantern down, grips my forearm and pulls hard, sending lightnings of pain through my wrist, and she is strong and determined, and my flesh and bones are weak and fragile. I cry out, "You can't break it, Miriam!" That doesn't stop her, but I see a light in the house. Yes, a light in the new wing. I turn away from the pain, blow on the whistle, gasp for air, and blow again. *Shadow, come to me, sweet Shadow. . . .*

Abruptly Miriam ceases jerking at my arm, shines the lantern on me, and I hide the whistle in the shawl, hear the rasping of my breath against hers. She stares at me for a long time. She doesn't seem aware of the distant barking, doesn't seem aware of anything but my face. And in her face I see the anger and frustration smooth away, see a smile press deep shadows into the corners of her mouth, and I'm struck with terror. I've been afraid to this point, but that smile throws terror into the equation.

She touches my cheek lightly, her voice as gentle as the moonlight.

"Oh, yes, I should've known you'd be here. The Lord has delivered His enemy unto me. Unto *me*!"

She rises, stands limned in the moonlight, and she shouts to the sky, "*The Lord be praised!* Thou hast delivered thine enemy unto *my* hands!" Again and again she shouts this affirmation as if the words were charged with potent magic, as if they rise from a wellspring of arcane power within her that can change entrails into portents, water into wine, blood into absolution.

And life into death.

I'm incapable of conscious decision, and perhaps it is my body that remembers to keep blowing on the whistle. And the sound of barking seems louder. Shadow—that's Shadow's bark. Yes, I'm sure of it, I think I'm sure of it. *Shadow, come to me, come to me. . . .*

Miriam's exultant litany stops suddenly. She looks down at me, then with a hoarse cry, lunges, snatches the shawl away from my face.

The whistle tangles in the shawl. She rips at it, finds the chain, tries to get it over my head. But I fight her for this, for my silent hope of help. The chain cuts into my neck and palm, and I kick at her, hear her yelp of pain. I see her fist coming, turn my head to make it a glancing blow, but the next one catches me at the side of my mouth, my head thuds against the door. She fumbles at my neck, muttering, "Mine enemy is delivered unto Thy hand . . . mine enemy . . ." And she pulls the chain off, tosses it away.

And her enemy is a witless old woman with a mouth full of blood, head raddled with pain, who can't even manage a coherent word to plead for her life. Or curse her killer.

I stare up at multiple moons, my ears ringing, yet I still hear her chanting, "Mine enemy . . . mine enemy . . ." And scraping sounds.

There's Miriam, wavering into focus. Miriam at the corner of the vault on her knees, digging in the ground with her bare hands and—a knife. Yes, she has a knife. It flashes in the lantern light, but I can't see what she's digging up; it's around the corner.

No. She's not digging up anything. She's digging a hole next to the foundation. She grunts, throws a rock out of her excavation, and it tumbles down the slope.

I hear a sound, insistent, continuous, and distant, and the ringing in my ears is abating. Barking. That's what I hear. Barking dogs. I look down toward Amarna, but all I can see is moonlit meadow and a swarm of stars twinkling in the black shadow clouds of trees.

Not stars. *Lanterns.* I can't be sure how many. I can't be sure my eyes aren't still multiplying the images.

I shout, "Help!" and nothing comes out but a rasping croak, and all the while Miriam is chanting and digging. The lights haven't reached the gate. I try again, head pounding with the effort.

"Help!" The sound dies in the still, balmy air, and Miriam rises. I put up my right hand to fend off the expected attack. But she ignores me. She sweeps up the dark bundle, takes it to the corner of the vault, uncovers it, and I can see the stacked dynamite sticks, the silver bullet of a blasting cap, all wrapped in a black ribbon of fuse.

I look down toward Amarna. The lights are past the gate, but the distance between me and that constellation of lights approaches infinity.

"Miriam, don't you see them?" I'm shouting, yet she doesn't seem to hear me. She places the dynamite in her excavation; her hands catch the lantern light, and they're streaked with her own blood.

"Miriam! The family—they're coming!"

And she chants, "Mine enemy . . . mine enemy is delivered . . ."

"Miriam, they'll *know* you destroyed the vault, they'll know you *murdered* me!"

She laughs ecstatically. "Yes, they'll know! Oh, Lord, I am the instrument of Thy will! And they'll *know*!"

There are four lights. I'm sure of that now. They're spread out in a bobbing line across the pasture, and the first has started up the steep slope. I can see small, dark shapes moving ahead of them, a flash of white ruff. Shadow. She is in the vanguard, barking incessantly.

And the plan worked. She has led the family to me, and they *will* know. They will know Miriam.

Too late.

The fuse coils in the grass like a thin, black snake. Miriam's bloody hands are shaking as she unfurls it, then, with an oblique look at me, cuts the fuse—cuts it only a foot long. I hear shouts in the distance, my name and Miriam's. Jerry's voice, Jonathan's, Stephen's.

She opens the glass face of the lantern, thrusts the end of the fuse in, and it erupts in a sputter of sparks, then seems to die. But there's no hope in the lack of visible flame. It is hideously alive, burning within itself, sending out spurting fingers of blue smoke and the acrid smell of smoldering tar. Miriam rises, shouts skyward, "I am the instrument of Thy will! The Lord be praised!" then begins a stumbling retreat down the slope, and she has left the lantern, left it so I can see the fuse trailing out from the corner, and I can see exactly how fast it is burning and exactly how much is left.

I wrench myself toward the dark snake that consumes itself second by second, stretch across the stone wall, straining against the handcuffs, but my free hand falls inches short of the fuse. The key. I fumble in my pocket, fingers closing on the key to the handcuffs. The barking and shouting are closer, and Miriam cries, "Go back! The Lord's wrath will strike! Go back!"

I can't find the lock. Angrily I jerk at the handcuffs, gasp at the pain. The lock, damn it—damn her!—find the lock. My hands are shaking, I hear my panting over the hiss of the fuse. There! Key in the lock. No, it slips against the metal, and I can't hear the deadly hiss for the barking in my ear. Shadow leaps at me in a frenzy of joy. She has found me, as I taught her. She has found me. And knocked the key out of my trembling hand and out of sight somewhere in the thick grass.

"Shadow, get away!" Less than six inches of fuse is visible. "Shadow, go back! Get away from me!" I strike out at her, and she yelps; she can't understand why I hit her, can't understand that she'll die if she stays with me.

I run my right hand through the grass by the stone plinth, vainly seeking the key. My hand closes instead on my cane, I stretch toward the fuse, beat at it with the curved head. But the spurts of smoke won't stop. I hook the cane around the corner to dislodge the dynamite and find no purchase. Shadow is barking hysterically, and I hear Jerry's voice near—too near. I look around, see him no more than twenty yards away, but Miriam is running toward him, she shrieks a warning, throws herself at him, and they fall together.

And the fuse has burned past the corner.

Shadow won't leave me, paws at me, whining, and it's too late for her now. I press my face into her satiny fur, remember the night I lay in Rachel's arms while she died. "I'm sorry. . . ."

And I wait. Listen to the sputter of the fuse. Such a small sound, yet it drowns out every other sound. Until it stops.

It simply stops.

I wait.

But there is no explosion. The sounds of the night—the frogs in the pasture, the murmur of the surf, the plaintive cry of an owl—softly fill the vacuum of silence in my mind.

The dynamite didn't explode.

Maybe Miriam didn't attach the blasting cap properly. Maybe the dynamite or the fuse were too old, stored too long in a damp climate.

It doesn't matter.

I begin to laugh. I shift, put my back against the door, hug Shadow to me, and I laugh. I laugh with relief, I laugh because I'm alive, I laugh at the sheer absurdity of this little drama, I laugh at the thought of Miriam playing with the technology of destruction born in an age she can't begin to understand, I laugh at myself for believing an artifact of that age would in her hands be a real threat, I laugh at the irony of Miriam witnessing the wretched failure of her act of god. I laugh until I cry, and the constriction in my chest seems only part of the laughter, the electric pain in my left arm only inevitable after the abuse it's had in the grip of the handcuffs.

The other witnesses to this failed act of god have drawn nearer, but now they stand transfixed. There's Jerry, with Jonathan and Stephen flanking him. Esther, her hand on Isaac's shoulder. Enid and Bernadette. Someone had the sense to keep the other children out of this. Grace must be with them.

These people aren't laughing with me, and I'm vaguely surprised. It's all so ludicrous. . . .

They're staring at Miriam.

And my laughter and tears cease when Miriam lifts her white-sleeved arms to form a ghostly crucifix, and the moonlight flashes on the knife still in her right hand, when she throws her head back, and from her throat emerges a single syllable stretched into a shivering cry of anger and anguish. *"No!"*

And I hear in that word other words unspoken: *My God, my God, why hast thou forsaken me?*

But Miriam hasn't forsaken her god.

She faces me, then moves suddenly, runs at me with the knife

366

raised, and I gaze at the translucent light shining through her gown, remember a picture I once saw of a snowy owl sweeping down on its prey, and it was as beautiful and terrifying as Miriam is in this instant of time that I recognize as my last.

"Mary!"

A blur of motion rushing at me from one side, an abrupt, crushing weight—something, someone falls on top of me, comes between me and the downward arc of the knife. *Stephen.* And Miriam staggers off balance as Shadow hurtles against her, teeth ripping into her forearm. Miriam shouts in pain, kicks at Shadow, sends her tumbling, yelping, and Jerry and Jonathan and Isaac close in. Isaac, his small face tormented with bewilderment, reaches out to her, wailing her name. But she doesn't hear. Like a hunted, cornered animal, she strikes out blindly, and the knife is still in her hand.

A dark fountain in the white light, and Miriam's gown is dappled with blood, and it still spills out as Isaac sinks into his mother's arms, as she sinks to her knees under his weight, and Isaac lies with his head canted back, Miriam's hand pressed to his throat to stem that hideous fountain, and blood pulses dark from between her fingers.

I cling to Stephen with my free arm as he clings to me, and Isaac's beautiful face is still, and if it weren't for that deluge of blood, I might think Miriam is only singing her son to sleep, but her lullaby is a broken whimpering rife with anguish, and her son will never wake again. The pressure in my chest has become adamant pain as if something unseen were trying to squeeze the lifeblood out of my heart as Isaac's has poured out. So willing, it seems, that outpouring, as if the sacrifice were embraced in ecstasy.

But the dark fountain has stopped.

None of us has moved through those endless seconds while Isaac died. We all watched stupefied, none of us believing one drop of that child's blood, none of us understanding it.

Now Jerry moves. Like a man transformed into stone, he moves ponderously toward Miriam and Isaac. He speaks, and his voice is the crack of boulders falling. "What have you *done?*"

I think he might have killed her, crushed her like an avalanche, but it is then that Miriam looks up, and he stops.

Her face is in full light, alabaster white. She doesn't see Jerry. Her eyes are dead with a fathomless despair that echoes in her voice as she cries out her son's name in a keening ululation that vibrates within me as if I were a tuning fork for that one terrible note.

Miriam understands everything at this moment.

When that cry dies into silence, her head falls forward, but that is her only movement.

Jerry leans down and takes Isaac's frail body out of her arms. He looks at me, finally forces the words out, and perhaps the questions are addressed to me.

"Who will forgive her? Who will forgive me?"

There is no answer to that. He knows there is no answer. He turns, carries Isaac away, down the long, moon-silvered slope. Jonathan follows him, his face nearly as lifeless as his brother's.

And I hear someone weeping. Stephen's head rests on my shoulder as if he were a sleepy child, but these aren't the easy tears of childhood. These are the labored tears of an adult. I press my cheek against his thick, curling hair, remember a day when I asked him if he'd do the same for me.

And he answered: *Yes, I'd do it for you, Mary.*

Esther and Bernadette come to help me find the lost key, help me free myself from my self-imposed bondage, help me make my way down from the Knob; I can't walk without their support. Stephen follows us, carrying Shadow. When we're halfway down the slope, I ask them to stop.

I look back, look for Miriam.

She had not once moved since her final cry of despair. Like Lot's wife, she seemed fixed in that one place, kneeling in the grass in her white gown blackened with blood.

But now, as I look back, I can't see her.

Stephen asks, "Where is she?"

The weight of the pain has made it too difficult to breathe. I can't answer that, even if I knew the answer.

I do not know what I may appear to the world; but to myself I seem to have been only a boy playing on the sea-shore, and diverting myself in now and then finding a smoother pebble or a prettier shell than ordinary, whilst the great ocean of truth lay all undiscovered before me.

—SIR ISAAC NEWTON (1642–1727)

The sun is moving south now as the summer wanes. Another August almost gone, another summer. At my age each season vanished is something precious lost.

Yet today I feel almost youthful with the golden seed heads of the grass rising around me, enveloping me in their piquant, dusty scents. I can forget, as I sit with my legs stretched out, one arm back to prop me, face turned up to the sun, that I will have to ask Jeremiah to help me when I decide to rise. But he'll offer his strong hand. He'd carry me if I asked. I won't. I'm still quite capable of walking with no other assistance than my cane, and I walk every

369

day. It keeps me strong. But it's gratifying to know I can depend on Jeremiah. I have at times no choice but to depend on him and the family since that night on the Knob, since Bernadette told me I had suffered a heart attack.

Jeremiah sits a few feet away near a mound of earth sparsely covered with grass. We are in the cemetery east of the orchard. Before May we didn't think of it as a cemetery. It was simply the place where Rebecca was buried. Now there are two graves, two wooden markers with names and dates carved on them. They remind me of all the poignant little cemeteries Rachel and I found after the End.

Every day when the children gather for school, I feel Isaac's absence. This grief was inevitable; he was too fey, too frail to survive many more years. But the manner of his death has given a trenchant edge to the inevitable.

I lean forward, stroke Shadow's head. She still limps a little, but I think I notice it more than she does. And I'm grateful I still have her.

I'm grateful for many things today. Grateful for the sun, grateful for my life, grateful for Jeremiah and the accepting silence between us. He sits cross-legged, looking down the long slope toward the barn and house. He has a book in his lap. It isn't a Bible. It is the collected poems of Emily Dickinson.

And all of us are especially grateful today. I attended the sabbath service this morning. I haven't altered my habits and convictions when it comes to the religious life of the family, and in the past four months I had set foot in the church only once. That was for Isaac's funeral. I made another exception today because on this sabbath Jeremiah baptized Esther's baby. Daniel. Healthy and strong, and that's the miracle I celebrated. I'm not concerned with his soul. Only his body now. Later I'll be concerned with his mind. No. Stephen will probably be the one concerned with Daniel's mind.

And so will Jeremiah, who is beginning to understand the value of the human mind, who has become in a way another student.

Rather, he has become a son. He has let me be the mother he wanted me to be.

I hear distant voices. Esther and Miriam are coming out of the henhouse, Esther with Daniel in a sling on her back, Miriam carrying a basket filled with eggs in her right hand. She has no left hand.

Our Astarte's perfect beauty is blemished. Like old Nehemiah, her arm has been amputated a few inches above the elbow.

I hear Jeremiah's hissing intake of breath. He's looking at Miriam, bewilderment and grief resurrected in his eyes. Part of the grief is for the sister he has, in a sense, lost. I wonder if he'll ever resolve that loss in his mind. He asked who would forgive her and forgive him. He's the only one who can.

And I wonder if I will ever look on this young woman laughing in the sun, her hair gilded with its light, without fear. Not for what she is now: for what she was, for what she could be again.

We thought she was dead.

For three days after she killed her son, Jeremiah and the others searched for her, and finally decided she had in her despair leapt off the Knob into the rock-strewn sea below. But I didn't believe that. I didn't believe Miriam would, however compelling her despair, defy the essential taboo against suicide encoded in her religion.

Yet in one sense I was wrong.

On the sixth day after that confrontation on the Knob, I had recovered enough for a walk to the tree, and Shadow had recovered enough to go with me. I wanted no human company; I was feeling smothered by solicitude. But I didn't get to the tree. Just past the east gate, Shadow stopped me with her barking. She stood sniffing the air, then limped off south down the road toward Shiloh, and all my calling and whistling wouldn't deter her. I followed her around the curve and saw something lying at the side of the road, tattered white and brown cloth nested in green fronds of bracken. Shadow's barking turned vicious, and I knew then what she had found.

Miriam. She hadn't fled her despair over the cliff at the Knob, but into the forest. She lay with her hair dull and tangled, her moonlight white gown stained with her son's blood, torn by branches and thorns. On her monstrously swollen left arm, I saw the gashes from Shadow's teeth. I remembered that purplish bronze color, that sweetly foul odor.

She was alive and conscious, terrified by Shadow's barking and perhaps by me. I quieted Shadow, then leaned over Miriam, and she looked back at me with fevered, fearful eyes. I knew she didn't recognize me even before she spoke, the words forced as if she weren't sure how to form them. "Who are you?"

I said, "I'm Mary Hope."

That meant nothing to her. She only stared at me until I asked, "Do you know who *you* are?"

She shook her head, grimacing. "No. I . . . don't know."

That was the way she committed suicide.

She couldn't kill her body, but she killed the self within her whose memories she couldn't tolerate.

But the self-death of amnesia might be transitory. To me, she was still Miriam, the priestess of the irrational, maniacally bent on murder—on my murder, on the murder of the past, on the murder of the future.

No one else at Amarna knew she was still alive. And she wouldn't be alive much longer if I left her here. Her eyes closed, and I couldn't see any sign of breath. I pressed my fingers under the curve of her jaw and finally found a faint pulse.

"Come on, Shadow." And I turned away, walked back to Amarna.

Jeremiah was in the barn. I told him where to find Miriam.

Bernadette performed the surgery on the dining-room table with opium for an anesthetic, and if I had been seeking revenge, I'd have had it in the next few weeks. But I took no pleasure in Miriam's pain, not the pain of recovery, nor the agonies she must have endured during those six days she was lost in the wilderness of forest and despair.

We told her only that her name was Miriam. No more. The family agreed with me on that, although it's hard for the younger children to accept. But it has been impressed on them that they are not to say anything to remind Miriam of the past. She has been born again, and like a child she is being taught to be a human being.

Jeremiah watches Miriam and Esther as they walk toward the house. He turns away, stares at Isaac's grave, and the twin griefs haunt his eyes.

"I wonder if she'll ever remember, Mary."

"She might. I hope not."

"For her sake, yes."

I don't add, *for our sakes, for the sake of the children.* I look down at the book in his hand. "Read to me, Jeremiah. Your eyes are better than mine."

He smiles. "But I can't read as well."

"Yes, you can. Please."

He opens the book, turns a few pages, then, pronouncing every word carefully, reads:

" 'The Poets light but Lamps—
Themselves—go out—
The Wicks they stimulate—
If vital Light

Inhere as do the Suns—
Each Age a Lens
Disseminating their
Circumference—' "

Vital light. Ancient light. I think of Miriam and the well of darkness hidden in the depths of her memory. I think of the survivalists Luke found in the Siskyou Mountains, and they are a tide of darkness. And if their children survive, their darkness will flow deeper, generation unto generation, and ultimately it could quench our light. And other survivors may one day discover Amarna, unknown factors of light or darkness.

I look toward the Knob, and I can only see a corner of the vault through the fruit trees. I can do no more to keep our light burning. All that's left me is hope, and that's all Rachel and I had to begin with.

Jeremiah is still poring over the book, frowning with concentration as he reads to himself. I don't disturb him. I think of the reclusive Emily reaching across an ivy-covered stone wall more than a century and a half thick to cast wildflowers in his path.

Then I raise one hand to shade my eyes. Stephen is coming up from the house. He walks with long strides, and I think he's grown half a foot this summer. Shadow rouses, runs to meet him, and he leans down to pet her. When they reach us, Jeremiah smiles and says, "Good day, Stephen. I suppose you've been hiding with a book somewhere."

"Well, I have to when my teacher gives me so much to read."

I laugh at that. "I hope you're not expecting sympathy from your teacher. But I'm glad you're here. Would you like to take a walk on the beach with me?"

He nods. "I was about to ask *you* that."

Jeremiah rises, and he and Stephen lift me to my feet. Jeremiah has my cane ready. I say, "Thank you, gentlemen." They laugh at that word, no doubt taking it literally, and that's apt enough.

Stephen and I walk to the house, where I make a short detour to my room, then we start down the beach path. Jonathan, Little Mary, Deborah, and Rachel join us, and when we reach the beach, they spill laughing and shouting onto the sand, with Shadow running joyfully around them. The sea is the quiet, glossy sea of summer, the sand pale and drifted like snow. Stephen shortens his stride to match my slow pace as we walk along in the firm, damp sand at the water's edge.

Finally, I stop, turn to face him, and take a small, black portfolio out of my pocket. I offer it to him.

"I have some more reading for you. I finished it last night, Stephen. The Chronicle of Rachel."

For a moment he only stares at the portfolio, then he takes it from me. "It's . . . finished?"

"Yes."

He opens it carefully, reads aloud from the first sheet, " 'And it came to pass in the days before the End of the last civilization, that Mary Hope left the city to come to the sea, and there she found at a place called Amarna a woman of wisdom and courage, and her name was Rachel Morrow. . . .' " He smiles, looks up at me. "I think now when I read this, I'll . . . understand."

"I know you will. You proved that." I look into his face, seeking the vanishing contours of childhood. "Stephen, there'll be so much for you to understand, and so many things will happen to you in your lifetime that will call for wisdom and courage. And I won't be here to help you, just as the day came when Rachel wasn't here to help me. In a way I grieve for you. It took me a long time to realize that Rachel grieved for me when she knew she was dying."

He frowns, and I know he doesn't like to talk about my dying. But he's learned a lot about death this thirteenth year of his life. And about wisdom and courage. Finally he says, "I wish I'd known Rachel."

I look out at the sea, chatoyant aquamarine, the surf casting up white laces of foam. "You know her, Stephen. And so will your children, generation unto generation. Even when her name is forgotten, they'll know her."

And I close my eyes to listen. *I am here . . . I am always here. . . .*

ABOUT THE AUTHOR

M. K. WREN, a widely acclaimed writer and painter, was born in Texas, the daughter of a geologist and a special education teacher. Twenty-five years ago she moved to the Pacific Northwest, where she wrote *Curiosity Didn't Kill the Cat; A Multitude of Sins; Oh, Bury Me Not; Nothing's Certain But Death; Seasons of Death; Wake Up, Darlin' Corey;* and the science-fiction trilogy, *The Phoenix Legacy.* As an artist, Ms. Wren has worked primarily in oil and transparent watercolor and has exhibited in numerous galleries and juried shows in Texas, Oklahoma, and the Northwest.